RYKER

SEAL SECURITY BOOK 1

SUSIE MCIVER

Copyright © 2023 by Susie McIver

All rights reserved.

No part of this publication may be reproduced, distributed, or transmitted in

any form or by any means, including photocopying, recording, or other electronic or mechanical methods, without the prior written permission of

the publisher, except as permitted by U.S. copyright law. For permission request, contact Susie McIver susie.mciver@yahoo.com

Book Cover by Amanda Walker

2023

❦ Created with Vellum

1

RYKER

I hadn't planned on being grumpy all the time, especially not around my fellow Seal buddies. However, since my fiancée humiliated me in front of our small town and my buddies by running off with her boss the day before our wedding, anger has consumed me.

Never again would I ask a woman to marry me. My anger isn't just because it happened; it's because I allowed it to happen. Hell, I'm not a child; I'm thirty-seven. The more I thought about how I felt, the more I realized I was furious because I was humiliated, not because my heart was as broken as I thought it should have been.

I was well-acquainted with most of the people in our town—hell, I grew up with most of them—and news of my wedding debacle spread rapidly. The entire town was invited, and it was meant to be a grand beachfront ceremony. Janet's mother broke the news to me, lacking the courage to do it herself. Walking through town became an ordeal as hushed whispers trailed me.

'Here comes Ryker Malone, the poor guy. I can't believe his fiancée ran off with another man,' they would murmur. I couldn't bear it; the humiliation was unbearable. So, I volunteered to work in other countries.

I eventually moved past the heartache in the first few months, but the anger lingered... much longer. Does that mean I dodged a bullet by not marrying Janet? Absolutely!

The wedding celebration still took place without me. All the food and alcohol I had ordered needed to be consumed. My mom said everyone had a fantastic time dancing the night away. It was reassuring to know that all the effort put into planning wasn't completely wasted.

I used to proclaim that true love didn't exist, and I was right. Who would commit to loving only one person for the rest of their life? I should have remembered that when I met Janet. She moved to town, and I thought she was almost perfect. God, I disgust myself.

I must admit there were a few things she did that bothered me. Her laugh grated on my nerves, and her obsession with her appearance annoyed the hell out of me. Her dislike for dogs should have been a deal-breaker.

In hindsight, there were plenty of red flags. She always ordered salads when we would go out for dinner, left the bathroom a mess, and never cleaned up after herself. At that moment, I chuckled and breathed a sigh of relief. That was a close one, Ryker. Too damn close!

I was a fucking idiot. I'll never fall into that trap again. I've been pissed off at myself for two years. I may have been growling at everyone, but that's because I was angry that I almost fell into the marriage trap. Wow, I nearly allowed myself to be shackled to one woman.

Those first few months, I was pissed at everyone, at least; that's what my buddy, Grayson, told me. But fuck, Janet ran off with her boss. What the hell were the two of them doing at work? Whatever it was, it saved my ass.

During the first year after her leaving me, I would sometimes put myself in dangerous situations. I had to get away from everyone feeling sorry for me, and I couldn't walk on the beach without someone approaching me. So I went to other countries to rescue people and had to be rescued myself. To top it off, the Army Rangers had to save me twice. It's not that I don't appreciate it; it's just that the Army Rangers had to rescue a Navy Seal, which made me angry at myself.

I admit I thought my heart was broken for a while and was a little reckless. I was foolish. Now I'm grateful. I'm back to my old self, dating whomever I pleased, whenever I want, without getting serious.

I returned late last night from an overseas mission. I stretched and looked at the clock. It was six in the morning. Why couldn't I sleep past six? Why couldn't I sleep at least until seven or eight? I knew why. My brain thought it would miss something, and then it fixated on that first cup of coffee. I had to be up and ready for the day as soon as my brain clicked on.

I carried my coffee out on my front porch and settled into my favorite chair. George, my Golden Retriever, lay at my feet. I was drinking my coffee and reading the newspaper. Life here remained as unchanged as ever.

A festival and a pie-baking contest were scheduled for this weekend. The paper even named the judges. I shook my head. Don't the ladies know by now that Judge Matthews always ensured his wife's pies would win?

I noticed a U-Haul truck over at Vic's place and was reminded that I'd miss those fresh vegetables he used to give me. Most of all, I'd miss our conversations. We used to have the best talks. Yep, I'd miss Vic more than I ever missed Janet.

Both George and I enjoyed visiting him. I hoped my new neighbor would be friendly and not a drunk. During my college years, I had a noisy neighbor who was drunk and noisy—always playing loud music and trying to sing along. He was also in college, but he went home after six months. The poor guy had too many parties, which ruined his scholarship.

I always knew I would return to my hometown after my Navy Seal service. I loved the Oregon coast. My buddies and I joined the Navy Seals after college. We pushed each other to the limit to ensure we all made it through.

Movement caught my eye next door, and I realized I was shirtless. Most people wore sweatshirts here, not me, and I was always hot. I looked over, and a teenage girl crawled into the back of the U-Haul truck. George perked up, wanting to investigate. The girl had long hair in two long braids all the way down to her hips.

I watched as she carried a large box to the edge, then she jumped down, grabbed the box, and took it back into the house. She was maybe thirteen or fourteen. I probably should have offered to help, but I didn't. I got up and went inside to grab my tee shirt. I filled my cup with coffee and went back to the front porch. It was the perfect weather for sitting outside.

A large dog emerged out of their front door. George's ears perked up. "Stay where you are, boy." George turned his head and glanced at me. I observed the girl's dog, hoping they didn't get her for protection.

I could have sworn the dog grinned at George before leaping into the back of the truck. I heard a voice singing to the dog from there. That was one sexy voice. What the hell was she doing back there? I heard scraping noises and saw a curvy backside wearing shorts walking backward. She jumped down and pulled a small desk halfway out. Before I could reach her, the girl was there helping.

I walked to the edge of my property, where the fence was, and looked at her. "Do you need a hand?"

She turned and looked at me, "No, thank you. We got it." She didn't even crack a smile.

Good. Once you start talking to them, they won't leave you alone. They carried the desk inside the house, and the dog followed. My heart started racing for some inexplicable reason. What the fuck is that about? I need to stay as far from her as I can get.

Her dark hair was held back with an old-fashioned turquoise comb, and her green eyes left me somewhat mesmerized. Just because I wouldn't get into a relationship with a woman that lasted longer than a month didn't mean I didn't enjoy being with them, and this one was a knockout —Hands off of your neighbor. This was too close for comfort.

No wonder my buddies laughed at me. A new woman arrives in town, and I start drooling. I returned to my porch and sat down, looking at George. "You stay away from that female dog, or I'll have to take you to the vet, and you know what he'll do. Snip-snip. George whined and retreated inside. I picked up my newspaper and resumed reading.

"Hi."

I lowered my paper. "Hello."

"My name is Madison Moore. We're neighbors now. This is my dog, Mona."

"Hey, Madison. I'm Ryker Malone. Is Mona a Bernese Mountain dog?"

She chuckled. "She is. Mom wanted a large dog to deter people from approaching us, but Mona loves everyone, so most people come closer to meet her. They love her because she's so calm."

"She's beautiful. Welcome to the neighborhood."

"Thank you. Your dog is pretty, too. Where did he go?"

"George walked back inside. I'm sure he's eavesdropping on our conversation and will come out at any moment." As if on cue, George walked out with his tail wagging.

"This house belonged to my great-grandfather; he left it to my mom. She spent a lot of time here when she was growing up. How long have you lived here?"

"I grew up in this town and bought this house two years ago." She didn't need to know I bought it for Janet, my ex-fiancée. "Vic was a good man to talk to. Plus, he had that incredible garden."

"My mom planted that garden for Granddad so he would stay outside and keep busy. We came here every spring and replanted the garden. Gramps had us add more vegetables each year."

"That was a good idea. He was continuously walking around checking on his plants. I remember him telling me his granddaughter helped him plant his garden."

"You were always gone when we came to visit. But I wanted to tell you that Granddad said you were a good man. He enjoyed talking to you."

I watched as she wiped her eyes. I could tell she missed Vic.

"Mom tried to keep him healthy so he could stay with us longer. But he said he was tired and wanted us to let him go. We miss him so much."

"I'm sorry. Remember the times you spent with him; it helps. I miss him too."

"Thanks. I have to register for school tomorrow."

"What grade are you in?"

"I'm a sophomore in high school."

"Do you like school?"

"Yeah, I enjoy it. I know people think I'm crazy because I like school. I hope I can meet some nice kids."

"Are you into sports?"

"No, I was on the newspaper and debate team. I might join the track team. I'm more of a nerd than into sports."

"It sounds like you stay busy."

"Sometimes. I change my mind a lot. My mom said she did the same thing. She didn't get to go to college because she became pregnant with me. I'll go to college and make her proud."

I wondered if she always told their family history when she first met someone. "What does your mom do?"

"My mom is a country singer."

"Wow, so do I have a famous person living next door?"

"She's pretty popular," she said with a wink. She looked toward their U-Haul, "Okay, I have to take more stuff into the house. It was nice to meet you finally. Bye."

"Bye."

I went inside and showered before meeting the other Seals at the office. George and I walked inside. He went automatically to his bed in the corner. The first thing Lincoln Harper said as we walked inside was that he heard I had a singer living next door. "Vic's great-granddaughter, that's who lives next door."

"I knew Gabby McKalister didn't move into that old house. It looks like it needs a lot of work."

Hmm... Is that who lives next door? She is famous. "It's Victorian, so it is old. I've been inside that home. It's beautiful. Everything is as if it was just built. The wood looks like it was just put in. Vic had a lady come weekly to do the dusting."

"Okay, I didn't ask for a lecture on the inside of your neighbor's house."

"Don't be a smart ass. What happened? Didn't you get any nookie last night?"

"Now you are being the smart ass. My brother got picked up again for fighting. He's out of control. He's taking my mom's death out on me and anyone around him. This is the third fight he's gotten into. He's not even out of high school. His grades are just so low at the moment; I'm going to have to see about hiring someone to help get his grades up."

"Damn, I'm sorry that you are going through that. It was a shock that your mom had that heart attack. What grade is Dustin in now?"

"He's a junior. It's been six months since mom died. Dustin acts like it happened yesterday. It really hit him hard. I was eighteen when Dustin was born. Mom and Dad were in shock when mom found out she was pregnant. She was so embarrassed she didn't tell me until it became obvious. Then Dad died when Dustin was twelve, so it's just been those two. I had to pick him up at the police station again. They would have taken him to the juvenile hall if Michael hadn't been working there."

"Maybe he needs grief counseling."

"I tried that. He's not interested."

I shook my head. I didn't want Dustin going the wrong way. "Dustin's a good kid. All I can say is to keep trying. The teenager who moved in next door might be able to help. She doesn't know anyone, and she could use a friend. Plus, she's smart. I'll ask her if she can help get his grades up."

"I'll never stop. I'll talk to Dustin and see what he says about letting her help him out. He won't be playing football this year if his grades don't improve."

"Well, that's an incentive: He's not going to like that."

2

GABBY

I WIPED MY EYES FOR THE HUNDREDTH TIME. *I can't believe Gramps is gone. I know he was ninety-six, but he was my family. I loved him so much.*

The rest of my family doesn't care about Madison and me. They contact me when they want something, which is the only time I hear from them. They are now madder than hell because Gramps left me this house. He knew I loved being here as much as he did. Mona rubbed her nose against my hand.

She always knew when Madison or I were sad. "I love you, Mona. Follow me, and we'll get some ice cream." Mona loves a spoonful of ice cream. I asked the vet if she could have ice cream, and he said yes, as long as it was not more than twice a week. So, I only gave her a spoonful.

I walked outside, "Madison, sweetie," I called. She was talking to our hot neighbor. It's a good thing I don't do hot or anything else anymore. He would be so tempting. "I have to take the truck back. Do you want to go?"

"How are you getting home?"

"The manager said she would bring me back."

"I'll follow you and bring you home," the hot guy said. I know his name because Gramps liked him a lot. He was good to my grandpa.

"Are you sure?"

"Of course, I'll grab my keys." He stopped and turned toward me, "My name is Ryker Malone. I'm sorry about Vic. He was a good man."

"Thank you. You can call me Gabby."

"It's nice to meet you, Gabby." I nodded and wiped a damn tear from my eye.

"I'll ride with Ryker," Madison said, following him.

Ryker didn't look too happy that he offered to pick me up. He might regret being friendly with the neighbor, but that made me chuckle for some reason. I climbed into the U-Haul and headed down the road. I couldn't believe we were living in Oregon again. I love living here. I should have moved back before now to spend more time with Gramps.

But thinking of Madison around my family again made me never want to move here. She's old enough to understand how my parents and siblings were. When Gramps got sick, I knew I needed to be with him.

I already knew he had left me this house. I've known it for years, but my family members went a little berserk when they found out. First, my mother demanded to know what I said to turn him against them.

It would have helped if they had visited him once in a while. They didn't even come to see him for the last three weeks of his life. I called them every other day during the first week. After that, I stopped calling.

Let me tell you something about my life: My parents have always treated me as the outcast of the family. I am not just saying that. Even when I was little, I felt left out of most things. My mother always said it was because I was the middle child, and that's why I felt that way. She claimed all middle children felt sorry for themselves.

I remember when I had to tell them I was pregnant, I was so scared. I knew my parents would be angry. Right out of high school, I got pregnant, and Gavin promised we would get married.

I'm glad we didn't do that. My parents refused to help me with college. They said I didn't need to go to college since I got pregnant. I had a responsibility to my child. I knew that, but I also knew I could still attend college. Mom's actual words were, 'You made your bed; now you can lay in it.'

They said I was a bad influence on my sister and brother. That was their excuse for kicking me out of the house. My sister was away at college, and my brother was sixteen. I don't know how I was a bad influence in their life.

My family never said anything about Madison, my sweet baby girl. They never treated her like she was their grandchild. They ignored her existence. They saw her when she was born, and I came home from the hospital for two months before they told me I had to leave. They laughed when I asked if I could have my college money.

Gavin, my boyfriend, and Madison's daddy stood by my side while I was pregnant. His mom and sister were excited about the baby, but his parents said Gavin was too young to settle down with a family.

I guess they thought since I was the one who was pregnant, I was old enough, but Gavin wasn't. Why people thought this was all my fault was beyond me. Gavin went away to college and met a lot of girls. At the time, I was heartbroken, and I didn't understand how someone who said they loved me could just stop loving me when they met someone else.

His mom was the one who told me Gavin was dating

other girls. She said he was young, and caring for a newborn baby for a nineteen-year-old boy was hard. I did all of it without help from my family and Gavin. Gramps saved me by letting me live with him.

I was so scared. I didn't know what to do. I had to move out of my parents' home. Gramps told me to come to him. That's what I did. I packed up everything I owned and moved out. It was just clothes, a few trinkets, and baby clothes. I bought my car when I was sixteen. I saved my own money and paid for it myself. I never went back home, not once. I stayed with Gramps until Madison was three.

I was always writing songs. I would sing my songs to Madison and Gramps. He was always telling me I would be famous one day. I sent one of the songs I wrote to Trisha Yearwood. She loved it and invited me to come and see her. I was afraid and nervous, but

Gramps said this was my chance.

So I agreed, and Madison and I went to visit Trisha Yearwood. When I sang the song I wrote for her, she cried and said she could never take that song from me. She wanted me to record it, and I did. That's how I became a country singer. I always thought of myself as a songwriter, but now I'm a singer and a songwriter.

And now, here I was, sitting in the back seat of the hot neighbor who was driving me back home. His vehicle was spotless and smelt as sexy as the man himself. I don't know what cologne he used, but I love the hell out of whatever it was. I could lay down on his back seat and stay here. I caught the chuckle before it went past my lips.

We pulled into his driveway. I thanked Ryker, and I opened my door. He was standing there looking at me with a frown on his face. I wondered what he was thinking. I frowned, thinking it must be me he was thinking about.

Then I smiled because I figured it out. He was mad because he had the hots for me, as I had the hots for him.

I remembered Gramps telling me Ryker's fiancée ran off with another man the day before the wedding. That proves what I always thought: falling in love is a piece of crap, and I would never fall for anyone again.

I heard a horn honk and turned around. *Great, just what I need right now.* Gavin Moore. I looked over at Madison. She smiled and walked to her dad's car. I stood there tapping my foot while the neighbor watched us.

"Hello, sweet cakes," Gavin said to Madison.

"Daddy, I'm so happy you came to see me. Would you please stop calling me sweet cakes?"

He hugged her and then walked over and embraced me. I never understood why he thought he could hug me whenever he wanted to. Does he not realize he left me to fend for myself and a newborn when I was eighteen?

"I have a lot of unpacking, so why don't you two take a walk on the beach or something."

"Why don't I order pizza? I haven't eaten yet. Have you?" he asked, looking at Madison.

"No, and I'm starving."

So he ordered pizza, and of course, he didn't offer to pay for it when it was delivered. He was like my family members. They thought because I made lots of money, they deserved some of it even though they treated me like crap.

I figured he had something he wanted to tell us as we sat around the small table on the front porch eating our pizza. I was feeding Mona pizza crust as she lay at my feet. He kept clearing his throat like he wanted to say something. Finally, he spoke.

"Look, I wanted to let you two know I'm getting married.

Nothing will change. You will still be my firstborn baby, who I love more than anyone," he said to Madison.

The thing is, I knew he loved Madison. He told her all the time he loved her. Then he looked at me, and I thought, *"Here it comes."*

"I wanted to ask you if Dani—that's who I'm marrying—" he cleared his throat again. "Would it be alright with you if we got married here, and could you sing at our wedding?"

I heard laughter and raised my head as my neighbor almost choked on the beer he was drinking. That's when I looked at Madison, who had a shocked look on her face. I chuckled; I couldn't help myself.

"No. And I can't believe you just asked me that. Have you lost your frigging marbles? I'm the pregnant teenager you dumped so you could date other girls. I'm the eighteen-year-old who was kicked out of her parent's home with a newborn baby to care for."

"Fuck no, you can't get married here, and fuck no, I won't sing at your wedding. You should be ashamed of yourself for asking me those questions."

"I'm sorry, Dani begged me to ask you. I promised I would—that's the only reason I asked."

"What is she, a teenager? Why would she think I would allow you to marry at my house and sing at your wedding?"

"No, she's not a teenager. She's twenty-one."

I rolled my eyes. "Congratulations!" I really did mean that. Now, maybe he would quit asking me out to dinner. Why he would think I would date him is beyond me. For Pete's sake, I can barely tolerate him coming around. I never realized how immature he was. But I would never keep him from coming to visit Madison. He loved his daughter.

"Gabriella…" I cringed every time he called me that.

Gavin is the only person who called me Gabriella. I never did like it.

"My name is Gabby; I feel like my mother's angry voice is talking to me when you call me by my full name. I know I've told you that several hundred times."

"Alright, Gabby, you must admit that you wouldn't be who you are today if we had gotten married as teenagers."

"Gavin, I never wanted to marry you, even though you promised we would get married. I'm glad we didn't. Why would you think I wanted to marry you?"

"Your mom told me once that the least I could have done was marry you since I got you pregnant."

"Why would you listen to anything my mom said?"

"I guess I felt guilty for not doing more. You gave me the best gift you could ever give me. I never thought I could love anyone as much as I love Madison. She will always have the biggest part of my heart."

"That's why you are a good father. But I didn't want a husband. Not then, not ever."

Gavin looked at Madison, "Do you want to go home with me for a few days?"

"Dad, I have school tomorrow. When are you getting married?"

I looked over and noticed my neighbor had gone back inside. "I will give the two of you time to spend together while I unpack some things."

I walked back inside and smiled. Damn, I was happy with the way my life turned out. Gavin was right. If we had stayed together, I would probably have been working in retail and would always be broke. I walked to my backyard as Madison and Gavin walked down the road that led to the beach. Mona ran after them.

3

RYKER

I was walking back up to my house after my run on the beach when Lincoln pulled up with Dustin. He smiled as I walked up behind his vehicle. "Hey, you two. What's up?"

"Your neighbor, Madison, is going to help Dustin get his grades up, or he'll be kicked off the football team."

"Cool. Have you talked to Madison yet?" I asked Dustin. I wanted to see the look on his face when he saw how cute she was.

"No. I haven't met her yet. But I hope she knows what she's doing and doesn't just want to get to know me. I'm tired of younger girls wanting to date me because I am the quarterback on my football team."

"You are such an ass. Why the fuck would you say that? Madison is brilliant, and I think I regret asking her to help you."

"Sorry. I didn't know you would get upset," he said as Madison walked out on their front porch, interrupting us. I looked over at Dustin. His big mouth hung open.

"Hey," Madison said, walking to the little fence between our properties. "Are you Dustin?"

He didn't say anything for more than three seconds, so Lincoln hit him on the arm.

"Yeah, I'm Dustin."

"Hey, Dustin, I'm Madison. Are you ready to start?"

"Sure. I'll grab my books." When he looked at me and gave me a thumbs-up, it made me a little nervous. I watched as he walked to where Madison stood.

"Let's get something straight first," she said. "I'm going to be helping you raise your grades. This is work only. If you think we'll be fooling around, then this won't work. Do you agree to let me teach you so you can pass your grades?"

I heard Dustin chuckle. "Yes, I agree."

"Great, we'll do this in the kitchen. Are you hungry? I'll make us a sandwich. I'm starving."

"Yeah, thanks. I would love one. I'll help you. It's nice meeting you, Madison."

"Yeah, you too. Why do you like playing football? You should join the debate team. You would like debating."

"Uh... Nope. I'll stick with football."

They walked into the house, and I could hear Gabby singing. She kept changing the words around, so I think she was writing a new song.

"Damn, I want to live in your house," Lincoln said, looking over at Gabby's home.

I laughed. "Too bad I'm staying here."

"I haven't seen Dustin smile once since Mom died. He meets Madison, and he chuckles."

"I told you there was something about Madison. She's so open, like her mom."

"Yeah, I wanna live here."

I laughed as he walked to his truck. "Tell Dustin he can walk home."

"Where's his car?"

"It's broken down again. If he wants that old car, he has to keep it running himself."

I was in the backyard when I saw Gabby in the garden. Then I heard her call my name. "Ryker, it's time for me to pull the vegetable garden up. Do you want to grab a basket and pick some of these veggies?"

"Sure." I picked up the bucket on the deck and walked over to her. George followed me. Mona was lying near the garden, and George lay next to her. "I see your dog is as good of a guard dog as mine," I said. She chuckled. "Are you going to keep planting the garden every year?"

"Yeah, I love working here. I want you to help yourself to anything in the garden—even the fruit trees. Sometimes I have to go out of town, so no one will be here to pick the vegetables. Now, let me be straight: do I need to stay inside with Madison and Dustin?"

I smiled. "No, Dustin is a good kid. He's been thrown off kilter since his mom died. Poor kid can't get over her passing."

"What? That's so sad."

I watched as she wiped her eyes. *Is she crying?* I allowed her a moment. "It's been six months, but it was such a shock. She had a heart attack at work. Lincoln, Dustin's brother, said Dustin is still having difficulties with it."

"Well, Madison will be good for him. If you haven't noticed, Madison is a no-nonsense teenager. She'll help him. So he now lives with his brother?"

"No. Lincoln moved back into his childhood home so that Dustin could stay in the same school district. He's renting his house out right now."

We talked some more, mostly because she wanted to know about Dustin. Eventually, it seemed that she was entirely okay with him being at her house.

I picked enough squash and tomatoes to last a few days. "Thanks for the veggies. I'll see you around."

"Yep, I'll see you around."

I walked back home and washed the vegetables before setting some aside for a meal later and putting away the rest. Thinking about Gabby McKalister, I wondered if she was seeing someone. Two hours later, I was cooking dinner, and Lincoln showed up.

"Is he still over there?"

"I guess he is. I haven't seen him."

"Hmm, I'll see if he's already walking home. I'll talk to you tomorrow."

I watched as he walked next door and knocked on the door. A moment later, he went inside. After I ate the fresh veggies I had cooked, I jumped in the shower. Lincoln was still there. An hour later, I sat out on the porch drinking a beer when Lincoln and Dustin walked out of Gabby's front door, laughing.

"Oh hey, Ryker. Thanks for introducing me to Madison. She's the coolest and smartest person I know."

"I thought so too."

"Here I was, worried about her wanting to meet me and hang out with me, and I see her, and it's like, wow! I think I want to marry her. You do know that's a song, right?"

"Oh yeah, the song."

Dustin laughed and shook his head. "Later, Ryker."

"Yeah, I'll see you around." I finished my beer, walked inside, turned my lights out, and locked up for the night. Then I thought, *did she lock her house up for the night?* So, like an idiot, George and I walked over and knocked on the door. I listened to footsteps walk toward the front door. Gabby opened it and raised an eyebrow.

"I wanted to remind you to lock up for the night."

"Thank you. Tomorrow, I will give you our phone number, and you can call us if you worry about the doors being locked. I did lock the house up for the night, but thank you for checking on us."

"I'm sorry. I know you have been doing this on your own for years. I'm sure you know how to lock your doors. Sometimes, my mind overthinks. Have a good night." I turned around and got the hell out of there. *Why the fuck did I do that? Damn it, Ryker, you are an idiot.*

4

RYKER

I looked at the others, but my mind was still on Gabby when she showed up at seven this morning to give me her phone number. I also gave her mine in case she needed me. "Hey, guys, are you ready to listen to what I say?" They shut up and gave me their attention.

"Three of us will need to go to Alaska and two to Colorado. I'm going to Alaska, let me know who wants to go with me. We will be guarding a woman from this guy she went out with several times. She said when she no longer wanted to date him, he got crazy and tried to kill her.

"In Colorado, two of you will have to stay with a married couple to keep them from killing each other—until they realize how stupid they are."

Lincoln sat up straighter. I knew he was ready to get down to business. "Who hired us to do this job?"

"His parents."

"Why do they want to kill each other?"

"He cheated on her, so she cheated on him. Now they want to kill each other."

"Why don't they just divorce?"

"You'll have to ask them that question. So I'll put you on here for Colorado. Who's going with Lincoln?"

A couple of hours later, I was picking George up at my place. He had to stay at the kennel until my mom got home. She was visiting a friend in California but would be home in two days.

"You'll be fine until grandma gets home. It won't be long. I'll tell them you don't like having the door locked on the cage they put you in. I'm sorry, buddy. I wish I could take you with me."

"Were you talking to me?"

I turned around and looked at Gabby. "No, I was trying to convince George that two days at the kennel won't be so bad. My mom will get him when she gets back to town. I'm so used to talking to him that I'm sure other people always think I have a screw loose."

"He can stay with us until your mom returns if you want."

Here it starts. Next thing you know, she'll have me over for dinner and want to do stuff for me. Nope, we aren't going there. I definitely don't want to date my neighbor. Let me rephrase that. I want to date her, but I won't because she's my neighbor. If she weren't my neighbor, I would take her to my bed in the blink of an eye. But since she's my neighbor, it would be too uncomfortable when I wanted to stop seeing her.

"I thank you for the offer, but George has already stayed there a few times. I don't want him thinking he can run to you every time I have to leave town," I said with a smile. "What are you doing?" She had wood and a saw. *This can't be good.*

"I'm making a bookshelf for the family room. Gramps used to have one, but he took it down when he got the large television. I took the television out of the family room, and now I'm going to make another built-in bookshelf."

"Have you done this before?"

"No, but I've been watching YouTube. It seems pretty straightforward."

Is she crazy? It's a frigging saw. You can get your fingers cut off or your hand. "Gabby, why don't you wait until I get back, and I'll make them for you?"

"That's awfully kind of you, but I'll be fine. I already know it's dangerous. I'll be very careful."

"Where the hell did you get the saw?"

"It was in the tool shed."

"It's the oldest saw I've ever seen. The blade must be rusted."

"Yes, it was, but I took it to the hardware store, and they put a new blade on it. It's incredibly sharp. See that piece of wood there," she pointed to a piece of wood that looked like a crazy person had cut it. "Well, I didn't know the saw would be so fast, so that piece got away from me. But I have a hang of it now. See this piece. Don't you think it's almost perfect?"

"I'll tell you what I think: I think you need to put this saw away and wait until I get back so I can cut the wood for you." I knew I blew it as soon as it came out of my mouth. "I'm sorry. I shouldn't have said that. I can cut a few for you now, and you watch me so you'll know how to place the wood."

"Okay, we can do that. But I want you to know I've been doing everything on my own for a long time, and I'm not used to people trying to take over."

"What are the measurements?" She showed me the paper she had written on, and I smiled. It was so cute. She drew pictures. "Okay, we are going to do the three-foot ones for now. See this here. It's a safety feature. Always use it, always. Where did you get the tape measure?"

"I found it in my grandmother's sewing basket."

"This is more for a woman to measure clothing or her measurements. Did you look in the shed to see if there was a measuring tape?"

"No, I'll go check right now."

"I'll go with you."

I walked into the shed and stood in awe at all the tools that had to be as old as the house. They were all in great shape; Vic took care of everything he had. He never let any of his tools get rusted. I opened a drawer and found the tape measure.

We returned to the saw, and I had cut six pieces of wood before I realized it was almost dark and the guys were waiting for me. I looked at Gabby. She was chewing on her bottom lip, looking at my buddies. The guys were here. I didn't even hear them.

"I think they want to leave," she said, nibbling on her bottom lip—those gorgeous, kissable lips. I shook myself out of those thoughts.

"I have to go. I guess time got away from me. Why don't you paint the wood, and I'll cut the rest when I get back?" She didn't say yes or no.

"I'll clean up. Thank you for helping me. Leave George with me. He and Mona get along great."

"Thanks. I think the kennel is closed now. My mom will be here in a couple of days to pick him up."

"He'll be fine."

I turned to the guys. My bag was already in the truck. "I'm ready." I locked up my house, hugged George, and we left.

"I'm in shock. I never thought I would see the day Ryker

Malone would have something going on with his neighbor," Blade said, chuckling.

"Back off. I don't have anything going on with my neighbor. She was out there cutting wood with a hundred-year-old saw. What was I supposed to do, for crying out loud? She could have cut her hand off. The piece she cut looked like a crazy person cut it. She said she didn't know the saw was so fast and sharp."

"Should I have let her keep cutting? She was using her grandmother's cloth tape, the kind a person uses for measuring body measurements." I chuckled. Then my heart flipped. *I should have locked up the saw.* I turned around to do just that.

"What are you doing?" Jackson asked, frowning.

"I'm locking that saw inside my house."

"Don't you think that's going a little far? Gabby said she would clean up the mess."

"That's what scares me. She has to pick it up to move it."

"Ryker, let it go. She got by for all these years without you saving her. She'll be fine."

"Fuck, you're right." I turned around and drove to the airport. We went to the plane, and I walked into the cockpit. I had to get my mind back on the job and remember that I don't date my neighbors. She might not even want to date me. Why do I think she would like to date me? I wouldn't ask her anyway.

5

RYKER

Alaska was cold. We knew it would be, so we were prepared for the weather. We picked up our rental Range Rover and headed to the address where the dad told us his daughter was hiding. The cabin was so far back we almost got stuck in the snow. This was not a good place to be. We would be sitting ducks if we had to hurry out of here. We could quickly get stuck in the snow. "We'll take her to the safe house. This place, we would be sitting ducks."

"Yeah, where the hell is this cabin? We've already gone five miles off the main road."

"The message says it's seven miles off the main road," Jackson said, "so we should be seeing it anytime now. What's that? There it is."

I pulled up to the cabin and parked. I saw a woman walk out on the porch holding a rifle. "You are trespassing. This is private property. The smartest thing you can do is turn around and get the hell out of here."

"Are you Darcy Hamilton?"

"Who wants to know?"

"We are from Seal Security."

"Why were you making so much noise? I could hear you the moment you turned off the main road."

I looked at her with my eyebrow raised. "We know how much noise we made. That was to chase anyone off who might be lurking in the area." She didn't look like she believed me, but that was fine with us.

"Will you ask us in, or will we stand out here talking all night?" Blade Wilder asked. Blade joined us a couple of years ago. He had come to town to visit Mace Cohen, who had lost his wife and two kids in a car accident a couple of years ago.

Mace was never in a good mood these days. He had started hanging out with a motorcycle gang. When Blade saw how Mace was, he came to see us. He was in the Navy Seals with us, and we invited him to join us in Seal Security. He took the job.

We walked inside, and I was surprised at the comfort. "Do you want to tell us what happened with your ex-boyfriend?"

"What's to tell? He didn't want to break up with me. I told him we were no longer a couple, and he went berserk. We only went out a couple of times, maybe three. He didn't hit me that time. I didn't know he was so unbalanced. He wouldn't leave me alone. He came to my work. I work for my parents. He slammed the door to my office in my mother's face. I was so angry, I told him to get out of my office and off the property, or I would call the police."

"What did he do?"

"He pushed me against the wall and attempted to rape me. I got away from him because my father broke the door down. Then he beat the hell out of Steve. That made him angrier. He kidnapped me and held me for two days before I got away. He beat me and raped me for two days."

"The police had him, but the district attorney wouldn't press charges because he needed more proof. He told me to tape our conversation about admitting what he had done to me. Then he kidnapped me again."

"This time, he not only beat me, but he also beat my mother. He took me into another State and tried to kill me. I still had some fight left in me, and I was able to hit him with a medal yard decoration. It knocked him out and I took off in the rental he had."

"I went straight to the police department. He was gone when they arrived at the place where he held me captive. I've been hiding ever since because I know he'll kill me the next time. My parents are also hiding from him. My mother is scared to death he'll find her."

"How come the district attorney didn't press charges?"

"Because they are cousins, he no longer has a job. What are we going to do?"

"We'll stay here tonight. Tomorrow, we'll go to a safe house. How long were you two dating?"

"We weren't dating as such. We went out two times, maybe three. I should have ditched him after the first date. But I felt sorry for him because he begged me to give him another try.

Then he sent me flowers and candy. He took me dancing. I knew something was wrong with him. I felt it each time I was around him. So, I told him I didn't want to date him anymore."

"Did he get angry?"

"He put a dead kitten by my front door. I know it was him because I told him I was going to get a kitten. He should be locked up in a mental hospital. If I see him, I'll shoot him. Let me tell you something that is a fact. This rifle will go with me when we leave here. When I see him, I will shoot him."

"Okay, but be careful with that," Blade told her.

I looked at the guys. "Let's eat, and then I'll take the first watch." I returned to the vehicle and brought in a bag of survival food.

"I made spaghetti and French bread," Darcy said, turning toward the kitchen.

"Yeah, spaghetti sounds way better," I said, putting the bag down.

There was no movement outside, so the night passed in silence. The following morning, we were packed up and ready to leave when the sun came up. "Whose cabin is this?"

"It belongs to Bill. He's a friend of my dad's. They went to college together. I hope the police catch this guy. He's really crazy. I told him he was crazy, and he beat his fist into the wall next to where he had me tied up on the bed. His hand was broken and bleeding, and the crazy man continued to hit the wall."

I nodded because I'd seen someone like that before. "When I was held prisoner, a Taliban man beat a cement wall with his fists until his hands were broken and shredded. The man was out of his mind. The other prisoners wanted to break out of there, and I told them we would wait. The guy would get his hands all infected, and then we'd take his gun and shoot him and the others.

"That's what we did. We killed him and the others. We released the other prisoners and got the hell out of there. So yeah, those people don't care about anything. They don't care about other people's pain if they can't feel their pain."

"I hope they kill him, or I will," Darcy said. "As long as he's alive, he will be after me. I'll be scared for the rest of my life."

"How did you meet him?" Jackson asked, frowning.

"My best friend's husband invited him to their home when they had a barbecue. I figured if Joel liked him enough to ask him to go to their home where their child was, he must be a nice guy. Joel and Sally were so upset that both cried when they found out what he had done. I called them and told them to keep their doors locked."

We soon pulled into the airport and made our way to the plane. We were on our way to Arizona. We had a safe house in the Red Mountains. I loved that place. I felt so much peace there. Every time I had a vacation, I went to the Red Mountains.

"Where are we going?" Darcy asked, walking on the plane.

"Arizona. We have safe houses all over the place."

"I've never been to Arizona. I've wanted to go, but I'm usually so busy working. My dad always likes his workers to work, especially his wife and daughter. We work all the time. I'm going to quit after this is over."

"I hate leaving my mom there to cover for me. At least she has time off now while they are hiding out. I wish Dad would hire four or five people and teach them how to do everything and take time off. They need to take a vacation. If this has taught me anything, it's that life is short, and you better live for the day."

"Maybe they are ready to take time off after this close call."

"Not my Dad. I'm thirty-one, and he hasn't taken a vacation since I was a little girl. If I remember correctly, I was twelve when they had their last vacation. My poor mom works all the time."

. . .

DARCY SLEPT for the rest of the trip. I got caught up on my paperwork, and then my mind drifted to my neighbor. I wondered what she was doing right now. Was she working in her garden? I hoped to hell she wasn't trying to use that massive old saw. *I'll call her when I reach Arizona.* Then I had a panic attack and decided to call her right then. I took out my phone and pushed the button with her name. Blade sat down across from me.

"Hello."

"Hello, Gabby. It's Ryker. I wondered if you were able to put that heavy saw away." I looked at Blade, and he rolled his eyes and smirked.

"Yes, I went to the hardware store and bought a smaller one. I'm going to finish cutting the shelves. Dustin and Madison are going to paint them after school today. I should have them cut by then."

She couldn't see me. If she could, she would know I was frowning. Blade knew because he was watching me. "Why don't I call one of the guys to come over and help you?" I looked at Blade, and he was shaking his head. I heard a sigh on the other end of the phone.

"Ryker, I'm thirty-three. I've taken care of myself my entire life. I have not cut my finger or my hand off. Will you please stop worrying? Please don't call me again unless you have something to discuss; that isn't if I locked my doors or touched that dangerous saw. I've decided to make birdhouses also. While you are gone, I'll make you one. Goodbye, Ryker."

I looked at the phone: she'd hung up on me. I smiled. Then I looked at Blade. He was grinning.

"You called her to see if her doors were locked for the night?"

"The first time, I knocked on her door to tell her to lock

up. Damn it, I can't help myself. She's so clumsy... No, not clumsy. That isn't the word I need. She's always rushing around. I watched her digging the back garden up, she had a hoe in her hand chopping the ground, and she swung so hard she missed the ground, and the hoe missed her leg by a tenth of an inch.

That massive dog she has walked in front of her. She fell while watering the flowers because the dog tripped her. That's only a few things I've seen. Imagine what I don't see."

"You need to stop right now. Gabby will think you're a stalker."

"Yes, you do need to stop. You can't check on her if you are not dating this woman. Lord, what were you thinking," Darcy said, peeking around the seat. She got up and joined us. "Tell me about your neighbor."

"My neighbor is Gabby McKalister."

"Oh, wow, the country singer Gabby McKalister."

"Yes."

"She's beautiful, and she plays with saws."

"Exactly. Gabby thinks she can do anything, and I guess she can. She's been caring for herself and Madison since she was eighteen."

"That's right. I forgot she has a daughter. How old is the daughter?"

"She's fifteen. Madison is a great kid."

"So you have a thing for the neighbor? Why don't you ask her out?"

"I would never date my neighbor, and she would never date me."

"Why?"

"I don't want to date my neighbor because living next door would be uncomfortable when we break up. I think we are better off staying friends."

"If you think that way, you should stop calling and checking on her. Otherwise, she'll think you want to be more than friends."

"Why? Friends can be concerned about each other. But I wouldn't want Gabby to think I'm interested in her. So I guess I'll take a step back."

I fell asleep and woke up when we were landing in Arizona. The sun was high in the sky, and it felt fantastic. I left the plane first, and then the others followed. I couldn't wait to get to Sedona. The house had a waterfall behind it with a pool at the bottom.

My favorite spot was that pool. George even enjoyed it. I put Darcy in a room between all of us. We bought this place because of all the bedrooms. It had six bedrooms, and each room had its own bathroom. That's what I loved. I never liked sharing my bathroom.

"I'll cook dinner tonight. We will have steaks," I said.

"How is your fridge filled with fresh fruit and fresh meat?"

"We have someone who works for us in town. I called and asked her if she would fill the fridge."

6
GABBY

I stepped back and looked at the birdhouse I had just made. It might be a little crooked, but I love it. It was beautiful. I was so proud of myself for making this birdhouse. All I did was look on Pinterest and copy it. I ended up getting a couple of different saws. *Hmm... Should I send a picture to Ryker and ask him what color he wants?*

I picked up my phone and started texting him. 'I decided to let you finish the bookshelves since you are so kind to do this for me. I made you a birdhouse. What color do you want me to paint it? I bought various colored paints that were returned to the hardware store.' My phone binged, and I smiled.

"I can't believe you made me a birdhouse. I love it." Ryker texted. "I will let you decide what color to paint it." I looked at the colors and decided on purple and green. *It'll look great. I hope he doesn't think I like him or something.* I looked up as a vehicle pulled into my driveway, and an older woman got out.

"Hello."

"Hello, I'm Ryker's mom. I came over to pick up George. My name is Wilma Malone."

"Hi, Wilma. I'm Gabby McKalister. We can keep George here with us. He's no trouble at all. He likes being lazy with Mona. Let's go inside, and I'll show you. They are best of friends. We walked inside, and both of us stopped in our tracks. George and Mona were mating. I threw my hands over my face and screamed. Wilma laughed. I peeked through my fingers at her, and she turned her back on the two love birds.

"What am I supposed to do now?"

"I don't think you can do much right now."

"How long will they be together?" I couldn't help it. I started crying. Mona was a baby. She wasn't old enough to have babies. I should have fixed her, but I wanted to wait until we moved here. I waited too long. I wiped my eyes, and Wilma wrapped her arms around me.

"Let's go back outside. You can show me your birdhouses. I'll take George home with me when those two are finished."

"Yes, that would be best. Every time I see George, I'll remember this. Wait until I tell Madison."

"Who's Madison?"

"She's my daughter. We got Mona when she was so tiny. She is still so young. I hope she'll be okay."

"You can take her to the vet in a few weeks, and he can advise you on what to do. Maybe she won't become pregnant."

"I never thought of that. I'm sure I'm worried for no reason. I'll show you my birdhouses. I just started making them. I made this one for Ryker because he cut the wood for my shelves."

"He's going to love it."

"I sent him a picture, and he does like it. I'm going to paint it purple and green."

"I'm sorry about your grandfather. Vic was such a nice man. He was an excellent friend to Ryker and everyone in this town."

"Thank you. I miss him a lot." I heard a noise and saw George and Mona walking off the front porch. I shook my head, and then I looked at Wilma. She was trying not to laugh, but I burst into laughter. "I feel like Mona needs a bath."

Wilma then burst into laughter, "I know what you mean. I can barely look at them."

We laughed for a while before Wilma said she had to leave. "I have to clean out my fridge. It went out while I was gone, and everything inside was ruined."

"Oh no. If you need me for anything, please feel free to call me. Here, I'll get you my number." I ran inside, grabbed a piece of paper, and wrote down my number. "Here you go. It was so nice meeting you."

"I'm glad I got to meet you too. If Mona has babies, can I please have one of them?"

"Of course, you get the first pick. That's the least I can do after you had to see the mating." We started laughing again.

"Mom, I'm home. I'm going to make Dustin and me something to eat."

I was busy painting Ryker's birdhouse. "Come and look at my birdhouse."

"Mom, you did this. It's beautiful."

I looked at Madison, and she had a crooked smile, which meant she wasn't being entirely truthful. "You don't like it?"

"Mom, I do like it, I promise. It's just... is it crooked?"

"Well, a little. It's for Ryker because he cut my shelves. I have something to tell you."

"What is it? Is it horrible? You have that look."

"Today, Wilma, that's Ryker's mom... She came to pick up George today, and when we went inside to get him, he and Mona were mating."

"Are you saying George and Mona were doing it?"

"I didn't say it like that. But yes, they were doing it. So we might be having puppies running around here." I looked at Dustin, "Would you like one?"

"Are you kidding? I would love one. This is the best gift I could have right now. Something new. Thank you!"

"You're welcome. Wilma is getting one, too. I'm not positive she will have any puppies, but we'll know soon enough. I'll take her to the vet in a couple of weeks. Okay, now you can get something to eat." I looked at Madison, and she had tears in her eyes. I knew how she felt; I did the same thing. "Are you okay?"

"Mona is only one year old. She's too young to have babies."

"That's what I thought, so I called the vet, who assured me she was old enough. I should have gotten her fixed, but I didn't. Now we have to wait and see what happens."

"If she has babies, then we don't have the right to give her babies away." She started to cry before I could reach for her; Dustin put his arm around her and patted her on the back.

"She may not even be pregnant. We won't worry about her babies until the time comes."

"Yeah, let's go inside and find something to eat," Dustin said.

I could hear Dustin explaining to her how puppies were

supposed to be shared with others. I shook my head. If Mona was pregnant, I knew I would have a fight on my hands trying to rip those puppies out of Madison's tight fist. I laughed out loud. Never a dull moment in our house. I looked at the birdhouse and took a picture.

7

RYKER

I laughed when I saw the photo of my birdhouse. I texted back. 'I love it.' My phone rang. I saw my mom's picture come up. I answered the call. "Hey, Mom, how was your trip?"

"I had a wonderful time. I went to pick up George, and I met your beautiful neighbor. I guess you know she's famous. I recognized her right off. She is so sweet." Mom began to laugh.

"I have to tell you this," she said, chuckling. "Gabby wanted me to see how good George and Mona got along. We walked into her house, and the dogs were stuck together."

"What! Fuck, that damn George. What did Gabby do?"

"She screamed and covered her eyes, and then she cried. Because Mona is still a baby, I don't know. I think she was more embarrassed than anything. The good news is that I get the pick of the litter."

"Mom, why did I let you talk me into not fixing George?"

"I didn't want George to get fixed because I wanted the pick of the litter from George's puppy... I hope Mona becomes pregnant."

My phone beeped, and I saw it was Gabby. "I gotta go, Mom." We said quick goodbyes, and I hung up and answered her call.

"Hey, I'm so sorry. My mom told me about my bad dog."

"George is a nasty dog. You will be the one who will be with Mona when it's her time to have the babies. Now Madison says we can't give Mona's puppies away. She thinks I am going to keep all of them. In nine months, make sure you are around to help her deliver those puppies."

"Umm, Gabby, a dog isn't pregnant for nine months. They are pregnant for nine weeks."

"What? Nine weeks. That's crazy. How can puppies be born in nine weeks? I have to go." She hung up on me.

So, we will be co-parenting Mona. Maybe I'll take a pup.

"We've been here for three weeks, and the police still have not caught Steve. We need to set him up and catch him ourselves. We'll stay at Darcy's house. I bet you anything he's watching that house."

"That's a great idea. I'm ready to catch him. I need my life back, and I'm sure you guys are ready to get going. Let's go to my house and wait for that bastard. Remember though, if I see him first, I'm shooting him."

"I wasn't planning on taking you with us, Darcy. That would be putting you in danger."

"I'll be safe with all of you there. Let's kill Steve. If we don't, he'll kill me."

Blade stood up. "Darcy's right. If we don't kill him, he'll kill her."

I paced back and forth. I knew he was right. "We can't

just kill someone. We'll leave in the morning. Darcy, if you ever decide to move and get another job, I would like it if you would come and work for us. We have to have help in the office. We are so busy that it's hard to run this business while guarding people."

"Well, hell, don't cry," Blade said.

"I'm just so happy. I've been worried about what I'm going to do, and I knew I would miss all of you when this was over. Yes, I will work for you. Wow, you have made me one happy woman. I can't wait to start. I want to move from my town. Where do *we* live?"

"We live on the Oregon coast."

"I love the Oregon coast."

"So you've been there before?"

"No, but I've seen pictures, and the coast looks so pretty." She sat down and sighed, wiping her tears. "I know this is crazy, but I feel like you are my brothers, and I'm safe around you."

"DAMN IT, Darcy, get back in here. I've told you to only go outside if we know you're going out there."

"I'm ready to go to my new home. I still have to find a place to live. My boxes are all packed. I'm ready to move to Oregon. I want him to see me, so he'll come and get me."

"He'll come, don't worry, and we'll be ready for him when he does."

Later that day, it was my shift when I heard the scraping sound. I tapped Blade and Jackson on the shoulder. I motioned for them to stay with Darcy. I went toward the noise. I was sitting on her bed when he crawled inside from the window. I let him get inside. I saw the ax in his hand. He raised his arm, and I fired. I got him in the heart. Then I called the police.

It was pretty crazy for a while, with Darcy's dad wanting her to start back working for him on Monday. That was only two days away. This was too crazy even for my mind to comprehend. I mean, his daughter had just been through something so dangerous and all he cared about was her coming back to work immediately. I listened to Darcy talking to him.

"Dad, I quit. I'm moving to Oregon, and I'm going to work in the office for Seal Security. I love you, but you will kill Mom, making her work all the time. If this taught me anything, it was that I had to live my life and not work all the time. Please retire and enjoy life before it's too late."

Darcy's mom hugged her then she looked at her husband, "I quit too. If you want to work until you die, you go right ahead, but I quit. I'll give you two weeks' notice, and that's it. I want to travel and enjoy my life while I'm alive."

"I want to quit, too," Darcy's dad said and all heads turned in his direction. A few gasps came from the room. Looking at his face, I could see he was just a man trying to look after his family the best way he knew how. I felt sorry for him and happy that he was being honest in this very moment. "I'll put the business up for sale, and we'll travel together all over the world."

When they returned to their car after telling her goodbye, Darcy still clapped her hands. She was so excited. "Let's get going!" she said eagerly. "I will have to come back to sell my house and get my furniture. I can't wait to meet George and Mona. I wonder if I could have a puppy. I just realized I'd be there when the puppies are born. I'm staying at your house, Ryker, and I want to see the birdhouses. Maybe Gabby will show me how to build them."

Blade chuckled, and I smiled. You couldn't help but love Darcy. She was friendly and talkative, just like a little sister.

8

GABBY

When Ryker got back, I was sitting on the front porch with Mona when I saw a pretty woman get out of his vehicle. Before I knew what she was doing, she was on my porch smiling at me. "Would you like a cup of coffee?" I asked.

"Oh, I would love a cup. My name is Darcy Hamilton. I'm so excited to meet you and Mona. Can I please have a puppy?" It must have been the look on my face; I'm sure it showed that I was just baffled by what was happening. She clarified things for me, "You must think I'm crazy. Seal Security guarded me against someone who tried to kill me. He's dead now."

"He sounds like he needed to be dead."

"That's for sure. I'm going to work for their company. But I wanted to meet you and see if you could teach me how to make birdhouses."

I chuckled. "I'm not very good at it."

"I saw Ryker's birdhouse and thought it was so cute. I've always wanted to do something like that. But I was always working. I just quit my job. Now my dad is selling his business, and he and mom are going to travel."

"That sounds like fun for them."

"I think so too. I have to find myself a place to live. You probably think I'm a child, the way I'm going on and on. I'm just excited to be here. I love your singing."

I chuckled again. "Thank you. Here you go. I'll pour a cup for Ryker, too."

"Thank you. I could use that coffee right now." I handed him his coffee.

"I see you've met Darcy."

"Yes, we introduced ourselves."

"Darcy will stay here until she finds a place of her own."

"I hope you find a place you like."

"Ryker's mom said there is a place over where she lives. I'll check it out tomorrow."

"Good luck. I wish I could help, but I'm leaving tomorrow."

"Where are you going?"

I looked at Ryker when he asked that question. I knew he was biting his tongue for asking me.

"I have some concerts I'm having."

"What about Maddison?" he asked.

"What about her?"

"Will she miss school?"

"No, she does it online. It's okay for a few weeks. We've done it this way since she started school. If you will excuse me, I need to do some packing."

"Thank you for the birdhouse."

"You're welcome. I'll see you when I get back."

"Yes, I'll see you then."

I heard our taxi pull into our driveway, and a text message confirmed that my driver had arrived. We were all packed and ready to go. "Maddison, the driver is here," I called out to her, unsure of where she was in the house.

"I'll be right there."

When I saw what she was wearing, I laughed. "Where did you get that sweatshirt?"

"Guess." The sweatshirt read, 'She is my teacher, so back off.' It also had a photo of Dustin on it. My heart skipped a beat. I wondered if Maddison was having a crush on Dustin or if they were having one on each other. I made a mental note to ask her later.

I was singing my third song when I suddenly had the chills go down my body; something was wrong. I looked at Levi, my base player. He walked to where I stood singing. I covered my mic. "Can you check on Madison?" He was back in twenty minutes, giving me a thumbs up. I let my body relax. The rest of the night dragged by. I couldn't wait to get to Madison. One more night, and we could go home. I couldn't wait.

We were in the RV getting ready for bed when my phone rang. "Hello."

"Hey, I just wanted to see how things were."

"It's going. I keep reminding myself that I'm taking a well-deserved year off in just one more night, one more live performance." I allowed a pause to linger before changing the topic. "Mona is so fat. I hope she doesn't have her babies until we get home. I'm driving the RV home. I had the strangest feeling come over me when I was singing. I don't know what it was, but it scared the hell out of me."

"Listen to me, Gabby. Go with your feelings. Lock your RV up good and tight tonight. Can you have someone stay in the RV with you?"

"They'll think I'm crazy."

"To hell with that. What is better? Yours and Madison's safety or your band members thinking you are crazy."

"You're right. I'll call Levi right now. I'll see you in a few days." I called Levi, and he came right over. "I'm sorry to ask you to stay with us, but I can't shake this feeling."

"Someone was lurking around out there, so I told the guard, and he said he would stick around the RVs."

"Good. Thank you. Madison is sleeping. I'm going to bed. Goodnight."

"Goodnight."

9

RYKER

I was drinking a beer on the front porch when Gabby drove up in a giant RV. That thing had to be the biggest RV I've ever seen. She called my name, and I walked over with Dustin, who eagerly awaited Madison's arrival.

"Hurry, Mona is delivering her puppies. Please help her."

Dustin dropped down next to Madison, and she hugged him.

"Why don't we let Mona have her puppies in peace? We'll stay nearby, but I don't want to upset her while she's having her puppies. Dogs know what to do."

"Ryker, I'm going into my house to unpack my suitcase. You can watch over Mona. I've had to listen to Madison crying over Mona being in pain for the last, I don't know how long, and I have a headache."

"There really isn't anything to do. You just stand by so she knows she's not alone."

"You can tell me when she's finished, and we'll bring all of them inside. I'm worn out. The last hundred miles were long. Between Madison crying and Mona breathing hard, I'm ready to pull my hair out."

I was smiling as she talked. "Welcome home." I handed her my beer, and she took a long drink.

"Thank you."

I watched as she walked into her house. Damn, I missed that woman! What the hell am I saying? I missed her because I was used to having my neighbor home. It's not for any other reason. It's not because I worried about her driving the freeway alone with only her daughter. I walked back to my porch.

I smiled and took a deep breath. I was so relieved she was home. I looked at my birdhouse hanging on the tree. She made this for me. After being unable to stop thinking about her, I got up and walked over to her house. The front door was open, and I stepped inside. She was in the kitchen; I could hear her singing. She looked at me, her eyes big.

"Did she have the babies? Should we take her to the vet?"

I didn't say anything. "Why are you looking at me like that? What are you doing?"

I stood in front of her. "I missed you."

"You did?"

"Yes, I did. I'm relieved you are home safe, where I can see that you are okay."

"What are you doing?"

"I'm going to kiss you," I said as my hands threaded through her hair. My mouth landed on hers and devoured her plump lips. I wrapped my arms around her and pulled her as close as possible. She had her arms around me, also.

"I don't think we should do this. We are neighbors who are friendly with each other. I don't want to mess that up."

"I want you."

"You want me?"

"Yes, I want you."

"Wow, I've never had anyone tell me they wanted me."

"You have now." That thought sunk in and instantly stopped me in my tracks. I pulled away from her and looked her in the eyes. "Wait, I can't believe no one has ever told you they wanted to make love to you all night long."

"Well, you didn't exactly say that, so I still haven't been told that either. But I have a daughter."

"So."

"I don't have sex with men because I have a daughter."

"Are you kidding me?"

"Be quiet. Someone might hear you."

"Listen, sweetheart, we can take this slow if that's what you want. But this is going to happen. I'll give you time." I pulled her back into my arms, and she kissed me. My arms were around her waist. She leaned back and looked at me.

"I don't need time. I want you to. We will have a date as soon as everything settles down with the pups."

"We will?"

"I'm not going to just sleep with you. You can have me over for dinner one night."

I smiled and kissed her lips. "Okay, Wednesday night; I will cook you dinner."

"It's a date. Now, let's check on the puppies."

We walked back to the RV, where three puppies had already been born. She was obviously still in labor. "Mama, how many babies will she have?"

"I don't know."

"She'll have maybe six. She's a big dog," Ryker told her.

"What! How can she have six? She will die if she has six puppies," Madison wailed loudly.

"Madison, I want you to go inside the house and shower

it'll make you feel better. Look at Mona. You're causing her to have a hard time because you're scaring her. She doesn't like you watching her and crying. I'll stay with her. I'm sorry, but I can't have you here while she has her puppies."

"Okay, as long as you stay here with her, I'll leave. I'm happy I'm going. It is just too hard watching her have these puppies."

"Come on, Dustin, you can make us a sandwich while I shower."

That's when I remembered I should have talked to Madison. When they left, I looked at my handsome neighbor. "I need to talk to Madison about Dustin. It seems like the two are becoming very close. I don't want what happened to me to happen to Madison."

"I'll talk to Dustin. How about you and I sit on that sofa over there?" I pulled her hand, walked her to the sofa, and onto my lap when I sat down. I wrapped my arms around her and kissed her.

"What if we end up hating each other and have to live next door to each other? I would have to build me a very tall fence. Because I'm telling you, I will not sell my house."

"I could never hate you. You are the only person I know who made me a birdhouse."

10

GABBY

Mona had ten puppies before the day was over. We carried them all into the house and put them in the laundry room, where it was warm. Mona was such a good mommy to her babies. But dang, they were loud, crying for her to feed them. I didn't worry about her needing to get out because she had a doggy door and could come and go whenever she wanted to.

Madison spent a lot of time with the puppies, and I spent a lot of time with Ryker. He was either at my house, or I was at his. I loved kissing him and the places his hands went was very welcomed. I was ready to crawl into his bed by the time Wednesday night came around.

"Madison?"

"Yeah?"

"Your dinner is ready. I'm going over to Ryker's for dinner."

"You are?" I didn't miss the silly grin she had on her face.

"Yes... I can't believe I'm going to say this out loud... I don't know how this came about. Okay, I do. I'm going to Ryker's on a date. I might be home late."

"What! I like Ryker. Mama, that's wonderful."

"It is?"

"Yes, it's about time you went on a date. If I need you, I'll call you. I don't want you worrying about me."

I heard the doorbell, and when I opened the door, Ryker stood there looking handsome. "Why are you here?"

"I'm picking up my date. You didn't think I would let you walk to my place alone, did you?"

"Well, I guess I did." I heard giggling and turned around. Madison stood there with a giant grin on her face.

"Hello, Madison. Your mom will be at my place if you need anything."

"I won't need anything. Besides, Dustin is coming over."

I looked at Ryker. I had been so busy with him lately I still hadn't given Madison that talk.

"I talked to Dustin, and you don't have to worry," he whispered. "He said they are best friends, not the boyfriend and girlfriend kind of friends."

"I'll still talk to her." I closed the door behind me as we began our short trek next door. "What are we having for dinner?"

"Spaghetti and meatballs. Do you like spaghetti?"

"Yes, it's one of my favorite foods." When we got into his house, he had made it romantic with soft music and candlelight. "This is beautiful."

"I'm glad you like it. He walked me to the dining room. The bread and salad were next to each other. I sat down and then he took the seat opposite mine. Neither of us talked. I took a bite of the bread and then dug into the salad. "This is really good. Where did you get your bread?"

"I made it."

"Wow, I'm impressed. It's delicious. Did you make the dressing too?"

"Yes, it's my special recipe."

I smiled and kept on eating. I was so nervous about today that I hadn't eaten anything. He brought in the spaghetti, and I devoured it also. "Everything is so good."

"Would you like some more? Or are you ready for dessert?" he asked as he poured more wine into my glass. I wasn't used to drinking anything but iced tea, so I decided not to drink any more of the wine.

"What are we having for dessert?"

"I made a chocolate cake. I also have ice cream."

"I'm ready for dessert. I'll help you dish it out," I said, getting up and carrying my plate into the kitchen. His kitchen was spotless. He didn't make messes like me when I cooked a meal. I turned with my back to the counter when he took me in his arms. He kissed me, and my body had a mind of its own.

My panties were wet within the firs two second. I pulled back and looked at him. "I want you."

"Right now?"

I smiled. "Yes, now." He took my hand and walked me to his bedroom. I pulled my dress up and over my head. I knew how this night would end, so I only had on my bikini panties. He looked at my body and stepped up to me, and his hands trailed lightly over my breast and further down. I pulled at his tee shirt. I heard him chuckle as he pulled it over his head. I've seen this body without a shirt on many times, and every time, I wanted to taste his skin, every muscle he had. I ran my fingers over him and down to his waist.

"Take them off," I said in a breathy whisper.

He unbuckled his jeans, and I pushed them down then he took off my panties. We stood naked together. Ryker pulled me into his arms as his hard erection pushed against me. His hand trailed down goosebumps spread over my body.

Ryker picked me up and put me on the bed. When his hands ran under me, he trailed his mouth all over my body. He pushed me up to meet his hot tongue as he tasted me. I cried out and spread my thighs further to give him better access. He pushed his fingers inside me and started moving in and out. I was overexcited, crying for more.

I knew I was going to explode, so I pulled him up. Ryker reached over and put a condom on, pushing his hot hard erection inside me. I orgasmed, and he kept pumping. "Yes, Ryker. Don't stop," I cried as I came again and again. I knew when he looked into my eyes he was going to come.

He lay over me, propped up by his elbows. He was staring into my eyes. I raised my head and licked his lips. That was all he needed. He devoured my lips as he moved over me again and pushed his hard erection inside me. I met him with each move, taking him deeper inside me. We made love until it was super late, and I knew I had to leave.

"I'm coming with you," Ryker said, pulling on his clothes.

"You are. Why?"

"Because I want to be with you all night."

"Okay. I want to be with you all night too."

He walked to me and pulled my dress over me but not before tasting my breast as his fingers went inside of me, and he took the time to make me come again. We ran to my house, and I prayed Madison was sleeping. It was dark, so I took his hand and ran upstairs. It only took a moment to undress and jump into bed.

"Your bed is too small."

"Nope. It's a strategy. This way, I have to squeeze next to you, and we can cuddle."

"I think I'll enjoy cuddling you."

I raised and climbed on him. I pushed his erection inside me and started moving. All the time, I watched him. He pushed himself hard into me each time I moved until I cried out, then he flipped me under him and started moving as I orgasmed. He never stopped, and I came again. When he orgasmed, I felt it go inside of me. We looked at each other in shock. I forgot he needed a condom when I put him inside of me.

"It's okay; I take the pill."

"Look at me, Gabby. Are you telling me the truth?"

"No, but it was only once. It'll be fine. I don't want you to worry. I don't want anything to mess this night up. It was perfect. I wish we would have started making love before now. It's so good."

He chuckled. "I'm getting you some condoms to put in your nightstand."

I lay in his arms and slept. When I woke up, he was gone. I got up and showered. Then I went downstairs for coffee. He was there with Madison. I felt my face burning as he winked at me. "I came over early to get you. You do remember we were going to that new antique store, don't you?"

"Yes, I'll have a cup of coffee, then we can leave. Madison, do you want to go with us.?"

"No, I will stay here. So, are you two dating now?"

"Yes, is that okay with you?" Ryker asked.

"Yes, I think it's great. I'll see you when you get back. I'm going with Dustin and some friends surfing."

"Madison, you be careful."

"I will be."

As soon as she walked out of the room, Ryker pulled me

into his arms. "Your lips taste good. In fact, all of you taste good. Can my tongue taste you this morning?"

"Yes, I want to taste all of you, also. Where are we going?"

"You're quick. I have a place in the mountains about an hour away from here. We are going to make love until the sun starts going down. Then we will come home, and I'll be in your bed tonight."

"That sounds perfect." I kissed him again.

We made love every night for a week before Ryker had to leave for work. "Where are you going?" I asked when he broke the news.

"Texas. It's a human trafficking case. Someone hired us to find his daughter. She's sixteen. I pray we find her before they drug her up."

"Why do they drug them?"

"To make them behave. They get them addicted to drugs, and they will do anything for their next fix."

"I'm going to miss you. I probably won't be able to sleep without you to cuddle up with."

"I'm going to miss you too. I want you to take care of yourself while I'm gone. I admit I have one of those minds that worry about everything."

"No kidding, I never would have thought that if you hadn't told me." We both chuckled, remembering how he was worried over the saw.

11

RYKER

I wanted to kill every one of these fuckers. We still haven't found Elizabeth, the girl we were hired to find, but we have found other girls. We were in disguise, so they wouldn't know we were the same men who asked for girls each time.

We needed to kill these bastards, and I will as soon as we find Elizabeth. I was waiting in my room when someone knocked. It was Juan. He was pulling a girl in behind him. I couldn't believe what I was seeing. There were two little girls, and both were crying. He slapped them, and then he took my money and left.

I held my fingers to my lips. These were the girls who went missing this morning. They were covered in bruises. "I'm not going to hurt you. I'm going to take you home. But we have to make sure Juan is gone first."

I called Lincoln. "I have the twins who went missing this morning. I need to get them out of here and back to their parents. Do you know if Juan is gone?"

"He just left here. Give it ten minutes. I'm going to take this woman to her husband. When you're ready, let me know. She's been missing for two months. She lives in Mexico. They forced her to come here, or they would kill her family. She's scared to go home, but she's going to go anyway. She said the cartel and some high-up politicians are working together trafficking women and girls."

"Bastards, that doesn't surprise me at all. Our government is so corrupt. You can take her to the vehicle first, and then I'll take the girls out."

I waited for ten minutes before I took the girls to the vehicle. They climbed into the back seat with the woman as I sat in the front. Lincoln drove. He was angry. I knew not to say anything to him. Lincoln was half-Mexican, and it pissed him off how the cartel treated the people who lived in Mexico.

I turned in my seat and looked at the girls. "Do you know your address?"

"Yes." They told us where they lived, and we drove two hours to their home. I knocked on the door because I wanted to make sure the police weren't there. When their father answered, I asked him to step outside.

"My name is Ryker. I'm a retired Navy Seal and my company was hired to find a sixteen-year-old girl. We found your daughters while looking for her. You can't tell anyone about us. It will destroy our cover, and then we won't be able to help anyone else."

"I won't tell a soul," he said through trembling lips. His eyes were filled with tears and hope. I guess hope that I was telling the truth and he was really about to be re-united with his daughters again.

"Okay, we'll pull into your garage, and the girls can get out of our vehicle. We have another victim with us. We are taking her to her family next." He ran inside, and the garage door opened. We drove inside, and it closed.

He and his wife were there. They jerked the back door open, and their little girls flew into their arms. "You need to call the police, but give it a few hours. Tell them your daughters were home. Don't tell them anything about us, and don't let them question your girls."

They were crying and nodding their heads. "Why don't you take your family on an extended vacation? Do you have any family you can visit?"

"Yes," he said nodding, tears running down his face. "We will visit my brother."

"Good idea."

"How can we ever thank you?"

"Just don't mention us. Now you can open your garage door."

We left the family together and made our way out of the neighborhood discretely. The same way we had come in. As if she'd been thinking about this strategy for a while, the young woman said, "You are doing good work. I don't think my husband will want me after I've been gone so long. I'm going to stay here and help others that the cartel kidnaps. I've seen lots of small children. It's mostly the kids that came over the border. But there are also white kids."

"How are you going to help them?"

"I will help them by helping you. If you can give Juan extra money, I can stay with you and help. But you have to pay him for me. I know where these children are held."

"Okay, I agree she can help us," Lincoln said.

"It's about to get very dangerous. You know Juan, he's nobody. The ones which cause us nightmares are the ones guarding the kids."

We drove to our hotel and took our disguises off. Then we put another one on. The woman refused to tell us her name and took a shower. She stayed in there until the water was ice cold. I knew she was trying to wash away the horror she had gone through.

We were in another vehicle as we drove past one house and then another and another. We decided to call the lady with us Haddy because she wouldn't give us her name. We had to plan. We couldn't just storm the house. We had to kill the men who held them captive.

"How many men watch the house?"

"Maybe three. The women and kids are locked inside the bedrooms. They don't get to leave the bedrooms."

"What if they have to use the bathroom?"

"The bedrooms I've been in have bathrooms."

We drove past one of the houses when something on the roof caught my attention. "Fuck, there's Elizabeth."

"She must have broken the window because all the windows are nailed shut," Haddy said with fear in her voice.

My heart stopped beating. That was a two-story house. "Go down the road. I'll get out and help her. We have to get her before the men see her."

I jumped out of the vehicle and ran back to where Elizabeth was. I saw her sitting on the roof of the house. I pulled myself onto the roof. She saw me, and I put my fingers to my lips. She wiped her eyes and nodded. I pulled myself up on the second roof, and she walked to where I was.

"Elizabeth, your dad sent me to find you. Don't say anything. I will get you off the roof. Do you see that black car down there?" She nodded. The moment your feet touch the ground, you run to it. Tell Lincoln, who is driving, to go. I'll catch up with him." She nodded again.

I helped her off the first roof and then the second one. As soon as she touched the ground, she did exactly as I told her to. I went to the broken window and saw the kids inside.

I held my hand to my lips, and they nodded. I motioned for them to come outside.

I wondered what I would do with them. I saw the neighbor lady watching me and held my finger to my lips. She nodded. Thank God for nosey neighbors. I loved my neighbor. Where the hell did that come from? I enjoy my neighbor. I don't love her.

I had three girls out of the window when the neighbor put up a ladder that led into her yard. The girls trusted us to help them. The woman wiped her eyes. She had guessed right that she lived next door to a home where they held trafficked children. There were fifteen girls in that room. One of the girls told me four bedrooms had girls in them.

I climbed down the ladder, and we went into the woman's home. "I knew something was going on at that house. I would sometimes hear girls crying. What do you want me to do?" she asked, confirming what I thought when I looked at her crying.

"What kind of vehicle do you have?"

"A large SUV."

"Put the girls in it and drive away. Make sure they stay down. Whatever you do, don't call the police yet. I have to get the other girls out before they show up with their sirens blaring." I looked over on the roof, and Lincoln was there. I wondered where the girl was.

"That's my friend, Lincoln. He will help me. Can you handle this?"

"Yes, I can. Don't worry about us."

I hid the ladder along the fence line in case we needed it again. I looked at Lincoln, "There were fifteen girls in that room. One of the girls said there were four bedrooms, and each had at least fifteen girls in them."

"How are we going to do this?"

"We will each take a window and break the glass as Elizabeth did. Then we will get them out, and they can go down the ladder."

"Okay, let's get started. If I see one of the cartels, I'll kill him."

"Yeah, we have to do what we have to do."

The room I looked into was full of little ones. They were all scared to death. When they saw me, they cried louder. I put my finger to my lips, and some calmed down. By the time I got most of them out of the window, I knew they wouldn't be able to go down the ladder. Lincoln came around from the other side, and he glanced at the children.

He looked at the kids with him and said something. Then, I watched each of the older kids pick up a little one. I put the ladder up and helped them down. I looked at the older kids. "How old are the kids in the last room?"

"They are women. I can sometimes hear them screaming in pain. I think they do a lot of sick stuff to them. I hope you can help them. But I think the men stay in there with the ladies. Their room is on the first floor. It's in the back of the house."

"Damn, that won't work. Go into this house and keep the doors locked until I call out. My name is Ryker, and my buddy is Lincoln." I took the ladder down again, pulling myself onto the roof. We were quiet as we walked to the back of the house.

That's when I saw a man on the phone walking in the backyard. I looked at Lincoln, and he took something from his pocket. A silencer. I watched as he pointed his gun and shot the guy in the chest. The man hit the ground and died before the phone fell from his hand.

We jumped to the ground and almost ran into the man who walked out the slider door. My fist connected with his face, and he went down. I saw him move, and Lincoln shot him in the heart.

We decided just to walk inside and see where the last man was. I opened a door, and he had his cock in a woman's mouth while he beat her with his belt. I cleared my throat, and he looked at me. I saw the fear in his eyes before Lincoln killed him. The woman got up and kicked him at least twenty times.

"How many men are here?"

"Three."

"Then they are all dead."

We finally called the police and explained what was going on. We refused to hand the kids over to them when they got there. One of the girls said some of the police were involved. So when the news people showed up, I told them why the kids were not leaving us unless it was with their family. Of course, that made it a lot longer before I would see Gabby.

12

GABBY

THE PUPPIES WERE THE CUTEST THINGS, BUT THEY WERE SO noisy, crying all the time, wanting Mona to feed them constantly. She didn't have time to walk around outside before they wanted her back with them. Wilma had been over and picked out the puppy she wanted. She named her puppy Sara. Dustin picked out his puppy, too.

Madison wasn't happy. She thought it was mean for us to take Mona's babies from her. We all explained to her that's how it worked. She decided that if we were giving the puppies away, she would pick their owners. I was surprised when she refused to let her dad and his new wife have a puppy.

"I don't trust them to take care of a puppy," she told me openly. "I'm sure the puppy would be locked outside all the time." Now her dad was upset because his young wife wanted a puppy. I told him to buy her one and tell her it was one of Mona's.

I missed Ryker; I thought of him all the time. I was just wondering if he thought of me, and then he called me. I was so excited to hear from him.

"We'll be here longer than I thought we would be. What are you doing?"

"I've been going crazy with these puppies. Ryker, I miss you and am not too fond of missing you. It's not like we've even been dating long. We dated for less than two weeks before you went away. But I do miss you. When are you coming home?"

"I'm not sure. I miss you too. I wouldn't say I like it either. We know how my love life was before you moved next door. I don't want to allow one person to have control of my happiness or my sadness. I want to be in control of all of my feelings: me and only me."

"Do you want us to go back to just being neighbors?"

"Hell no. This is why I knew this wouldn't be a good idea. I don't want to hurt you. I don't want you to get hurt if I want to date another woman."

"Is this why you called? Do you want to date another woman?"

"No, I only want you."

"Good, I'll see you when you get home. You are going to have to take a puppy. Madison has already picked one out for you. I think she plans on keeping them close to her. She has given Sofie and Noah one already. I think she is making your friends take the puppies."

"Darcy has one, Madison tried to give her two, but Darcy said no, she only wanted one. Your mom has two of them..." I heard laughing, and he couldn't stop. "You can stop laughing. My daughter is obsessed."

"I'm sorry. It's good to laugh again."

"Is it horrible?"

"Yes, it is. The cartel will take anyone. The younger, the better. They're everywhere. Make sure you keep your doors locked."

"Always. Goodnight, Ryker."

"Goodnight, sweetheart."

It's been six weeks since I've seen Ryker. He made sure those kids were back with their families before he left. Now he was on his way home, and I was a nervous wreck. I've taken two showers. I even changed my clothes three times. Finally, I put on shorts and a tee shirt so Ryker wouldn't think I was waiting for him.

At eleven, I went to bed. Ryker wasn't home, and I was worn out by being excited all day. I had to stop this. I was sleeping when I heard a noise. I raised and looked around. I got out of bed when I heard shouting.

I ran downstairs and into a horror film. A man was fighting Dustin while another man held my daughter by her hair. I picked up a large brass lamp and charged the man as he cut Madison's ponytail off. I screamed as I hit him on the back of the head. He fell and landed on the floor, then I ran and went to hit the man fighting with Dustin when I saw his knife enter Dustin's body.

Madison screamed and ran to Dustin when the man grabbed her and pointed the knife against her neck.

"Get the fuck away from my daughter, or I will kill you right now!" I roared. He started laughing, and I saw blood as he stuck the knife deeper into her neck. "Stop! What do you want?"

"What we want is money. Lots of money," the man I'd hit over the head said.

Damn, I was hoping he was dead. They were high on drugs. I've seen it before. There were sores on their faces. They looked to be in their forties. He walked up behind me, and his fist hit me in the face. I knew instantly that my nose was broken. I fell to the floor. I heard Madison scream for me. I got back up and looked at the man who hit me. They were a couple of ugly bastards.

"I will give you as much money as you want. I'll go with you right now. Just leave my daughter here. If you touch her again, I will never give you anything."

"Let's go. Joe, you stay here with them."

"No, don't let him leave you here. He just wants all the money." I thought if I could get them fighting, then they would both go. I didn't care if they took me, but I had to keep them away from Madison. I prayed they would leave her here.

"Is that what you were thinking? To take her, and then you would leave me here to go to jail. I'm going with you."

"Grab the girl. We take her with us."

"No! She stays, or I won't get your money!" I screamed.

"Leave her. Let's go," he shrugged.

"Mama, no."

"I'll be okay.

13

RYKER

IT WAS LATE, AND I WAS TIRED. A BAD ACCIDENT ON THE freeway held us back a couple of hours, as we volunteered to help the fire department clean everything up. "What the fuck is going on?" I shouted as Lincoln and I pulled into the driveway. I jumped from the vehicle as it was rolling. We both ran to Gabby's house, where the ambulance and three police cars were. Lights were flashing, and a siren was still blaring. I reached into the police car and turned it off. My heart stopped beating.

We ran inside. Madison was crying hysterically. She wouldn't let go of Dustin's hand. In her other hand was her ponytail. I let out a roar so loud. Madison ran to me. "They have Mama. One man hit her, and her nose is broken. They cut my ponytail off."

I was in shock, looking at Dustin on the stretcher. He looked like he might be dead. Lincoln was ready to kill everyone as much as I was when he saw his brother on that stretcher. I looked at Madison holding her ponytail. I wrapped my arms around her. "I'll find her. I promise you. Does she have her phone or anything with her?"

"No, she was sleeping. She's in her pajamas. You have to find her. They stabbed Dustin. I thought he was dead," she cried, "but he's alive."

"Those men are mean, and Mama hit one over the head with a lamp. He's the one who hit her. They want money. They were going to take me too, but Mama said she wouldn't give them money if they took me."

The puppies and Mona were going crazy in the laundry room. "What bank does she use?"

"I don't know. Oh, wait, Mama goes to the Bank of Oregon."

"I'm going to have my mom come over and take you to her house. You can stay with her until I find your mom. Do you want to get some things together?"

"Okay, I have to take the puppies and Mona."

"I'll take them to my house."

"You aren't going to be home."

"Okay, you can take them with you." I walked over and looked at Dustin. He was white as a sheet. He must have bled a lot. "I'm going to find Gabby. I have no idea where to start looking, but I think if we follow her debit card, we might find her. I'll call Sofie and see if she can find her online. If anyone can do it, it's Sofie," I said, looking at Lincoln.

When my mom walked inside, Madison threw her arms around her. "Oh, my God, what happened here?"

"They took Mama," Madison cried. "They broke her nose and stabbed Dustin."

"Ryker will find your mom. I'm taking you home with me."

"We have to take the puppies and Mona."

"Okay, we can do that."

"I have to tell Dustin I'm leaving. They are taking him to

the hospital. They won't let me go with him. I don't know what to do."

Madison threw her arms around me. I wasn't used to handling teenage girls. I patted her on the back and wrapped my arms around her. "Let's get the puppies," I said, trying to calm her down a little.

Madison walked to where they were getting ready to take Dustin to the hospital. "Dustin, you listen to me. You better get better, or I swear I will be so angry at you. Dustin, I love you. You're my best friend. Please wake up."

"Madison, I'll be okay. I love you too."

"Mama, I'm going to let you take care of Madison and the pups. I have to go."

"Go, honey, bring Gabby home. I'll take care of things here."

"Ryker, I'll catch up with you."

"Okay, take care of Dustin first. Noah and Jackson are meeting me at the bank."

I drove to the bank. I knew Gabby wasn't there, but I had to start somewhere. I saw Noah and Jackson already there. I explained to them what had happened. Noah's phone rang. "It's Sofie," he handed me the phone.

"I have a picture I'm sending you. It's a horrible photo. Try to keep your cool."

"Show me the damn picture... Fuckers! Those fuckers are going to be dead!" The photo showed Gabby's face covered in blood, trying to get more money from the ATM. Her nose was swollen, obviously broken.

"Here's another one."

I shouted as loud as I could. The fat one slugged Gabby in the face, knocking her down. She was out cold. I saw him kick her.

I brought up a shot of the vehicle and the license plate, and I immediately sent a shot to the police.

I saw the old car and license plate. "I love you, Sofie. We'll catch these bastards." I showed the others the vehicle. "We'll catch them hopefully before daylight. We must find them before they do something she'll have to live with for the rest of her life."

"Why don't we split up?" Jackson suggested. "We can cover more ground that way. They will get angry once they find out you can only draw a thousand dollars daily from the ATM."

"You're right. Whoever finds these fuckers, promise me you will break their bones before you kill them."

"I agree," Noah said.

"Me too," Jackson said. "Let's find them."

I drove until the sun came up. My phone rang. It was Sofie. "Hey, Sofie, what's up?"

"They're in Bend. They tried getting money from an ATM, and I could see their car. They are on fifteenth street, at the bank."

"Thanks for helping, Sofie. I appreciate you staying up all night helping me find Gabby."

"Of course, I will stay up until Gabby is safe with you. I would also like to kill those bastards."

I got on the freeway and headed toward Bend. It took me an hour to get there, and then I looked at the Banks. I googled each Bank until I found the one that Gabby used. As soon as I pulled into the parking lot, I saw the vehicle. I could hear Gabby screaming. Where the hell were the police?

I ran my SUV into the back of the vehicle, then jumped out and pulled the driver's door open. I knocked that first guy out. That's not the one I wanted to start with. I jerked the other fat man out of the back seat. He was the one I wanted to hurt. I gave Gabby a quick kiss. Then I broke a few bones.

The other man pulled a gun out of his pants, and both were dead in a blink. I opened the other door and helped Gabby out of the car and over to my vehicle. She was crying and her body shook. As I held her in my arms, I was sure I was shaking also. Then I called the police and then Madison. "Madison, I have your mom."

"Mama," she cried.

"Don't talk long. I'm taking her to get her nose checked." I didn't say anything about her body being beaten, battered, and bruised. If they weren't dead, I'd kill them again. I stood close to Gabby and guarded her against anyone who came by.

When the police pulled into the parking lot, they pointed their guns at us. I growled at them, "Put those damn guns down! Gabby was kidnapped and beaten. I'm taking her to the hospital. If you want to ask questions, you'll have to wait."

"Those bastards are dead. If they weren't, I would kill them all over again." Gabby grabbed my shirt. She wanted me to be careful.

"I'm taking Gabby to the hospital." I gave him my SEAL Security card, then I turned to Gabby. "Hey, sweetheart. I'm taking you to be looked over. I'll check on Dustin while I'm there. How do you feel?"

"I'm so thankful you found me." Tears started falling from her eyes. I pulled her into my arms and held her. "We could have all been murdered. They stabbed Dustin and cut Madison's hair with the same knife. I was so scared they would take Madison."

"They'll never bother you again." I buckled Gabby in

and then went to the driver's side. I reached over and held her hand. As we drove back to Cedar Falls, I never wanted to let her go. My heart was finally starting to get back to normal.

When I pulled into the emergency entrance, Madison came running to us. She was crying. Gabby hugged her and touched her everywhere, ensuring her baby was safe. Her hair was a mess. She walked into the hospital with us. My mom stood up and came over and hugged Gabby. I noticed when someone would touch Gabby, she winced. She must be in pain.

They thought I would stay with my mom and Madison in the waiting room. They didn't know me. We were shown to the cubicle, where a nurse started to undress her. "Wait, Ryker can help me, but why am I getting undressed?"

"We are going to do a rape test on you."

"I wasn't raped. I was beaten up. I have a broken nose. If the doctor can fix it, I want to see how Dustin is doing." An hour later, we walked into Dustin's room. Lincoln was sleeping in the chair, Dustin was sleeping on the bed, and Madison lay next to him sleeping.

Gabby tapped her on the shoulder, and she opened her eyes. "Time to go home, honey."

"I don't want to go home."

"Okay, then we will stay at Ryker's tonight. But tomorrow we are going home. Those men are dead. They will never bother us again."

"They cut my hair."

"I know, baby. I'll call Allie, and she'll come here to make it cute for you."

"Okay... I'm scared."

"I know, sweetheart. I'm scared, too. I'll put an alarm in

the house." She looked at me. "Can we stay with you tonight? I'm sorry, I didn't even ask first."

"You can stay with me for as long as you want to stay with me."

Dustin opened his eyes and took Madison's hand. "Hey, I think your hair looks great."

"How do you feel?" she asked, hugging him. "If you hadn't been there, they would have killed me. Thank you for saving my life."

"I would do it again anytime. I told you I love you. You're my best friend, right?"

"Right, I love you too."

I saw the look in Dustin's eyes. He really loved her. "Hey buddy, I'll see you tomorrow," I said, patting his shoulder.

"I'll see you tomorrow. Goodbye, Maddie."

"Bye." She bent her head and kissed him.

14

GABBY

I sat in Ryker's living room, curled up on his sofa, drinking hot chocolate. "When I was in Nashville, I felt someone watching me. I even had a band member stay in the RV with me. It was these jerks. They followed me home so they could kidnap me and rob me. Can you believe that? They came all the way here from Nashville."

"You will never know how a crook operates because their mind thinks differently than others. I'm just glad we found you before they killed you. I don't doubt for a second they would have. I'm surprised they didn't kill you and take your debit card."

"They were going to, but they wanted to wait until Monday so I could go inside the bank and take out fifty thousand dollars. They didn't realize you couldn't get it out that fast. They make you wait for it. I had already planned never coming out of the bank."

"Are you scared?"

"No, I know they are gone. I will sleep with Madison tonight. Thank you for letting us stay here."

"You can stay here for as long as you want, Gabby."

"We'll go back home tomorrow. I have to get back to normal, or Madison won't ever want to go home. I'll see you in the morning."

"Yes, I'll see you then."

I walked into the bedroom and crawled into bed with Madison. She cuddled up next to me. I inhaled. My body hurt everywhere. Allie would be here in the morning to do Madison's hair. Allie Bennett was our dear friend and the woman who did my hair when I lived in Nashville.

I lay there thinking about what had happened. We were so lucky to be alive. I will buy a gun, and if anyone ever came into my house to harm my family, I will kill them. I couldn't count on anyone except myself. I knew how to shoot a gun; I learned how to aim it. I took lessons a long time ago when I first moved to Tennessee. I got rid of that gun because I didn't like having it in the house.

I was up before anyone, went to our house, and cleaned it. I was thankful the fireman cleaned the blood off the wood floor, or it would have ruined it. The lamp was a mess. It needed a new shade. I threw the old one away. I'd pick one up later. The door opened, and Ryker handed me a cup of coffee.

"How do you feel?"

"My body feels like crap. I must have bruises all over. I'm buying a gun. I used to have one, but I got rid of it."

"Do you know how to use a gun?"

"Yes, I took lessons when I bought my first gun in Tennessee."

"I'm going to put some ointment on your body to help with the pain."

"Does it work?"

"I believe it does. We all use it. I'll get it."

He was back in a minute. "Is this a homemade ointment?"

"Yes, Sofie makes it."

"Sofie is amazing; how did she meet Noah?"

"Her car broke down, and Noah was visiting his brother in Nevada, and he picked her up with his brother's tow truck. First, he hired her to work for us. Because she's brilliant with computers, then he asked her to marry him. And the rest is history."

"What a great story."

"Yes, it is. Now, let's put this on you."

"It's mostly my back. I can do the rest if you take care of that part." He helped me with my blouse, and then I turned around. He actually growled. He sounded like a tiger growling. He didn't do anything at first. And then I heard him taking deep breaths. I felt his lips kissing my back. And then his hand softly touched my back as he started putting the ointment on. He kissed my neck.

"I'm sorry this happened to you. I wish I could kill them over and over a million times. I should have been here with you."

"Stop it! You should not have been here. You were at your job. You and I aren't in that place where you can say this. We are seeing each other, but you are not responsible for me. I have my house, and you have yours. I don't want you to blame yourself. You saved my life, which is the most you could have done."

"I wouldn't be here if you hadn't shown up. They were going to kill me. They told me they were." I turned around and took his face in my hands. "Thank you for saving me."

"I want to be responsible for you. I want to be more than someone who is seeing you and lives next door."

"No, you don't. I know you don't want to be with only one woman. You told me that yourself."

"I was stupid back then."

"It was only six weeks ago."

"A lot can happen in six weeks. Turn back around. You are too tempting facing me without anything on."

I smiled and kissed him. "I'm becoming fond of you too." Ryker was quiet for a few minutes. "Wear my shirt. It's loose and won't rub your skin." He took it off and put it on me himself.

"Take this and put it where you hurt. I'm sleeping in your bed tonight. We don't have to make love. I want to be with you."

"I want to be with you too. We'll stay here. I can't let Madison be afraid to come back home."

"Okay, I'll order us a pizza for dinner."

"Mama, where are you?" Madison cried.

"I ran to the door as she reached it. I'm right here, sweetie. I was cleaning a few things. Why don't you go with Ryker and bring Mona and the puppies home?"

"I want you to go with us. You can't stay here alone."

"Madison, those men are gone. Ryker killed them," she glanced at Ryker. And then she took his hand. "I'll lock the door. I'll be fine, I promise you. Allie will be here soon. No one wants to hurt us anymore."

"Promise to keep the doors locked."

"I promise."

I had just gotten out of the shower when I heard the doorbell. I put my housecoat on and walked downstairs. I looked out the window, and my friend Allie was there. I met Allie when I first went to Nashville. She lived next door to us, and I begged her to move in with us when I made enough to buy a home.

"Allie, I'm so happy to see you. Thank God you are here," I said, opening the door to welcome my friend.

"What happened to you? You look like a pack of dogs dragged you through a bunch of rocks. Your entire face is bruised."

"Yeah, my nose is broken. Let me show you to your room. Madison went with our neighbor to get Mona and her babies."

"I can't wait to see those puppies. Tell me, what happened to you?"

"Let's go to my room, and I can get dressed before Ryker and Madison return."

"This place is still beautiful."

"Can you put this ointment on my back, and I'll do the rest."

"Oh my god, your entire body is bruised. I want you to start from the beginning."

"I woke up because I heard a strange noise. When I came downstairs, a man had cut off My baby's ponytail, and another stabbed Dustin. Do you remember the boy Madison told you about? I hit one over the head with a lamp and didn't give him another thought."

"My only thought was helping Dustin. Then that guy woke up and slugged me in the face, he broke my nose, and they kidnapped me. It was a horrible nightmare. You have to fix Madison's hair. She's so scared. She didn't want to leave me here alone. But I knew she was scared to be here without Ryker."

"What happened to those men?"

"Ryker killed them. He rescued me and killed those men."

"I bet he's hotter than hell without looking at the man."

"Yes, he is, and he's mine."

"Oh, this is a first for you. He must be good in bed."

"I'm not discussing that with you?"

"Why not? I always discussed everything with you."

"Allie, I didn't ask you to tell me everything," I chuckled. It was so good having her here with us. She was more of a sister to me than my own sister who I didn't even know.

"Just tell me one thing: Is that his tee shirt you just put on?"

"Yes, it feels better because it's loose. Oh, they're home. Let's let Madison see you. I know she will feel better seeing her Aunt Allie."

We walked downstairs, and as soon as Madison saw Allie, both started crying. Two of the puppies were being squished between them. I saved the puppies, and Allie and Madison disappeared outside.

"I'll introduce you when they come back inside. They are very close. Allie lived with us the in Nashville, then we all moved in with her family. Sometimes she would come here with us for Christmas. She didn't like Madison being so far from her at Christmas.

"Does she have family?"

"Yes, she is very close to her family, and we are also close to her family."

He pulled me gently into his arms and kissed me. "I have to go to a meeting. Are you going to be okay?"

"Yes, we'll be fine. Allie is probably cutting Madison's hair right now. We will visit Dustin later today."

"I'll see you this evening."

"Okay, I'll see you then."

15

RYKER

I heard someone at my back door in the middle of the night. Thinking it was Gabby, I didn't bother pulling on my sweats. When I opened the door, the woman I was lucky not to marry stood there smiling.

"Well, look at you. You're as beautiful as you were the last time I saw you. Do you always answer the door in your boxers?"

"What do you want, Janet?"

"I need a place to stay for a few days, and my parents are still not talking to me."

"What about your boss? Doesn't he have a place for you to stay?"

"He left me at the hotel a week after we ran off. Plus, he left me with the bill. I tried calling you, but you wouldn't answer your phone."

"I didn't want to talk to you, and I still don't. So no, you can't stay with me for even one night."

"But I have no other place to go."

"Then sleep in your vehicle. Goodbye." I shut the door, knowing she wouldn't leave. Two seconds later, she was banging on it again. I opened the door, angry that she thought she could come here for a place to stay.

"Can I stay two nights until my work deposits my check in the bank?"

"Why are you back here?"

"Because I have a child. And he needs a place to sleep that isn't the car."

That threw me off. I couldn't imagine her with a child. "I'm surprised you have a child."

"You are no more surprised than I was. Allen refused to help me with him."

"Who is Allen?"

"His father. Can I please bring him inside?"

"You can stay tonight and only tonight. Take the child to your parents or anywhere else, but you are not staying here."

"I'll leave tomorrow. Let me go get him."

I put some clothes on and waited for her and the child to return. When she did, I was surprised to see a newborn baby sleeping in a baby car seat. "How old is your baby?"

"He's three weeks. I've done many things in my life that weren't right. But I'm responsible for this little guy, and I'll take care of him. Do you have a tee shirt I can sleep in?"

"Did you not bring your clothes with you?"

"No, I didn't have time to get anything. Allen was going to take my baby from me. I heard him talking to his mother. He can afford a lawyer; I can't. So I'm not taking any chance that he will take the baby from me. You can think what you want of me, but this is my baby, and I will keep him." She took a deep breath and looked at me. "I need you to marry me right away."

I walked into my room and got her a tee shirt. Then, I showed her where she would sleep. "I wouldn't marry you if you were the last woman on earth. I count myself the luckiest man on earth by not marrying you."

"Thank you very much. Shouldn't you be thanking me if you feel so damn lucky?"

"Good night, Janet."

I was in the backyard when I heard a woman's voice. I walked around the front in time to hear Janet speaking.

"I'm Janet, Ryker's fiancée." She stood on my front porch with a cup of coffee, my tee shirt, and nothing else.

"You are not my fiancée. Get your clothes on." I looked over, and Gabby, Allie, and Madison were getting ready to go somewhere. "Good morning, ladies. I allowed her to stay one night because she has a newborn baby, and I couldn't let a baby sleep in the car."

"Of course, you couldn't," Allie said. I heard her whisper to Gabby. "This is getting interesting."

"Can I see the baby?" Madison asked.

"We don't have time for you to see the baby. We promised Allie we would watch that movie with her."

"What're a few minutes? I want to see the baby, too," Allie said. She and Madison walked upon the porch, and I opened my door for them to enter.

I looked at Gabby, "Do you want to see the baby?"

"No, I don't. The last time I saw you was after midnight. What time did Janet show up?"

"Around three. I told her to leave until she told me about the baby. Her parents still won't have anything to do with her. The child's father wants to take him away from her. So she ran away."

"She should get a lawyer. She can't keep running."

"Are you saying you believe everything I just told you?"

"Yes, why? Was it not the truth?"

"Yes, it was, as far as I know. But she was wearing my tee

shirt and nothing else. I thought for sure you would jump to conclusions."

"I don't do that. Besides, you have no reason to explain things to me."

"Sure I do. We are seeing each other, and I..." I almost told her I loved her. That's not something I would say to a woman ever again.

"You what?"

"I like you, and we are dating, sort of." I pulled her to me for a long deep kiss. Gabby licked her lips.

"That tasted good. Do you want to get together tonight? I'm almost completely healed. We are having tacos tonight."

"I love tacos. I would love to get together with you tonight." I walked her up against the wall and kissed her. Then, looking at her, I said, "I want you."

"I want you too."

I chuckled. "Do we have time before Allie and Madison get back?"

"No, I hear them right now."

We walked back around as they stepped off the porch. "Mom, Allie is going to help Janet keep her baby."

I looked at Allie like she was crazy. "What? Allie, what is she talking about?"

"I'm just going to help her find a lawyer to help her with her child," Allie replied.

"But she doesn't live here. She lives in another place," Gabby explained.

"She said she's staying here with Ryker," Allie frowned.

"She is not staying with me," I said.

"I'll let you and your ex-fiancé settle this. I'm late for a movie," Gabby said walking away.

I watched as Gabby turned and walked away. That's when Jackson drove up, and Janet walked out on the porch.

"Hi, Jackson. How are you doing?" Janet greeted him.

"What the fuck is Janet doing here? Have you lost your freaking mind? I've come to pick you up. You know what? Drive yourself."

"Where were we going?" I asked.

"There is a meeting in thirty minutes."

Fuck, the last thing I need right now is to see all the guys. I knew Jackson was angry seeing Janet here. "Janet, I have a meeting. I want you out of here when I get home."

"But Allie is going to help me find a free lawyer, so Allen can't take the baby from me. Please let me stay here. I don't know what to do. Everyone I know doesn't like me. My baby is more important to me than anything in the world."

"I'm not listening," I said.

"I don't have money for gas."

"I'll give you the money. Here," I reached into my pocket and pulled out some money, "Take this three-hundred-dollars, and I want you gone when I get back."

She stood there looking stubborn. I didn't have a good feeling. Driving to our office, I wished I had stayed there until she left.

Lincoln met me at the door. "I can't fucking believe you let that damn Janet stay at your house. Why are you screwing it up with Gabby? Does Gabby know that you were once engaged to marry Janet? If Janet hadn't left, you would be married to her now."

"Yes, she knows. I'll say this one time for all of you to hear. Janet stayed one night because she has a newborn baby. Did you want me to have them sleep in the car? She is broke, she has no money," I tried explaining. She going to be gone before I get back.

"Oh, hell! Tell me you didn't fall for that trick again. Janet kept your pockets empty the entire time you were dating. Did she tell you she needed money?" Lincoln demanded to know.

I didn't answer. I walked into the room and sat down. "Let me know what we have. I'm not saying another word about Janet."

"We have to go to Vegas. The cartel is taking kids from the little town where Sofie grew up. Sofie and Noah are already on their way. They think it's because Sofie caught the computers that the cartel had hacked into. So that cost them a ton of money, and they weren't happy. I don't know how they knew Sofie did that unless someone was forced to spill the beans. Anyway, we are leaving tomorrow at seven in the morning. We have to ensure we catch them, or they might come after Sofie."

I hated leaving Gabby. I couldn't wait for tonight. I drove home and saw Janet's vehicle still in my driveway. When I got out of my truck, she walked onto the porch.

"I know, I know. I'm leaving. The lawyer Allie found me is coming over to talk to me, and then I'll find a place to live."

"Why are you moving here? You said yourself that no one liked you. I don't want you to screw with my life."

"I'm not. I needed help, and then I'm leaving." Her fake alligator tears started falling down her face.

"Why the fuck are you here?" I demanded.

"I told you," she cried.

"I don't believe you. I don't want you causing trouble."

"I won't."

I walked over to Gabby's house. I saw Allie in the kitchen and headed that way. "Allie, I'm going to tell you something about Janet. She isn't to be trusted. You can't believe anything she says."

"I find it strange that a woman who had a child three

weeks ago can wear skin-tight jeans without a bulge. She doesn't act like she is in any pain. I don't want you getting her mixed up in Madison and Gabby's life."

"Have you seen that baby? He is not three weeks old—he's at least six weeks old. She didn't fool me for an instant. She has no mommy instinct at all. She doesn't cuddle the baby; she only gives him a bottle. She doesn't even like to change his diaper. I think she might have stolen the baby. No lawyer is coming over. He's an undercover guy I've worked with before."

"Are you a hairstylist?"

"No, I'm an undercover detective."

"But why did Gabby say you were coming to fix Madison's hair?"

"I've done everyone's hair since I was fourteen. I have six sisters, and they all had me do their hair before they went on a date. I'm number five on the chain. So, as you can imagine, I've done a lot of hair. So, back to what I was saying: I think it would be a good idea if you let Janet stay at your place until we see if that child is stolen."

"Wait, are you telling me that Janet might have stolen that child? Shouldn't the baby be over here if that's what you think?"

"She's bringing him over here. Watch how she holds the child."

"Where would she have taken him from?"

"I don't know where she came from. I think she's trying to find a man to care for her. You were damn lucky," she said, glancing at me.

"Don't I know it? I have no interest in being anywhere near her. I don't want her anywhere near Gabby and Madison."

"Don't worry; I'll keep an eye on them. I'm moving here," she said, grinning.

"That's wonderful. I'm so happy for Gabby and Madison; they love you."

"I love them right back. Oh, someone is here."

I turned as Dustin walked inside with Madison. "Dustin, how are you doing."

"I feel good. The doctor said I was as good as new. I'm staying here while Lincoln is gone," Dustin said.

As Gabby walked in from the back door, I raised my eyes to her. She was covered in dirt, and she was beautiful. She smiled when she saw me. "Did Allie tell you what she thinks?"

"Yes. If she believes the baby is stolen, we need to call the police."

"Allie is the police."

"What if Janet harms the baby?" I worried.

"I'm going to bring the baby here," Gabby said.

"I'm going to get him right now. If someone's child is missing, I want to find out who it is. They must be scared to death," Allie said. She left through the front door to get the baby.

I wanted to pull Gabby into my arms, but others were standing around, so I would have to wait. "When is the lawyer or whoever is coming here?"

When Allie returned, she was carrying a diaper bag and a baby. "Why don't we call Sofie and see what she can dig up about missing babies?"

"What a great idea," Gabby said.

"Damn, I forgot they left for Nevada. I'll call her, and she can see if there is a missing baby boy when their plane lands."

"Good idea. Would that be Sofie Taylor from Franklin, Nevada?" Allie asked.

"Yes, do you know her?"

"She's my cousin. When my mom was sixteen, she said her cousin, who was sixteen at the time, moved to Franklin, Nevada. That would be Sofie's mom. She just up and moved from Tennessee. Olivia Taylor was pregnant with Sofie, but no one knew that until later. We have always kept in touch with them."

"I thought Olivia was the only family Sofie had," I said.

"She's the only family who lives in Nevada," Allie explained.

Gabby was smiling as she looked at me. "I didn't mention this to you Ryker, but Allie likes to talk and tell everything she knows to people she first meets. She never keeps anything inside her like most people. You'll know about her entire family within an hour," Gabby said.

"What's wrong with that?" Allie demanded. "I'm not saying anything wrong about my family."

"What if Sofie doesn't want everyone to know that her mom moved across the country at sixteen because she was pregnant?" Gabby demanded.

"Hmm, I never thought about that. Listen, I don't want any of you to mention what I said about Sofie's mom," Allie said, giving all of us the evil eye.

Everyone chuckled and promised to keep the secret. "Sixteen, that's so young. What happened to the dad?" Dustin asked.

"She never told a soul who he was," Allie said.

"Wow, I can't believe you didn't try to find out about him. I mean, you are always trying to figure out everyone you meet. Did you find out who he was?" Madison asked, knowing damn well Allie tried finding out or she already knew who he was.

"That's no one's business except Aunt Olivia's," Allie said.

"Oh, he must be someone important. I bet you Sofie knows who he is. I remember you telling me she could find anything on that damn computer of hers," Madison said.

"I think you remember too much. I don't want you to ask any more questions about Sofie's dad. I didn't know this Sofie was your cousin," Gabby said.

"I'm sorry. I won't say another thing about him. What about this little guy? I mean, she doesn't have a name picked for him yet. That's just pure stupid. Don't you have to put their name on the birth certificate when the babies are born? I've watched babies, and this one is no newborn. He's playful and laughs out loud."

As I listened to these two talk, I looked over at Gabby. She was smiling, and so was Dustin. "I take it Madison wants to be a detective?"

"No!" everyone said at once.

"I haven't decided what I'm going to be. But I don't want to do anything dangerous. Allie carries a gun on her all the time."

"I didn't notice you carried a gun," I said.

"I wouldn't be much of an undercover agent if you knew I carried one now, would I?" Allie said.

"I guess not. With you here, I won't have to worry about Gabby and Madison while I'm away," I said.

"Why would you worry about us anyway?" Madison asked. I looked at Gabby, and she was smiling.

"Why wouldn't I worry about you?" I was saved from answering when there was a knock on the door.

When Dustin opened the door, a man in a suit stood there. He saw Allie and walked to her, "She's gone."

"What do you mean she's gone?"

"I told her I would need a blood test from her and the baby. She excused herself and grabbed her purse, and she left."

Gabby was shaking her head. "This poor baby. His family must be frantic right now. Okay, we need to find the baby's family now. Where could she have stolen him from?" She wondered out loud.

"Her license plate says Montana," Dustin said.

"If you will all excuse me, I need to get back to work," the guy said.

"Thanks, Thomas."

"Anytime."

16

GABBY

"I have to be quiet. If I start crying out loud for more, stop me. I'm sure these walls are thick, but I don't want to take any chances that my daughter will hear me."

"Baby, you can cry for anything you want; my mouth will cover yours, and no one will hear a thing." Ryker was checking the bruises on my body. Most were gone, but he was kissing the others. When he spread my thighs, I moaned, and he put his finger over my lips to quiet me.

"I'm going to make you feel so good, and you'll want to scream, but don't because I'm going to be busy down here."

"Okay, I won't." I moaned as his tongue touched me. His fingers parted me, and I threw the pillow over my head as I screamed into it. His fingers moved in and out so fast while his tongue made me crazy. I pushed up as his mouth devoured me.

My legs wrapped around his shoulders, and my fingers ran through his hair. I held the pillow tight against my face when I orgasmed. When he entered me, he moved the pillow, and his mouth covered mine as his hard erection moved fast and hard inside me.

His mouth caught every scream I uttered. When I orgasmed over and over, I was moving like a wild animal, clawing at him as I came. Then he slammed inside me, and he released. *Damn, I shouldn't have told him I was on the pill. I'm sure it'll be okay. Yeah, it'll be okay.*

He gazed into my eyes as he started moving again. I smiled as I raised and met him for each move. We made love until two, and I fell asleep in his arms. I woke up at five and got into the shower. I stood under the shower when I felt Ryker's arms come around me. Ryker turned me around, picked me up, and slid me down onto his stiff erection. He pushed me against the shower wall as he moved inside me fast. I threw my head back, and his mouth went over my breast. I clawed his back as he pounded inside me. "Yes!" I screamed. "Oh, yes!" His mouth covered mine as he came deep inside of me, my orgasm lasting forever as I cried out into his mouth. When I stopped, he looked at me and kissed me again.

"I love you, Gabby. I love you more than anything in this world."

I wanted to tell him I loved him, but I was afraid I would mess everything up. Then I gazed into his eyes. "I love you too. I love you so much that it scares me. If you ever stopped loving me, I would die."

"I will never stop loving you, not ever."

We made love again, and then he had to leave. "Please be careful. I don't want anything to happen to you. I love you."

He kissed me hard and long. "I will be careful, I promise. I love you. If that crazy Janet comes back, please stay away from her. There is no telling what she would do if she stole a baby."

"Don't worry about me. Worry about yourself."
"I never thought I would fall in love like this. I love you!"
"Go, you'll be late." He kissed me one last time.

17

RYKER

I saw Sofie at the airport. She was picking us up and taking us to the motel in Franklin, Nevada. "I wanted to talk to you about a baby boy who might be stolen. I'm pretty sure he is." I told her about Janet. "Allie noticed immediately that the baby was too big for a three-week-old baby."

"Allie, who?"

"Allie Taylor is your cousin. She already told us about being related to you."

"Oh God, Allie loves all of us, but she tends to talk to people like they are all her family. So her friend Gabby, who I've heard about for years, is your neighbor. I wonder why she has never told me that. I'm sorry. Please keep telling me about the baby."

She was driving down the road with Lincoln, Jackson, and me. "Janet pretended to have a newborn. We think he was stolen. Her license plate said, Montana. If you could check if a baby was stolen from Montana, he's at Gabby's house."

"Why is he at Gabby's house?"

"Because Janet ran off and left him there."

"She'll be back." The way she said it made my heart take a dive.

"She sounds kind of psycho to me. I think you should call them and tell them to leave. Have them go to a hotel far away and then call the police and tell them everything you told me."

"Do you think that's necessary?"

"I don't know. Do you think it's not?"

"FUCK!" I picked up my phone and called Gabby, "Hey, sweetheart," I said when she answered her phone, ignoring the looks the others sent me. "I think you all, even Dustin, should take the baby and get a hotel somewhere."

"Why do you think that?"

"Because Sofie says Janet sounds psycho to her, and she thinks you should. I don't want a crazy lady around all of you."

"Okay, that's what we will do. Call me if you find anything out about if he's stolen. And if he isn't, then we will probably end up in jail."

"No, that won't happen. I'll call you later."

"Okay, I'll talk to you later."

When I hung the phone up, I wished I was home with her so I knew for sure that she was safe.

"You don't have to worry about Gabby and Madison. Allie is very good at her job. She has always wanted to be a detective. Here we are. There is Noah. We don't dare go to Mamas. I'm afraid they will hurt her if they know we are related. I would love it if one of you would get her for me and bring her here."

"I'll get her. Don't worry about her. While you look up the baby, I'll take Noah with me."

"Noah won't leave me. I'll give you the address. Is that okay?"

"Yes, I don't mind. Do we have a rental?"

"Yes, it's that black SUV."

I unloaded my stuff to my room and left to retrieve Sofie's mom. I drove for an hour when I saw the very unique mobile home park. Six people came out and watched me when I pulled into space eleven and parked. I knew something was wrong before I got out of the vehicle.

I knocked on the door. When she didn't answer, I turned to the people watching me. "Is Olivia gone?"

"Yes, her daughter sent someone to pick her up. I didn't have a good feeling about it. I tried to tell her to stay here. I bet you it was the cartel. They are angry with Sofie. If you see her, tell her not to come to town. They'll be watching out for her."

I got in the car and called Noah as I drove back to the motel at breakneck speed. "Noah, the cartel has Sofie's mom. You have to guard Sofie. They are angry with her."

"What?"

"The people from the trailer park said someone picked her up and said her daughter sent them. They told me the cartel was angry with Sofie. Get her somewhere safe. They're after her."

"Fuck!" The phone went dead.

When I got back to the motel, Lincoln met me outside.

"Sofie said to give you this."

It was a piece of paper. "The baby is missing from Butte, Montana. Here is the information you will need. Please find my mama."

"How are we going to find her mom?"

"We'll let them find us. Then we'll find Sofie's mom. I hope she's still alive."

I called Gabby. "Hey, sweetheart, I only have a moment.

The baby is stolen. I will text you the information, and you can give it to Allie. I love you."

"I love you too. Please be careful."

"I will. Bye, sweetheart."

I walked into the room and grabbed my bag. "Let's go. We need to find Olivia."

"Why don't we stay around here? I'm sure they'll find us."

"I don't think we have that much time. We go to Franklin and talk to people who will get us noticed. If we're lucky, she will be where the kids are."

"How many kids are missing?"

"Five, I think."

We jumped in the SUV and headed for the town of Franklin. It was a small desert town. I pulled into the café parking. It was small, which was perfect for the size of the town. We went inside and sat at the bar and ordered dinner."

"Are you three men on your way to Las Vegas?"

"No, we are here to find the missing children. Plus, now we need to find Olivia Taylor.

"Who are you?" a man sitting at the bar asked.

"My name is Ryker, this is Lincoln, and that one is Jackson. We are ex-Navy Seals. We came here to save the kids that are missing. Can anyone tell me anything that could help us?"

"Yeah, I can tell you something. My eight-year-old grandson was taken on his way to the neighbor's house. I'll tell you what will help. You give Sofie to the cartel, and they'll give us our kids back."

"Did the cartel tell you this?"

"They don't have to tell us anything. We know how

angry they are because Sofie called the FBI when she spotted those computer glitches."

"Do you mean when she discovered that all the computers in the area were hooked up to the people's bank accounts? Do you have a computer for your business?"

"I don't own one of those things."

"People who have businesses need to have computers, and they don't deserve to have their bank accounts cleared out."

"I'm so happy that Sofie told all of us about that. We all used the same repair guy. Who would have thought he put that bug inside for the cartel? He had already taken four thousand from our account. That is the money we need to pay our employees. We were lucky we had terrific employees who let us wait until the next month to pay their total wages," Tammy said.

"I know you lost a lot of money, but is it worth losing our Bobby over?"

"No, it's not. I'm not saying that. I'm saying the cartel needs to be run out of here. Why are they here in our small town? I'll tell you why. It's because they are using this place to traffic women and kids. I pray they don't traffic our kids, but that is what they do. They traffic other kids, and if we give a thought to them, it's only a moment's thought. We need to run them out of our country."

"And how are we going to do that, Tammy? We are a community of forty-five hundred. The cartel picked our town because we are close enough to Las Vegas that they can drive the women there and back every few days. I see what they are doing. I do not live far from that big house they built. Why don't the police raid that place? It's because it's the cartel, and they want to live. Or maybe they are paying them off. We don't know anything because we do nothing."

"Are the kids and Olivia at that house in the country?"

"We don't know."

"Has anyone checked?" Jackson asked.

"My son went out there to get Bobby and was shot in the shoulder and told to bring Sofie to them."

"What did the police do?"

"They told him they would take care of everything." The grandpa said.

"Wait, are you telling me there has been no arrest?" I asked.

"The police told them that he's lucky that he didn't get killed."

Right then, a policeman came inside the café. He walked straight to us, "What are you doing in our town?"

"We are ordering dinner."

"After you eat, you should leave. It's not safe around here for strangers."

"I heard. It's not safe for kids either, but it's safe for the police. You allow the cartel to kidnap hundreds of people, including the kids in town. Did they send you here to chase us out of town?" I asked.

"How would you like it if I haul your ass down to the jail? You don't know what is going on around this town. I save the women in our town from getting kidnapped."

"But you didn't save the kids."

"You don't know what the fuck you are talking about. My son and the other kids are missing. My wife is going crazy with worry. I'm trying to find all of those kids."

"So they aren't at the house in the country?"

"I don't know. All I know is that I'm doing everything I can to save this town's people. I don't take money from them. All I want is for them to leave our people alone. If Sofie would come back and give herself up to these people, they would let the kids go."

"Sofie is not going to hand herself over to these monsters. We will get the kids. All you have to do is stay out of it. We will take care of rescuing the kids."

"You don't understand what I'm talking about. They will go through town and start shooting everybody."

"Listen, I'm going to call a few friends. And we will take care of everything."

Lincoln looked at me, "Who are you going to call?"

"I'm calling The Band of Navy Seals, and I'm calling the Army Rangers. Whoever they can spare, I'll walk outside and call right now. Order me a steak. I'm starving."

"Ryker wants a steak, and we'll take the same thing."

18

GABBY

Hearing that the baby was stolen is entirely different from thinking he might be stolen. Now I was scared. Janet might come for the baby. We needed to get a room somewhere. Wait, I have to call the police. First, I would call the parents. I looked at the phone as I walked around and gathered everyone together.

"Outside," I told all of them, "bring the baby," I said to Allie. "We're moving hotels.

"Where are we going?" she said.

"Away from here," I said. I dialed the number Ryker gave me.

I heard a voice answer the phone, "Hello."

"Hello, you don't know me, but I think we have your baby."

The next thing I knew, there was shouting, and someone else got on the phone. "I am FBI agent William Thomas. Who am I speaking to?"

"I don't have a lot of time right now. I'm driving to a different hotel, so Janet can't find us."

"So Janet took the child?"

I heard more screaming. A woman shouted that she was leaving someone's ass if she didn't kill him first. Then she took the phone, and I heard a tearful voice, "Is my baby okay?"

"Yes, he's perfect. We thought he might have been stolen, so we took him from that crazy Janet."

"I'm going to fly out to you. What state are you in?"

"Oregon," I told her the name of our town. "We'll be at the Marriott hotel. I'll be waiting for your call when you get to town."

"Thank you so much. Goodbye."

"What was that about?" Allie said.

"That was baby boy's mommy. She will meet us at the hotel. This has a happy ending, after all," Gabby replied.

"Don't count your chickens before they hatch," Allie said.

"Allie, please don't spoil my happy ending."

"I'm not trying to spoil anything, but you always jump to conclusions. Who gave you the phone number for the parents?"

"Ryker."

"Ryker, how did he get the number?"

"I'm sure Sofie got it for him."

"Sofie, then I'm sure everything is okay."

"I don't remember meeting Sofie. Did she ever visit your family?"

"No, Sofie never went anywhere, but I guess since she married Noah, she came to Oregon. I'm surprised. We visited her and Olivia in Nevada. Olivia is Sofie's mom. She has OCD. She never goes anywhere. Did she come here for Sofie's wedding?"

"I don't know. I lived in Nashville."

"Oh, yeah. Silly me. I'm sure she did. She might be getting better. I hope she is."

"Ryker said the cartel took her."

"What?" Allie asked in a panic. "They took her. I have to leave. I have to help find her."

"I know you do. I'll take you to the airport."

"But I can't leave you."

"Yes, you can. I'll be fine, and Madison will be fine. We have Dustin here with us. We'll take care of the baby; his mommy will be here in a few hours. So please don't worry about us. I can handle everything here."

She nodded and smiled, "Yes, you can. If you see anyone that looks like Janet, then keep going. She might be in a different vehicle now. She knows by now that we are on to her. She might have rented another car. So be prepared for everything."

"I will. All of us will. Isn't that right—Dustin, Madison?" I asked the kids, sitting in the back seat.

"Yes, we will guard this child. She will not get him back," Dustin said, kissing the baby on his forehead. A thought entered my head, and I thought he would be a perfect husband for Madison in about ten years. Who knows, maybe that will happen, or perhaps someone else will come along when Madison is twenty-five or thirty, and she'll fall deeply in love. Whatever happens, I want her to be happy.

"Mama, are you daydreaming? Allie asked you a question three times."

"Yes, I'm sorry, Allie, I was daydreaming."

"Were you writing a song in your head again?"

"Yes, I think this may be my favorite song of all. Writing might take a while, but that's the joy of writing the perfect song. You can take as long as you want. You have complete control over everything you write. Here we are." I pulled into line at the crowded airport. I hugged Allie and wiped a tear away. "Promise you will take care of yourself."

"I promise. I will. You do the same thing."

"We will." We watched as she stormed into the airport, and the bells went off as they detected her gun. Allie turned and winked at us. I smiled. Allie loved this because when she told them she was hurrying to rescue some children and a woman who had been taken in Nevada, they offered to take her to the first available plane. She wouldn't have to wait for a plane.

"How about we get Carl's Junior before we get our rooms?"

Dustin rubbed his hands together. "Yes, I'm starving."

"Me too," Madison said.

We were sitting in our room watching television when someone knocked at our door. A woman and man stood there. The baby spotted them and cried. His parents rushed inside and picked him up. Then she turned to me, crying, "Thank you so much. Oh, my God. You're Gabby McKalister, the singer."

I put my fingers to my lips. "I don't want anyone knowing about the baby and me. This is about your family getting your baby back. Please don't tell anyone about me."

"I won't say a word. Neither will John. Isn't that right, John?"

"Yes, I'll never say a word." They took the baby's diaper bag and left.

They went out the door. I opened the door and said, "Hey, what is the baby's name?"

"His name is Little John."

"Little John," I repeated before bidding them farewell again. I shut the door and looked at Dustin and Madison, "His name is Little John."

"I like that name," Madison said, and Dustin nodded.

We watched television until bedtime. We had a suite, so each of us had a room. "I'm off to bed. Don't answer the door for anyone."

"Okay, Mom, we won't. I hope they catch that woman soon. I'm not too fond of the idea of her being after us."

"She won't know where we are—goodnight, you two."

"Goodnight."

"Goodnight, Gabby," Dustin said.

A whole week passed before they found Janet and took her back to Montana to stand trial for the kidnapping of little John. We were glad to get back home. I missed Ryker and wondered what took them so long to find the kids and Olivia.

19

RYKER

I looked around at the people who came to help this little town, and I prayed I didn't screw up and one of our friends get killed. I looked at Ash Beckham. He was from the Band of Navy Seals; Killian and Luke were with him. Jax, Matt, and Ryan from the Army Rangers also came to help us with this case.

I explained to them what the hell was going on. "It might get bloody, so I'm warning you now, if you want to change your mind, do it now," I finished.

There was a knock at our door, and I answered it. Two policemen stood there. One was the officer that I talked to yesterday. "We want to join you," one of them said.

I nodded. "Just don't get in the way of bullets or fists."

When Allie showed up, I was pissed. "You are supposed to be watching over Gabby and Madison."

"Dustin is watching over her. The parents have their baby. Gabby, Madison, and Dustin are at the Marriott. Stop worrying so much."

I thought she was crazy to say Dustin was watching them but decided not to say anything more. Dustin was a kid and had just gotten out of the hospital recently. I left it alone.

Now, here we were a week later, with nothing to go on still. The house was empty. Something wasn't right. The more I thought, I got the idea that one of the cops was on the other side, so I confronted them.

"Which one of you is working for them?" Paul, Bobby's father, was shocked. I saw it instantly; then he turned and started beating the hell out of the other cop. I let them fight for a while because the guy deserved it.

"Why would you work with the cartel?" Paul demanded.

"You know why. It's the money. I make more off the cartel in a week than a year as a policeman."

"They have my fucking son! My son!" Paul shouted.

"They said they wouldn't hurt him or the others. I didn't ask about Olivia, but the next time I talk to the head honcho, I'll ask about her. I know you didn't want their money. You have your own home. Now we can buy a home."

"How will you do that behind bars, you fucking bastard?" he bellowed before his fist plowed into the guy's face again.

"Do you think I didn't plan for this? I prepared for everything. Look around you. There is nothing but desert, and that helicopter is coming straight for you." He thought he would jump in the vehicle and take off.

I grabbed him back and threw him on the ground as we all took off, zig-zagging across the desert. I saw Ash Beckham jump on top of one of the vehicles and start shooting. I did the same thing. We fired until the helicopter fell from the sky.

"Here comes another one. Hurry! We need to get out of here." I grabbed the top of the SUV and held on as we flew in the desert. I saw Ash pull himself inside the vehicle he was on. I had a feeling this was not going to end well for me. Then I saw Lincoln come halfway out of the vehicle.

"Give me your hands?"

Is he crazy? What the hell would I hold onto? *You'll hold onto his hands. Do it, Ryker!* I reached my hand out to him, and he grabbed me. I forgot how strong and stubborn Lincoln was. He pulled me around and held my other hand. Before I knew it, he jerked me inside the vehicle.

"Damn, that was close. Jackson, we need to follow Killian. He knows where he's going." We were flying when suddenly, we saw Killian go through the sand hill. "Follow him," I shouted.

"What the fuck," Jackson said as we went through the side of the mountain. We kept following them deeper into the hill, and then we stopped and waited. I saw Killian and the others get out of their vehicles. We got out of our vehicle as well.

"How did you know about this?"

"That's all we did for years—hunt the cartel. This large cave was here for years. I saw things here when we first found this place. Some of the stuff was from the forties. They should leave soon. I wonder if they killed the other cop."

I watched Paul as he shrugged his shoulders. All this time, he thought Jim was his friend. Boy, was he wrong? "I don't know what would be worse, him going to prison and constantly being afraid for his life or dying right now. I think him dying now is the easier way. Do you think we'll find Bobby and the others?"

"I think so. Because if they hurt any of those townspeople, they know their history. You should call the FBI to clean up this place after we get everyone back."

"I think you're right. I sure can't do it on my own. I grew

up in this town as Sofie did. Nothing ever happened. Then six months ago, someone bought the old mayor's home. We thought someone famous bought it. Then we discovered who it was at a town meeting, and the cartel showed up. They said, 'If you leave us alone, we'll leave you alone.' They held women; now I know kids were also in that house. Do you think kids have always been there? They picked our town because it was close to Las Vegas."

I looked at everyone. "I hear something. Allie, get in the vehicle."

"You don't have to tell me twice."

"I hear the helicopter. They're checking the area out. What if they find out where we are? Is there another way out of here?"

"Not by car. We can run for it or stay here and fight."

"I say we stay. We will be seen when we leave this mountain. I say we see what the hell is going on. Otherwise, they will bring more men here. You're right. Let's take the vehicles to the opening in the mountain."

We jumped in the vehicles and backed up to the cave opening. We could hear the helicopter still outside. We stopped and got out of the vehicles when we saw the opening. I could hear the aircraft, and it sounded like it was away from where we were.

I walked out and pressed myself against the mountain. I saw movement from the corner of my eye and turned with my gun pointed at the two men. They were as surprised as me. We fired our guns at the same time. Then we all fell at the same time. The others ran out of the opening. Lincoln dragged me back inside the cave. Then he ripped my shirt from the front.

"Why the hell did you rip my shirt? I would have taken it off."

"Sorry, I'm strung up from being inside this cave. When I saw the blood all over you, it shook me up. Damn it, you got yourself shot twice."

"You make it sound like I meant to get shot."

"You are the one who ran out there like this cave was on fire."

"That's because I knew you would do it if I didn't, and you have a brother who needs you."

"What about you—"

Before Lincoln could finish talking, Killian interrupted us, "Shut up! You two argue like an old married couple. How bad is his wound?"

"It's not that bad. The bullets went through, so nothing had to be taken out. I'll close it up."

"Wait, all you need to do is pour some disinfectant on it and put on a band-aid."

"And every time you move your body, it bleeds. I'm sewing you up."

"No, I want you to let Jackson sew it."

"Oh, please, are you still afraid because I thought you already had your skin deadened that one time I sewed you up?"

"We don't have time to argue. There is still a helicopter out there," Killian reminded us.

Finally, he put a bandage on my wounds. I tried to make my way to the SUV when Allie approached me, and she helped me.

"I'm going to look at your wounds. I'm trained. I was an EMT for two years. Then I became a detective. Lay back so I can see."

"Allie, I'm fine."

"No, you are not. One of those bullets must have nudged something inside, or you wouldn't be in so much pain. Look,

Ryker, Gabby, and Madison are my family. Maybe not biological, but they are. Gabby loves you. I have to fix you so Gabby won't lose you."

"Do you have an x-ray machine?"

"Don't be a smart ass."

I watched as she looked at one wound and then another. I had to bite down on my teeth to stop wincing from the pain. "Are you finished?"

"No, you have shrapnel in here, like the bullets left behind some pieces of metal before exiting on the other side. You cannot get up and walk around."

"What do you mean?"

"I mean, infection will start showing up if you don't get these cleaned, especially if any desert sand gets inside."

"Are you sure?"

"Yes, I'm sure. You have to go to the hospital. I'm going to see if I can push some of this shrapnel out."

"Fuck, what the hell are you doing? That hurts."

"This shrapnel has hooks like a fish hook. They must be made for the cartel. I don't know what to do about them. But if they make their own bullets, do you think they can also put poison on them?"

"You're full of joy. Check on the others. I need to get to a hospital. And then we have to find those kids and Olivia. There are so many women and kids being mistreated right now. I don't know how we will save all of them."

"We won't save all of them because there are too many, and we don't know where they are. We have to save the ones we came here to save and my aunt Olivia."

"I can't believe you and Sofie are cousins. You are nothing alike. Sofie is quiet, and you aren't."

"I will take that as a compliment even if it wasn't." I chuckled. Allie started explaining more to me about her cousin Sofie. "We haven't been around each other much. We would have to visit her here because Olivia refused to leave her home. I think it was because she didn't want people back home to talk about Sofie."

Lincoln ran to the vehicle. "We're leaving. The Army Rangers shot the Helicopter down. Now Nick will drive us crazy by telling us how he and Matt ran to the top of the mountain and waited until the copter was close enough that they targeted the pilot and shot him, and they crashed."

"I don't care who shot it down; I need to get to the hospital." We explained to Lincoln about the shrapnel. Of course, he had to see it, as did Jackson. "As soon as they get this cleaned up, I want to get out of there. I'm not staying in the hospital."

We talked to the group and decided Allie would take me to the hospital so everyone could keep looking for the others. I wondered if they had another house around Las Vegas.

We came upon the cop, who was a traitor. Allie stopped to see if he was dead. He wasn't dead, but he didn't have long to live.

"He's not dead." I heard her talking to him. "Do you know where the kids and Olivia are?"

"They are in another house in Las Vegas. I don't know where it is. I tried finding it, but I wasn't able to."

I saw him on the ground, and he threw up blood. "Ask him what he wants us to tell his wife."

"Tell her I hid some money under the floor under our bed." Every time he talked, he spat up more blood. "I lost my life for that money. Please don't let my family know I worked with the cartel." He spat up more blood, and then he took his last breath.

"What should I do with him?"

I looked at the guy who did nothing for those kids. "Leave him. He let those kids and Olivia stay captured by the cartel. He can stay here until someone comes for him."

By the time we made it to the hospital, I was vomiting. I knew for sure I was poisoned. It took six days before I could leave the hospital. I still felt like crap, but the poison was gone and the damn shrapnel was all gone.

20

ALLIE

I WAS READY TO KILL RYKER. HE WOULDN'T STOP complaining. The only reason they released him was that he wouldn't shut up.

They pushed him out of the hospital in a wheelchair. I swear they could hear him on the moon.

"I can walk myself. Why do I have to ride in a wheelchair like an invalid?"

"It's not me who makes the rules, as I've told you a million times this week. I would have let you walk out of the hospital six days ago if it were up to me. Oh, wait, we couldn't do that. You had pieces of bullets in you, and you were poisoned and dying. We had to save your life," the nurse said, smiling.

"You're right. I'm wrong again. Why are you pushing me out of the hospital?"

"Because I wanted the privilege of being the one to push you out of the hospital. Behind me, you will see the others from our floor cheering as you get pushed out the door."

Ryker turned the same time I did; sure enough, some nurses followed and recorded his exit from the hospital. "It's not that I wanted to hurry all of you. I want to catch the bastards that have kidnapped those children and Olivia. We all know it's the cartel," Ryker explained.

"Shhh, they are everywhere and can hear everything we say," she whispered.

"I don't give a damn what they hear. Do you ever get women in here that you think might be trafficked?"

"Yes, I even know where they live," she whispered. "You can't even tell the police because everyone has their hand in the pot..." She was whispering, but I stopped walking. "Oh, here is that joke I was going to let you read," I said as I took the paper and a pen from my bag. The nurse read it and wrote something down. Then she laughed like it was a funny joke.

We pulled out of the parking lot before I handed Ryker the piece of paper. On it was an address at the end of Carter Street. She noted that it was a huge house.

"Let's get the others before doing anything. If we go in now, we'll be dead before we blink our eyes."

I knew what he was going to say before he said it. "Let's drive down the street. Google the address for Carter Street."

We found Carter Street in all this traffic. I swear it was as bad as driving in Los Angeles. I never liked driving in traffic. Carter Street was dead-end, so I turned before we got there. That wasn't good. They would have you trapped before you could back out of there. The thing to do was not to drive in; we would have to walk in.

"They probably have these homes like this all over this city. This might not be the one we want."

"Yeah, but it might be. We'll never know unless we try. Where is everyone right now?"

"They are in Henderson at a hotel there. We stay at a hotel for a couple of days, then move on. We don't all stay in one place together, but we aren't far apart. In case we need each other. They all know you are getting out of the hospital today. They'll be happy to hear about the Carter house."

"I do hope that they are at that house. I hope lots of them are. Anyway, we'll figure that out later. How long have you known Gabby?"

"I met them when they moved to Nashville. Madison was three. A man had just taken off with Gabby's purse, and I ran after him and got it back. I could tell Gabby was scared. They were house hunting, and it so happened that my ex-boyfriend had moved out of the house I was renting. So Gabby and Madison moved in with me. I was at the police academy at that time. So I needed a renter. I knew I could trust Gabby because she had a little girl."

"What happened to the guy who stole her purse?"

"I kicked him, and he ran off. When Gabby started to become known, I would go with her and do her hair. That made me a small fortune working with all the other singers. We always got there early. Or I would go to their homes. The country singers are down-to-earth people."

"Pop singers are all into themselves. They wanted to be treated like they were special. I treated them how they wanted to be treated because I made so much money doing their hair."

"Wow, so the country music awards are coming up. Does that mean you'll be fixing the singer's hair? Is Gabby singing at the CMT Awards?"

"Yes, she sings there every year. But this year, she's singing her new hit. Are you coming with us?"

"I don't know. We'll see."

I knew he wanted to go so he could hear Gabby sing. I will put a bug in her ear to invite Ryker. We pulled into the parking lot, and the guys stood outside waiting for us.

"Welcome back, Ryker."

"Hey, we might know where the kids and Olivia are. One of the nurses told us about this house on Carter Street in Vegas. It's at a dead end, so we'll have to walk in and have someone waiting in the vehicles to take off once we have the kids."

"Do we leave tonight?"

"Yeah, let's talk to the others. Where are they?"

"They'll be here soon. They called before you got here and are getting antsy. They said they weren't used to sitting around for this long."

"As soon as they get here, we'll plan to leave. I'm surprised they are still hanging around."

"Some had to leave. Hopefully, we can finish this and get these kids home to their parents."

"Where are Noah and Sofie hiding out?"

"They are at her mom's place, disguised as hippies. I saw them, and they indeed looked just like hippies, except Noah is a little broad at the shoulders."

I looked at the others and said. "I'll drive one of the vehicles." My phone rang, and I answered, "Gabby, you know you aren't supposed to call me while I'm here. I told you the guys lectured me for hours the last time."

"I want to know how Ryker is doing. His and Lincoln's phones are turned off."

"Mine is supposed to be turned off as well. You weren't supposed to mention that I told you about Ryker getting shot. Goodbye."

"Wait! Hand the phone to Ryker if he's there." Ryker took the phone from my hand. He and the others heard my conversation with Gabby. I felt my face burning and looked down at the ground.

"Don't worry about Ryker getting angry about the phone, but you won't get your phone back until this is over."

I nodded. "What if my mom or one of my sisters tries calling me?"

"I'll tell you what, here, use my phone and tell your mom you won't be able to use yours for a while. She can tell the others."

I took his phone and called my mom. "I can't use my phone. I'm undercover," I told her after our quick hellos.

"Whose are you using?"

"A friend's. Tell the others, and I will call you as soon as I get home. I love you. Goodbye."

Before Jackson could turn his phone off, it rang. "Hello, no, she can't come to the phone. Didn't your mom tell you she's undercover and busy?"

"I want to talk to my little sister. I don't know who you are. She might have been kidnapped."

"She hasn't been kidnapped. What's your name?"

"Never you mind what my name is. What's yours?"

"Jackson."

"Mine is Isa."

"Hello, Isa. Allie will call you when this job is over. Goodbye, sweetheart."

He hung up on her. I didn't say anything, but I was sure Isa would give him an earful when she saw him, and she would see him. I was sure of it.

"Gabby, sweetheart, I'm fine. I'm out of the hospital. We are about to wrap this up."

"I called to see if you want to attend the CMA awards with us."

"I would love to go with you to the awards. I love you, but I have to go. Gabby, Allie won't have her phone anymore, so don't bother calling her."

"I love you too, bye."

"Allie, I will keep your phone until this is over. Everyone knows to turn off phones. What if we were sneaking into the house where the kids are, and your phone rang? We would all be dead."

"I'm sorry. I was playing a game on it earlier and forgot to turn it off."

"Have you turned it off at all?"

"Yes, I turned it off when we were in the cave."

"That was good. I'm not sure I want you to go with us. Gabby would never forgive me if you were shot."

"I'm an undercover detective. I know what I'm doing. So I will drive the car. I've been friends with Gabby for a long time, and I've been an undercover detective for eight years. I'm being transferred to Cedar Falls, so I might as well learn to work with your team now. You never know: we might need each other down the road."

"Okay, you can join us. Here they are."

I was glad that he succumbed. I smiled internally.

21

RYKER

"We all know this would be dangerous, but we are all professionals. We knew what we were doing. We go in and get the kids, Olivia, and any other kids you see. We get them out of there and make sure everyone's guns are loaded. Make sure you wear your vests. I don't want anyone to take a chance at getting killed. Are we ready?"

"We're ready," Killian said.

"We are ready," Matt confirmed.

"As we climbed into our vehicles, the hippies walked up to us.

"We're going with you, Noah said. I have to save Olivia. She's my family."

"I want my mama, and Allie is my cousin, so I'm going with you too."

"Sofie, you do know these people are dangerous. I don't think you should go."

"That's okay. Noah said I could go."

Noah looked at me. "I didn't actually say she could go," he shrugged. "She said she doesn't give a damn what I say as she's going."

"Let's go." I didn't have time to argue. We had gone ten miles when Paul pulled us over.

"I'm going with you."

"I figured that. Get in."

When we got to Las Vegas, it was dark. We made our way to Carter Street. "You two listen to me. No talking. Allie, you'll be the driver. Sofie, you will sit in the third seat. I don't want either of you to speak to each other. You listen to us. You get ready to take off if you see us running with kids. Watch for the other guys. If you see them take off, you take off."

"I'll wait until you are in this vehicle before I take off."

"Allie, don't argue with me. Do as I say."

"You're too damn bossy, and I'm sure Gabby hasn't seen this side of you."

I shut the door. It was the only thing that would shut her up. I looked at Sofie, climbed over the seat, and zipped my lips, hoping she at least listened to me. I did wonder what kind of undercover work Allie did.

The house was dark. I felt it was dark drapes, and they wanted everyone to think the lights were out. When I got close, I spotted the cameras and took out my paintball gun. It was loaded with black paint. I shot one, and another was on the trees. Before we could get on the grass, seven cameras were shot with black paint.

We nodded to each other, and then we took off. The windows were all locked. I pulled myself up on the roof to check the windows on the second floor. Paul was right next to me. The first window we tried was locked, then the curtain was pulled back, and Olivia looked at us. I put my fingers to my lips. She nodded then she looked at Paul.

She pulled the curtain up, and we saw all the kids inside with her. She got a piece of paper and wrote on it, 'If you raise the window, the alarm will go off,' it read. I looked over the side, and Killian was taking the alarm apart. I went back and held my hand up. Paul walked to the side of the house. He would let us know when Killian was finished disarming the alarm. Everyone was on the roof and ready to go through this window and check all the rooms. I hoped there wouldn't be too many men guarding this place. I knew men would die; I hoped it wasn't any of us.

As soon as the alarm was disconnected, I broke the window. I knew it was nailed down; I could see the nails on the other side. Paul was the first to go into the house. He grabbed his son in his arms and then another boy.

He handed them through the window, and then we passed them to the guys on the ground. All eight kids were rescued, and then Olivia came through the window.

As soon as they were on the ground, they ran with Paul for our vehicle, where Allie would drive them to town. As soon as we saw the vehicle headlights leaving, we broke the lock on the door and cracked it open slowly. We went through every room upstairs.

There were women and children. We snuck them out through the broken window. I heard shouting, and we leaned against the wall. I looked around. I didn't see any of the other Seal team. Then I heard Ash shouting, and I ran toward his voice. Three men had their guns pointed at him.

"Well, it looks like we caught some cartel men," I said as Ash hit the floor.

"We own the police. Nothing will happen to us," one of them menaced, his face screwed up as he spat on the floor towards Ash.

"I didn't say we were handing you over to the police. We know how corrupt the government is. I raised my gun and fired, as did Lincoln and Jackson. The men lay on the floor dead, I heard someone crying, and I opened a door. A teenage girl sat on the floor crying.

"You're safe now. We'll take you home."

"You're not going to hurt me?"

"No, we won't hurt you." She came out of the room and mouthed, "He's behind the door." I pushed her behind me and watched as Lincoln Jumped in front of me and fired. He was hit before his bullet killed the guy.

I knew we had to hurry. I threw Lincoln over my shoulder, and we all left. When I came to the vehicles, Allie was waiting. "I told you to leave."

"I knew you would need me. Let me see him. Put him in the back. We have to get him to the hospital."

"Who went with Sofie?"

"Noah did."

When we arrived at the hospital, Allie got into an argument with the staff until she showed her badge. We were able to stay close to Lincoln while they checked him. The nurse looked at me, "You're back already."

"We just rescued some women and children from the cartel."

"They need to run every one of them out of our country," the doctor said. He cut Lincoln's shirt off of him, and I looked at the wound, which was close to his heart. "He's lost a lot of blood. We might have to give him more blood. We'll check his type."

"He's O+."

"Me too," Allie said.

"Do you want to give him some of your blood?"

"Of course, I will. He's one of the good guys." The tone of her voice made me give her a double take. I hope she was not falling for Lincoln. He is not the type to get serious with anyone. I'd hint that to Gabby when I get the chance.

Allie donated blood for Lincoln, and we made ourselves comfortable in the waiting room. "How about I go grab our bags?" Jackson offered. "We can go to the airport from here."

"I'm all for that. I am so ready to go home. I'll see how everything is going with Lincoln."

I walked down the hall and saw the nurse talking to Allie.

"They brought those children in," I heard her say. "Everyone is angry that the cartel has been getting away with what they're doing. These kids have been through hell. No one reports them missing because they are the kids that have crossed the border."

"It makes me sick. Our government knows about this, and they won't do anything. They are taking money from the cartel. I'm thinking of staying here to help find the missing kids that no one wants or cares for."

"Allie, that is not a good idea. The cartel is deadly. They'll kill you. Gabby will not like you doing this."

"I'll be okay. I sometimes seem flakey, but I'm good at my job. I'll be fine. I've already talked to the border patrol. They know more than anyone about the cartel. I'm going to save the children. I have to. I can't leave them alone. Someone has to help them."

"I know. It's just that you get so emotionally involved."

"Don't they deserve someone to get emotional for them?"

"Yes, they do." I hugged her. "Jackson went to get our things. Where are you going to stay?"

"I'm staying with my aunt, Olivia, for now. Then I'm moving to the border town."

"Be careful. Remember, when something sounds too good or even good, it probably is someone you shouldn't trust. Everyone's pockets are greased, as they say."

"I'll be careful. You can call Gabby and tell her what is going on. That way, she will already know before I get home."

"I'll call her tonight. And she can get the anger out of her system before you get home."

"Good, Jackson will be back soon. Have they said anything about Lincoln?"

"No, not yet. I think he'll be okay. After all, he has some of my blood." I walked back to the waiting room. I was sleeping on the plastic sofa when Jackson came back. He woke me up when the doctor came in.

"Well, Mr. Harper was lucky. The bullet missed any main arteries and any vital organs. He lost a lot of blood, but that was taken care of. So he can leave tomorrow. He will need to take it easy. No hunting killers or running through jungles and jumping out of planes. In other words, he can't do anything for two weeks and still has to take it easy after that."

"I'll tell him what you said. So he gets to leave tomorrow?"

"Not until tomorrow. No sneaking out until I release him. He is a fortunate man to be alive. I won't say that again." He nodded and left.

Three hours later, I went in to see Lincoln. Allie was there with him. "Why are you two arguing?"

"She thinks she's staying here to catch the cartel. Like she's going to be a hero and ride off into the night. No, she can't stay here. Tell her she has to go home with us."

"I can't tell her what to do, and neither can you. She knows what she wants to do with her life. She's staying with her aunt. Allie will be fine. She's a survivor." He wouldn't take his eyes from hers. I could feel the tension in the air.

"Goodbye. I'll see you when I visit Gabby and Madison,"

Allie said, turning to me. I hugged her goodbye. I gave her phone back to her. Lincoln wouldn't look at her. I knew if he did, he would start shouting. She sniffed and hurried out of the room.

"Why the hell did you make her cry?"

"I'm done talking about Allie. Help me up. We're leaving."

"The doctor said you can't leave until tomorrow."

"I don't give a fuck what he said. I'm leaving."

22

GABBY

I PACED BACK AND FORTH, WAITING FOR RYKER TO GET HOME. I was so anxious to see him. I also wanted to know why he let Allie stay there to fight the cartel. Hell, she didn't know anything about the cartel. *They'll see her beautiful face and want her for themselves. She makes me so mad.* I almost went there and made her come home.

I called her family and thought maybe I shouldn't have done that. Isa and Cinda were shouting over the phone. Then I reminded them next month was the CMA Awards and Allie would be there. So they agreed to wait and see her until the awards.

I looked up when I heard a car. I ran outside and saw Ryker and Lincoln. They must have dropped off Jackson on the way. I ran into Ryker's arms and got the longest hottest kiss. I knew we would be at it all night. Ryker told me on the phone that he would keep me up all night. Lincoln was limping, and that reminded me of Allie.

"I can't believe you didn't tie her up and make her come back with you. I know when Allie gets it into her head to do something, she won't let anything stop her. She's going to get herself killed." We walked over to Ryker's and I watched Lincoln barely make it up the steps. I stopped and turned to him. Then I pulled his shirt up and he had a large band-aid covered in blood. "What happened to you?"

"He was shot. He's lucky the bullet missed his organs."

"Please get me some clean bandages. Lincoln, get on the bed. I can't believe the doctor let you leave the hospital." No one said anything, so I looked at both of them. "Let me guess, you left on your own."

I walked into the bathroom and got some scissors. I cut his bandage off and saw how red and swollen his injury was. "I think you might have to go to the hospital." Still, Lincoln didn't say a word. I cleaned up the wound with some disinfectant Ryker gave me. Lincoln looked angry, so I asked him what he was mad about.

"Your stupid friend is going to get herself killed. Do you know how many people the cartel kills? Of course, you don't. Nobody knows how many they kill because they are fucking killers."

Before I knew what happened, Ryker's hand was on Lincoln's throat. "Don't you ever raise your voice to her? I'll kill your ass right now. Tell her you're sorry."

"Ryker, his face is turning purple."

"Tell her."

"He can't tell me because you are choking him. Move your hand right now."

Ryker did as I asked. He stared at Lincoln who was holding his throat and looking at me. I could tell he simply respected Ryker, it's not that he couldn't fight back.

"I'm sorry. I shouldn't have yelled at you. I'm so pissed at Allie. She doesn't know what she's getting herself into. She wants to save the children. She's one person. What is she going to do?"

"I feel the same way. I am so angry with her. Allie gets like this. You can't even talk to her. She is so pigheaded."

"Yes, she is. Does she think she's a superwoman?"

"Sometimes she does. I mean, she's good at her job. But she's so trusting of people. I'll try calling her again to see if I can change her mind." I put his bandage on then I turned to Ryker, "I missed you."

"I missed you too. I couldn't wait to get home. Where are Madison and Dustin?"

"They went to get ice cream. They'll be here in a little bit. Lincoln, you'll have to stay here in case you need to go to the hospital."

"I'll be fine. Dustin can take care of me. I heal fast. I'll wait here until he gets back. I'm sure you two are in a hurry to be alone."

"You're right. We are. We'll just walk over to Gabby's house. You need to rest. You didn't sleep an hour last night."

We left him lying there. I was sure his eyes were closing before we left the room. When we got to my house, Ryker carried me to my room and pulled my top over my head, and then he pulled his over his. That's when I saw the bullet holes. He told me they were nothing. I could see by looking at them that they were far more than nothing.

My hand trailed down to both of them, Ryker picked me up, and I wrapped my legs around him as his lips took mine. His kiss made me want to cry. I loved this man so much. If a kiss could make me cry, I needed help.

"I love you," he whispered against my neck.

"I love you so much. I worry about you. Now that I see the bullet wounds, I'm more worried. I never really thought much about your job until today. I see how dangerous it is. Lincoln has a bullet wound, and you have two of them."

"Sweetheart, it's not always like this. We went to fight a

war that wasn't ours because we wanted to save those kids and Olivia. It is never as bad as it was this time."

I didn't believe him. I let it go for now. Ryker had us both undressed before I knew he had my pants off. I wanted him. I wanted his hard erection in me.

"I want you hard and fast. We only have a little time before Madison returns. Hurry, give it to me." Ryker chuckled at that. He pushed his hard erection inside me and moved so fast and hard, I begged for all of it. When I orgasmed, I cried. Ryker kept going, giving me more and more. My body was on fire. I orgasmed again, and then Ryker had his release.

"Why are you crying?" He kissed my tears and my mouth. He kissed my closed eyes. He kissed my neck.

"I don't know why; it's just that I love you so much. I'm a little shaken up. Making love with you does that to me. Ignore me. I'm being silly."

"You're never silly." He pulled me on top of him, "I love you. I will love you for the rest of my life."

"I will love you forever. Now I need to get up before Madison gets home."

We got up and jumped in the shower. We laughed as we made love in the shower, trying to hurry. By the time Madison was home, Ryker was at his house, and I was sitting on the front porch drinking hot chocolate.

"Your brother is over at Ryker's right now resting. You will probably stay another night because he is healing from a wound."

"Lincoln's hurt?"

"Where is Allie?"

"She stayed there to help rescue more kids. She's being stubborn as usual."

"She must be crazy. Does Isa know she stayed where the cartels live?"

"I've talked to all of them. I reminded her sisters that the CMA awards are next month, and she never misses it."

"I'm going to see Ryker. Come on, Dustin, you can see Lincoln. Tell Ryker and Lincoln we are having tacos tonight. They are welcome to have dinner with us."

"Okay, I'll tell them."

I smiled to myself as they walked over to Ryker's. I needed to make a doctor's appointment and get something for birth control. I felt that Ryker and I would be like a pair of rabbits around here.

23

RYKER

I SMILED AS I SAT AT THE TABLE EATING TACOS WITH GABBY, Madison, and Dustin. Lincoln was still sleeping, which was good. He needed all the sleep he could get right now. That's what would heal him. I looked at Gabby. She was watching me. I smiled, and my hand touched her knee under the table.

She put her hand on top of mine. Gabby looked over at me and smiled. I had a feeling come over me like I never had before. *I love this woman.* I wanted to be with her every minute of every day. I looked at her, and before I knew what I was going to say, I said it, "Gabby McKalister, will you marry me? Will you have my babies? Will you spend the rest of your life with me? Will you let me be a father to Madison even though she's fifteen? She may not want me to be her father but I love her already as if she was my own daughter. Well, what do you have to say?"

"You want to marry me? I thought you didn't want to ever get married."

"I knew I wanted to be with you every day and night. I don't want to be alone; I don't want to wake up in my house alone. I want to wake up with you in my arms. I want to be with you forever. I want us to have lots of babies together."

"How many babies do you want?" she chuckled. And tears fell down her face. "Yes, I will marry you. Yes, we can have babies. I love you and want to spend the rest of my life with you. I am not getting married on the beach. We're getting married right here in my home where grandpa can see us. His best friend and his granddaughter are going to be married."

Madison and Dustin jumped up and started hugging us. There were tears and cheers.

"I only want our family and close friends at my wedding. I can't believe we are getting married." Gabby looked at me and started crying.

"Are you going to be crying for the rest of the day? I don't mind if you do. I just want to know to prepare myself for tears. You made me so happy. After dinner, I'll call Mom and let her know. She's going to be so happy."

"I can't wait to be married to you," Gabby said, putting her arms around me. "I want us to be happy and grow old together."

"We're going to be so happy together. You just wait and see. I will go over and check on Lincoln and see how he's doing. He can be my best man."

"I'll make him some tacos you can take to him." She looked at Madison, "We have to go shopping to buy each of us beautiful dresses. You will be my maid of honor."

"Mama, I'm so happy you found Ryker, or he found you. Whichever way it went, I am so thrilled. My dream of you finding someone to love you the way you should be loved makes me want to cry." And then she burst into tears.

Gabby gathered her in her arms. "Now, when I go away

to college, I won't have to worry about you. When you go to Nashville to sign papers, you'll have Ryker with you."

"You sound like you are handing over a job to Ryker. He might not be able to go with me, but I can take care of myself. I didn't know you worried so much about me. That's my job to be the worrier, not yours. I don't want you to worry anymore."

"Okay, I won't."

"Now, I'm going to make Lincoln some tacos. You two finish eating your dinner."

I watched Madison and Dustin make themselves some more tacos. I walked into the kitchen where Gabby went. She was wiping her eyes. I gathered her into my arms.

"She didn't mean it the way it sounded. She was just happy that you have somebody with you now and she doesn't have to worry when she goes away to school."

"I know; I just didn't know I was a job for her. I didn't know she worried about me every time she wanted to go somewhere. Did I keep her from enjoying her life? Is that why she is so smart? Is she so smart because she stayed home with me and studied instead of having friends and going to parties with them?"

"Gabby, stop it. You're lucky she didn't want to go to parties. There are all kinds of weirdos at parties. Madison did what Madison wanted to do. She told me that she loves working with the school newspaper."

"She didn't want to be a cheerleader. She wanted to be on the debate team. She would have been a cheerleader if she had wanted to be a cheerleader. You have a very happy daughter. You did nothing to think otherwise. Now, let's get those tacos and take them over to Lincoln."

"You make me so happy. Look at you making it all make sense. You already sound like a father. I can't believe you want to marry me and not just that but also love my daughter as your own. Do you know what you are getting yourself into? I'm very forgetful."

"I'm sure you have someone for that."

"Yes, I do."

"I have to let Allie know I'm getting married. I'll have to ask her family. They adopted Madison and me when we moved to Nashville."

"Are you asking your family?"

"Hell no. Those people kicked me out onto the street when Madison was a tiny baby. We don't have anything to do with each other."

"I'm sorry."

"Don't be. My family never once tried to have me as a part of their family. They have always treated me this way. I'm used to it. Are you inviting all of your Navy Seal buddies?"

"Yes, I want all of them there. Some of them are on a rescue ship, but I'll get hold of them. When do you want to get married?"

"I don't know. Let's first see if we can get hold of your buddies and Allie. I don't want to wait more than a month."

I picked her up and swung her around. "No wonder I love you. You're perfect."

"I am far from perfect. Do you like two weeks from this coming Saturday?"

"I love that date."

"Good, me too."

We walked to my place with Lincoln's tacos, and everything went to hell. "Call an ambulance. He's burning up. That bullet must have had poison on it."

Dustin looked scared to death. Madison held his hand while the EMTs worked on Lincoln before they put him in the ambulance and drove him to the hospital. We followed. No one said a word. When we got to the hospital, Jackson, Noah, and Sofie showed up.

"So you think it's the poison like yours was."

"I don't know. I shouldn't have just let him sleep. I knew he was tired. I thought sleeping would help him."

"Of course, you did. Everyone would think that. You had no reason to think otherwise. Lincoln is strong. He'll pull out of it, you'll see."

I heard Gabby's phone ring, and she answered it, "Allie, are you alright?"

"No, I feel something is wrong with someone I love. Mama and the others are all fine. So are you and Madison okay?"

Gabby put the phone to my ear so I could hear Allie. "Lincoln is in the hospital. His fever is so high they are trying to get it down. Allie, it doesn't look good. Poor Dustin is so upset. I don't know what to say to him."

"Hug him and tell him you are there for him. All people need is a hug. I'll be there in a couple of hours."

"You're coming home?"

"Yes, I've given Lincoln some blood. Wait, that was only yesterday. So much has happened in such a short time."

"When you get here, I have some other news to give you."

"Tell me now. I need some good news."

"Ryker and I are getting married."

"What, you finally asked him?" Gabby chuckled and I almost did too.

"I'll see you when you get here."

"You might have a call from the others to make sure you are okay."

"I'll be sure and answer. Bye."

"Goodbye."

She turned to face me, pretending I didn't just overhear her best friend saying she was going to ask me to marry her. I played along. "Allie will be here in a couple of hours. She says she might have to give him blood," she told me.

"Yeah, she did that before in Las Vegas. He lost a lot of blood then. It might be my imagination, but I felt a vibe between those two. I walked in on them once arguing, and Allie was wiping her eyes. They shut up, but I felt something."

"That would explain Allie calling me. Anytime something happens with someone she cares for, she feels it. Allie's grandma was a gypsy. She died a few years back. She was one hundred and two and as strong as a sixty-year-old.

"She was killed in a tornado while visiting her twin sister. The sisters were holding on to each other as tightly as possible when they were found. They had to pry their fingers apart. Rose, that's Allie's mom, said they went out of this world the same way they came in. It was always told that when they were born they were holding hands. And the day before they died, both had a premonition that they would die. They didn't know where or anything. They only knew that they wanted to be together."

"Wow, does that mean Allie has premonitions?"

"No, but of course, Allie might not say if she does. She doesn't want anything to do with gypsy magic. She only tells us she can feel when someone she cares for is hurting."

Madison leaned in closer, "Grandma told me that when Allie was born, her eyes were wide open, and she was staring right into their eyes. She said it gave her the creeps. Her Daddy only laughed. He thought she was the cutest baby at the hospital."

Ryker was counting ages on his fingers. "The grandma was too old to have a child, wasn't she?"

"Well, grandma never had a child until late in life. She wanted a baby, but she had never fallen in love. But she went to a bar and was sitting all alone. She watched the men who came and went."

"She did this for a month because she didn't want a drunk. She wanted someone who could hold their liquor. And then she saw him walk inside the bar. She had seen him before and hoped she would see him again. Grandma was as beautiful as Allie. Even though she was fifty-five, she looked thirty. She picked this man out of all the ones she saw. She slept with him three times until she knew she was pregnant."

"Did she love this man?"

"She fell madly in love with him, and he loved her so much, but he was already married to an invalid wife at home. He had no children, so their son was his only child. When he died, he left everything to his son."

Dustin was making a face. "Eww, did he know that she was an old lady?"

Gabby chuckled. "No, I don't think he did."

"Is Allie an old lady?" Dustin asked.

"No, she's thirty-two."

"She doesn't look thirty-two, and she doesn't act like thirty-two either," he said.

"Sometimes she does. Don't forget she's a detective."

"That's right. I forgot about that."

"Don't tell her we told you her story."

"We won't say a word, will we, Dustin?"

"No, I won't say anything."

I couldn't help it; I was nosey. "Did Allie's dad know about the man?"

"Yes, he always knew. He worked for his dad after he got out of college. The girls knew about him as well. They called him Grandpa. But he and Grandma never met up again. He died ten years ago. Grandma and the entire family grieved his death."

"When did his wife die?"

"She died when Allie was still little."

"Mom, will you tell them about Allie when she saw the man's wife?"

"When Allie was two, she was with her mom and grandma at the doctor's office. The lady saw them and thought Allie was the cutest baby. She reached into her bag and pulled out a silver bell."

"She told Allie that whenever she needed help, she had to ring the bell. But the bell was what the woman used when she needed help. So when she opened the wrong door, she didn't have the bell to ring for help and fell down the stairs to her death."

"Are you telling us the truth?"

"Yes, we are."

"What happened to the bell?"

"Allie's grandpa took it and buried it with his wife."

Dustin looked at Gabby big-eyed. "If you tell me Allie hears a bell ringing when she senses something, I'm sitting over there."

"I'm not saying anything."

"That is frigging crazy."

24

GABBY

We were walking to get a coffee when Allie showed up. She ran to us and hugged all of us.

"How is he?"

"They took him back into surgery. The bullets had poison on them," Ryker said, looking at her as if she was going to cast a spell or something.

"I want to see him."

"He's in surgery."

"I need to get in there."

"Allie, that's crazy."

Dustin was staring at Allie. I knew he would say something to her. "It can't be any crazier than Allie's life. We have to get her in there with Lincoln. I don't even care why she needs to be in there. She heard the bell," Dustin said.

"Did you tell him about the bell? Really?"

"He's very upset about his brother, and you know how I get. I just started talking about your intuitions. Before I knew it, the time was flying by."

"Congratulations, you two. I can't wait for your wedding."

"Are you thirty-two? You look more like twenty," Dustin said. "I mean, you are beautiful. I bet you look like your grandma."

Allie smiled and hugged him. "I'm sorry you are upset about Lincoln. But you are never supposed to ask a woman her age. And yes, I am thirty-two. And I, indeed, look just like my grandma. Now, let's find out what surgery room he's in."

"I'll ask the nurse where he is, and you can figure out how to get in there with him," I said, walking away.

Dustin was still watching her. "Why do you think your intuition is telling you to get in there with him?"

"I don't know, but I'm in a panic right now, and if I don't do something, I'll have a panic attack and pass out."

"I'll help you."

"You will."

"Sure, you love my brother, right?"

We all looked at her. "No, that's silly. I gave Lincoln some of my blood in Vegas; I feel he might need more. Lord, I can tell you've been around Gabby and Madison too long. You're starting to sound like them. Well, go find out where he is. I'll be hunting up a disguise. I'll meet you back here in ten minutes. I'll have my disguise by then."

We stood there and watched Allie run off down the hall. Dustin laughed loudly and took off to talk to the nurse. "Let's just wait a moment. I have to see what happens."

"I wouldn't move for anything," Ryker said as he drew me close and put his other arm around Madison. "Madison, I don't want you to think I'm taking your mom from you. I look at it like she's sharing you with me."

"That's how I feel too. I'm so happy that you are going to be in our family. Here comes Dustin. Is that Aunt Allie?"

I looked, and I thought it was a doctor. But the more I

looked, the more I saw Allie. "She's going to pretend to be a doctor and sneak into where Lincoln is. Why is she doing this? I have never seen her act like this."

"Allie, this could ruin your career. You can't do this."

"I'm sorry but I have to. Something is pushing me to get in there. I'll see you in a little bit. Go get a cup of coffee."

And then she was gone. I looked at Ryker, "I know my friend is strange. She's always been like this, but she is the best friend in the world, and I love her. Plus, she is a good detective. Let's go get our coffee." I took his hand, and we walked into the cafeteria.

"I would love to be a fly on the wall," I said as we all entered the cafeteria.

"Mama, let's eat something. I'm starving."

"Me too," we all said together.

"I wonder what the heck she's doing in there," Dustin said to everyone sitting at the table eating lunch.

"I'm sure she has the doctors and nurses as confused as we are."

25

ALLIE

I WAS SURPRISED WHEN I WALKED INTO THE OPERATION ROOM that they didn't stop me. I walked up to where Lincoln was on the table. I looked at his wound, I could see shrapnel, but I didn't think the doctor saw it. "He has some shrapnel. Can you see it?"

"What? Where do you see that?"

"Right there," I said, pointing my finger. I was glad I put the plastic gloves on, or he would have seen all the scratches on my hand from climbing up those rocks the other day.

"Why in the world would he have shrapnel in his wound?"

"Because the cartel made the bullets to kill. There is poison on them."

"Do you know this man?"

"Yes, I do."

"He keeps having his heart going up high and then way down. I've thought he would have a major heart attack several times."

That's when Lincoln's heart started soaring. The doctor was shouting at the nurses. I took my glove off and took

Lincoln's hand, whispering soothingly in his ear, telling him I was right here with him and everything would be alright. The doctor ignored me as I whispered to Lincoln. His heart went back to normal, but I didn't let go of his hand. I kept hold of it until the surgery was over, then I got up and walked out.

I found Gabby and the others. I looked at Dustin, "Everything is going to be alright. Lincoln will probably be going home in a couple of days." I hugged them and looked at Gabby, "I might not be able to be here for your wedding. You know I love you so much. I am so happy that you and Ryker are getting married. Now, Madison can stop worrying about going away to college. I love all of you." I knew it would be too good to be true if I could get away that easy. Ryker stood in front of me and blocked my way.

"You didn't really think we would just let you go, did you?"

"I hoped you would have. What can I do for you, Ryker?"

"You can start by telling me what happened in that operating room."

"Please don't tell Lincoln about me going in there. They didn't even question me. The doctor didn't see the shrapnel, so I pointed it out to him as I told him about the poison. Then he told me Lincoln kept having heart problems. I knew this was why I was here."

"I took his hand and whispered encouragement, telling him I was there and everything would be alright. His heart went back to normal, so I held his hand until the surgery was over. Then I left in case the doctor wanted me to sew him up.

"You know, in the movies, they always say, 'You can take over doctor so and so.' What would I have done? Would I start sewing as I do when sewing a rip in my socks? I wasn't about to take a chance. And here I am, and now I have to leave."

"You know Lincoln was a boxer. He was the best. He could beat any man they put him up against. Then he quit, just like that. I asked him why he left boxing. He told me because he had a dream about the woman he loved. He hadn't met her but knew he had to save her. In his dream, he kept boxing, and on the way to a fight one night, the small plane crashed, and he died, and because of him still boxing, he wasn't able to save the woman he loved."

"Why are you telling me a story that I'm pretty damn sure Lincoln didn't want you repeating?"

"Because I want to know if you are that woman?"

"Oh my God, and I thought my family was crazy!" I looked over at Gabby. You are marrying into a family that has friends who are pure crazy. I would give anything to be in this family." I laughed and threw my arms around everyone. "And all I wanted was a hug," I teased, then I left.

26

RYKER

I was lying in bed with Gabby. I no longer snuck into her bed. I now stayed in it as ours. "This question has been driving me crazy, but what did Allie mean when she said, 'All I wanted was a hug?'

"I don't know what she meant with Lincoln, but with us, she said when she saw Madison, all she wanted was a hug, but then she fell in love with her."

"Those two seem to be taking the long way around to finding each other. I pulled her under me. I knew what I wanted the moment I saw you. I knew you were made for me. I didn't need any gypsy blood to tell me anything." I bent my head and slowly kissed her entire face. "I love you. I bet if I had met you years ago, we would have kids running all over this house."

"I think we might have one here in a few months."

"What?" My heart slammed in my chest. I couldn't breathe.

"Have you stopped breathing? Breathe, Ryker." She slapped me on the back.

"We are having a baby?" I couldn't stop the damn water

falling out of my eyes. I lay on my back and pulled her with me. "God, this is the best gift I could ever get. A baby girl who looks like her mommy and her big sister. Thank you."

"Ryker, are you okay?"

"Yes, I am. I'm just a little shaken. When will our baby be here?"

"I'm not sure. When did we first make love, with out a condom?"

"Are you saying we made our baby the first night we were together?"

"Well, I'm not on birth control, and you only used a condom once that night, and we made love four or five times that night."

"That means you could be five months pregnant. I can't even tell." My hand splayed across her tummy, where I could now feel her baby bump. "Is this why your breasts are tender?"

"Yes."

"How come you didn't tell me?"

"I didn't want to pressure you into marrying me. I love you, but I would never force you to marry me. I'm starting to show, so I'm happy we are getting married soon. We still have to go to the CMA awards... Why do you have that look on your face?"

"You should stay in the house until our baby is born," I said.

"That is not going to happen. We leave for the awards in Nashville in two days, and then we get married on Saturday. I am not staying in the house until our child is born. No matter how much I love you."

"Okay, but I'm not leaving your side the entire time."

"I know. That's why I love you so much. We'll tell Madison about the baby together."

"Okay, I hope she doesn't get her feelings hurt."

"Madison will be so excited and happy she will not have hurt feelings."

We were eating pancakes when Madison sat down at the table. I ran my fingers through my hair, fidgeting like a child, thinking I was about to get into trouble. Gabby sat next to her and took her hand. "Madison, we have something to tell you. Something exciting."

"Tell me," she said.

"We are having a baby."

She looked at her mom, then at me. She jumped up and twirled around. "We're having a baby. A real baby. That will stay here with us. Yes!" she cried. A baby. I can't wait for my baby sister," she looked at me or my brother." She sat back down and started crying. "This is the best news. I'm so happy."

"I knew you would be sweetheart," Gabby said.

"You cannot go to Nashville. It would be best if you stayed calm. When will the baby be here?" She asked. She looked at us, and her face turned pink.

"Three months," Gabby said. Then she burst into laughter.

"We have an appointment at one to view the baby and see what we are having. Would you like to go with us?" I asked Madison.

"Try keeping me away. Oh, this is wonderful. Way better than the puppies. Even though I miss them, I guess we won't have more puppies now that Mona is fixed. Wow, I could eat five pancakes. I'm so excited. Why must we wait so long to see what we are having? Has anyone talked to Allie? We have to tell her." Madison said.

"Her phone has been off, but she'll never miss the

awards; she makes half her income from the awards ceremony."

"I was going to stay here, but now I am definitely going with you. I have to guard your tummy in those overcrowded bathrooms. Are we taking the RV?" Madison asked.

"No, we are staying with Allie's family. They wouldn't take no for an answer. I love all of the Bennett's, but they are all so bossy. And when they find out I'm having a baby, they'll be two times as bad."

"Then, please, let's get a room somewhere else," I said.

"Their feelings will be hurt if we do. So let's have everything we need for our trip so we won't run around like crazy people." Gabby said.

"What about Dustin? I told him he could go with us. He and I can stay backstage. That way, he can see all of the singers."

"Is Lincoln able to be alone?" Gabby asked.

"Yes, I saw him chopping wood yesterday," Madison said.

"Damn him. What is his problem?" Ryker asked.

"Dustin said he keeps having the same dream at night, which keeps him awake. Is that Dustin's motorcycle?" Madison said. We were standing at the kitchen door when Dustin pulled up with another girl. I looked at Madison to see what she thought. I couldn't read her feelings, but I was pissed on her behalf. He shouldn't bring girls here.

"Hey, everyone. Madison, do you know Heather?" Dustin asked, coming in with the girl.

"No, not exactly," Madison said.

"We hang out with different people. Mine are the cool kids, and Madison's are the nerds. That's why Dustin hangs with her; she's tutoring him so he can play football. That's so sweet of you."

I didn't want to get involved, but this Heather girl was

rude to my daughter. Were she not a child, I would have stepped in. I groaned internally, hoping she wouldn't say another smart-ass remark.

"Well, this is Madison, and this is Heather. Are there any more puppies?"

"No."

The cute cheerleader pouted. "Darn, I wanted one. I keep playing with Dusty's. They are so cute."

Madison frowned as she looked at Dustin. "Dusty. You actually let someone call you Dusty."

"Everyone calls him Dusty."

"I don't like that name. Call me Dustin. That's my name."

"Dustin. You've always liked for me to call you Dusty," she said, putting her arms around him and kissing him on the mouth.

"Knock it off, Heather."

"What's the matter? You were enjoying all of my kisses earlier. In fact, you were enjoying all of me earlier. Will I have to remind you?"

Madison turned and walked out of the room, "I'll see you guys around."

I followed her. "I'm sorry if Dustin bringing that girl here was upsetting," I said when I sat beside on the deck sofa.

"It wasn't upsetting. Dustin can hang out with whoever he wants to. I just forgot there for a while that I was his tutor, not his friend."

"That's a damn lie, and you know it," I heard Dustin say behind me. "Look at me. You're my best friend. Don't ever forget it. It's you I like hanging with. You didn't say goodbye."

"Goodbye, Dustin," she said sarcastically.

I know Dustin thought the same way I did. I felt that goodbye sounded final. I looked at Gabby, and she wiped a tear from her eye as she turned around. I wondered if she knew something that I didn't. She went back into the kitchen, and we both followed her. I gave Dustin a look to let him know he needed to fix this. Madison walked over to the sink and began cleaning the dishes.

Madison asked me, "What do you think we are having?"

I decided to go along with her and change the subject. "I think we are having a girl. One as beautiful as her sister. I'm so excited. I wonder if we went early, would they let us in?"

Heather was standing in the doorway, playing with her hair. "Dusty, can we go, please?"

Dustin looked to me as if he needed my help but my focus was making sure Madison was okay. I shrugged, and he followed Heather out the door, saying goodbye to the three of us.

"Maybe someone will cancel. Let's go," Madison said, drying her wet hands with a dishtowel. "Mama, hurry. We are going early to the baby viewing."

"Why are we going early?"

"Because someone is going to cancel, we need to leave now."

"Let me grab my bag."

It made me smile the way Gabby agreed to most things. Even if it sounded far-fetched, she would go along with it. We climbed into the vehicle and went to view our baby. As we walked into the room, a lady at the reception desk asked Gabby her name.

"Gabrielle McKalister."

"Oh, I was going to call you. Someone canceled this morning. Take a seat and fill out these forms. You'll be seen soon."

Madison clapped her hands. We sat down and were shown into a room less than fifteen minutes later. Gabby lay on a table, and they squirted some stuff on her tummy. Gabby made a noise.

Sorry, it's cold at first. I held onto her hand, and Madison had the other one. I couldn't even swallow. I think I stopped breathing. I inhaled sharply when the screen came up with the baby on it. It was a three-D display. The baby's face was right there. Her eyes were closed. She was beautiful. Madison started to cry. I blinked because, damn it, I'm a strong alpha man. I can't cry over my baby in the safe tummy of her mommy. "She's beautiful," I said out loud.

"You mean he's beautiful," the woman running the sonogram said.

"He."

"I have a brother. I have a brother!" Madison laughed and looked at me. "He will look just like his handsome father."

I bent and kissed Gabby. "Are you two going to act like this every time we come to see more pictures of him?"

"How often do we get to come?" I asked.

"You can come next month and see his progress. If you talk to him, he'll recognize your voice when he's born."

"I wish I could hold him," Madison said.

"You'll get all the holding you want after he's born. I hope he's as good of a baby as his sister was. You were an angel." Gabby said, looking at Madison.

"I'm so happy, Mama. How many babies are you and Ryker having?"

Gabby chuckled. Before she could answer, I said, "Four!"

"Good, he'll need someone to play with. I'll be away at college. I'm going to miss them so much. I swear I have a pressure headache trying not to cry. I'm such a big crybaby."

We all chuckled. Every one of us had water in our eyes. "The only reason I'm not bawling my head off is that I'm supposed to be the strong male figure in the family."

"How would you like me to print a copy out?" the lady asked.

Madison looked at her. "Can you print me one to keep in my room?"

"I need one for my mom and one for my truck."

"How about four copies?"

"That will be perfect, thank you," Gabby said.

We talked about the baby all the way to my mom's house. We had to pick out a name. "His first name will be Ryker. You can pick a middle name, and that is what we will call him," Gabby said.

I bent and gave her another kiss. "I love you."

"I love you too. Oh, look, there's your mom walking the dogs."

We pulled into the driveway, and Mom and the puppies ran to us. "Here, Mom, let me take the puppies, and you can have this."

"What is this?" Madison stood next to her. She held her hand over her heart. "Are we having a baby?" That's all Madison needed—the word baby.

"I'm going to have a brother; can you believe it? I'm going to have a brother."

"A baby boy? Your dad would have been so proud to have a grandson. I am so happy," Mom said, looking at me and Gabby.

She put her hands over her face and cried. "Come on, you two, let's get inside," I said with my arm around my mom. I looked back, and Madison was carrying the puppies while Gabby walked in front of us. I was one lucky guy.

27

RYKER

"I AM SO HAPPY YOU CAME WITH US TO NASHVILLE, MOM. I need to make sure Gabby doesn't overdo it."

"Thank you for asking me to come along with you. Are you sure the Bennett's will have enough room?"

"They have plenty of room. I want you to enjoy your visit and have a blast. The Bennett's are very popular with the Grand Ole Opry. I'm sure Mama Bennett will be dragging you all over the place. You have to be forceful with these people. I love them more than anything, but they are so bossy," Gabby said.

"I can't wait to see them. I miss them so much. I wish they would visit us more. I will tell them I want to see them more than every few months. I'm used to being with them. When I go away to college, things are going to change," Madison said.

"Why don't you go to the University of Oregon? Then you won't have to go anywhere," I asked Madison. "Unless you want to spread your wings."

"The University of Oregon. Mama, what do you think?"

"Well, I know what I want, but this is your life. You

decide what you want to do. Isn't Dustin going to the University of Oregon?"

"Yes, that's what I want. I want to go to the University where I'm not far from home, and I can see my little brother and the other three kids you will have."

"Wow, it's like a weight has been lifted off my shoulders. Thank you, Ryker. You always seem to know what I want," Gabby said, hugging me.

Isa and Oda met us at the airport, and they pulled Madison and Gabby into a hug. All of them were crying. They were breathtaking, like Allie. I wondered if they were anything like Allie.

"You can't stay away for so long. Why haven't you been to see us?"

"I'm sorry, sweets, we have been so busy. Look at you. You're as tall as me," Isa said, hugging her. Then she looked at Gabby and touched her tummy. When is the baby due?"

"In three and a half months. I would have told everybody sooner, but I wanted to tell Ryker first, and I waited to hear him say how much he loved me."

"So I take it he loves you a lot."

"Yes, I do. I told Gabby before how much I loved her. I guess she had to believe it first."

"I'm so glad you are staying with us," Oda said with her arm around Madison. "I missed you so much, Madison. Oh, by the way, I have a boyfriend. His name is Michael."

"Tell me about him."

"He's handsome. They talked, walking behind us."

"Have you heard from Allie?"

"No, I was going to ask you. The awards are tomorrow, and she hasn't even called us."

"If she is tracking someone or hiding from them, she has

to keep her phone turned off," I said, walking with my arm around Gabby.

"Why is she doing this?"

"Because she saw how bad it was for the children they sent over at the border, they say they are taking them to family, and it's a lie. They'll send them all over, and that's when they are trafficked."

"This makes me angry. She should have never gotten involved in this. Why did she?"

"Because Olivia was kidnapped, and when the Seals Security went over there, she went with them. She was upset because the border kids have no one fighting for them."

"That sounds like our Allie. Always one to protect the kids. I'll do your hair if she doesn't show up."

"Thank you. I worry about her. She is so stubborn. We told her to stay away from the cartel, but she wouldn't listen."

"Are you singing your new song tomorrow?"

"How do you know about that?"

"Madison told me about it. She let me listen to you when you were singing it last week. It's a beautiful song. I guess you wrote it for Ryker."

"You wrote a song for me?"

"Yes, but you can't hear it until tomorrow."

"Your phone is ringing," I told Isa.

"Hello, Allie. Where are you? We are all worried about you." A moment passed as she listened to Allie, then replied, "It would be best if you came home right now... She hung up on me," she said to us as we looked at her.

"Can you believe that? She said to apologize to everyone and let you all know that she won't be coming. Apparently, she is in hiding and can't show her face. This is way too dangerous for Allie. She's too kind-hearted for her own good. What are we going to do?"

"I'll call a few people and have them check on her." I said trying to calm the sister's down.

"Thank you. Let's not say how dangerous this is in front of Mom and Dad. They worry all the time."

We were now standing beside a large Limousine. Madison and Gabby acted like this was their usual way of life here. We drove to the country over beautiful hills. Mom talked like she had known these people all her life.

The landscaping was perfect. Forty-five minutes later, we pulled up to an electric gate. That opened when we stopped. I looked around, and when I saw the resort, I smiled—nothing like a private resort. When we stopped and got out of the vehicle, a beautiful woman ran down the steps, threw her arms around Madison, then hugged Gabby.

"I have missed you two so much. Your hair is beautiful, Madison."

"Mom, we decided we wouldn't mention Madison's hair."

"Well, that was when I thought it was to her scalp. I think it looks beautiful. It suits the older Madison. It's very stylish. Allie did a great job. Where is she, by the way?"

"She just called me and won't be able to make it this year. She's too busy with Aunt Olivia," Isa answered quickly.

"I'll have to give her a good talking to. How is grandma's favorite girl doing?"

"I'm good, Grandma. Oh, this is Ryker Malone. He and Mama are getting married."And this is his mother, Wilma Malone, who will be my grandma.

"I figured he was her fiancé. He's so handsome, and I was a little shy to say anything to him."

Everyone busted out laughing. Gabby put her arm through Rose's arm. "We are having a boy."

"A boy. Oh, I'm so happy for you three. You are so lucky to have a baby in the family."

"What are you talking about? You are my family. He will be in your family as well."

"Well, then, I'm going to have a grandson. I'm so excited. Thank you for including us in everything. I'm so happy to meet you, Wilma. I know we will be good friends."

"Mama, will you keep them outside the entire time they are here?" Her husband said, walking outside.

I watched Madison run to him, and he twirled her around. "You are more beautiful every time I see you.'"

Madison kissed his cheek. "Grandpa, we are having a boy."

"A boy," he said jubilantly. "I can't believe there will be a boy in our family. Gabby, you have made me so happy. You too," he said, looking at me.

"Papa, this is Ryker, the man I told you about. And this is my mother-in-law. This is John. He and Rose are my family. He adopted Madison and me when I was twenty-one and Madison was three."

"Ryker, it is a pleasure to meet you. Why don't we have the wedding here?"

"We are having the wedding in Oregon. You have to come to my house. If you want to visit your grandkids, you'll have to get used to it anyway."

"I know, come inside. We'll have some iced tea and sandwiches. Let's go to the kitchen."

I looked around once I was inside I realized this was their home, which looked comfortable for a mansion. The kitchen was a chef's dream. The stove was eight burners. We sat around the wide island on the most comfortable bar stools I'd ever sat on. I watched as John made the best-looking and tasting sandwich I'd had.

"Are you a chef?"

"Yes, I am. Has Gabby not told you we have a line of food we sell at the markets?" I almost fell off my stool when he told me the family name.

"Gabby forgot to mention a few things to me."

"So, where is my Allie?"

I enjoyed my sandwich as the others told him about Allie. I felt someone watching me, and I looked around. It was Madison watching me. I smiled as she brought her iced tea and sandwich over to where I sat. I hugged her and kissed her forehead. "Are you as excited as I am to hold your baby brother?"

"Yes, I wish I could see him again." Then she took the photo of the baby out of her backpack and handed it to Rose, who started crying. Then the image was passed around.

"That was perfect timing. Madison," Gabby said, squeezing in between us. "I waited because I knew Grandpa would become angry because Allie wasn't here."

28

RYKER

I stayed next to Gabby the entire time we were at the CMA awards. She went backstage before she was to sing. I went with her. There were too many people; I didn't want to lose her. Madison was talking to the Bennett's. The family was welcome everywhere they went. They had their very own sitting area.

When it was time for Gabby to sing, I saw Madison walk up, and she went to a microphone where the backup singer would be. *She sings backup for Gabby.* I was astonished. I've heard Gabby go around singing all the time, but I never heard Madison sing.

Isa walked up to me as I stood backstage. "Are you surprised to see Madison as a backup singer?"

"I have never heard her sing before. Gabby always goes around singing, but Madison doesn't."

"Madison is shy. But her voice is the most beautiful I've ever heard. I talked her into singing backup on a couple of Gabby's songs because I want her to get used to singing in front of people. I'm Gabby's manager."

I looked at her, "I'm glad she has someone who she can trust. Someone who doesn't only think of the money."

"I'm glad she and Madison have you. I watched you with them, and I can tell you love them as much as they love you. I can't wait to meet Rye."

"Rye?"

"Our baby boy, we always give a nickname to our family members. Except for Madison, she threw such a fit every time we would give her a nickname we had to call her Madison."

"Thank you. I like that name."

I watched Gabby walk over and kiss Madison, and the music started. Gabby walked onto the stage, and the audience was enthralled. I saw her look at me, then she walked over and took my hand, pulling me on stage, as she sang her beautiful love song.

Without thinking, I bent my head and kissed her. The crowd erupted. I gazed into her eyes as Madison's voice drifted to us. Then I smiled and gave her another quick kiss before she finished the song.

"I want to introduce my man to all of you. Ryker Malone, these people," she said, her arms going wide, "are my family. And this guy here is my man, Ryker Malone."

I pulled her into my arms and kissed her so everyone would know she was mine forever. The woman who would forever be in my heart. Madison threw her arms around us. I raised my head and kissed her on the cheek. I was so lucky that I moved into the house I bought for my other fiancé. If I hadn't moved there, I would never have met the love of my life.

THE END

Dear reader.

Thank you, for your continued support. I really appreciate that you read my books.

If you can please leave me a review for this book, I would appreciate it enormously.

Your reviews allow me to get validation I need to keep going as an Indie author.

Just a moment of your time is all that is needed. I will try my best to give you the
    best books I can write.

Keep reading for a look at book two in the Seals Security

LINCOLN

Dustin, my younger brother, wouldn't stop staring at me. "Why are you staring at me?"

"Because you almost died. Do you even know how sick you were? Your heart nearly exploded. I don't want to go away to college if you are still ill. It's a good thing Allie came back. She snuck into the operating room and showed the surgeon where the shrapnel was and that there was poison on them. Then when your heart soared, she held your hand and whispered words of encouragement."

I couldn't believe Allie came here while I was in the hospital. They should have tied her down while she was here and not let her go back to fight for those border children. She couldn't fight the damn cartel alone. "Why the hell was Allie even here? I thought she was supposed to be saving kids from the cartel. Tell me what she did?"

"She dressed like a doctor, went into the operating room, and pretended to be a doctor. Allie had a premonition that something terrible was going to happen to someone she cared about. When Gabby told her about you being so sick, she flew back here in case you needed something."

"Why would she think she could fix it if I did need something? You don't have to worry about me. Besides, you're going to the university of Oregon, so you'll be an hour away."

"I know, but I still worry. You're the only family I have left."

"Hey, I'm going to be fine. You take care of yourself when you're away."

"Don't worry about me."

"What happened with you and Madison? You two were like best friends. You did everything together."

"I want Madison to meet other guys. She's falling in love with me. I could see it when she looked at me. It's not fair for Madison. She needs to meet other guys."

"I thought you were the one falling for her."

"Yes, well, there is that too. I'm not going to get serious about anyone right now. I have college to get through, and then I'm joining the Seals. You know that has been my dream since I was little."

"I know. I think you are right, but you can't just drop Madison. She's your friend."

"I know I took Heather with me the last time I went there. I could see Madison's hurt, but I think it worked."

"I'm sure it did." I walked outside and thought about the beautiful Allie Bennet. She took way too many chances. She was too hot for her own good, and I wanted her the moment I laid eyes on her. I chuckled, thinking about her pretending to be a doctor. *How did she know I needed her to tell the doctor what happened to me?*

We rescued kids and women from the cartel in Vegas when I was shot. I left before the surgeon told me I could. That's why I became so sick. I know I should have stayed at the hospital in Vegas, but I was so angry at Allie for staying there to help the children the cartel sent over the border. Why does she think she can help those kids and women from the cartel?

I knew why I was angry. It was because Allie was starting to get under my skin. I couldn't allow that. I didn't want to start a relationship with Allie or any woman. I was waiting for that one woman. Okay, this might sound crazy, but I'll tell you anyway.

I used to be a boxer and was pretty damn famous for boxing for the Seals going all over the world. Then I had the most real dream I could have. I dreamed that the woman I loved needed me. I had to save her. I didn't know who she was or anything about her. At first, I ignored the dream, but after having the dream every night for a week straight, I stopped boxing. I had to be healthy and ready when my lady needed me.

That's why I didn't allow myself to get involved with Allie. I didn't want to hurt her when I had to save the woman I loved. Besides, she gets on my nerves. She never knows when to shut up. I hope to hell she doesn't lead the cartel to her by talking so damn much.

I don't want to go down that rabbit hole again, thinking of Allie again. The last time I went there, I wanted her naked beneath me every time I saw her. It took me getting shot to stop thinking of her. I couldn't believe Sofie was her cousin.

They are entirely different in every way. Sofie barely speaks, and when she does, she's quiet. Allie is beautiful, loud, and never shuts up. If she thinks you deserve to be yelled at, then that is what she would do e*ven if you are the cartel!*

"Fuck, I picked up the phone and called Gabby. Hey,

Gabby, have you heard from Allie? I wanted to thank her for everything she did for me in the operating room."

"You weren't supposed to know about that. No, I haven't heard from her. But Ryker said she probably has her phone turned off. How are you feeling?"

"I feel great. It's been two weeks since the surgery, so I'm ready to return to work. If you hear from Allie, will you please let me know?"

"I sure will. Bye."

"I'll talk to you later. Wait, I have a question. Do you think Allie would yell at the cartel men if she's angry?"

"I've tried not to think of that. Allie is an excellent detective. I don't know how she would be as someone rescuing kids from the cartel. She has a fierce temper, and if she sees them with the children, she might do something crazy."

"How crazy?"

"Crazy, like yelling at whoever has the kids or whoever is mistreating women. She is very protective. She doesn't like mean people, period."

"Do you think she might need help?"

"Allie usually works better on her own, but I'm worried because she won't answer her phone. I've been trying to call her for over a week."

30

ALLIE

I KNEW THE MOMENT WHEN I WAS DISCOVERED. WHEN I heard the kids crying, I moved too fast because I was afraid they would leave with the kids. I couldn't allow that. So I made a noise so they would notice me. I had a disguise, so they didn't know I was a woman who most men thought was beautiful. Instead, they thought I was an old lady.

Bastards kicked an old lady, or who they thought was an old lady, and they kicked me again when I fell. I didn't dare talk because my voice was low, and some men told me I had a sexy voice, maybe if I mumbled.

"Get up."

It's a good thing I speak Spanish. I pretended like it was hard for this old lady to get up. I stumbled like an old lady."

"Why do you have an old lady?"

"She was nosey. We saw her walking toward the kids."

"Why were you in this area?"

"I prayed I could fake my voice. "I heard babies crying."

"Then she can take care of the kids until we get our money for them. Then you can kill her."

Lord, what am I going to do? I'll run off with the little ones if they leave me alone with them.

Get her out of here. Why do you two always put more shit on my head? Can you not do anything I ask you to do? Get her out of here!" he shouted.

I knew this guy was going to be hard to fool. The other one pushed me into the room where the kids were. He shoved me, and I fell. One child, a little boy about eight, helped me up. He looked at me, and I recognized him. "Why are you here?"

The man took me when I walked to school." Why the hell would his parents let him walk to school? My God, he has been kidnapped once already. I want to wring their necks. Did they think he was safe? No kids are safe since the government let the cartel come inside our borders.

I wish I had some help. I didn't want to die. But I did want to see who the buyers were.

Whoever is buying these trafficked kids needs to be shot dead. I felt behind me, and there it was, my gun. If I have a chance to use it, I will. I'll kill who I have to.

"Are there any other kids?"

Yes, they are in another room." That's when they brought the other kids into the room with us.

"You can watch all of them. Here are the other ones," he said, handing me two babies. He threw a diaper bag into the room. I sat on the floor to be at eye level with the kids. The babies looked a little like they were in shock. I wondered if the parents sold these kids. They couldn't pull them out of my arms if these were my children.

I need help. Don't start getting weepy. You can do this. No, I can't. I need help. I looked at all the kids and knew they would most likely die a horrific death if I didn't get them away from here. And I couldn't let that happen.

I saw a few older kids. Maybe they could help me. If we could make it to my vehicle, we could go to that tunnel in the desert. I need to get rid of the guards. I heard a car outside and looked out the window. It was the man who told them to kill me. He was leaving. That left the two men to get rid of. I needed to plan.

I got up and walked to a corner. I pushed a button and waited for her to answer.

"Allie, where the heck are you?"

"I can't talk. I need help. Send someone." I hung up and shut my phone off. Then I turned and smiled at the kids. I sat on the floor and gathered them around me. We are going to escape. I won't let anyone hurt you. I held one baby in my arms, and a little girl held the other. She looked like she's carried babies before.

Okay, how was I going to get us out of here? One of the men walked in and took a little girl by the hand. There was no fucking way I was going to allow this. So it was starting now. I walked over and pulled her away from him. His fist went straight for my face, and I ducked.

He dropped the girl's hand and came after me. I wasn't a homicide detective for nothing. I did have to learn something about fighting. So when he charged me, I tripped him. While he was down, I hit him over the head with an empty whiskey bottle. He was out cold. I couldn't let him have the chance to wake up. I looked at the kids and put my fingers to my lips.

I whispered to the older kids to take the younger kids to the other side of the room. When they did, I hit the guy in the head again. I'm positive he's dead. I would get the other one when he came to find his friend. I waited next to the door for thirty minutes before the second guy came to find his friend.

As soon as he stepped inside, I hit him. I was as tall as the guy, which helped me with my swing. His legs buckled, but he turned and aimed his gun. He shot as I swung. He was dead, I looked at my arm, and it had a little hole where the bullet entered. I hoped it exited as well.

"Let's go. Hold hands. We have to stay quiet, and that's when I realized I was talking in English, so I changed and spoke Spanish. The baby started crying. I grabbed the diaper bag and made a bottle. Who would give these babies away?

My vehicle wasn't far, but it took a while before we reached it. Then I hurried and put the kids inside. The bigger kids held onto the little ones as I drove away. I took a deep breath and called aunt Olivia.

"Where are you? Gabby called and said Lincoln was on his way over here. They want you to stay put. So he can find you."

"Tell Lincoln and only Lincoln I'm in the cave in the desert. Can you please get as much food as you can get? I have twelve children, but I haven't figured out what to do with them. I'll be by your house in an hour. If you can ask your neighbors if they can also get food and water together, that would be wonderful. Thank you, aunt Olivia."

"What have you gotten yourself into?"

"I'll talk to you when I see you. Also, I will need bandages and antiseptic."

"Why do you need that?"

"I have an injury to my arm."

"What kind of injury?"

"Auntie, can I explain everything when I see you?"

"Yes, if you can get peanut butter and jelly as well as other food, that would be great. You know I love peanut butter and jelly. Now I have to drive. I can't keep talking. Oh lord, I can't believe it's Lincoln. He doesn't like me."

"I'm sure that's not true. Everyone loves you. You are kind and the sweetest child I know besides my Sofie. He better watch out. I will pull his ear off if he says anything about you to me."

I giggled. I couldn't help it. "I'm hanging up now. Goodbye."

"I'll see you later."

Lincoln, I'm not sure I want him to help me. He's handsome and doesn't like being around me without arguing.

31

LINCOLN

I looked at Gabby like she was crazy. "What do you mean she needs help?"

"She called me and said she needs help. I'm scared, and Ryker isn't here. I think she must have confronted some cartel men. I don't know what the heck she means. She said she needed help. The thing with Allie is people think because she talks so much that, she is a tuff cookie. She's a homicide detective, but she is so sweet. Please help her."

"Give me your aunt's phone number. I'll leave now." For some reason, I was starting to have a panic attack. What was taking so long for Gabby to get me that phone number?

"Here you go. Thank you, Lincoln. As soon as I hear from...." I had already turned around and left out the front door. "Lock my house up," I called over my shoulder. I tossed my keys, and she caught them.

Link for Lincoln
My Book

Here is a link for a bonus story of Noah and Sofie.

https://BookHip.com/ZQDMFVD

JOIN me on social media Follow me on BookBub
https://www.bookbub.com/profile/susie-mciver

NEWSLETTER SIGN UP HTTP://BIT.LY/SUSIEMCIVER_NEWSLETTER

FACEBOOK GROUP: https://www.susiemciver.com/

HTTPS://WWW.SUSIEMCIVER.COM/

HTTPS://WWW.INSTAGRAM.COM/SUSIEMCIVERAUTHOR/

BAND OF NAVY SEALS
KILLIAN BOOK 1
My Book

ROWAN BOOK 2
My Book

ZANE BOOK 3
My Book

. . .

STORM BOOK 4
https://www.amazon.com/dp/B08Y7C9D4Z

ASH BOOK 5
My Book

JONAH BOOK 6
My Book

KANE BOOK 7
My Book

AUSTIN BOOK 8
My Book
LUKE
My Book
RYES
My Book

ARMY RANGERS SPECIAL OPS
KASH
My Book
ANGEL
My Book
MATT
My Book
JAX
My Book

RYAN
My Book
TREY
My BookJ
CONNER
My Book
ASHER
My Book

Printed in Dunstable, United Kingdom

PAUL WHITEMAN

BIKINI STATE RED

Copyright © 2020 Paul Whiteman

The moral right of the author has been asserted.

Apart from any fair dealing for the purposes of research or private study, or criticism or review, as permitted under the Copyright, Designs and Patents Act 1988, this publication may only be reproduced, stored or transmitted, in any form or by any means, with the prior permission in writing of the publishers, or in the case of reprographic reproduction in accordance with the terms of licences issued by the Copyright Licensing Agency. Enquiries concerning reproduction outside those terms should be sent to the publishers.

This is a work of fiction. Names, characters, businesses, places, events and incidents are either the products of the author's imagination or used in a fictitious manner. Any resemblance to actual persons, living or dead, or actual events is purely coincidental.

Matador
9 Priory Business Park,
Wistow Road, Kibworth Beauchamp,
Leicestershire. LE8 0RX
Tel: 0116 279 2299
Email: books@troubador.co.uk
Web: www.troubador.co.uk/matador
Twitter: @matadorbooks

ISBN 978 1838591 502

British Library Cataloguing in Publication Data.
A catalogue record for this book is available from the British Library.

Printed and bound in Great Britain by 4edge Limited
Typeset in 10.5pt Adobe Jenson Pro by Troubador Publishing Ltd, Leicester, UK

Matador is an imprint of Troubador Publishing Ltd

For Janet

A map of the United Kingdom and surrounding waters is provided on the last page of the book. This shows towns, ports and coastal areas relevant to the story.

PART ONE

ATHENA

Born, fully armed, from the head of Zeus, she is the virgin goddess of wisdom and prudent warfare.

1

This is a tale of events in the early 1990s.

Sunday 27th September

The coincidence was unfortunate.

The salt marshes of North Norfolk stretch out to the North Sea. The land is flat and prone to flooding. In places the heaped shingle sea defences separate marsh and shoreline. It's a birdwatcher's paradise, free from the usual paraphernalia of coastal resorts. That was why John McAdam was there. The others were there because it is secluded and desolate, and an ideal place to smuggle in goods via the North Sea.

As twilight dwindled, Charles Fisher turned the motor launch towards a deserted stretch of shore between Cley Beach and Blakeney Point. A few minutes later he cut the engine to run the boat gently aground in front of the sea defences. Jimmy Tarrant fixed a temporary mooring line to steady the boat against the rising tide. Fisher and Tarrant were ex-marines. They had served with the SBS, the Special Boat Service – the naval equivalent of the SAS. Now they were mercenaries. The other man aboard, known only as Tremain, was coordinator of the operation. He called them into the cabin for a final briefing and handed over the first payment. Tremain was running late and needed to make the long trek across the shingles and marshes to get to the village of Cley-next-the-Sea, where his car was waiting.

'From now on we contact each other using the agreed procedure.' Tremain started to climb ashore.

'Hold on!' urged Tarrant. 'Someone's coming.'

Lieutenant John McAdam strolled slowly along the shore, enjoying the late-September evening, imbibing the gentle roar of the sea and the swishing of the waves as they broke over the sand and shingle. There was a hint of rain in the air. The small boat in the distance had not yet caught his attention. His thoughts were elsewhere. He was glad Mary had made the decision to take the children to her mother's house in London. The boys constantly demanded his attention. He wanted desperately to spend the last few days of his leave alone with Mary. She understood – she always did. And she never complained about his long periods at sea – though he knew they made her unhappy. He began to think about how things might work out after his retirement from the navy in two years' time. There was no chance of promotion now. It wasn't just the kudos – the pension too. 'Pity,' he muttered, forcing back a pang of resentment.

His attention turned to the boat perched upright on its bilge keels on the shingle. She was a little beauty. The light was fading fast but he just had to look her over before turning back.

Tremain grabbed his binoculars.

'Looks like a bloody birdwatcher – they get everywhere,' remarked Tarrant.

Tremain adjusted the focus, straining his eyes to get a good view of the face in the fading light. The blue serge naval-issue jumper confirmed his worst suspicions. 'Damn and blast! I know that man. If he recognises me the operation is compromised.'

'You mean cancelled?' Fisher's thoughts focused immediately on the prospect of diminishing revenue.

'Hope not,' replied Tremain. 'Let's see if he minds his own business. If he is who I think he is, we have a problem.'

'There's no one else around – what if he *disappears?*' suggested Tarrant.

'You're mad,' retorted Fisher.

Tremain ushered them back into the cabin. 'We'll have to play it by ear.'

The lieutenant continued walking towards the boat. Tremain jumped over the side onto the sea-covered shingle and marched towards him. McAdam stopped in his tracks.

'McAdam, isn't it?'

'Yes – but…'

'Well, well – what a coincidence! Now, old chap, no need for formalities.' Tremain grasped the lieutenant's arm just above the elbow and led him away from the boat. 'So, what are you doing here?'

'I'm on leave.'

'Do you live here?'

'No – just having a short holiday.'

'I see – on your own, are you?'

'I am today. My wife's meeting me in Cley tomorrow.'

'Look here, old chap, I'll have to take you into my confidence. You've stumbled across an important undercover operation. Don't discuss this with anyone – including your naval colleagues. Understand?'

'No problem.'

'Is there anyone else with you who might have seen us, or might come looking for you here?'

'No.'

'Did you see anyone else on your way here?'

'No, it's deserted now; not even a car at Cley Beach.'

'Except yours?' enquired Tremain.

'Not even mine, the wife's got it. I walked from Cley.'

'Really?' Tremain squeezed the lieutenant's arm encouragingly. 'Is someone expecting you back tonight?'

McAdam hesitated before answering. 'No, I'm alone in the cottage tonight.'

'Excellent!' responded Tremain. 'Then I expect you would like to look over the boat.'

McAdam was intrigued and climbed eagerly aboard.

Tremain stood in the wheelhouse, blocking the entrance to the forecabin. 'Quite an instrument panel for a small boat, eh?'

'Fantastic!' McAdam recognised some of the equipment, the latest in electronic navigation. The other devices were less familiar.

Before the conversation could develop further, Tremain called out to Fisher and Tarrant. McAdam's curiosity turned to unease when two Viking-like characters built like the proverbial brick houses emerged from the cabin.

'Meet my friends, Charles and James.'

Fisher shook hands briefly. Tremain nodded. Tarrant suddenly grasped McAdam's extended hand and flung him face downwards onto the deck. The lieutenant was silenced by a heavy blow to the back of the head.

*

John McAdam struggled to wake up from his bad dream, but the throbbing pain in his head and the pounding noise intensified.

'What the bloody hell…?' His mind jolted to consciousness – and with reality came fear.

It was a moonless night. The navigation lights were off. In the open-backed wheelhouse of the launch, two men shouted to each other above the rush of the sea and a large diesel engine pumping away at full power. McAdam lay motionless on the deck near the stern among a large heap of mouldy-smelling ropes. The boat was planing with bow high and stern close to the swirling sea. The showers of cold spray sharpened his senses. But he felt sick and dizzy and his head was still throbbing.

Suddenly, one of the men clambered towards him. McAdam feigned coma and gritted his teeth. He managed to stifle a yell and remain motionless after a painful kick in the back.

Tarrant returned to the wheelhouse. 'He's not going anywhere.'

'We'll dump him soon and get the hell out of here,' replied Fisher.

It started to rain.

McAdam knew he had only one chance. He slowly lifted his head to gain sight of the men over the top of the large engine casing which loomed above him amidships. Their backs were towards him. He thought he could see shore lights astern. McAdam struggled to remove his boots, took a deep inhalation of air and slid quickly over the starboard side into the foaming sea. He forced himself down three metres and stayed underwater for a good minute. The noise of the motor cruiser got progressively fainter. The sea was rough for swimming but provided cover. The rain, now heavy, further decreased visibility. The lieutenant struck out for land. Soon he could hear nothing but sea and wind.

The sound of the engine returned. McAdam stopped his steady crawling stroke, trod water and looked around. A light searched across the sea, catching the spray and causing luminescent halos. The boat passed by at speed. The light suddenly flashed his way. He dipped under the water momentarily but had no stamina left for prolonged submersion. The rain and the waves sheltered his head from view. The boat made several more excursions but none came near.

The exhausted lieutenant struggled on. The tidal stream swept him east of Cley. His steady stroke had become a thrashing motion, and he was only just keeping his head above water. He was choking and almost on the verge of giving up when the dark outline of the dyke appeared before him. With a final desperate effort he lurched towards it and, unexpectedly soon, his feet touched the sandy shingle. He managed to crawl halfway up the embankment before collapsing.

*

The shrill chanting of seabirds aroused McAdam some hours later. Cold, dazed and feverish, he lay there, too weak to get up. The shore was deserted and misty. Somehow it seemed safer now that dawn had broken. But the head injury was taking its toll. The lieutenant passed in and out of consciousness.

He heard vague sounds of trudging feet. Soon hands were lifting him off the shingle. McAdam opened his eyes and tried to focus. The images were blurred – but he saw enough.

2

Monday 28th September

Alice Silk bounded effortlessly through the waves of humanity in London's West End. Commander Tom Falconer trailed wearily behind.

'We're going in here,' she instructed, guiding Tom into the third clothes shop.

'Navigating frigates through busy shipping lanes was easier than this,' joked Tom.

'This is it!' announced Alice, snatching a jacket from a rack. 'It's you, it really is.'

Alice was twenty-six, tall and elegant. And, thanks to grooming at a well-known ladies' college, she had confidence and style. Her persuasive posturing was beginning to attract attention in Jaeger. Tom bought the jacket, grabbed Alice's hand, hauled her out of the store and hailed a passing taxi. They sank into the soft, welcoming seats and simultaneously burst into laughter.

Commander Falconer had recently turned forty. After twenty years' service as a seaman officer, and much against the advice of Rear Admiral Richard Claydon, he had taken early retirement from the Royal Navy. He met Alice at an exhibition at the Royal Academy. He was on leave at the time. Oil painting was his hobby. Alice was a professional in the world of the fine arts, a cognoscente. It was all they had in common – but they soon became lovers. Tom moved into Alice's small, but valuable, flat in a fashionable mews in Belgravia. Thanks to the navy they had so far spent only short periods together during their two-year affair.

Tom stared thoughtfully out of the cab window. He was now a civilian. Tonight would be a landmark. He had arranged to meet a few close naval colleagues at a Turkish restaurant in town. They were all officers on his frigate. The old crew would soon be splitting up – they were due back from leave at the end of the week.

It was late afternoon when their taxi turned off Belgrave Square into the mews, a quaint little lane providing a village-like haven in the metropolis.

'We've an hour before Scottie arrives,' Tom called from the bathroom.

Alice entered and handed him a cognac. She sat briefly and admired her man. He was physically tough, a bit on the chubby side, with unruly brown-Labrador-coloured hair and a wicked twinkle in his eyes. The thick but well-trimmed ginger beard gave him that nautical look.

'Hope you don't mind being chauffeur tonight?' said Tom.

'Of course not – and I'll meet your friends at last. Don't be too long in that bath – I want to look my best with all those prime male specimens around.' Alice giggled as she left the bathroom.

He didn't reply.

'You're not jealous, are you?'

Tom laughed. 'Oh no – apart from the fact they're younger than me.'

The bath was not as relaxing as usual – Tom hastily finished washing. Alice had met John McAdam and his wife, Mary, but not the others. What would they think of his beautiful young girlfriend? And this was his final farewell to a life at sea and the comradeship peculiar to the navy.

*

Surgeon Lieutenant Commander Paul Scott emerged from Knightsbridge Underground Station into drizzling rain and made his way briskly towards Belgravia. 'Scottie' had joined the navy as a surgeon at the age of thirty-one. He had just completed his training period of general officer duties, spending the last few months aboard Tom Falconer's frigate in the North Atlantic. The two men had become good friends.

Alice opened the door, hesitating momentarily as the good-looking man with blond hair stood awkwardly on the step.

'Alice! It's wonderful to meet you at last.' Paul kissed her precipitously on the cheek. He removed his wet raincoat to reveal an expensive, well-tailored dark blue suit. Alice was pleased she had managed to persuade Tom to buy a new outfit.

Tom appeared and ushered them into the small lounge. Scottie opened a carrier bag and produced a bottle of Glenfiddich single malt. The conversation was pleasant but Alice was slightly unnerved by their guest. His display of panache was a bit overpowering, even for her.

Paul Scott mentally analysed Alice's features – her tall, slender build, elfin nose, black urchin-styled hair, warm, sensuous lips and those questioning pale blue eyes. Sensing her discomfort, he quickly became self-conscious of his indulgence.

'So, Paul – why did you leave the NHS and join the navy?' asked Alice pointedly.

'I'd finished my specialist training as an accident surgeon but got fed up with waiting for a suitable consultant appointment.'

'A lot of competition, I suppose,' added Alice.

'I just felt like a change – and I love the sea.'

'So, what's your next move?' asked Tom.

'I'm due for a stint of shore-based training, but before that I may be on another mission with Nigel and Mike.'

'What's it all about?'

'Haven't a clue yet. I'm hoping Nigel will enlighten me tonight.'

'It's nice to know that some of the old crew will still be together,' added Tom. 'I believe poor John McAdam will be shore-based at Devonport for a while.'

'Why "poor"?' asked Alice.

Tom explained. 'When John joined the navy he was too old to get a full career commission. Promotion is less automatic. That's why he's still a lieutenant. It's a sensitive point.'

*

The traffic and parking in London were as unpredictable as ever. They arrived at the restaurant later than intended. Lieutenant Commander Nigel Hannay and Lieutenant Mike Morris were already well ensconced at the bar. After the introductions an exuberant Hannay insisted on champagne all round. Alice basked in the toasts and admiring glances. Hannay bubbled with good humour. He was a bear-like man and well over six feet. His light brown hair was receding and he looked older than his thirty-eight years. He smiled and laughed with his whole face.

The waiter arrived to take orders.

'Where on earth is John McAdam?' asked Mike Morris. 'It's not like him to be late.'

'John and Mary are coming back from Norfolk today – maybe they got held up somewhere,' replied Tom as he turned to the waiter. 'Give us another ten minutes.'

John McAdam did not arrive.

Alice arranged to pick Tom up later. She returned to the flat to catch up on paperwork. The last few days had been hectic, and wonderful, but her new business venture was also demanding serious attention.

Back in the restaurant, the conversation centred initially on Alice – and the flat in Belgravia. No one asked about managing on the naval pension. But Morris came up with the question Tom was most dreading.

'Have you decided what to do next?'

'Nothing for a while,' replied Tom. 'I'm going to settle into a civilian way of life and examine my options carefully before committing myself.'

'Sounds sensible,' said Mike unconvincingly.

The food arrived. Scottie took the opportunity to change the subject. 'Nigel, I'll probably be joining you and Mike in about three weeks. What's this next mission about?'

Hannay went coy and dithered uncharacteristically.

Tom laughed. 'You can whisper in Scottie's ear if you wish, but I'm still subject to the Official Secrets Act.'

'Sure, Tom, why shouldn't you know – it's just another weapons trial in the North Atlantic with yet another top-secret widget about which, to date, we have been told virtually nothing. On return from leave, Mike and I will be holed up for a couple of weeks with the boffins at AWRE.'

'At least I now know where we're going,' said Scottie. 'Pity it's not somewhere warmer.'

The floor show started. The men turned their attention from matters naval to the belly dancer who had just made a flamboyant, whirling entrance onto the stage. The shapely young woman, who could have passed for Turkish, danced her heart out for the sparse Monday-night audience. Inevitably, she descended from the stage and danced for each table in turn. By the time she reached the naval officers she already had several ten-pound notes tucked into her scanty attire.

Tom was the first to receive her attention, with a dazzling back-bend shimmy. The men admired her athleticism, and her body. Unable to keep a straight face, Tom soon gave in and tucked a note gently under her hip-band. Hannay teased her mercilessly with a twenty-pound note until she danced on the table. Wearing a cocky leer, Mike Morris made the girl work overlong before he clumsily pushed a carefully rolled-up crisp new note under her bra strap. She winced as the sharp edges abraded her soft, silky skin. Mike apologised. The girl laughed it off – she was used to such things. Pointedly, she turned to Paul Scott and danced for him. He was enticed onto the stage and, much to the delight of the audience, gave a stylish display of dancing with the girl. Mike put on a brave face and joined in the revelry.

As the dancer made her exit the waiter appeared with a message. It was Alice – on the telephone.

'Tom, Mary McAdam just phoned from Norfolk. She's distraught – John's disappeared.'

'What?! When did she last see him?'

'Yesterday, but they planned to meet at their cottage in Cley this morning. She thought he went birdwatching while she was away. She's contacted police and hospitals – absolutely nothing. Tom, I told her you would phone – she's desperate.'

'Alice, could you drive me to Norfolk tonight?'

'No problem – but it'll be late.'

'I doubt Mary will be sleeping. Throw a few things in a case and tell her we're coming. Oh, and bring my binoculars too – I might need to scour the coast and the marshes.'

Tom looked distracted when he returned to the table.

'Problem, Tom?' asked Scottie.

'Yes. Mary McAdam phoned to say that John is missing. It seems he went birdwatching but failed to return.'

'Oh dear,' said Mike. 'He likes to do that in isolated parts of the North Norfolk coast. There are nasty rip currents in some places.'

'I'm sure John would have known about that,' replied Tom.

In solemn mood, they waited for Alice.

3

Tuesday 29th September

Alice drove and Tom navigated. After more than a hundred miles of unlit road they arrived at Blakeney in North Norfolk. It was 2am. They turned eastwards, taking the A149 coast road towards Cley-next-the-Sea. The roadside shrubs glowed in the headlights but nothing else was visible in the eerie blackness extending outwards in all directions. The short high street chicane of the village suddenly appeared out of nowhere. They soon found the cottage – the lights were still on.

Mary looked pale and exhausted. Her eyes were red and swollen from crying. She was a petite, friendly woman. Her long black hair was neatly tied back and she was still wearing a pretty new blue dress. Alice's heart went out to her.

Mary had packed ready to leave. 'It's our third holiday here. We rent the cottage – should have left by now. I can't think what to do next. I've contacted police and hospitals, checked pubs, traced John's favourite walk – absolutely nothing.'

'What are the police doing?' asked Tom.

'I don't know – two men called before midnight and asked a lot of questions.'

Mary went over the events of the previous two days.

Tom summarised. 'So, a neighbour saw John leaving the cottage early Sunday evening wearing the jumper, jeans, boots and rucksack that are still missing. He didn't have the car. And you said the bed was not slept in.'

'That's right,' said Mary. 'It's exactly as I left it on Sunday morning. John said he would pack before I returned, to give us a free day – but everything is just as it was.'

'Was John his usual self – any problems?' asked Tom gently.

'The police asked that too. No, not as far as I know. He was fine when I left him on Sunday.'

'And he seemed OK when I saw him a couple of weeks ago,' added Tom.

The unthinkable loomed in Mary's mind. Was John injured – or dead? Would she never see him again? What would she tell the children? Tears began to trickle down her cheeks.

They tried to comfort her. Alice made tea.

Tom phoned the Sheringham police – but they weren't forthcoming. 'I'll visit them in the morning and make some other enquiries,' added Tom. 'Meanwhile I think we should try to get some sleep.'

Mary was awake most of the night – waiting, listening and hoping. Prompted by his watch alarm, Tom struggled out of a deep sleep at 8am. Alice tried to appear alert and cheerful as she handed him a mug of hot coffee.

Tom borrowed Alice's Mini and took the coast road to Sheringham. Alice accompanied Mary back to her mother's house in South London. She arranged to meet Tom later at Sheringham Station.

*

The local police insisted that Tom return again to Sheringham in the afternoon to see the Ministry of Defence Police (MDP) when they arrived from Devonport. The base commander's office at Devonport was sympathetic but unable to help. Nothing appeared to be happening in Norfolk. Tom raced back along the coast road via Cley to Blakeney, where Mary had recommended a hotel.

The old village of Blakeney lies seaward to the A149 coast road. Its quaint, narrow high street passes down to the quay and is blessed by the absence of fast-moving traffic. The impressive view lightened Tom's mood – the exquisite natural harbour and the salt marshes stretching into the distance. The hotel was on the quay, blending well with the picturesque surroundings. Tom booked a double room on the first floor with a view of the harbour.

Outside, his attention was drawn once again to the marshes extending in all directions. Searching for evidence of John McAdam along this coastline would be difficult. There was a marine chandlery in Blakeney. He bought an east coast yachting chart.

On his way back towards Sheringham, Tom turned off the road at Cley onto a narrow, winding track which cut through the green marshes towards the coast. Two-thirds of a mile from the road it ended in a rough shingle car park at Cley Beach. There were half a dozen cars and a closed cafe with an unoccupied coastguard's lookout post above it. Dominating the view was a heaped shingle sea defence stretching into the distance. Tom walked up the steep incline to the top. On the other side the North Sea stretched into the distance. The desolate shoreline disappeared towards Blakeney Point to the west and merged with cliffs near the horizon towards the east. Inland, Cley and its windmill were visible across the marshes.

Tom started on the trek to Blakeney Point, a blob of land at the end of a shingle-covered spit reaching five miles to the west of Cley Beach. The narrow spit ran parallel to the mainland in front of the salt marshes of Blakeney and Morston, a village to the west of Blakeney. It was one of John McAdam's favourite walks. Walking on the shingle was slow going. Tom stopped frequently to scour the surroundings with the binoculars. There was nothing suspicious. After an hour he turned back – he would have to move fast to get to Sheringham on time.

*

Inspector Adrian Lomax of the Ministry of Defence Police, and his sergeant, had arrived. Communications soon reached shouting pitch. After haranguing the local inspector for allowing Falconer to interfere, Lomax turned his attention to the young WPC before she could escape from the room.

'I can't drink this gnat's piss – get me a hot, strong cup of coffee.'

The superintendent was about to join in the fracas when Lomax suddenly changed tack and turned to the inspector again.

'Give me all the facts you have – I'll only interrupt to clarify things. Sergeant – take notes. We must hurry if we are to do anything before dusk.'

*

Tom Falconer arrived.

'Good luck, mate,' said the desk sergeant as Tom was ushered into Lomax's temporary office.

'Ah! The intrepid *Mr* Falconer, I presume,' said Lomax sarcastically.

Tom sat down and crossed his arms. He had not spoken to Lomax before but knew of his reputation – a bastard, but a bastard who got results.

'You've buggered things up here, haven't you, *sir?*' jibed Lomax.

'What?!'

'You sent Mary McAdam back to London. You disturbed what little evidence we have. You created misunderstandings at Devonport. In short, you are obstructing us.'

'Look here, Lomax, John McAdam has been missing for two days. His wife reported his disappearance yesterday morning. Damn all has been done so far. It's a shambles. Helicopters should have been out yesterday.'

Lomax was unmoved. 'There are many causes of disappearance. What is your relationship with Mary McAdam?'

'What the hell do you mean?'

'Falconer, I know little about you, what you are doing in Norfolk and why the lieutenant is missing. I need facts, man, facts. Tell me all you know about the McAdams, their habits and the events of the last few weeks.'

After a lengthy one-way flow of information, Lomax showed Tom the door.

'That's all for now. Stay around, and leave an address and phone number, in case we need you. God help us.'

Tom resisted the urge to retaliate – and the urge to find a pub. He parked the car near the station and sat there until Alice's train was due. He met her on the platform – she looked exhausted. They made straight for the hotel. As they turned onto the quayside at Blakeney they saw the Westland Lynx military helicopter. It was flying low over the marshes.

*

Even in affluent times, the suggestion of a 'fast-track development project' struck fear into the hearts of Whitehall civil servants. Their traditional caution was now compounded by an austere economic climate, and by the lingering memories of delays and escalating costs associated with earlier military development programmes – such as the Command and Control System (CACS) at the heart of NATO marine warfare operations.

Military leaders were frustrated by the two-faced rhetoric of politicians. Defence budgets were under constant threat. Sensible long-term planning had become virtually impossible. Yet the navy was expected to be ready to send a modern fleet with state-of-the-art weaponry into a conflagration in the Middle East, or the Balkans, at a moment's notice.

Despite this, and after three months' gestation in MoD committees and a difficult labour, Project Athena was born.

Rear Admiral Richard Claydon had pulled strings to secure approval from the Weapons Controllerate for the first sea trials on a new intelligent missile system developed at the Admiralty

Weapons Research Establishment (AWRE). The Advanced Missile Navigation Control System, inevitably reduced to the acronym AMNACS, was the brainchild of Dr Peter Tolley's innovative artificial intelligence research at AWRE. Claydon was determined to explore the full military potential of this work as soon as possible.

Unarmed missiles would be used in the first sea trial. The frigate HMS *Athena* was available and would require only minor conversions at Devonport. Conveniently, a flotilla currently engaged in other trials in the North Atlantic could provide the necessary backup without much additional resource. Claydon had made it clear that any postponement would escalate costs.

*

Captain Andrew Fox spread the last of the Admiralty navigation charts across the highly polished conference table in the rear admiral's spacious Whitehall office. They had finally agreed the schedule for Project Athena.

Fox had a distinguished record as a principal warfare officer and had also commanded one of the navy's most prestigious modern frigates. He had recently taken a keen interest in project management. It came as an unexpected but welcome surprise when he was invited to join the Admiralty Project Athena team as project leader with overall strategic and operational responsibility for the first sea trial.

Fox proceeded to pack the project plans and Gantt charts into his brief case. 'The trial finishes on the last day of October and we'll be making our way back via the North Sea on 1st November.'

'However did we cope without computers and professional

project managers in days gone by?' replied Claydon with a wry smile.

'Judging by some of the previous cock-ups, perhaps we didn't,' retorted Fox.

'Well, old chap, we had better get this one right, for AWRE's sake if nothing else.' Claydon buzzed his assistant for more tea and cakes. 'You'll have a good crew. Nigel Hannay was an excellent principal warfare officer under Tom Falconer's command – they were involved in several weapons trials.'

'My main anxiety,' replied Fox, 'is having a civilian aboard, actually working with a new weapons team.'

'We'd avoid it if we could, but the device is complicated. It would be impossible to train up our engineers on every aspect in time for the trial. You could operate the system to a limited extent without Tolley, but you'd need him to troubleshoot any malfunctions. Also, his being aboard provides the opportunity to modify and optimise the system in the field. It will save us months.'

'Aren't we expecting a lot of him in two weeks?'

'Andrew – the man's a genius. This trial could put us years ahead of the field.'

Jill entered with the refreshments.

Fox was still uneasy about some of the arrangements. But he intended to exploit this rare opportunity to the full.

4

The Falklands and Gulf Wars had dramatically demonstrated the formidable power of modern electronic warfare. Revolutionary developments in the field of artificial intelligence were further advancing the capabilities of guided weapons systems. At the cutting edge, Peter Tolley had successfully combined improved sensing devices with fast parallel-processing electronics and novel neural network computing. The result was AMNACS.

Tolley had gained a PhD and a fast-growing scientific reputation by his twenty-first birthday. Top brass in the MoD spotted the potential of his research while he was working with Associated Avionics Ltd. The company ran into financial problems soon after Tolley joined. It cut its R&D budget drastically. Encouraged by Rear Admiral Richard Claydon, the Admiralty took advantage of the situation and snapped up Tolley by making him an offer he wouldn't refuse – a senior position, reasonable freedom for exploratory research, and plentiful resources. He had now been at AWRE for three years.

Wednesday 30th September

Tolley arrived early to finish the report on his final validation tests. Deadlines had been met. Prototype devices were already wired into unarmed missiles in a hangar across the field.

Lieutenant David Llewellyn, a bright young weapons engineer officer seconded to work alongside Tolley's team, walked briskly to the main gate to meet Captain Fox. After security clearance they parked near the laboratory complex.

Fox sat silently for a while and then turned to Llewellyn. 'You've worked closely with Dr Tolley.'

'Yes, sir – for three months. I've nearly got the hang of AMNACS.'

'I hope so. You and he will be the only ones aboard with real in-depth knowledge.'

'Well – I know how to use it with the test weapons, not how all of it works – in detail, that is,' added Llewellyn as an afterthought.

'That bloody complicated, is it?'

'Afraid so – only Tolley and his assistant Martin Smith have the computing expertise required for modifying the key cognitive processes.'

'Is Tolley happy in his work?' enquired Fox.

'More or less – apart from the Official Secrets Act.'

'You mean the restriction on publication?'

'Yes. But he's pleased about the sea trials and seeing the full potential of his work develop. I can't see any immediate difficulties.'

'What's he like to work with?'

'Keeps to himself – but seems to like working alongside us naval types. Doesn't suffer fools easily.'

'I get the picture. Let's go in. And, David, informality is the order of the day – I'm Andrew.'

Fox made a brief courtesy call on the R&D director who had been working closely with the ministry. They all proceeded to the meetings room. A security guard double-checked their passes before allowing them in. Fox suppressed a grin. The director made the introductions at exactly 9am, ensured that refreshments were in place and left Fox alone with Tolley and Llewellyn.

Somewhat self-consciously, Fox produced agenda papers and project plans from his case. He wanted to tread a path between businesslike efficiency and informality.

'Let me start with a few introductory points. Firstly, this project has the highest security rating because of its obvious potential military value. The slightest leak could activate extremely unsavoury activities from several quarters – including some that are supposed to be friendly. Look out for possible security risks. Ask for help if in doubt.'

Tolley interjected impatiently. 'We have been through all this with Security here. And I am aware of the importance of my work.'

'I'm sorry to state the obvious,' replied Fox firmly, 'but I must ensure that the concerns of the MoD are hammered home to all members of the project. In these matters we are talking about real risks, not imaginary ones.

'Next, a somewhat trivial item,' he continued. 'The ministry, in its wisdom, has given a name to the forthcoming sea trials – Project Athena.'

'That should confuse the enemy,' quipped Tolley.

Fox smiled. 'The civil service has a penchant for the classics. HMS *Athena* is the frigate we will be using for the tests.'

He went on to explain his overall operational responsibility for the project. As the meeting progressed, Tolley became more impressed by Fox's efficient style and his ability to rapidly assimilate and understand technicalities. Fox had done his homework on the research director's regular reports to the ministry. By 11am they were putting together a list of action points. Fox then announced the dates.

'The Project Athena team will congregate here at AWRE next Tuesday for two weeks' intensive training, and then transfer immediately on Sunday 18th October to HMS *Athena* at Devonport – destination North Atlantic.'

*

It was a cold, dull and wet day in North Norfolk. The police were still busy in and around Cley and the military were assisting with the search.

Tom and Alice felt better for a good night's sleep. They could think of nothing else useful to do in Norfolk. They drove to Cley Beach. A policeman was leaning on his car, pouring a hot drink from a flask. Tom recognised him as one of the constables from Sheringham.

'I'm impressed with all this activity,' said Tom. 'Is it all down to Inspector Lomax?'

'Some is,' replied the constable grudgingly. 'We did what we could with our limited manpower before he arrived.'

'I know Lomax thinks we're interfering, but John McAdam was a friend and served with me for many years in the navy. I'm sure you can understand my concern.'

'I can, sir, but there's not much you can do, and you could get in the way.'

'You're so right,' said Alice, hanging on the policeman's every word. 'It must be very difficult to coordinate the operation with different police forces and the military.'

'You can say that again!' he replied, warming to Alice's interest. 'Well, we haven't got very far for all the effort.'

'Nothing at all?' enquired Tom.

'Lomax's sergeant visited Mrs McAdam and brought back a few of the lieutenant's things for the dogs to sniff.'

'Oh!' said Tom enthusiastically. 'Any luck?'

'Dogs seemed interested in one bit of beach – but it hasn't led to anything, as far as I know.'

'May we see?' asked Alice.

'It's cordoned off – you'd best keep out of the way. You can just see it from the top of the sea defences.'

About half a mile to the east, stakes and tape marked out a small area on the shingle dyke. Tom and Alice took turns with the binoculars. There was no activity and nothing else to see.

'Well, we're going home tomorrow morning,' said Tom, giving the constable their Belgravia address and telephone number. 'Is there anything we can pass on to Mary McAdam?'

'Not really, Inspector Lomax is dealing with all that.'

They thanked him and started to head back to the hotel.

'What do you make of that?' asked Alice.

'I don't know. All we can assume is that John went for a walk, probably to do some birdwatching, and at some point may have been on that bit of beach. Then he disappears without trace. He could be anywhere – inland or out at sea. It's weird.'

'Tom, let's give it a rest. We've done all we can here.'

'Absolutely!'

Back at the hotel, they relaxed with a drink in the lounge and admired the panoramic view of Blakeney Harbour. It was mid-afternoon.

'It's amazing how the tide transforms the harbour,' said Alice, looking out over the drained inlets. 'All the boats are high and dry on the mud.'

'Yes,' said Tom vacantly as he gazed into the brandy swirling around in his glass. The vaguely nautical allusion rattled something in his brain. 'Sorry, darling, what did you say about tides?'

Alice reiterated.

'Yes – yes, of course,' replied Tom. 'It's a new moon. That's why it was so dark when we drove down here on Monday night.'

'So?'

'Well, in a nutshell,' explained Tom carefully, 'at new and full moons the tidal ranges are at their greatest, so the low tides are very low and the high tides are very high. We saw the boats making their way on the high tide this morning.'

'Oh, I see,' said Alice. 'You mean spring tides.'

'That's right – spring tides. Probably just a coincidence.'

5

Saturday 3rd October

The invite from Clarissa Hannay brought mixed reactions. Tom wasn't keen and didn't want to stay overnight. 'All seems a bit sudden – Nigel's going back to Devonport tomorrow.'

'Tom, I'd love to meet the wives,' said Alice. 'We'll have to accept their offer to stay over. It's a long drive back from the New Forest – and we'll be drinking.'

*

Gusts of wind buffeted the car on the open forest road. It was a barren landscape with the trees visible in the distance. They soon reached the outskirts of Lyndhurst, a delightful little town in the middle of the New Forest. The track leading to the Hannays' property was less easy to find. They drove past it first time round – the few houses there looked far too grand.

Eventually, they stopped by a large stone archway with open wrought-iron gates.

'This must be it,' announced Tom.

The long, well-tended drive and surrounding lawns stretched away in front of them to meet a wide-fronted house with a large portico and classical columns, giving the appearance of a minor stately home.

'My God – it's a palace!' exclaimed Alice. 'I didn't realise they were that wealthy.'

'Lieutenant commanders do boast royalty among their ranks,' replied Tom sarcastically, 'but, in this case, I think it's Clarissa who has the money and contacts. A bit like us, I suppose.'

'Tom – I wish you hadn't said that. Is it a problem?'

He laughed. 'Not at all!'

'As you know,' added Alice, 'Granny left me the flat in her will. We should both be grateful.'

'Oh, I am, believe me. You must tell me more about Granny sometime.'

'I shall – perhaps on our way back tomorrow.'

Tom parked the Mini next to a pristine vintage Jaguar.

Clarissa Hannay met them at the door. She was tastefully dressed in an elegant but unobtrusive haute couture evening frock. Her charm immediately disarmed Alice.

The entrance lobby led into a huge reception hall, from which an impressive open staircase wound upwards to a large gallery overlooking the hall. Clarissa showed them to their bedroom and then escorted them to the spacious lounge, where they were welcomed by Nigel Hannay and Paul Scott.

'Don't fight over Alice,' said Clarissa, as she took Tom's arm and led him across the room to the bar. 'I was flabbergasted to hear that you're leaving the navy – couldn't understand what possessed you. Now I can – Tom, she's gorgeous,' she added with a wicked grin.

'Alice wasn't the only reason. I'd had the best years of the navy. I had to decide whether to change altogether or stay on until retirement in my dotage, or redundancy after more defence cuts.'

'Nigel was convinced you were going on to higher things.'

'You mean a desk in Whitehall? No thanks.'

'Not keen on politics, Tom?'

'Dead right!'

They joined the others.

'We're so glad you came,' said Nigel. 'Mike and Jane Morris couldn't make it.'

'Oh, what happened to them?' asked Tom.

'Not sure – but you know Mike and CTPs; he's never at ease with them.'

'CTPs?' enquired Alice.

'Naval jargon for cocktail parties,' said Paul Scott. 'We all get trained in etiquette and diplomacy at Dartmouth. You know – what to do if you meet a foreign ambassador, and all that. It wasn't Mike's best subject.'

Nigel took Alice's arm. 'Let's go to the library. I'd like you to see a couple of paintings Clarissa bought.'

Alice was taken aback by the vast collection of books; not the usual for-display-only material but books and journals on a wide range of academic subjects. The library was obviously a workroom – there was a powerful-looking PC and a laser printer on the desk. The two Victorian paintings were not half bad, by lesser-known artists enjoying a revival.

'I'm impressed,' said Alice. 'I like them – this sort of thing is becoming quite popular now.'

'Any idea of their value?' asked Nigel enthusiastically.

After the usual caveats, Alice suggested a slightly generous figure 'for insurance purposes'. Nigel seemed pleased.

A gong beckoned them to dinner.

The oak table and its attendant twelve antique dining chairs looked lonely in the centre of the large oak-panelled dining room. The spread was a match for the Senior Gunroom at the Britannia. The resident housekeeper, a shy lady in her fifties, proceeded to serve.

'Is there any news of John McAdam?' asked Alice.

Clarissa stared thoughtfully into her soup.

'No, nothing. He'll be officially AWOL tomorrow,' replied Nigel.

'Poor Mary,' said Clarissa. 'I would have invited them here today, but in the circumstances – well, you know.'

'It's difficult to know what to do to help her,' said Tom. 'If there's no news in a week or so I'll contact her. She might run into problems with the navy, like getting money out of them – doubt they'll be wonderfully cooperative at the moment, given the circumstances. I may be able to help Mary with the negotiations.'

'Excellent idea,' said Paul Scott.

'They seemed such a happy couple – it's so sad,' added Clarissa. 'They had quite different backgrounds too. Come to think of it, I suppose we all do.'

'How did you and Nigel meet?' asked Alice, seizing the opening.

'I almost hesitate to say,' replied Clarissa coyly. 'Actually, it was at a CTP in a British Embassy in Continental Europe.'

'Good heavens, what were you doing there?'

'Just a minion in the Diplomatic Corps – then my knight came along from a visiting warship and whisked me away.'

'It was love at first sight,' said Nigel.

'Weren't you at Oxbridge?' asked Scottie.

'Cambridge,' replied Clarissa.

'And she got a double first,' added Nigel proudly.

Clarissa looked uncomfortable and intervened. 'Darling, our guests don't want to be bored out of their minds with the history of my adolescence.'

'Well, I'm very impressed,' said Alice as she turned to Paul Scott. 'Anyone special at the moment, Paul?'

'No – I fell for the old routine.'

'Doctors and nurses?' quipped Nigel.

'No, doctors and doctors – it was fatally flawed.' The memory of the broken engagement was still painful. 'I never quite got to the altar.'

'Tom – did your sleuthing in Norfolk turn up anything?' asked Clarissa.

'Not really, I probably just got in the way.'

'What about the police?'

'Not sure – didn't seem to be getting anywhere. Nigel might get more news at Devonport.'

'But someone must have a theory or something, surely,' insisted Clarissa.

'I had one or two,' replied Tom, 'but they're all improbable. I'd rather not speculate.'

Nigel Hannay tried to vary the conversation but it kept returning to John McAdam.

*

Tom and Alice left early the next morning.

'Can't wait to get back home,' said Tom as they left the forest.

'They made us very welcome,' replied Alice, adding, 'and Clarissa made a special effort to satisfy my vegetarian food fad.'

'I just felt the evening gradually became excessively focused on John's disappearance,' said Tom. 'Perhaps it was the main reason for the invitation.'

'Getting back to my granny,' said Alice, changing the subject, 'it's a complicated family affair – not easy to talk about. My mother's family were from a line of well-heeled landed gentry. Her mother inherited everything and ensured that we were well looked after. When my father lost his job in the City he took to drink and his gambling got worse. He virtually drained my mother of funds. So, Granny paid for my private education at a good boarding school and left me her London flat in her will. She tried to ensure that I would be protected from him financially.'

'So what's the situation with your mother now?' enquired Tom.

'Well, as you know, Mum's separated from my father. She lives alone in my grandmother's other property at Frinton-on-Sea in Essex. She has local connections and good neighbours, who are very supportive. Dad's more or less stopped bothering her now.'

'Thanks for putting me in the picture,' replied Tom. 'If I can help in any way please don't hesitate to ask.'

'Thanks, Tom – that means a lot. And we must get round to meeting each other's parents at some stage – but not just yet if you don't mind.'

'I agree – we've a lot to sort out at present.'

Monday 5th October, Devonport

Flaunting her majestic light grey lines, in the company of a dozen other warships, HMS *Athena* floated idly in HM

Dockyards, Devonport. Typical of an Amazon-Class Type 21, she was a good general-purpose frigate built in the 1970s to a commercial design. Compared to the newer Type 22 and 23 frigates, her weaponry was limited. But she was still formidable, with four Exocet missiles, a Seacat surface-to-air missile system, torpedoes, two 20mm close-range guns and, on the foredeck, a powerful Mk 8 automatic 4.5-inch gun with high-explosive shells. She could, but rarely did, carry a Lynx helicopter armed with torpedoes and air-to-surface missiles.

At 9.27am Commander Appleby boarded HMS *Athena* via the starboard access at the rear of the ship. He briefly inspected the modifications being made to the helicopter landing platform and hangar. With a disapproving grunt he turned heel and proceeded to negotiate the gangways and ladders leading to the wardroom in the interior of the ship. During the previous two years Appleby had commanded *Athena* with reasonable autonomy. The forthcoming mission would be different.

Andrew Fox, Nigel Hannay, Mike Morris and David Llewellyn were already in the wardroom. Fox made the introductions. Morris, Llewellyn and Appleby had not met before. Hannay and Appleby had met aboard the ship the previous evening – camaraderie was already evident.

'It is important,' said Fox, 'that we all understand the rules of command for Project Athena. Commander Appleby will, of course, have full responsibility for the working of the ship, including standard operation of the weapons. Nigel, as principal warfare officer you will report directly to him. Mike, you will join the ship's weapons engineering team. However, modifications to AMNACS will be my responsibility. Dr Tolley, and you, David, will report directly to me. Mike and David will work together on issues concerning installation of AMNACS in the test missiles. Thereafter, *Athena*'s weapons team will be responsible for the installation of missiles into the launching canisters, and for normal electronic tracking.

'This might all seem a bit complicated,' he continued, 'but I'm sure you appreciate the need for the division of labour and responsibility.'

'Frankly, no,' replied Appleby, po-faced. 'This has been cobbled together in unnecessary haste. I and my crew should have been properly briefed from the start.'

'It's an unusual situation,' responded Fox, 'and it needs a *creative* approach.'

'No, I disagree,' said Appleby, taking the opportunity to air further grievances. 'It's become a problem because some of my key officers have been transferred to other ships at short notice, including my principal warfare officer. No offence to you, Nigel, or you, Mike; I'm glad to have you aboard, even at this late hour. I suppose we will just have to make the best of an unsatisfactory situation.'

'I'll take that as a positive contribution,' retorted Fox. 'We are talking about a novel and important advancement – it needs professional non-blinkered support from us.'

He continued. 'Missile prototypes are ready at AWRE but the AMNACS units may need special adjustments as the trial progresses. That is why we are having a portion of the hangar partitioned off for Dr Tolley and David to work in. Tolley will need a small office area there as well as electronic workshop facilities. Operating this way, we could cut a year off development time. Any problems, David?'

'No. Tolley is happy with the plans and everything is on schedule.'

'Good,' replied Fox. 'Over the next two weeks some remaining issues will be finalised at AWRE and the relevant equipment will be installed on *Athena*.'

'I'm not happy with a civilian working in the vicinity of the firing area,' added Appleby. 'He isn't paid to take risks and he could be a risk to others.'

'Absolutely right,' replied Fox. 'That brings me to an important operational point. Tolley must only work on AMNACS units detached from the missiles. Only authorised naval personnel will be allowed in the vicinity of the flight deck and hangar during the actual tests.'

The meeting continued for another hour. The quiet David Llewellyn expanded on some of the technical details. His first-class honours degree in engineering from Imperial College became a personal but unexpressed bone of contention with Mike Morris, who had studied for his degree at the Royal Naval College of Engineering at Manadon, near Plymouth.

Fox and Llewellyn left for AWRE. Mike Morris and Nigel Hannay joined Appleby for lunch. Mike was rankled by David Llewellyn's obvious academic prowess. He enjoyed the bitching session which followed. Appleby made no attempt to conceal his concerns, or his resentment of Andrew Fox and his sidekick.

Monday 5th October; dusk descends over Moscow

The shibboleths of political leaders have a habit of backfiring. Mikhail Gorbachev's glasnost and perestroika had already become objects of ridicule. Old KGB factions were now vying for power and the Russian economy was on the brink of disaster.

Admiral Alexai Mendeleyev was admitted to the President's room in the inner sanctum of the Kremlin. The President pointed to a chair on the other side of the large, shiny wooden table.

'Alexai, my advisers tell me I should be spending more money on new weapons. What is your opinion?'

'Comrade, the problem is quality – not just quantity. Our conventional weapons capability is now dangerously behind that of the United States and Western Europe. The technology gap is widening every year, and these days new information is less easily bought.'

'Ah!' retorted the exasperated President. 'So you too think we should pour even more money into a bottomless pit. But you also have another plan – yes?'

'AMNACS?' queried the admiral.

'Yes – AMNACS. The reports are interesting. The prospect of advancing our missile capabilities at a stroke without a massive research budget is tantalising. How's it shaping?'

'Tremain and his agents are active,' replied Mendeleyev. 'We communicate indirectly via the embassy in London. I'm not sure exactly how he intends to get the device and documents away from the Royal Navy – but it will involve a sleeper on the frigate. He then plans to deliver it to us inconspicuously in international waters sometime after the sea trials finish and the fuss has died down. We will use a fast submarine for the pick-up – it will not need to surface.'

'The plan is daring,' said the President, 'and it is risky for our agents in Britain. You must shut down the operation if there is any hint of trouble. Any problems – come straight to me. Good luck.'

On his way out, Mendeleyev noticed General Chkalov of Russian Intelligence waiting impatiently for his audience with the President. He also had secret agents in Britain.

6

On Monday 19th October, HMS *Athena* set sail from Plymouth for the North Atlantic. Commander Appleby steered a course well to the west of Ireland and the Outer Hebrides. The frigate reached her destination on Wednesday evening, where she joined the small flotilla of warships north of Cape Wrath. The flotilla had journeyed south from the deeper waters of the North Atlantic to the shallower continental shelf waters to participate in Project Athena.

Wednesday 21st to Thursday 29th October

The unarmed, experimental surface-to-surface anti-ship missiles were ready for sea trials. The missile heads contained an array of complex optical and radar devices linked to AMNACS. The effecter systems had been redesigned to give the missile increased manoeuvrability. The initial test firing gave Tolley and Llewellyn enough information to make critical adjustments to the sensors and control system.

Subsequent tests used an old barge as a target, with attendant frigates attempting to protect it with anti-missile weaponry. In the crucial second test a frigate fired a Sea Wolf missile to intercept the test missile. Tolley's intelligent system sensed the attack and executed complex avoidance tactics. The Sea Wolf missed and the test weapon sailed on towards its target.

The third test was a repeat of the second, but with the addition of a CIWS 'goalkeeper', a robotic close-range anti-missile gun, firing from a Type 22 frigate in a last-ditch attempt to stop the missile. The Sea Wolf failed again, but the goalkeeper destroyed the missile in the last few seconds. Tolley was confident he could make the necessary adjustments to give a good chance of avoiding the robotic gun. He and Llewellyn worked day and night in the hangar workshop, which had been specially heated to combat the bitter cold.

At 7.40am on Wednesday 28th October, a tired and unshaven Peter Tolley burst into the wardroom. 'Done it!' he announced. 'Over to the boys in blue.'

'Well done,' said Fox.

Appleby seconded the sentiment. Whatever differences there may have been over the organisation of the operation, no one had any doubts left about Tolley's ability. Tolley scoffed down some toast and coffee and then retired to his cabin for a couple of hours' sleep before the final test firing.

A fresh-to-strong breeze was blowing up over the cold grey-green North Atlantic. Under the experienced eye of the officer-of-the-watch, Lieutenant Commander Paul Scott was taking one of his few chances to practise navigation on the high seas. Commander Appleby, Captain Fox and Dr Tolley joined them on the ship's bridge. The day's main event was about to begin. The missile, primed with the modified AMNACS unit, was in its canister ready for launch. The engineers had made their contribution and now the operations room was the centre of activity.

The principal warfare officer (PWO) is responsible for 'fighting a ship', and most of this he does with a team of men, and now women, working at electronic consoles in the operations room. Nigel Hannay, HMS *Athena*'s new PWO, came up through the hatch onto the bridge.

'Everything's ready,' he announced, borrowing a pair of binoculars. 'Air, radar and sonar surveillance show no other vessels or activities within thirty miles.'

'Keep them waiting fifteen minutes,' ordered Appleby.

Hannay scanned the horizon briefly before returning to the operations room to prepare for firing.

HMS *Athena* was positioned four miles from the target. A Type 22 frigate was stationed strategically to protect the target from the missile. After fifteen minutes, *Athena*'s radar locked onto the target. The missile's independent radar and electro-optic systems came into operation immediately after firing.

Travelling at high speed, the missile took an unpredictable and circuitous course. The Sea Wolf attempted interception two miles from the target. The test missile executed successful avoidance manoeuvres. In the last few seconds a CIWS automatic gun fired from the Type 22 frigate. A cheer went up on the bridge of *Athena* as a puff of red smoke appeared in the distance – Tolley's missile had reached its target.

The test missile had also been modified to eject the section holding the AMNACS unit just before hitting its target. Tolley was more anxious about the recovery of the unit than he was about the outcome of the day's trial – for him the latter was a foregone conclusion. HMS *Athena* joined the other ships. Before dusk the ejected AMNACS unit had been retrieved from the sea and returned to Tolley's workshop.

*

Andrew Fox managed to prise Tolley out of the hangar at 7pm by inviting him to join the officers for a small celebration. The excellent dinner and the ambience of the wardroom gave Tolley much pleasure. The coolness evident earlier between him and the officers had changed to a healthy mutual respect. He could also hold his liquor. That impressed Mike Morris, who without much difficulty persuaded him to have a third pint. But there was little danger of Peter Tolley becoming 'one of the boys' – looking at his watch twice in five minutes, his obsessive workaholic drive was beginning to surface.

'Peter – your system seemed to be playing chess with the enemy,' commented Appleby.

'Probably closer to poker,' replied Tolley.

'How long would it take to think up a countermeasure to AMNACS?' enquired Nigel Hannay.

'A few weeks once they know how AMNACS works,' said Tolley, adding, 'But thinking is one thing – getting it developed is another.'

David Llewellyn was becoming uncharacteristically effusive. 'The big question is,' he blurted, 'will the British continue to back AMNACS?'

No-one responded immediately.

'Quite. Well – we're all used to being political footballs,' said Appleby.

Tolley looked at his watch again – it was 10pm. 'I was thinking of writing up a few details before turning in – but I'm too tired now.'

'I should think you are,' said Fox.

With distinctly slurred speech, David Llewellyn interjected. 'I find I write a load of gobbledegook after a few drinks.'

It was obvious to all that the slightly built Llewellyn was the worse for wear. Morris could not completely suppress a triumphant smirk. 'Well – you might have to accompany David to the hangar this time,' he said, pointing his remark to Peter Tolley.

'I don't need David to get into the hangar – I memorised the security code when he entered it.'

'Tut, tut,' said Fox jovially, adding, 'One of the reasons for accompanying you is to make sure you don't get injured on the way – lots of nasty obstacles on warships.'

'Well, tonight I think I am less likely to fall overboard than David,' replied Tolley. 'Anyway, I'm going to bed.'

David Llewellyn had difficulty standing up. Paul Scott helped him to his cabin.

*

The 'sleeper' was wide awake – it was 1am. AMNACS was a success – there was no going back now. He would make a practice run tonight. If seen, he could easily talk his way out. It would be different next time in the North Sea. He waited for signs of activity to disappear and then slid quietly out of his cabin.

He followed a well-planned route to the stern, noting potential places to hide in an emergency.

Within minutes he reached the hangar on the flight deck. It was secluded and dark with little moonlight. There were no signs of life. He shone his torch on the electronic lock and punched in the code. The sleeper entered the hangar, closed the door and switched on the lights. He carefully noted where everything was. The remaining and recovered AMNACS units were all neatly labelled.

The sleeper returned to his cabin. He was now confident – and ready.

Sunday 1st to Monday 2nd November

By Sunday evening HMS *Athena* was well into the North Sea, homeward bound. The atmosphere in the wardroom gave Tolley déjà vu. Once again he had an urge to get back to the hangar to finish off some work. After just a few drinks David Llewellyn was, once again, incapable. At 11pm Paul Scott and Mike Morris helped the almost-comatose lieutenant to his cabin. Fox was not amused. Scottie gave Llewellyn a cursory medical examination to make sure his vital functions were still intact and then left him to sleep it off. There was something odd about Llewellyn's breath but it didn't ring any obvious medical alarm bells.

Tolley stopped looking at his watch and made a conscious effort to socialise with the officers. They had looked after him well – he knew he ought to make the most of this unique opportunity rarely open to a civilian. Commander Appleby had promised to show him the navigation equipment on the bridge

– he was looking forward to that. Tolley, Morris and Scott were the last to leave the wardroom for their cabins.

Tolley could not sleep. Ideas were whirling around in his head. He got up and paced about the cabin. He thought he heard someone in the gangway outside his door. It was 1am. He sat listening for five minutes – there were no more signs of activity.

'Sod it,' he muttered. Two hours' work and he could finish off everything tonight.

Tolley put on warm clothes and sneaked quietly out of his cabin. As he left the warm, protective interior of the ship he experienced an unexpected feeling of anxiety. The fierce, cold wind blew a heavy spray over the open decks. The crescent moon was obscured by cloud. It was dark and the atmosphere distinctly eerie. Tolley hurried along the port side to the ladder leading down to the flight deck. There was no one about. As usual, he slipped on the last few rungs and bruised his knees. He felt more at ease on the secluded flight deck. But as he groped for the security lock he realised that the hangar door was already unlocked.

Gingerly, he started to open the door. His pulse was racing. Inquisitiveness got the better of him – he went in. Suddenly, he was dazzled by a torch beam shining straight into his eyes. His heart jumped. He stood fixed to the spot, speechless. He remembered the light switch close by. With courage he never knew he possessed, he lurched towards the bulkhead, scrambling in all directions for the switch. The torch came nearer. He found the switch and flooded the hangar with light. Immediately in front of him stood a large figure clad in a blue serge jumper and with a balaclava helmet masking his face.

'What do you want?' screeched Tolley.

There was no response.

He looked around wildly. His worst suspicions were confirmed. There was a large waterproof bag on the floor with his notes and computer disks beside it – and an AMNACS unit was missing. He attempted to dash towards the hangar door, but the masked figure grabbed him and flung him hard against the bulkhead.

Tolley crumpled to the deck. A large metal wrench crashed down towards his head.

The short, gurgling scream of terror ended abruptly.

*

Fox was finishing off a substantial breakfast in the wardroom. 'Where's Llewellyn?' he asked tersely.

'Dead to the world, I should think,' replied Morris.

'Don't say that, I gave him the once-over last night,' joked Scottie.

'Well, he had better look lively. I want everything destined for AWRE to be organised and packed before we dock at Devonport,' said Fox coldly.

'I'll go and check,' said Morris.

He knocked on Llewellyn's door – there was no reply, so he went in. Llewellyn was snoring.

'Come on, mate, get up, or you will be in hot water with Fox,' said Morris, showing a rare flash of compassion as he tried to rouse him.

The bleary-eyed lieutenant struggled out of bed and shook himself awake, aided by the cold, wet flannel handed to him by Morris. He got to the wardroom just in time to snatch some breakfast.

'You had better lay off alcohol,' snapped Fox.

Llewellyn blushed with embarrassment. 'Yes, sir, you're right. I can't understand it – I'm not much of a drinker, but I never used to get inebriated so easily. Is Peter up yet?'

'Haven't seen him either,' retorted Fox.

'That's odd, he never misses breakfast and we were supposed to be in the hangar by...' Llewellyn looked at his watch. 'Er – well, by now.'

Fox stared at him. Llewellyn got up and went to search for Tolley. His cabin was empty and there was no sign of him in the officers' quarters. Not keen on facing Fox again, he made his way to the hangar.

The hangar was locked. Llewellyn entered the code and opened the door. No one was there but the place looked oddly untidy. There was something spilt on the deck by the bulkhead. He bent down and examined the substance with his fingers. He recoiled in horror when he realised what the sticky dark red mess was.

Llewellyn's complexion was deathly white when Fox and Appleby arrived at the hangar.

'Have you found Tolley yet?' asked Appleby.

'No, sir,' replied Llewellyn, pointing to a trail of blood leading out of the hangar.

'Christ!' exclaimed Fox.

'There's something else,' added Llewellyn hesitantly.

'Well, let's have it,' snapped Fox.

'I think one of the AMNACS units is missing – and some of Tolley's papers too.'

Fox was stunned into silence.

'I'm holding an immediate investigation,' said Appleby. 'All but essential crew will be confined to quarters and I shall have the ship thoroughly searched.'

*

Within ten minutes the master-at-arms had swung the long arm of the law into operation. The officers were congregated in the wardroom while their cabins were searched. After half an hour the door burst open, exposing a grim-faced Appleby accompanied by Fox and an armed guard.

'Llewellyn, come with us,' ordered Appleby.

The lieutenant was marched off to an unused cabin.

'What's all this about?'

'Speak when you are told to,' ordered Appleby.

'Why is there blood in your cabin?' asked Fox.

'I don't know what you are talking about – what blood?'

Appleby intervened. 'Lieutenant David Llewellyn, you are being placed under armed guard until we reach Devonport, where you will be handed over to the MoD Police.'

The beleaguered young officer sat quietly, trying desperately to remember the events of the preceding night. None of it made any sense.

An hour later the door to Llewellyn's 'cell' swung open and Paul Scott entered with a medical kit. The guard locked the door and left them alone.

'Relax, David, I want to help. I managed to persuade Appleby to let me get blood and urine samples from you – a bit of a pretext, really.'

'What the hell is happening?' pleaded Llewellyn.

'God knows! Can't get much information – everyone's closed up like clams. But Tolley's still missing, that's for sure.'

'And I'm to blame? Do they think I murdered him or something? I haven't been formally charged with anything yet. It's a bloody disgrace.'

'Appleby and Fox seem to think you were up to something last night. I gathered that much from their reaction to my suggestion that you weren't capable of doing anything. Fox thinks you were shamming drunkenness as a cover. That's why I'm here – officially.'

'I was out cold all night.'

'I believe you,' said Scott. 'David, these tests might help you rather than them.'

'I'll agree to anything if it'll get me out of this mess.'

Scottie examined Llewellyn and obtained the samples. Something was wrong but he wasn't sure what.

*

HMS *Athena* arrived at Devonport on Monday night to be greeted by armed guards, Ministry of Defence Police and flashing vehicles. The missing device was not on board, and neither was Peter Tolley.

PART TWO

TROUBLED WATERS

7

Tuesday 3rd November

Tom Falconer had arrived early for his appointment at St Katharine Docks, the upmarket yacht haven near Tower Bridge. An acquaintance had put him in touch with a businessman, David Price, who wanted to start a motor cruising school on his boat. Tom wasn't too hopeful – but the possibilities were intriguing.

The sun was spinning a web of silver ripples across the River Thames. A police boat cruising under the bridge caught his eye – there was no more news of John McAdam. Tom wandered round the marina, looking at the people, the boats and the posh shops. Some of it seemed a bit pseud, but there was plenty of money about – he could live with it. He recognised a Grand Banks, a large, well-designed motor cruiser, moored on a floating pontoon in the West Dock. Sure enough, she was *Binnacles II*. Tom called out and climbed aboard.

Almost immediately, Jenny, a blonde in her mid-twenties, appeared on the deck to greet him. She was smartly dressed in a navy-blue suit with a short skirt which clung tightly to her shapely hips. She led the way to a spacious cabin where David Price was typing away with an air of businesslike efficiency on his laptop. He was a dynamic, rakish character with a bony face and short black hair. The loosely fitting but smart, trendy grey suit gave him the appearance of a well-dressed stick insect. They waited in silence as Price rattled the keys to a halt. He swung round on his chair. Jenny made the introductions with the professionalism of an experienced personal assistant.

In digital motion, Price stood up, paced one step forward and pushed out a spidery hand as he beamed with an expression of delighted surprise. 'My goodness! Commander, you really look the part – and image is so important. Great stuff!'

Before Tom could open his mouth, Price raced on.

'Make yourself comfortable and I'll tell you about my plan – but first let's have some coffee, yah?'

Tom nodded approval.

'Be a dear, Jenny,' said Price.

Jenny gave a dutiful smile.

'Great stuff! Tom, I bought this boat a couple of years ago – originally had a berth at Brighton Marina. A few months ago I had to meet some clients here at the Tower Hotel. It was then that the idea struck me – to bring the boat to St Katharine's and use it as a business asset. I now use her for entertaining clients. It's been a hit. But most of the time she's lying idle. So I thought about the possibility of setting up some sort of motor cruising school. I'm aiming for the wealthier end of the market, of course – no riffraff. The bottom line is, I need someone with the right credentials to run it. Tom – how does it grab you?'

'It sounds fascinating, but are there enough customers around at the moment?'

'Yes,' replied Price with confidence. 'There is a definite gap in the market. Jenny has done some preliminary scouting around in this part of the City. What is needed is a high-class operation that makes the most of these facilities. The question is, Tom,' he continued, 'what can *you* offer *us?*'

Jenny busied herself elsewhere on the boat.

Tom had prepared his spiel. This was hardly comparable to a Navy Board interview. He reeled off a list of relevant qualifications, skills and experience, and then offered some ideas of his own on how the courses might be organised. 'We would need to get the training facility recognised by the Royal Yachting Association before we could issue their certificates,' he added.

'Well, Tom, that would be your department. Do you anticipate problems?'

'Probably not – I'd need to make enquiries.'

'Could you start this week?' asked Price.

'I could,' replied Tom.

'Wonderful stuff!' said Price, looking at his watch. 'We both need to think it over and I have to go for a meeting in the City now. Sorry about this, but something came up unexpectedly this morning. Have a look around the boat with Jenny. I'll give you a ring early evening – if that's OK with you?'

'That's fine,' said Tom, 'but I do need to know what's in it for me – we haven't discussed remuneration.'

'Quite so,' replied Price, looking again at his watch. His body language changed to that of a hard-nosed salesman dealing with an obstacle. 'Well, it's not salaried and I don't want to be bothered with stamps and all that stuff. Off the top of my head

I suggest we run it on some sort of consultancy contract basis. Let's discuss it in detail later.'

Price flashed an animated grin as he landed his hand firmly on Tom's shoulder.

'Tom, dear chap, great to have met you – but I really must dash.'

*

Jenny showed Tom around the boat.

'This must be small fry compared to the boats you skippered,' she said, as they finished the short tour and ended up in the salon.

'Yes, but it's an excellent boat for small navigation classes.'

'So are you keen, then?' asked Jenny.

'Well, yes and no – I need to know more about the set-up.'

'Oh! Tom – let's open up the bar for a proper drink.'

'Now you're talking – a cognac please, Jenny. Tell me, what line of business is David Price in?'

'He's basically a sort of estate agent – although he would murder me if he heard me say that. He rents good-quality flats in the City to businesspeople on short visits from abroad. Some City firms use him regularly.'

'How many staff?'

Jenny smiled. 'It's just him and me. I'm secretary, PA and general factotum – and, in case you're wondering, it's strictly a business arrangement.'

Tom found Jenny's company exceedingly pleasant. After half an hour, and another cognac, he decided to leave before he outstayed his welcome.

*

The table was carefully laid, complete with candles. The rice was cooked and the oil was heating in the wok. Tom started the stir-fry the moment the Mini turned into the mews. Alice was taken aback as much by the sight of Tom cooking as by the wall of steam and overheated oil vapour which greeted her.

'Wow, I'm impressed. Are we celebrating?' she said, as she sidled as inconspicuously as possible towards the extractor fan switch.

'Sort of, but it's also time I pulled my weight around here to help a hard-working girl.'

'Tom Falconer, don't give me the blarney. What happened about the job?'

He handed her a glass of cold dry white wine. 'I've been offered the job in principle.'

'And…?' replied Alice impatiently.

'And I accepted – in principle.'

'What's all this "in principle" business about?'

Tom recounted the day's events to Alice. He had more or less agreed terms with David Price over the phone, but wanted the details in writing. He had some doubts about Price but decided to keep that to himself.

'The venture may be a little risky but I won't be putting my money into it.'

'Pity you haven't got your own boat,' said Alice.

'Some people run motor cruising courses on hired boats – but one thing at a time,' replied Tom.

'So when do you start?'

'Tomorrow,' said Tom enthusiastically.

Alice was pleased for him – but she wasn't too sure about Jenny.

Wednesday 4th November

The events on HMS *Athena* had led to a considerable tightening of security at HMS *Drake*, the other name for HMNB (Her Majesty's Naval Base) Devonport. Everything and everybody entering and leaving the base was double-checked and recorded. The atmosphere was tense.

The officers of the *Athena* had been separated from each other during the interrogations. Paul Scott had got off lightly compared to his colleagues. He had had little to do with AMNACS at any stage and was eliminated from suspicion early in the proceedings. He had also managed to secure a pass for the day to attend a prearranged surgical training session at the Royal Naval Hospital, Haslar, near Portsmouth. But Scott was nervous – there were unofficial activities on his agenda this morning too. In his pocket, wrapped in a handkerchief, were two small, unlabelled tubes containing aliquots of the samples he had obtained from Lieutenant David Llewellyn.

Scott pulled his car to a halt a few yards short of the exit gates in time to hear the final salvos of a contretemps between the guards and an officer. In the cold early-morning air an uppity young lieutenant returning from leave was venting his spleen on the guards for being officious and wasting his time. Head high, the officer marched off in an air of self-righteous indignation. The two young guards, who were already waiting impatiently for their watch to end, were now in belligerent mood.

With trepidation, Scott drew closer to the gates. If they found the specimens he would have some explaining to do. The smaller of the two guards blocked the exit, cocking his self-loading rifle in a menacing pose, while the other, a gruff, stocky man, hovered impatiently by the driver's window. To divert attention Scott placed his small case conspicuously on the front passenger seat and then fumbled absent-mindedly through several pockets for his identity card and pass.

The gruff guard scrutinised the documents. 'These seem to be in order. Where are you going, sir?'

Scott told him and prepared to drive off through the gates.

'Not so fast, sir, we haven't finished yet.'

Scott's heart jumped. Clumsily, he tried to control the situation. 'I hope this won't take long or I'll be late – I've a long journey ahead of me.'

'I have strict orders, sir,' said the guard as he looked inside the car. 'Please open the boot, and then your case.'

Scott obliged.

The guards made a thorough inspection, finally rounding on the ophthalmoscope in the case. Scott gave them a concise account of the use of the instrument and opened its battery housing for inspection.

'That's the most interesting thing I've seen this morning. Have a nice day, sir,' said the gruff man, permitting a hint of a smile.

Scottie had a 170-mile journey ahead of him. He would have to motor fast to reach Haslar by 10am – and he needed to sort out the other matter first. At least he would have a good excuse for being late.

He reached the outskirts of Portsmouth at 9.30am and stopped at a railway station with a nearby minicab office. Quickly, he took the samples from his pocket and labelled them with a false name. He then scribbled a short letter on notepaper headed with his own private London address. It read:

> *Re: Blood & urine from Mr P. Grimes, age 30 (ref. PP1019)*
> *Please analyse samples for alcohol, drugs and drug-related substances.*
> *Levels may be low. Confirm with mass spectrometry if necessary.*
> *Send results and invoice to above address ASAP.*
> *Paul Scott, MB, BS, FRCS.*

He put the letter and samples into an envelope and addressed it to a private pathology laboratory in Harley Street, London. He then ran the few yards to the minicab office and paid cash in advance to have the package delivered urgently by car. He hurried to the station and used a public telephone to warn the laboratory that the samples were on their way. Scottie then phoned Tom Falconer's Belgravia number.

Tom was busy preparing notes for the first seamanship course when the phone rang.

'Thank God you're in – Paul Scott here. I can't talk for long.'

'Scottie! Good to hear from you. What's up?'

'All hell's let loose at Devonport. I can't go into all the details now but the bottom line is that the new missile device disappeared from *Athena* while we were at sea. And, worse, so did the boffin from AWRE.'

'Good heavens!' replied Tom.

'But here's the rub – they must have disappeared while we were in the North Sea. Our course took us through the Outer Dowsing Channel so we must have passed quite close to the Norfolk coast. A bit of a coincidence, don't you think?'

'Incredible!' replied Tom, dumbfounded.

'I'm supposed to be attending a course in London next week – we could meet then,' said Scottie.

'We must!'

'Great. I'll be in touch if and when I get to London. Tom – I know you won't, but not a word to anyone. I must go now.'

Paul Scott rushed back to his car. It was nearly 10am.

Tom searched through the boxes in his cupboard and retrieved the east coast navigation charts.

*

Earlier that morning, Rear Admiral Richard Claydon had been subjected to an inquisition at Whitehall. Then, after a tiresome journey from London, he had to suffer a grilling by the special investigation team at Devonport. Now it was someone else's turn to take the heat. He quickly organised the loan of an office and summoned Captain Andrew Fox.

'I blew it,' said Claydon, looking out of the window. He turned to Fox, fixing him with menacing dark eyes. 'I blew it by choosing you as project leader, and you blew it by sheer incompetence.'

Fox refused to be made the scapegoat. 'That's just not true. The project itself was highly successful – everything went to plan.'

Claydon stood up and was about to wade in when Fox angrily thumped his fist on the table, stood up and snapped back again.

'You don't expect weapons and scientists to disappear on a battleship in the middle of the sea. You approved all the plans I drew up. And you selected some of the key officers – one of them may be involved. So, you are in this mess as deeply as me.'

Claydon was unmoved. 'You fool. You had carte blanche to make all the security arrangements. You were so obsessed with bloody Gantt charts and all that baloney that common sense went out the window.'

'In my view the security arrangements for Project Athena were adequate for the purpose,' retorted Fox.

'Idiot!' blasted Claydon. 'Even if you are right, no one else will interpret it that way. Appleby is already making a meal out of this. He's complained about your security arrangements. He's criticised the Admiralty, and me in particular, for a hastily and poorly planned operation. He intends to come out as Mr Clean – and the mud's coming our way.'

Fox knew that his ambitions had got the better of prudence. 'Perhaps Appleby has a point,' he admitted. 'But we shouldn't be totally negative – we now know that AMNACS works brilliantly and most of the data will be available for AWRE.'

Claydon paused for a while – now was the time to change tack. 'Andrew, you're right. We should emphasise the positive aspects and hope that blame can be directed firmly towards an identifiable traitor.'

'I suppose nothing came of the searches in the North Sea?' asked Fox.

'As soon as I got your message from *Athena* I organised searches in the most likely areas, but the time of the event was too vague to be useful,' replied Claydon. 'Nothing was found up to yesterday afternoon – but the whole thing has been taken out of my hands now.'

Claydon was curious to know more about the events on HMS *Athena* – due to heightened security he knew less than Fox realised.

'Andrew, let's think things through carefully. What do you think actually happened?'

Fox recounted events as he saw them.

'And do you really believe that Lieutenant Llewellyn removed AMNACS and got rid of Tolley?' asked Claydon.

'I know it seems incredible, but the evidence is stacked up against him more than anyone else,' said Fox.

'Well,' added Claydon, 'we need to try to cover each other's backsides whatever the outcome – I'll put in a word for you if I get the chance.'

Fox was unconvinced about support from Claydon. He secretly hoped that Llewellyn would be found guilty – that would be neat and convenient.

*

Much to the chagrin of his seniors, Inspector Adrian Lomax and his sergeant had been seconded to the special investigation team. The SIS investigators had completed their own enquiries at Devonport and had returned to London. They left Lomax in charge of the local operation.

By now Lomax should have made detective chief inspector but his propensity to upset people in high places had not helped his career progression. This was of no consequence to the SIS, which had enlisted his services on a previous occasion and recognised his talents.

But Lomax had not spared his tongue when dealing with his new colleagues. He was unhappy with the proposed release of Llewellyn. The SIS won the day – Llewellyn was to be released and Lomax was instructed to keep track of events.

*

Mike Morris and Nigel Hannay had been supping in the base wardroom since dinner. It was 9.30pm when Paul Scott joined them, having just returned from Portsmouth.

'So, they've let you off for good behaviour,' said Scottie, attempting to lighten the situation.

'Lulling us into a false sense of security, more like,' replied Hannay.

'At least you got away for the day – lucky dog,' added Morris.

'Yes, but I've missed all the action – what's happening?'

At that moment Andrew Fox entered the room. 'I should have known you reprobates would be in here. Let me get a round, and in return you can tell me what you make of this ghastly affair.'

The discussion was short on facts and peppered with guarded probing. There was general incredulity at the idea of David Llewellyn being a secret agent.

'Presumably, in real life, agents do not look or behave like James Bond,' observed Fox.

'Who else could have done it?' asked Scottie.

Morris took the bait. 'Any of us – except you, I guess. We all had access to the hangar and we all knew enough about AMNACS to do the necessary. There were a couple of senior rates who might also be implicated at a pinch.'

'But Mike,' asked Hannay, 'if it were you, what would you have done with AMNACS – thrown it in the sea?'

'Why not? A boat or submarine could have picked it up given an accurate location.'

'We detected nothing near us around that time,' said Fox.

'And searching the seabed would take forever without amazingly accurate bearings,' added Morris.

'Do we have any idea what time these events took place?' asked Scottie, hoping for a clue to the likely bearing of the ship.

'We've been over that several times,' said Morris. 'The consensus is that it must have been between midnight and 4am.'

Fox was called to the phone. 'Well, well! They've released Llewellyn,' he announced. 'He's in his room and would appreciate some company.'

Hannay procured a bottle of whisky and they all left for Llewellyn's room.

*

The young lieutenant looked shattered, with tired eyes peeping through dark halos. He had been interrogated for many hours with little sleep. Nigel poured him two fingers of neat whisky, which he accepted gratefully.

'You need sleep, man,' said Scottie, stating the obvious to break the awkward silence.

'Did they actually charge you with anything, David?' asked Fox.

'God knows what they are playing at. I was accused of murder and treachery during the interrogation but I don't appear to be under arrest. Christ, you chaps, you don't think I did it, do you?'

'We think you are innocent,' said Mike, overstating the general consensus in an attempt to console the lieutenant.

Llewellyn continued. 'The fact is, I did not steal the damned AMNACS, or Tolley's work. I did nothing to Tolley – and if I had I certainly wouldn't have planted the incriminating evidence in my cabin. I ask you, am I that stupid? But who did, then? The answer is simple – it must be a colleague.'

'What exactly was planted in your cabin?' asked Scottie.

'It's laughable,' retorted Llewellyn. 'They say they found one of Tolley's papers smeared with his blood – a bit too obvious, don't you think?'

'David, are you saying it must be one of us?' asked Morris.

'That's it,' replied Llewellyn, gulping down a large mouthful of whisky and coughing. 'Apart from you, Scottie, the most likely suspects are in my room.'

'I know you've been through a lot but there's no need to be impertinent,' snapped Fox.

Llewellyn laughed and started shouting at no one in particular. 'I don't give a fuck. My career's been ruined and I might still be locked up. However long it takes, I'm going to nail the bastard that did this.'

'Don't give him any more whisky, Hannay; you know he can't hold his drink,' said Fox angrily.

Not sure what to do next, Fox ordered everyone to leave so Llewellyn could get some sleep.

Paul Scott went immediately to his quarters, waited a short while and then returned. Llewellyn was pacing the room like a caged animal when Scottie knocked. He opened the door hesitantly and peered through the gap. Seeing a friendly face, he let out a sigh of relief.

'Sorry about the outburst,' he said. 'It was not directed at you.'

'I'm surprised you trust anyone,' said Scottie. 'You say you don't suspect me, but maybe I could have done it if someone had given me sufficient information.'

'No, Scottie – too many variables to take into account. Whoever did this knew a lot about the arrangements. We are dealing with a cool customer.'

'And a dangerous one – we must be careful,' added Scottie. 'There was one thing I wanted to check with you again. When we took you to your cabin on Sunday night you were dead to the world, but I didn't think you had had that much alcohol. Are you sure you didn't take any sort of drug or medicine which might have interacted with alcohol? I'm thinking of things like tranquillisers, sleeping pills, antihistamines etc.'

'Not even an aspirin,' replied Llewellyn thoughtfully. 'You are not the only one who thinks it's odd – that swine Lomax suggested I was putting it on to strengthen my alibi.'

'There is another possibility,' added Scottie. 'Someone may have drugged you.'

'You mean laced my drinks? That doesn't bear thinking about.'

'Exactly – David, I'm telling you this in complete confidence, putting my neck on the block. I sent some of your samples off to a private lab for drug analysis. If they find something it might strengthen your case. The forensics boys were probably concentrating on the alcohol levels – initially at least.'

'When will you know the results?'

'At the weekend, I hope. I'll let you know as soon as I can. If the results show anything important I'll have to tell the police – and take the flak. Keep this to yourself for now.'

'Thanks a million, Scottie – at least someone's on my side.'

Paul Scott went straight to his bed. It had been a long and tiring day.

*

The sleeper was restless. He was waiting for the opportunity to pass on the information required to retrieve AMNACS from the bottom of the North Sea. Security was too tight at the moment.

He did not know the identity of his contact, but they certainly knew his. He felt like a vulnerable pawn.

Also, the plan had badly misfired. Why the hell did Tolley have to turn up in the middle of things? David Llewellyn was the perfect patsy for espionage, but not for Tolley's murder as well. And what was going on now? Why had they released Llewellyn? Was it a trick of the SIS? He needed to point the finger of suspicion firmly back to Llewellyn. He would have to move fast – they might not expect that. How great if he could use their ploy to his advantage.

The sleeper set to work on his next move.

8

Thursday 5th November

The smart little shop in the busy Hampstead street was warm and comfortable. Helen Lane watched the chilled people bustling along under the street lights outside. The loneliness she felt following her divorce was fading fast. Now life was fun and exciting again. She enjoyed Alice's company and eagerly awaited her return from the afternoon stint of delivering business leaflets to local residents. Alice and Helen had taken the plunge. Their joint venture, Silk-Lane Arts & Crafts, was now in its eighth week. Tonight they were having a girls' night out.

It was just after 5pm when Alice bounced into the shop, full of beans. She was cold and shivering. Helen started to make some tea.

'Anything?' asked Alice.

'A couple came in for a browse, probably to get warm. Oh, and Tom phoned – he may be late back from St Katharine's – didn't say why, but not to worry.'

*

Tom Falconer's plans had already run into difficulties. Despite his knowledge and experience, he would still have to attend a course for instructors before the motor cruising school could be accredited to run officially recognised certificate courses. To get things moving as soon as possible, he turned to the idea of short introductory courses for absolute beginners, just providing tuition on basic boat handling and some practical experience at sea. He wondered how David Price would react to the proposal.

Tom had done his homework on Thames navigation and had talked at length to the lock-keeper at St Katharine's. This was fortunate because Price had just turned up unexpectedly and insisted on a short trip down the river. Tom skippered *Binnacles II* with ease through the lock gates and down to the Thames Barrier at Woolwich, and back again, giving a nautical commentary on the way. Price was impressed, and so was Jenny. It soon became apparent that Price knew little about boats, navigation and seamanship. But he made the most of the free lesson.

David Price stayed on till early evening. Fifth of November fireworks were already popping in the distance. The water lapped vigorously against the boats in the marina. The three relaxed in the warm, comfortable salon. Price was enthusiastic about the short courses for beginners – Tom had managed to paper over the accreditation problem. Jenny had put the finishing touches to the leaflets she would be taking to the printers in the morning.

'So, Tom,' announced Price, 'you're well on the way. Excellent stuff! You'll need these – the keys. Come and go as you please. She's in your hands now – the boat, I mean,' he added, winking at Jenny.

David Price handed Tom a set of boat keys. Jenny beamed. Price performed his usual staccato farewell ritual and left.

'I'm going to prepare the victuals while you carry on with your work,' said Jenny.

'You're cooking?'

'I certainly am. We're going to wine and dine in style tonight. Just a one-off, you understand.'

Tom felt slightly uncomfortable and busied himself in the engine room. When he returned to the salon he found the dining table laid for a three-course meal complete with wine, crystal glasses, a small bowl of flowers and a silver candelabrum.

'I'm trying to compete with the captain's table,' called Jenny from the galley, 'and I'm serving now.'

Tom tried to hide his embarrassment. 'You shouldn't have gone to all this trouble.'

'Sit down and enjoy,' demanded Jenny. She raised her glass and laughed. 'Don't look so worried. I was thinking of our clients. This is a practice run. I thought the odd course dinner, wardroom style, might go down well – high-class stuff and all that, remember. What do you think?'

'Great idea! It's worth a try on the longer courses,' replied Tom with some relief.

After an excellent meal Jenny brought coffee to the salon and sat next to Tom. Several times she caught his eyes and smiled. He resisted temptation.

'Tom, you get on and leave the clearing up to me, I insist,' she said, getting up from her chair. 'You will have to entertain the customers after dinner, so I need to get used to being galley hand.'

Tom shifted a few papers around aimlessly. He felt the need for fresh air, and went outside to check the lights. After walking round the deck he stepped lightly onto the floating pontoon and then ambled slowly towards the dockside. The subdued strains of a Brandenburg concerto filtered through the cold night air. The music got louder as someone climbed out of an illuminated hatch onto the deck of the large white powerboat just ahead of him. Tom stopped by the boat – he remembered seeing it in the daylight. It had sleek aerodynamic lines with dark-tinted windows, and could have passed for an intergalactic spaceship.

'Good evening,' said Tom, inviting conversation.

The well-built middle-aged man in neat white trousers and jumper looked up. Wary of strangers on the pontoons at night, he responded cautiously. 'Good evening to you,' the man replied in a soft American accent.

'This looks like a powerful beast – a forty-five-footer, I guess?' said Tom.

'Nearer fifty. Do you have a boat?' enquired the American.

'I'm from *Binnacles II*, the Grand Banks moored at the end of this pontoon. Name's Tom Falconer.'

'Well – OK,' said the American as he stepped onto the pontoon and shook Tom's hand. 'I'm Dan Bush, from Texas – people call me Tex.'

After a brief, friendly exchange, the Texan suggested Tom join him later for a drink in the Yacht Club. Tom accepted gladly and returned to fetch Jenny. She insisted he go on ahead.

Jenny freshened up, put on her face and let down her long blonde hair. She liked Tom, but resolved not to overdo the teasing.

Dan Bush was the European general manager of an American-based oil technology firm with offices in the City of London. The two men were just getting down to serious conversation when Dan's attention was diverted by the glamorous blonde making her way towards them.

Tom introduced Jenny.

At 9pm, after a pleasurable hour, Tom announced that he had to leave and ordered a taxi. He wanted to get home before Alice. Tex and Jenny seemed happy to stay on.

*

David Llewellyn switched off the light, opened the curtains of his third-floor room in the old accommodation block and peered out into the darkness. The shadowy figure he had seen earlier on the narrow access road at the back of the building had gone.

It was dark and slightly misty, with the smell of fireworks still in the air. The road looked damp and uninviting. There was nothing to see apart from the black outlines of storage sheds. He thought he saw one of Lomax's men following him in Plymouth in the afternoon – he wondered if he was becoming paranoid. He closed the curtains, put on the light and poured himself a stiff whisky.

Lomax did not have the manpower available for total surveillance. There was no police presence outside Llewellyn's block tonight.

But someone else was there, lurking unseen in the shadows. The sleeper was about to put his plan into action. He was one of the colleagues who had called on Llewellyn earlier that evening. He had left the building through a non-alarmed rear fire exit, leaving the door closed but unlatched with the aid of a stiff piece of plastic.

Wearing powder-free surgical gloves, the sleeper pulled open the fire door. He took out a pair of shoes from his zip bag and placed them on the vinyl-covered floor. He then removed his damp soiled shoes, placed them in the bag and slipped into the dry, soft shoes. He closed the door behind him as quietly as possible, leaving it imperceptibly ajar for a quiet exit. The sleeper took off the gloves and made his way stealthily up the stairs and along the corridor to Llewellyn's room. He tapped lightly on the door.

Only after the second set of tapping noises did Llewellyn realise that someone was outside his room. Nervously, he opened the door to see a familiar face smiling at him with a finger to his lips indicating the need for silence.

'I must tell you something, but for goodness' sake be quiet,' whispered the visitor.

Llewellyn let him in and pointed to the whisky bottle.

'David, it's almost unbelievable but I've found an electronic bug in my room. You may have one too. Question is – is it friend or foe?'

Under cover of soft background music from a radio, they searched carefully for twenty minutes. They found nothing, but continued to drink and chat until 1am. Llewellyn was becoming incoherent. The deception had worked so far – the sleeper now had to finish the job. He stood up and pulled a handkerchief from his pocket, dropping several pound coins onto the carpet. The lieutenant bent down in front of him to help pick them up. This was the moment. The sleeper delivered a sharp rabbit punch to the back of Llewellyn's neck, sending him collapsing to the floor.

Llewellyn was unconscious but still breathing. The sleeper put on gloves and rolled his victim into a semi-prone position. He opened his bag and extracted a carefully measured length of rope with a hangman's noose at one end. He rubbed the rope over the carpet and Llewellyn's clothes and hands to embellish the forensic evidence. He then switched off the light and opened the curtains and the large window. The free end of the rope was fixed tightly around the back of a heavy armchair moved against the wall, close to the window. Llewellyn was still unconscious. The sleeper pulled him towards the window and placed the noose around his neck. He tightened the rope until the large knot rested firmly against the lieutenant's cervical vertebrae. With difficulty he managed to get him onto the windowsill and struggled to apply Llewellyn's fingerprints to the window frame. The lieutenant groaned and began to move as the noose was again adjusted round his neck. With a sudden heave he was launched off the sill and clear of the building. He dropped freely until the rope drew taut with a sickening crack.

Dangling at the end of the rope, the tormented body writhed for a few seconds before it fell silent and motionless.

For a moment the sleeper was stunned, his concentration disturbed. A flashlight flickered in the distance. It jolted him back into action. He had to make it look like suicide. But first he had to close the curtains and put on the light to clear away incriminating evidence – a disposable plastic cup, the coins still on the floor. Finally, he switched off the light and left the curtains wide open.

The corridor was clear; no signs of life. Carefully, he closed the door with one hand, using the other to prevent a slam as the lock clicked back into place. He went swiftly to the rear exit, changed his shoes again and closed the fire door behind him. No one was about. It was only a short distance to his building. He slid along close to the walls and soon reached his entrance. He took off his shoes and walked on tiptoe to his room. His heart was pounding. He opened his door with painstaking care. At last he was inside and safe.

Immediately the sleeper set to work – diligently cleaning and disposing. At 3am he set his alarm and climbed into bed. He tried to sleep but his mind was buzzing – tracing every step, every event. How lucky he had been. But would they suspect suicide or murder? Had he left any incriminating evidence? The more he thought about it, the more confident he became.

The sleeper was fast asleep when the police vehicles started to appear on the roads outside.

9

Monday 9th November

It was 3am when Paul Scott arrived at his London flat. After a short sleep he was woken abruptly at 7.45am. His hand thrashed about the bedside table, knocked over a cup and finally silenced the jangling alarm clock. He had to move fast to get to the first lecture on time. As the mists of sleep lifted, a sickly feeling of panic hit him.

The horrific events at Devonport rolled around in his head. Getting a pass had been tricky this time – Lomax was decidedly against him leaving the base. He had half expected to find his flat turned over by the police, the SIS or worse. His thoughts turned to Llewellyn – he now knew how it felt not knowing who was friend and who was foe. And the samples – those damned samples. The results from the Harley Street laboratories confirmed his worst suspicions. He had not told the police yet – he could be in big trouble.

He went to the phone and then paused. Thank goodness Tom hadn't tried to phone him at Devonport – everything was being monitored. Perhaps his phone was tapped too. He decided to use a public payphone. On his way out, the letter from the laboratories caught his eye. He read it once again – a cold shiver went up his spine.

*

As usual, Alice left early in her Mini to pick up Helen en route to Hampstead. Tom was hanging on to avoid the worst of the London rush hour. He was still in the flat when Paul Scott rang. The call was short and cryptic. They arranged to meet at 7pm at St Katharine's.

Jenny arrived at the boat soon after Tom. She was clutching a cheque and a parcel. 'Well,' she said, 'at least we have two takers for this weekend's course – they've paid a deposit.'

'Good,' replied Tom, playing down his relief.

'Quite a few people are interested,' added Jenny, 'but most would rather wait until warmer weather.'

'Not surprised – but we might squeeze in another one or two short courses before winter sets in if we keep up the pressure. Another couple of people are coming to see me later today.'

'It's not exactly big bucks though, Tom, considering all the effort we're putting in.'

'I guess not.'

'By the way,' added Jenny, 'here is your package from the printers.'

Tom opened it and pored over the contents – neat, fresh-smelling documents he had prepared for the course.

'What are they?' asked Jenny.

'Certificates of attendance,' he replied. 'They'll act as a log of boating experience – although they won't carry much weight officially.'

'Oh, that's good.' Jenny tried to sound enthusiastic.

'There shouldn't be any more incidental expenses apart from food, drink and fuel on the course itself,' added Tom.

'Thank goodness for that – getting David Price to part with money isn't easy,' replied Jenny, looking at her watch. 'I must fly – he's expecting me at the office. Will you be here this evening?'

'Up to seven o'clock; I'm meeting a friend here.'

'Mind if I call round later?' asked Jenny cautiously.

'Not at all – I'll introduce you to Paul, another naval officer.'

Tom found himself viewing his new venture in a different light. Suddenly it all seemed a bit of a non-entity: a small business with small returns for a lot of effort – and a lot of niggling problems, like David Price. Characteristically, the fleeting string of negative thoughts kicked him back into positive action mode. He locked up the boat and made for the Barbican to deliver more leaflets.

Jenny reappeared at 6.30pm to find Tom shaking hands with a young couple who were just about to leave. Tom introduced her as the 'course administrator'. She didn't balk at the new title.

'Let's celebrate,' announced Tom as soon as the couple had gone. 'They're also coming on the course this weekend.'

*

Paul Scott picked his way around St Katharine Docks in the dark. There appeared to be only one large motor cruiser with signs of life aboard in the western reaches of the yacht haven. He made his way along the pontoons towards her. He was checking the name when a cabin door opened to reveal a familiar figure silhouetted against the light, glass in hand.

'Tom, you old devil, what's this – John Brown's navy?'

'Come aboard and meet the crew. Jenny, meet Paul Scott, known as Scottie – he's still in the navy.'

'And an officer too?' enquired Jenny, hoping to extract more information about the handsome specimen standing before her.

'He's a lieutenant commander – an officer and a gentleman,' added Tom.

Scottie laughed and gratefully clutched a gin and tonic.

'So, how's Barts?' asked Tom.

'It hasn't changed much since I was last there, apart from the gloom and doom from threats of closure.'

'Surely you don't mean St Bartholomew's Hospital?' asked Jenny, even more intrigued.

'Oh yes, I forgot to tell you; he's a surgeon too – just a little Saturday job on the side,' quipped Tom.

Scott made an effort to be sociable. But Tom noticed the dampening of his normally extroverted personality. After a short exchange of pleasantries Tom insisted they had to leave but promised Jenny they would all meet up again before Paul returned to Devonport.

The two men found a quiet bar nearby.

'I've contacted Alice – she's expecting us in about an hour or so,' said Tom. 'So we've plenty of time to talk.'

'Sorry I didn't get in touch with you earlier,' said Scottie, 'but things just went from bad to worse at Devonport.'

'What the hell is going on?'

Scottie paused, hardly knowing where to start. 'I shouldn't be talking to you at all, but I've got to talk to someone I can trust.

You might even help solve this whole sordid business. Tom, what do you know about AMNACS?'

'It rings a faint bell – no more than that. What exactly is it?'

'It's a new guided missile control system developed at AWRE by a civilian scientist called Peter Tolley. It was the subject of our weapons trial in the North Atlantic. Have you ever met Dr Tolley or Lieutenant David Llewellyn?' asked Scottie.

'No. Who is David Llewellyn?'

'He was a naval weapons engineer working alongside Tolley at AWRE – they were both transferred to HMS *Athena* for the trials.'

'Did you say Tolley was a civilian?' asked Tom.

'Yes; there was a bit of a rumpus about him going but apparently he was needed to optimise the device during the trials. Anyway,' continued Scottie, 'before leaving Devonport those involved with the test weapons, including Nigel Hannay and Mike Morris, went to AWRE for intensive briefing and training. As a mere medic I didn't get to know anything about AMNACS until we were at sea.'

'Who was in command?' asked Tom.

'That was another bone of contention. Commander Appleby was in command of HMS *Athena* as usual, but Captain Andrew Fox was aboard as project leader responsible for AMNACS trials.'

'Say no more,' said Tom. 'Fox is an ambitious, pushy so-and-so – I'll bet Appleby's nose was out of joint.'

'It was. Anyway, the trials in the North Atlantic were a great success. But on the way back via the North Sea, it all happened.'

Scottie paused for a moment, trying to assess Tom's reactions. Could he trust him? It was odd that Hannay, Morris and McAdam were all on Tom's frigate.

'Go on,' said Tom impatiently.

'Right,' said Scottie, taking a deep breath. 'While we were in the North Sea, Tolley disappeared and so did one of the AMNACS devices and some key data. There was blood leading out of the hangar where Tolley worked – it was later confirmed to be his blood.'

'Remind me when this happened?' asked Tom.

'Early morning of 2nd November – probably between midnight and 4am. Fortunately, I was taking an active interest in navigation, so I do know roughly what course we were on.'

'Good,' said Tom. 'We'll look at the navigation charts when we get to the flat.'

'It gets worse, Tom.'

'You're joking!'

'No. After all the interrogations on the ship, Lieutenant Llewellyn was accused of Tolley's murder.'

'Good God – on what basis?'

'Apparently one of Tolley's documents, stained with his blood, was found in Llewellyn's cabin. Llewellyn insisted he had been set up.'

'What do you think?' asked Tom.

'Let me go on,' continued Scottie, 'it gets even worse. At Devonport on 4th November, Llewellyn was released – I don't know why. He insisted he'd been framed. Then the morning after Guy Fawkes, we were all rounded up for questioning once again. Llewellyn had been found dead – hanging at the end of a rope.'

'Unbelievable!' exclaimed Tom. 'Suicide?'

'That's the consensus,' replied Scottie. 'It all fits, doesn't it? Llewellyn knew all about AMNACS and worked with Tolley during the trials. There was damning evidence in his cabin. Presumably Tolley inadvertently got in the way and had to be disposed of. Then guilt and remorse drove Llewellyn to suicide. Very neat!'

'You sound sceptical, Scottie.'

'Yes, Tom – I believe Llewellyn was set up all the way and then murdered.'

'Do you have evidence?'

Scott continued. 'The night before the disappearance of AMNACS and Tolley, we were celebrating in the wardroom. Llewellyn was so drunk that I had to help him to his cabin – but he didn't appear to have had that much alcohol. Some have suggested that Llewellyn was faking drunkenness to provide an alibi for his intended activities that night. I persuaded Appleby to let me get blood and urine samples that might provide important evidence – like actual alcohol levels. But I split the samples and sent a set to a private lab as soon as I could get away from Devonport. There was something odd about Tolley's breath after that wardroom party. The lab results solved the puzzle. In addition to alcohol, they also showed that he had taken chloral.'

'What's chloral?'

'It's a hypnotic which can be used as a sleeping draught. Mixed with alcohol it's potent – a Mickey Finn. Tom, it means someone probably laced Llewellyn's drink. If so, we may be dealing with a cold-blooded killer who is still at large – and he may be one of our colleagues.'

'So who is on your list of suspects?' asked Tom calmly.

'Taking everything into account, I think the front runners must be Andrew Fox, Nigel Hannay and Mike Morris.'

'What made you think Llewellyn was murdered?' asked Tom.

'Can't be certain – but he didn't seem suicidal when I last saw him. Tom – do you think John McAdam's presence in Norfolk was a coincidence?'

'Having a holiday in Norfolk is one thing, but disappearing without trace is just too much of a coincidence,' Tom continued. 'That won't be lost on the police. Who is leading the investigation?'

'Apart from the pack of wolves from London, an Inspector Lomax seems to be in charge,' replied Scottie.

'Oh dear!' exclaimed Tom. 'He was investigating John McAdam's disappearance too.'

Scott summoned up the courage to push the discussion further. 'Tom, it is possible that John is involved in some way with Mike or Nigel.'

'Yes, and they were all under my command – great. It's a wonder I haven't had another visit from Lomax,' replied Tom coldly. 'Surely Fox is a better candidate – he had more time and opportunity to plan things well in advance.'

'True, but it doesn't let John McAdam off the hook, does it?'

'He's not on a fucking hook – he's just missing,' replied Tom sharply.

Tom broke the long silence that followed. 'Sorry, Scottie, didn't mean to snap, but the implications are indigestible.'

'Join the club,' Scott replied, feeling some relief at having shared the burden.

*

The taxi arrived to take them to Belgravia.

The delicious fragrance of Alice's haute cuisine greeted them as they entered the flat. She dashed to meet them. Scottie kissed her on the cheek and gave her a hug. His problem shared, his lively personality was emerging again.

'My God, that smells wonderful,' exclaimed Scottie, his appetite returning for the first time in days.

Alice lined up the drinks and returned to the kitchen to finish cooking.

Tom grasped the opportunity and retrieved the east coast navigation chart. 'You said the time interval during which AMNACS and Dr Tolley disappeared was probably between midnight and 4am,' he said in a hushed voice. 'If I were up to no good and sneaking around a frigate at night, I would do it well clear of the watch changes – so let's call it between 00.30 and 03.30.'

Scottie plotted his best estimate of HMS *Athena*'s course during that time interval.

'You were right,' said Tom. 'You were probably coming through the Outer Dowsing Channel during that period. That's enough for tonight, Scottie – I need to have a good think. Let's relax.'

Tom's niggling thoughts continued. If John McAdam's disappearance was connected in some way to the retrieval of AMNACS from the North Sea, then an incredible amount of planning must have been done before his trip to North Norfolk.

Alice called them to the table.

Scottie was curious to know more about Tom's enterprise at St Katharine's, but was diplomatic enough not to mention the lovely Jenny. Tom enlarged, and then announced that the first course was definitely on for the coming weekend.

Alice was delighted and relieved.

'So, you've lost him to the sea again, Alice,' joked Scottie.

'As long as it's only the sea,' she replied.

No one took the bait.

'Did you say you intended to sail out to coastal waters?' asked Scottie.

'That's right – just to give the students some offshore experience.'

'Tom, I'm free in London this weekend – could I come along and give you a hand?'

'That would be a great help,' said Tom, seeing the possibilities.

*

Paul Scott returned to his flat.

Alice was keen to tell Tom about her latest plan to sell the paintings she had recently restored.

'So, if it all works out well tomorrow I may be at a fine arts and antiques fayre in the City on Saturday,' she concluded enthusiastically.

'Shame I'm running the course on the same day,' said Tom, adding, 'I'd love to keep you company.'

'That's sweet of you Tom, but you can't,' she replied, pleased by the sentiment.

Tom looked distracted and fidgety.

'Is everything all right?' asked Alice.

'What? Oh, yes – just tired. Let's go to bed.'

Alice snuggled into Tom and was soon fast asleep. Tom couldn't sleep. He slipped out of bed and went to the lounge. He plotted out the sequence of events from before McAdam's disappearance up to the present, and worked through various scenarios. Then he remembered the new moon and the spring tides when they visited Norfolk. He looked at his diary – there was a full moon this week.

He needed to get back to North Norfolk as soon as possible.

10

Tuesday 10th November, London

As usual, Alice woke up just before the alarm clock went off. She gently roused the snoring mass beside her. 'It's your turn,' she said.

Tom staggered to the kitchen and returned to the bedroom with two cups of coffee. 'I need to go back to North Norfolk for a few days,' he announced suddenly.

'Why?' asked Alice, taken aback.

'There's something going on – it could be important.'

'What? What's going on?'

'Alice, I can't tell you any more, it's too dangerous,' replied Tom, biting his lip and wishing he had thought before putting his foot in it.

'I don't understand – my God, what are you involved in?'

'Trust me, Alice, please trust me.'

'I might if I knew what the hell you are talking about,' she snapped.

Tom tried to put his arms around her. She pushed him away.
'It's nothing to worry about, really.'
'Why, Tom – why?'
'It might help solve John's disappearance.' Tom consoled himself that this was at least partly true.

Her pale, silky face flushed. 'Why not let the police do it? We've done our bit already.' She felt the tears welling up and forced them back.

Tom had never seen Alice so angry. He was shaken. 'Let's talk it over tonight,' he said.

'What is the point?'

Without another word Alice went straight to the bathroom and locked the door. Tears were flowing down her cheeks. She lowered her head over the basin for a few minutes. The confused feeling of anger, misery and fear changed gradually to one of dogged determination. She took a few deep breaths, pressed a cold, wet flannel to her face and then proceeded about her business.

Alice had other important things to do this morning – she resolved to take the day by storm.

*

'Fifteen love!' Alice called to herself as she shot the Mini into a much-sought-after parking space, leaving the contestants, an immaculate new Porsche and its driver, fuming in the middle of Carlton House Terrace. Jenkins the art dealer would not yet be open. She sat in the car rehearsing her campaign. After half an hour she touched up her face and then strode purposefully towards Piccadilly, clutching a large, carefully wrapped package under her arm.

George Hutchinson of Jenkins Fine Arts was pleased to be doing business again with Alice. He was a smarmy, podgy man in his forties with immaculately trimmed black hair. He was also an outrageous snob. Alice did not much care for George but she needed his help now. After coffee, biscuits and social chitchat she unwrapped her package to reveal two well-restored Victorian paintings. George was impressed with Alice's work, although the paintings were not quite to his taste. But, after listening to her well-thought-out and persuasive argument, he conceded that they were the type of thing now sought by collectors. After a tense hesitation (Hutchinson had to think of his reputation), he agreed to display the paintings on Saturday on the Jenkins stand at the fine arts and antiques fayre in the City. George agreed to a very nominal commission on sale only and insisted Alice join him and his colleagues at the fayre. He also suggested she might join him for a drink or a meal one evening. She decided to hang on to that string – she didn't say no.

Alice left the paintings in George's safe hands and motored northwards to Silk-Lane Arts & Crafts. Business was not brilliant – she was pinning her hopes on the fayre. A row with Tom was the last thing she needed at the moment.

*

Dazed by events and feeling uncomfortable with his own company, Tom left earlier than usual for St Katharine's. He set to work on the boat at a brisk pace. By midmorning all essential tasks were completed – *Binnacles II* was ready to go. Anything else could wait until Saturday.

While attacking his well-earned brunch in the Tower Hotel, Tom came to a decision, if not the important one. He was spending too much time at St Katharine's – enough was enough. He returned to the flat, packed everything ready for the course on Saturday and then phoned Jenny at her office.

'We can accommodate another two people on the course, so if anyone else is interested could you give them the details and I will see them first thing Saturday morning?' said Tom after a short series of directives.

Jenny was taken aback by his instructional tone. 'Will you not be visiting the boat before Saturday, then?' she queried.

'That's right. Jenny – something tricky has come up which needs my urgent attention. I'd be most grateful if you could take the helm for a couple of days.'

'Of course – I'll put on my general factotum hat.'

'Also, I think I'm spending too much time on the project given the likely reward,' Tom added.

Jenny was hurt. She didn't respond.

'By the way, Paul Scott will be coming along to help me with this first course. See you Saturday then,' said Tom, adding, 'We'll take you out for a drink after the course – take care now.'

'Big deal!' Jenny muttered to herself, only just resisting the temptation to slam down the phone.

Tom wrestled with the pros and cons of going to Norfolk. Was one of his colleagues a traitor? Where did John McAdam fit in – if at all? The need to know drove him forward – the thought of a rift with Alice held him back. He tried to be pragmatic. The chance of finding anything was remote – the trip would probably be a waste of time and money. But he did have some new ideas, and unless he took action now it might be too late. Tom found the phone number of the woman who had rented the cottage in Cley-next-the-Sea to the McAdams. She was in. And yes, the cottage was available for Wednesday and Thursday nights. The decision was made – he arranged to be at the cottage in the morning.

*

Helen Lane's sixth sense quickly detected a hint of domestic tension. She empathised with Alice's undeclared problem. With gushing gratitude she accepted Alice's invitation to join her at the fine arts and antiques fayre. On the way home Alice agreed to stop for a while at Helen's flat in Camden Town. But she soon became agitated, and then irritated. She resented Helen's increasingly overt intrusions into her personal affairs. Within the hour, while they were still on speaking terms, she left.

Tom was pacing the lounge, unable to concentrate on anything, when he heard the key turn in the lock. Again, this time hastily, he rearranged the flowers he had bought, hoping Alice would not see them as a cheap gesture.

Quietly and cautiously, Alice entered the lounge. They eyed each other sheepishly. She saw the flowers.

'For me?' she said, allowing a strained smile.

'I'm not trying to get round you, sweetheart – it's to say I love you,' replied Tom awkwardly.

Silently they embraced – it felt good. Alice knew she had to get things into perspective, but Tom had been unreasonable and selfish.

'How was your day?' asked Tom.

'My trip to Jenkins worked out OK,' she replied, not bothering to enlarge further.

'Good; let's hope it's a success.'

Tom avoided those beautiful, questioning blue eyes.

'Any news for me?' asked Alice pensively.

'You won't like it,' said Tom. 'I must go to North Norfolk. I've rented the cottage the McAdams used. I'm leaving tomorrow morning and I'll be back on Friday.'

'That's that, then. Pity you don't trust me enough to tell me anything. Where will that Jenny be while all this is going on?'

'That's ridiculous, Alice. This is all tied up with the navy and the Official Secrets Act – there isn't a woman in sight. One day I'll tell you – but not now.' Tom ran his hand through his beard. 'You can come with me if you want to. I could use help – especially with that camera of yours,' he said thoughtfully.

'I have a business to run,' Alice replied pointedly, 'and, come to think of it, so do you – it won't go far if you keep swanning off.'

'To be frank, it's not going very far anyway,' replied Tom.

Visibly surprised and upset, Alice resigned herself to the inevitable and poured them both a stiff drink. 'How are you travelling?' she asked.

'I'll have to hire a car.'

'My God! You are throwing money away, idiot – take my car, damn you.'

'I didn't like to ask. Are you sure?' asked Tom, exuding guilt.

'Yes. And Helen can make her own way to Hampstead for a change.'

'Things not working out?'

'Tom, they are not working out in any direction.'

He took Alice's hand. She let him. He put his arm around her shoulders and kissed her. Reluctantly, she pulled away. There were tears in her eyes.

'If you are going, go – just be careful,' she pleaded.

'I promise,' said Tom, who was by now feeling quite wretched.

'And now, sir, what would you like for dinner?' she added sarcastically.

11

Wednesday 11th November

Alice was half asleep when they exchanged farewells. By 10am Tom had arrived at the cottage in Cley-next-the-Sea. He called on Mrs Blackburn, a neighbour living opposite who held the keys for the owner. A well-covered, motherly sort, eager to please but slightly overbearing, she welcomed Tom in for a coffee.

'It's such a shame about John and Mary. I knew them well, you know – there's no more news, I suppose?' asked Mrs Blackburn.

'No, it's a mystery,' replied Tom.

'And how is Mary coping?' she continued.

'As well as can be expected. Tell me,' said Tom, changing the subject, 'did John have any friends in these parts – anyone I can talk to?'

'Not sure, dear – but he might have known some of the regular birdwatchers. He often visited Blakeney Point.'

Mrs Blackburn settled down, ready for a gossip. 'I hope you don't mind me asking, but who was that lovely young lady who helped Mary when John disappeared?'

'You mean Alice?'

'Oh yes, that's right, dear, Alice.'

'She's my young lady,' replied Tom, bemused.

'Oh really; your wife, you mean?' she asked, unable to suppress a hint of surprise.

'Yes.' Tom looked at his watch. To get away gracefully he would have to tell another white lie. 'Goodness, I had better get a move on or I'll be late for my appointment in Blakeney. Many thanks for the coffee.'

'That's all right, dear – call in if you need anything.'

Tom dumped a few things in the cottage and, armed with flask, wellies, compass, maps, notebook, binoculars and Alice's camera, set off to explore the coast and marshes.

*

Tom mulled over his plan, which was based on several assumptions. Given accurate bearings a small boat could, with suitable equipment, search for AMNACS in the North Sea. Several excursions might be needed to locate the goods. The boat could shelter unobtrusively between times in a small harbour or inlet on the North Norfolk coast. Spring tides could be a factor – and they were occurring around now. John McAdam's disappearance may not have been an unrelated coincidence. If so, the likely boat haven could be near Cley. It was a long shot and time was limited. He quickly visited several coastal locations within a few miles to the east and west of Cley. Some could be crossed off the list – poor access by boat or car, unsuitable mooring facilities, the presence of regulations and officials to enforce them, lack of seclusion – anything affecting ease of operation for an imaginary smuggler.

Mid-afternoon, tired and hungry, he stopped at the hotel in Blakeney for a non-alcoholic lunch. He examined his notes from the morning's work and produced the shortlist. Tom's best bets narrowed down to the creeks in the marshes at Blakeney and Morston, the little village two miles west of Blakeney. The creeks of both Blakeney and Morston marshes ran into the common waters of Blakeney Harbour, which reached out to Blakeney Point to meet the North Sea. He decided to revisit Morston, which offered some advantages.

The quay there was largely mud and shingle, with the odd track and landing stage. It was more secluded than Blakeney. There was also a bird observation post, which was currently unoccupied and locked – but on the outside of the building was a flight of stairs leading to a well-raised veranda overlooking the harbour. Tom realised he could use it to keep a check on boats coming in or out of Blakeney as well as Morston. High tide was due in a couple of hours. He decided to stay on the observation platform until about two hours after high tide. It was getting dark. He yearned for an infrared telescope but made the most of the binoculars in the moonlight. There was nothing of interest – no people or boats on the move. At 10pm he left for the cottage. He needed to phone Alice – she would be worried.

Thursday 12th November

The next morning Tom returned to Morston to continue surveillance and take photographs in the light. After an hour of nothing, he suddenly felt a flutter of adrenaline – a small boat was moving in the harbour on the now-receding tide. It appeared to have come from Blakeney, and was making its way towards the Point. Tom hurriedly focused the camera and took several shots. He couldn't see a name or registration mark but it looked like a small steel vessel with a prominent cabin and radar mast. He watched the boat until it disappeared out of sight. It was almost certainly making for the open sea. Tom motored to Blakeney to take more photographs and quickly realised that one of the boats moored to the quayside by the hotel was missing.

He returned to the cottage for a wash and a change of clothes, and retrieved a photograph of John McAdam from his luggage. He needed to do a lunchtime round of hostelries to pick the brains of the locals. In Cley a couple of regulars recognised McAdam – the police had been doing their rounds with his photo a few weeks earlier. Yes, they had seen him before, he had visited the pub, but they knew nothing about him or his business. They certainly had not seen him since the police descended on Cley.

Tom drove back to Blakeney again and made for the pub in the quaint, narrow high street. Instinctively he made his way towards the barnacled old fossil anchored to a stool at the bar. Jo's florid white hair and beard formed a halo around his ruddy, weather-beaten face. His eyes lit up when Tom offered him a pint and settled on the next stool. Retired from the merchant navy, Jo was only too pleased to share his experiences with the friendly commander. They were soon on first-name terms but Tom did not push too hard – Jo was nobody's fool. Tom replenished his low-alcohol lager and ordered a second pint for the old salt. Another ten minutes passed with Jo doing most of the talking – then the course of the conversation turned to Blakeney Harbour. Tom edged towards the main business.

'Do you know many of the local boat owners?'

'Some – not as many as yer might think, though,' replied the old man, matter-of-factly. 'I'm not a proper local – only lived 'ere five years. Haven't a clue who owns most of those boats in Blakeney Pit.'

Tom knew of the pit from the charts – a pool of deeper water beyond the salt marshes but within the natural harbour, and hidden from the North Sea by the spit of land forming Blakeney Point. 'Are many boats moored there?' he asked.

'Goodness, I'll say; some decent-sized ones too.'

'I'd love to take a trip out there on the high tide first thing tomorrow, before I return to London – don't suppose you know anyone who might be interested in making a few quid?' enquired Tom.

'Well I can't; gammy legs and sold my little boat – but I know some who might. The regular ferries to Blakeney Point are scarce this time of year – that's if they run at all. Then there's me old mate Chalky – 'e's got a boat moored in the pit; goes to and from it in a little dory with an outboard.'

'How can I contact him?' asked Tom enthusiastically.

'Ah, there's the problem – with difficulty. But if 'e's ashore 'e'll be in Blakeney. I'll see what I can do.'

'Jo, please try. I'll make it worthwhile. Could you meet me here at about nine o'clock tonight? If Chalky can't make it we'll have a drink together anyway.'

'I'll try. Trouble is, 'e spends a lot of time on 'is boat these days – lost 'is wife a couple of years ago; affected 'im badly. Needs taking out of 'imself. Well, I'd better get moving or yer certainly won't get yer boat trip.'

Jo grabbed a stout, knobbly walking stick. After two hours of sitting his arthritic left leg had stiffened up. With a helping hand from Tom, he hobbled the few yards to Blakeney Quay.

'Jo, I saw a small boat with a prominent wheelhouse going out of the harbour this morning – looked like an old steel fishing boat. I think it came from round here. Is there a boat missing?'

Jo knew the boat immediately and glanced along the quay to check. 'Yup, it was here, now it's gone. Good riddance,' he announced.

'Who owns it?'

'A couple of louts, if yer ask me,' replied Jo.

'What makes you say that?'

'They hang about here banging and drilling, trying to repair the old tub, radio blaring away. No consideration – nasty pieces of work. They use this harbour because it's free. The more people get to know about this lovely little place, the sooner we'll end up with a harbour master – then there'll be mooring charges for everyone.'

'What do these men look like?' asked Tom, trying to avoid a long ride on Jo's hobbyhorse.

'Big blokes, in their twenties – gorblimeys.'

'What do they do then, fish?'

'Nothing, if yer ask me.'

'How long have they been here?'

'Since the summer – on and off,' replied Jo, who was now getting curious. 'Come to think of it, Tom, what are you doing here? Yer beginning to sound like a policeman.'

'It's a long story. I'll tell you about it tonight.'

*

After a meal and a few hours of unproductive surveillance, Tom returned to the pub in Blakeney.

Propped up at the bar, Jo was holding court with his friend, a wiry, clean-shaven man. Chalky was sixty-five but could have passed for fifty-five, unlike Jo who looked his seventy-five years. Their eyes fixed on Tom as he came through the door.

Harry White, alias Chalky, introduced himself with a firm handshake. No sooner had Tom set up a round of drinks than Jo launched an enquiry into Tom's business in Blakeney. Tom went along with it for a while, admitting his friend was missing and showing them the photograph. As Jo continued the interrogation, Harry suddenly cut him short in mid sentence.

'Look here, you old buzzard, the man only wants a trip round the harbour – not the Spanish Inquisition.'

'Could you take me first thing tomorrow?' asked Tom, seizing the opportunity.

'I can take you out – problem is, I wasn't planning on returning to Blakeney.'

'Could you drop me off at Blakeney Point afterwards? That would be close to your boat and I can walk back to Cley,' suggested Tom.

'That's no problem – in fact I was going to suggest it,' replied Harry.

Tom raised his glass in gratitude. Harry reciprocated.

'What about yer fee?' demanded Jo.

Harry was embarrassed.

Quickly, Tom pressed three twenty-pound notes into his hand. 'Will that be enough?'

'It'll be more than enough,' protested Harry.

'There's an end to it, then,' said Tom as he ordered another round, including a pint of the real stuff for himself – he needed it.

Tom arranged to meet Harry at 8.30am at the Blakeney slipway. He gave Jo his 'commission' and left them supping in their cloud of pipe and cigarette smoke.

Friday 13th November

The high tide was just on the turn when Tom arrived at the slipway in the cold, damp and foggy morning air. Harry White had already launched the tender and was busy trying to make room between the toolboxes, tins of paint, pieces of plywood, water canisters and bags of provisions. He intended to stay aboard his ketch for a few days to refurbish the cabin. Tom squeezed into a space between the obstacles.

Passing the short row of closely moored boats the little dory chugged slowly to the end of Blakeney Quay. It then veered north into the main creek running out through the salt marshes. A navigable channel was marked out by withies, long, spidery twigs poking up above the water, and later by small buoys as it meandered gradually westwards towards the more expansive and choppier waters of the harbour. It took half an hour to reach the deeper waters of the pit.

For Tom the scene was exciting and yet frustrating. There certainly were some interesting boats out here – but how could he possibly monitor them? He had to return home today, on pain of death. Tom pulled the navigation chart and a well-used hand compass from his bag, asked Harry to stop the boat, unwrapped Alice's camera from its protective towel and, in cramped, rocking conditions, proceeded with difficulty to take photographs and make notes. To Harry's incredulity, Tom expressed a wish to repeat the procedure in other parts of the harbour. Now more fascinated than wary, Harry decided to help.

'Why don't you come aboard my boat? Then you can do all this in comfort – and you'll have a better view.'

'Where is it?'

'You've just photographed it, old chap – over there, the ketch in the middle of the pit.'

'She's beautiful!' said Tom sincerely – words guaranteed to go straight to the heart of any skipper. He accepted the offer gratefully.

'Right then,' replied Harry. 'We'll go a bit further round Blakeney Point and then double back to the pit.'

Tom continued to scour the coast and then noticed a group of black-and-grey masses lolloping on an isolated stretch of sand ahead of them. 'Common seals,' he announced, pointing to the colony on the West Sands.

'Yes, they like to keep to themselves – like me,' said Harry.

'Weren't there problems with the seals here a few years ago?' asked Tom.

'That's right, the seal epidemic in 1988 – it reduced their numbers from over seven hundred to around two hundred. Anyway, they've survived – that's something.'

At that moment, just as Harry was turning the small dory around, another boat appeared, coming into the harbour from behind the Blakeney Point. It was the old steel fishing boat with the prominent wheelhouse.

'Oh dear, it's the likely lads; they're cutting it fine today,' remarked Harry.

'Do you know them?' asked Tom, taking more photographs.

'Well, I've talked to them. Why?'

'Jo thinks they are up to no good.'

'Well he would, the sour old puss. Of course they might be – who knows? This is the perfect place for smuggling, but they're a bit obvious, don't you think? Stick out like a sore thumb.'

'What do they do?'

'They're redundant welders – always wanted a boat, so they spent their redundancy money on one they could do up. Suppose they are on the dole – good luck to them, I say.'

The fishing boat passed by as they were boarding Harry's boat. It slowed down to reduce the wash. Harry waved an acknowledgement – the young men waved back.

'See what I mean?' said Harry. 'They may not fit well into Blakeney village life, but they're not all bad.'

Tom speculated as to who was the better judge of character – he was inclined to believe Harry.

Things were looking up. Harry was in the galley rustling up some breakfast. Tom was finishing his reconnaissance in relative comfort standing on the cabin. He had some more questions, and Harry probably had the answers.

The two men were still weighing each other up as they sat peering over the tops of their steaming mugs of coffee.

'So you think this is a good place for smuggling, then, Harry?'

'No doubt about it.'

'What about other harbours round here, like Brancaster, Overy Staithe and Wells-next-the-Sea?'

'Oh yes, all possibilities, but this is better. It's more secluded and there are fewer interfering busybodies. It's hardly ever checked by the coastguards – they're as stretched as hell to cover the bigger ports and harbours, let alone this one.'

'What about the people at the bird observatory at Blakeney Point?' asked Tom. 'Surely they must have a superb view of everything coming in and out.'

'Not this time of year, old chap. The warden and his students live there in the spring and summer but it's closed at the end of September. So you could come and go from here without anyone noticing.'

'Except you.'

'Well, that's a point,' said Harry, laughing.

'Look, Harry, I'll come as clean as I can without breaking the Official Secrets Act. I need help, someone who can keep an eye out for small seagoing boats creeping in and out of here suspiciously, especially strangers to the area. If you happen to be on your boat and see anything out of the ordinary, could you ring me? It's important. I'll pay for your time.'

'Has this got anything to do with drugs?' asked Harry warily.

'Absolutely not,' replied Tom firmly.

Harry was enticed by the hint of adventure, and he needed a boost. 'OK, I'll keep my eyes open when I'm out here. But I don't want paying – you can buy me a drink if I spot something.'

They talked for some time. The tide was well on its way out when they boarded the tender to take Tom the short distance to the point. Once there, Tom stepped onto the sea-covered shingle and, with a hefty shove, launched the dory back into the water. He waved farewell and watched the little boat until it was well on its way back to the ketch.

Tom started on the long trek back. His legs were already aching by the time he reached Cley, and he still had to walk along the coast road to Blakeney to get the car. He drove back to the cottage to pick up his things and hand in the keys to Mrs Blackburn. He was very grateful for the cup of tea she made him, and chatted with her for ten minutes before leaving.

He had had enough – and he wasn't expecting much sympathy from Alice. He looked at his watch – the date was Friday the 13th. That said it all, thought Tom.

*

The missing AMNACS and associated items were still hiding in a camouflaged waterproof bag at the bottom of the sea about thirty miles north of the North Norfolk coast. Only the sleeper knew the exact bearings of HMS *Athena* when he threw the package overboard. At last he had been able to safely pass on the key information. In turn, the intermediary phoned Tremain.

'Harry's not well. Can you come?'

'Yes, at once,' replied Tremain.

This was the signal for Tremain to return the call. He strolled out to the street, ostensibly to get some fresh afternoon air. He mingled with the public for a few minutes before going to a payphone. He got through straight away. The anonymous contact relayed the message from the sleeper.

*

With uncharacteristic patience, Charles Fisher had waited several days longer than expected for the call to action stations. To pass the time this afternoon, and to avoid another inquisition from his wife, he had taken his two young boys on an expedition to the local woods. He enjoyed their childish games and wished he could recall such pleasures from his own childhood. As dusk descended the dark ogre-like trees appeared to press in on them. The boys were frightened and wanted to go home. No sooner had they reached the van than Fisher's new mobile phone demanded his attention.

Tremain's message was short. 'Fifty-three degrees twenty-six minutes north, one degree one minute east; Plan B; good luck.'

The plans had been well rehearsed. Fisher knew exactly what to do. Now he had to contact Jimmy Tarrant to get things moving. But first, a more difficult task – thinking up more lies and excuses for going away again. His wife was no fool. She would go berserk if she knew what he was up to. And she never did like Tarrant.

12

Saturday 14th November, London

Their brief overnight reunion was something special. Now they would be parted for another two days. Tom was running late and Alice insisted on driving him to St Katharine's before going on to the fine arts and antiques fayre.

As they retrieved the luggage from the car and made their way to the dockside, Tom summarised his itinerary. 'We'll be spending the morning on introductions, coffee and some practical tuition. As soon as the lock gates open I'll get the boat into the Thames and take her round to the Essex coast. We'll berth her at Burnham-on-Crouch overnight.'

He handed Alice a piece of paper with the VHF marine call sign and some telephone numbers scribbled on it.

'Did you say you were staying on the boat overnight when you return on Sunday evening?' asked Alice.

'That's right. We'll be back late and the lock gates don't open after 6pm at this time of year. So I'll stay with the boat overnight at Tower Pier. The others can climb ashore on the landing stage. I'll get her into the marina on Monday morning.'

'What about Paul Scott?' asked Alice.

'He's due back on his course on Monday, so he may not want to hang around.'

A small crowd awaited them on the pontoon – everyone was there. Tom introduced Alice. Jenny and Alice eyed each other analytically.

'We were beginning to think we'd be skipperless,' joked Paul Scott.

'Sorry I'm a bit late,' replied Tom, suddenly noticing the extra person.

The young woman peeped out shyly from behind the others. Jenny introduced her. 'Tom, this is Sue – she decided to come along at the last minute.'

'Brilliant – the more the merrier.'

At that point Jenny dropped her bombshell. 'Tom, I've decided to come along too – I'm sure you men could use an extra body.' Smiling wryly, she turned to Alice and whispered in her ear. 'And I'd better chaperone that young Sue. God, she's only eighteen – makes me feel ancient.'

'I didn't realise you were coming this time,' said Tom.

'A woman can change her mind.'

Tom looked uncomfortable. 'Are there enough berths to go round?'

'No problem,' said Jenny. 'I've sorted out the sleeping arrangements – we'll all squeeze in nicely to everyone's satisfaction.'

Alice was lost for words.

'I'll keep my eye on Tom,' said Scottie, winking at her.

'Well, come on then, better get aboard,' announced Tom. 'We've a lot to cover before the lock gates open.'

He kissed Alice goodbye. 'Good luck at the arts fayre. I'll call you as soon as we dock on Sunday evening.'

'Please do,' replied Alice, trying to look cheery.

She stayed on the pontoon and watched them disappear into the cosy cabin. Jenny made a point of teasing Tom and Scottie and then waved to Alice.

'Damn little tart,' Alice muttered to herself.

*

Alice arrived at the Barbican before Helen Lane. The fayre was already in full swing. The air of excitement lifted her spirits. There was so much to see – she was tempted to stop and window-shop for a while.

A podgy hand at the end of a pinstripe sleeve waved at her over the heads of the crowd. It was George Hutchinson. 'Alice, come with me; we're over there.'

George led the way to the Jenkins stand, where Alice's Victorian paintings were already on display with a dozen others of similar age. He opened his arms and embraced her flamboyantly. 'And how are you, my dear?'

'Can't complain,' replied Alice confidently.

Full of himself and acting as though she was his latest conquest, George introduced her to his colleagues. Two rival art dealers also joined them for a chat. They were all consumed in the parlance of the aesthete when Helen arrived. Alice did her best to make her feel at home.

'Isn't this just wonderful? I mean, the atmosphere,' said Helen nervously in a slightly overdone pseudo-public-school accent.

'I'd rather be at Grosvenor House,' said George, sensing her insecurity.

'Oh, what goes on there?' asked Helen.

'My dear, where have you been?' remarked George condescendingly.

'I think I'll go and look at some real antiques. Silver and porcelain – more my cup of tea,' said Helen, giving the paintings a disapproving look.

'Watch out for the barrow boys,' said George.

Helen stood her ground and then, putting on the style, gravitated to more familiar territories.

'Where did you dredge her up?' teased George.

'Stop it, George – she is my partner, and she's an expert in her own field,' retorted Alice, adding, 'Anyway, let's get down to our business and try selling paintings.'

'Quite right,' said George, feeling slightly chastened.

There was keen interest in the Jenkins collection, including from Japanese and American visitors. George and his rivals on the adjacent stands were impressed with Alice's stylish and knowledgeable handling of discerning customers and collectors. After a very protracted but ultimately abortive soft sell to an attentive and polite Japanese couple, she decided to take a break and went in search of Helen.

Helen was busy discussing the origins of a porcelain piece with a dealer from Brighton. Alice waited for her to finish and then suggested they went for lunch. She made no secret of her distaste for George Hutchinson. For the sake of selling the paintings they agreed to pander to his eccentricities for the rest of the day. Helen insisted she was not intimidated by misogynistic worms like George, but her self-esteem had taken a battering.

With an air of esprit de corps Helen bluffed her way through the afternoon, holding her own with George. Alice was surprised at her resilience and power of adaptation. With only an hour to closure, Jenkins had managed three sales – but none for Silk-Lane Arts & Crafts. Another American appeared. Alice went through her routine yet again. He was buying for a gallery in Baltimore with a brief to expand their collection of Victorian genre paintings. He was a dilettante and they spoke the same language. Helen watched and listened, spellbound. With George nodding his approval, Alice suggested their two paintings might be offered as a set at a discount. The American took the bait and reserved the two restored paintings.

'Fantastic!' announced George.

Alice was visibly relieved and tired. Helen gave her a big hug.

Sunday 15th November

The demand for their attention was such that Tom Falconer and Paul Scott found little extra time to talk discreetly about events in Norfolk and Devonport. It was already dark as *Binnacles II* made the last leg of her voyage to the Tower of London. They had just passed through the Thames Barrier at Woolwich. Tom scored the course a success, technically at least. The younger couple, who started as complete novices, were now converted to boating for life. They encouraged Tom to produce the next course as soon as possible. The other man would have joined in the enthusiasm had his wife not spent much of the trip puking over the side in force-four seas. She never, ever wanted to see a boat again. The shy young Sue had soon blossomed and was now more interested in getting as much personal attention as possible from Paul Scott.

Romance, or for that matter sex, had not figured much in Scottie's life for some time. There had been few opportunities in recent months. Yet the desire for at least one steady relationship in one port was kindling. The intimate setting with the young women aboard *Binnacles II* over the weekend had further aroused his interest.

Sue may not have been as obviously glamorous as Jenny, but she had a delicate, sensuous charm and the compelling attractiveness of a young flower. She took a final turn at the helm under Scottie's instruction, and he sat close by and made a fuss of her. She liked it. Within their view Jenny was helping Tom with odds and ends, laughing and giggling, occasionally touching him and whispering in his ear. Scottie wondered if there was something between them, or was Jenny just making a point because of all the attention that had been lavished on Sue? He continued to eye the erotic Jenny, fascinated, interested. Young Sue noticed the distraction and demanded his attention.

After mooring at Tower Pier, Tom handed out the course certificates. Amid a flurry of compliments and farewells the students started to disembark into the gloom to pick up the threads of their normal Sunday-evening routines. Sue was reluctant to leave. Paul Scott accompanied her ashore. He returned fifteen minutes later, alone.

'That was quick. So she didn't seduce you, then?' remarked Jenny flippantly.

'Do I look like a paedophile?'

'What does one look like?' quizzed Jenny. 'Anyway, that was no child.'

'She certainly wasn't,' added Tom, amused by the crossfire. 'Well, you two, thanks for all your help. You certainly made it a lively trip.'

'But I haven't finished yet, Tom,' said Jenny. 'In fact I thought I might stay overnight and give you a hand with the boat in the morning.'

There was a painful silence, interrupted by Jenny again.

'And why don't you stay too, Paul? Let's have an intimate little party – it's horrible outside.'

Scottie wanted to get back to his flat tonight, but he did not relish the idea of leaving Tom and Jenny alone. Besides, he fancied her.

'Tell you what,' said Tom, 'I'll invite Alice to join us, then you two can decide what you want to do later.'

*

Alice arrived with a large shoulder bag.

'Shame you couldn't come with us – we had a whale of a time,' said Jenny.

'So I hear, and I gather the course was a success too,' replied Alice. 'So what's next?'

'Tom has some ideas but we need to discuss them with David Price.'

'Yes, I need to see him about several things,' added Tom thoughtfully. 'Anyway, Alice's business coup yesterday is a real reason for celebration – it's in a different league to this.'

'Alice, tell us more,' said Scottie, intrigued.

She explained.

'That's brilliant, congratulations,' said Jenny sincerely.

'I could end up being a kept man,' joked Tom.

Jenny gave him a look which suggested she thought he already was.

Tom then announced that Alice was staying with him on the boat overnight. She opened her bag and produced a set of clean sheets ready for the state room.

'Why don't we both stay too?' said Jenny, turning to Paul Scott.

Scottie hedged.

'Three's a crowd – I don't want to be gooseberry,' continued Jenny, trying to catch his attention.

'Four's even more of a crowd in the circumstances. I've a better idea,' replied Paul, looking her full in the face. 'The night is still young, so let me take you out and show you a good time, as they say.'

'Oh, what a good idea,' replied Jenny without hesitation.

As she stood up, Jenny tossed her head in the air triumphantly and laughed. The golden-blonde hair bounced over her face and shoulders.

Scottie looked pleased with himself.

Tom and Alice were stunned. Tom eventually managed some noises of encouragement.

'You're jealous,' blurted Alice after they had gone.

'You mean you are.'

'I am not,' she protested. 'Oh, this is silly.'

They sat for a while and shared concerns about their activities. Gradually the tension eased and tenderness blossomed. Alice took Tom's hand and led him to the state room.

'Tom, darling – let me into your life. Let me help you,' she whispered softly in his ear.

He kissed her warm, sensuous lips. 'I'll tell you everything tomorrow, I promise.'

Tuesday 17th November

Tom had an appointment with David Price in the afternoon. The office amounted to a very small room above a shop in High Holborn. Jenny sheepishly welcomed Tom in and then, diplomatically, went out to do some shopping.

'I imagined you had a much larger empire.'

'Overheads, Tom, overheads; must keep them down. This is the nerve centre – I see most of my customers outside at their convenience.'

Unimpressed, Tom got straight to the point. 'David, I've put the show on the road. The first course was a success.'

'Great stuff – so what's next?'

'There's the rub. We won't get much more business over the winter months, so I suggest we concentrate on recruiting students for next year.'

'I'm disappointed,' replied Price with a hangdog expression.

'Only a few are interested this time of year – it's not worth all the effort involved.'

Price shook his head disapprovingly. 'Bad show, bad sh—'

Tom interrupted. 'It's not a bad show – it's been a bloody good show so far. I've put in a lot of graft to get this thing off the ground in just two weeks – and you already have the first cheques in your hand.'

'But it's not what we agreed.'

'We don't have an agreement. I have nothing in writing yet.' Tom made a conscious effort to keep his cool. 'Look, here is my proposal. First pay me for my work to date, sort out a contract for running courses next year, then I'll help round up more customers.'

'I'll think about it and let you know – must get on,' said Price, jerking out of his chair and showing Tom the door.

'Let me know by the end of the week, or it's all off,' demanded Tom. 'And here is my bill for running the first course.'

'You must be joking,' replied Price sarcastically.

'Price, this is not something for you to think over. You had better send me a cheque in the next few days or there will be trouble.'

'Don't threaten me, Falconer. I said I'll think about it — OK?!'

'You make damn sure you do.'

13

Thursday 19th November, London

Having shared with Alice his knowledge of the tragic events in the North Sea and at Devonport, Tom had hoped to feel more at ease with himself. He could rely on her being discreet – that was not the problem. What was still nagging him was the run of seemingly fruitless activities into which he had landed himself since leaving the navy. The row with David Price was the last straw.

Alice, however, was almost beside herself with excitement over Tom's revelations of espionage and murder. She encouraged him to carry on sleuthing – but now with her help. She worked through the afternoon, using her equipment to enlarge and develop the photographs Tom had taken in Norfolk. He was struck by the close-ups of the boats – a spark of interest was rekindling. They settled down together and sifted through the information.

*

Paul Scott and Jenny had seen each other every evening since the weekend – they were now more than just good friends. This evening they were meeting at St Katharine's. Jenny wanted to pick up the last of her things from *Binnacles II*. Scottie took the opportunity to invite Tom and Alice to join them in the Yacht Club.

When Tom and Alice arrived, they found Paul and Jenny ensconced in conversation at the bar with Dan Bush, the Texan. He greeted Tom like an old friend and was plainly delighted to meet yet another lovely female. Not wishing to impose on their evening, Tex soon made a tactful attempt to leave. Tom and Scottie would have none of it and persuaded him to stay for at least one more drink.

'John here told me about your voyage at the weekend – sounds like a great success,' said Dan.

'In more ways than one,' replied Tom, laughing, but not enlarging on the statement. 'But I doubt we'll be doing any more for a while. Let's just say I'm having a few differences of opinion with the boat owner.'

Jenny winced but kept quiet.

'I'd love to have you naval types accompany me round the east coast sometime – I mean that, now,' said Tex.

'I might hold you to that,' said Tom.

'Tom, I'm banking on it – and the ladies are welcome too, of course.'

'Dan produced a business card from his wallet and wrote his home number on it. 'Mustn't do this in Japan – defacing your card is like insulting yourself,' he said as he handed the card to Tom.

'Yes, it's true,' confirmed Alice.

'You guys give me a call soon, now. You're all invited aboard for some American hospitality,' commanded Tex.

Determined not to outstay his welcome, he returned to his boat.

'An interesting character,' observed Scottie.

'He certainly is,' said Alice, looking at the business card.

'Yes, and quite a catch,' added Jenny.

'We had better watch out then, Scottie,' said Tom.

Jenny was having her own problems with David Price. He had been particularly evasive since Tom's visit. She pressed Tom to enlarge on his throwaway remark on the future of the courses. He obliged with a crisp résumé.

'So, I gave him an ultimatum – and he didn't like it,' he concluded.

'Oh dear, that explains things. I think that's the end of the motor cruising school, Tom.'

'Really, why do you think that, Jenny?' asked Tom, who had already more or less resigned himself to that probability.

'I think he is in financial difficulties. He's just sold his beloved Merc – and has a large outstanding mortgage on the boat. He's clutching at straws – and you were one of them.'

'Well, that's that, then – looks like I'll be paying him another visit.'

'Anyway, I've had enough of his stupid behaviour,' added Jenny assertively. 'I'm handing in my notice.'

'Gosh, this is all a bit final – sounds like the end of an era,' observed Alice.

'Ah, but the start of a new one,' said Scottie, putting his arm around Jenny's shoulder.

'Hush, you,' said Jenny, blushing.

'Oh, I see,' said Alice, her eyes lighting up in anticipation. 'Don't keep us in suspense.'

'Tell you what,' said Paul. 'First of all, let Tom and I book a table for dinner, then we can all have a good natter.'

The two women settled down to a quiet heart-to-heart. Scottie needed a few minutes to talk to Tom. Tentatively, he revealed the Jenny situation. To his relief, Tom welcomed the news. Scottie was planning to take Jenny to Devonport for the weekend before returning for duty there. But he had another plan up his sleeve too.

'Tom, I'm trying to arrange a little get-together on Saturday evening at the hotel Jenny's staying at in Plymouth. Mike and Nigel, and hopefully their wives, might be there. It would be marvellous if you and Alice could come too. There might be some interesting spin-offs for us if we keep our eyes and ears open.'

'Yes indeed! Fascinating. It's short notice, but I suspect I might be able to persuade Alice to join us,' replied Tom, knowing wild horses would not keep her away.

'Good, I'll arrange a room for you and Alice in Jenny's hotel. It's one of those little places in Lockyer Street, just by Plymouth Hoe – Alice will love the view of the Sound.'

'Excellent, Scottie – excellent!'

They rejoined the ladies.

'Seems congratulations are in order,' said Tom in good humour.

'We're doing a Tom-and-Alice,' replied Jenny.

'You're ahead of us,' said Tom. 'I haven't shown Alice the bright lights of Plymouth yet.'

'Where are they?' quipped Scottie, only just managing to restrain himself from making a joke about Union Street and the ladies of the night.

'Wonderful – don't lose touch with us, will you?' said Alice.

'Not much chance of that,' replied Scottie.

Friday 20th November

It was Alice's turn to mind the shop. Tom wanted to accompany her. It was a first – she was delighted. They would have a lovely day together in Hampstead. Still on a romantic high, they chatted away cheerfully over an unhurried breakfast. As Tom had predicted, Alice was more than eager to go to the party in Plymouth tomorrow. She was just in the process of admonishing him light-heartedly for reminding her about being discreet, when she heard the postman push a letter through the front door. It was for her. She sat down again and continued chatting, waiting for Tom to finish his coffee, as she opened the letter without giving it much attention at first. She rapidly became distracted, and then riveted into silence. The letter was from an art dealer in Piccadilly; not George Hutchinson of Jenkins, but a very prestigious rival.

Tom caught her eyes as they flashed away – she looked uncomfortable. 'Trouble, sweetheart?' he asked, concerned.

'Not really; quite the opposite. I've been offered a job out of the blue.'

She handed Tom the letter. The offer was more than just tempting – it was a crème de la crème appointment in the esoteric world of the fine arts. She was stunned, and thrilled – but… but she was also very nervous.

'My God,' said Tom, wide-eyed, 'you've been head-hunted and poached all in one go. You can hardly turn it down. Can you?'

'What about the business?' replied Alice, hedging.

'I'm sure you can work something out, dear. I love this passage,' continued Tom, paraphrasing the letter. '*We would suggest a salary in the region of da-de-da, but would of course be open to negotiation on terms and conditions…*'

Ironically, it was the large *da-de-da* salary and the commission Tom quickly skipped over that gave Alice cause for concern. She tried to gauge Tom's reaction. He was not giving much away, but he seemed pleased for her.

'You must think about this very seriously – you may become the main breadwinner,' said Tom, hesitating. 'In fact you already are – my pension hardly compares.'

'Does it bother you, Tom? Please be honest.'

'Well, it's a bit of a ball-crusher for an old, macho pig like me – but on the other hand I think I could get used to a life of luxury and leisure,' replied Tom, smiling at Alice.

She walked round the table and hugged him. 'You are a big man, and I love you.'

'And I love you. Don't worry about me.'

Tom wished some success would come his way. But he wasn't going to spoil Alice's day by feeling sorry for himself.

'I'll sit on the offer for a few days – there's a lot to think about,' said Alice cautiously.

'Good idea. Anyway, we had better set off soon or you will be late opening the shop.'

Saturday 21st November, Devon

The drive consumed most of the day. An early dusk was setting in on the last leg of the journey through the Devon countryside with its gentle rolling hills. A cold, foggy evening welcomed Tom and Alice to Plymouth.

The Drum Hotel was small and cosy. It was one of the many such billets on the Hoe catering for a mixed clientele, from tourists in warmer months to those with diverse maritime and military affiliations all year round. Tom was relieved to find no familiar faces in the lobby. A chatty young woman, who seemed like a teenager to Tom, popped up at the reception desk and coped with several distractions simultaneously while checking them in fast and efficiently. They were keen to get straight to their room to relax, freshen up and change.

The time for the rendezvous approached. Urging towards punctuality, the influence of years of military routine, Tom was soon champing at the bit. Alice preferred to arrive slightly late at parties, on principle. Eventually, late of course, with the air of a relaxed, happy couple, they descended the stairs to the lounge bar. They were happy – but also slightly nervous at the prospect of the intriguing, and possibly risky, evening ahead.

They were all there – Scottie, Nigel, Mike and the ladies. Dressed to kill in a chic little number from the latest Christian Lacroix collection, Clarissa swept across the room to greet them like long-lost friends. Alice imbibed Clarissa's exquisite French perfume, which matched her outfit and jewellery in taste and expense.

'I'm staying overnight too. Us girls can have a really good chinwag later – I say, Jenny's a live wire,' said Clarissa, exuding excitement.

'That's super. Is Nigel staying too?' asked Alice.

'Oh no – Nigel and Mike have to return to base tonight. Poor Tom and Paul will be left to contend with us bubbling, or should I say babbling, females. By the way,' continued Clarissa, turning to Alice, 'I don't think you've met Mike's wife yet, have you?' She turned her eyes discreetly towards Jane Morris, who was glued to Mike's side at the other end of the lounge. 'We've managed to get them along this time – with difficulty, I should add.'

Jenny was in her element, lapping up the attention being lavished on her by the extrovert duo, Paul and Nigel. Mike was making a manful effort to be sociable. He hadn't been keen to come, but the two lieutenant commanders had applied a gentle but persuasive pressure. Unusually chatty, for Mike, he encouraged Jane into the conversation at every opportunity. She was obviously there under duress. Unlike the other women, she had a young child to think about. Making arrangements for CTPs and the like was always a pain – and besides, she hated all the snobbery. But she did her best, for Mike's sake.

The exuberant Hannays skilfully steered the conversation and circulation. Even Mike was beginning to relax and enjoy himself. To Tom everything seemed natural enough; the lively gathering, the flowing conversation, the comradeship forged by past adventures, the stuff lasting friendships were made from – it was all here. Was there really some hideous problem? Could Nigel or Mike possibly be a spy or a murderer? Tom had doubts – Scottie could be wrong. He had only heard his version of events.

The men avoided talking shop for what seemed like an unusually long time. Tom felt compelled to ease a toe into the water. 'So, what's next Nigel? What does the navy have in store for you chaps?'

'Damn all at the moment,' said Nigel, quick as a flash.

'Come on now, both you and Mike have great careers ahead of you, and even Scottie's found a special niche,' said Tom.

'I certainly have,' replied Paul, giving Jenny a hug.

'Seriously – are there problems?' continued Tom.

'Our prospects are changing with the wind – let's just say there's trouble at t'mill,' replied Nigel, frowning and looking to Mike for support.

'That's right – we are marking time at the moment.'

'Tell me more; what's happening?' insisted Tom, urging them on.

Clarissa interrupted. 'I'm glad I'm not the only one in the dark. Something's going on all right, Tom. Nigel's leave was cancelled without warning, there were cryptic messages from the base and then to cap it all detectives turned up out of the blue and gave me the third degree. Jane, you live in married quarters; surely you must have heard something?'

'Well, there are lots of rumours…' Jane hesitated and looked at Mike – the worry lines on his face halted her flow.

'We are all under strict orders – can't say anything,' said Mike, trying to take control of the situation.

'Mike's absolutely right,' confirmed Nigel. 'Look, Tom, things didn't go too well on our last voyage and there's a cloud hanging over all of us until things get sorted out. Daren't say more than that.'

'Oh dear! I won't press you further then.'

'I'll tell you this, though,' said Nigel with his Dutch uncle smile, 'it's enough to make me think of doing a Tom Falconer and taking early retirement. Trouble is – Clarissa has set her heart on being an admiral's wife.'

They all laughed, except Jane Morris, who thought it was probably true.

*

Paul Scott had almost given up on his trump card, when it suddenly materialised in the doorway. It was Captain Andrew Fox.

Fox was not inclined to spend his time at parties unless they were conducive to his career prospects. He certainly would not normally have wasted his time on subordinates. But the suitably embellished remarks dropped by Scottie about Tom's sorties into North Norfolk were reason enough to accept this invitation.

Mike and Nigel looked uneasy as Scottie made the introductions. Clarissa and Nigel attempted to keep everyone circulating but the atmosphere had changed and the men congregated into a separate group. Fox latched on to Tom. They were soon reminiscing over weapons trials.

'What on earth are these chaps up to now?' asked Tom, feigning innocence. 'I'm aware of the Official Secrets Act, but they're as tight as clams about their last trip.'

'You haven't heard anything, then, Tom?' said Fox.

'I knew they were off to the North Atlantic; that's it.'

'What do you know about AMNACS?' asked Fox.

'Not much; something to do with new weapons systems – it was still hush-hush when I left,' replied Tom. 'Why do you ask – is that the reason for all this secrecy?'

'Let's just say there are problems.'

'Christ – that's what everyone keeps saying. Whatever it is, it must be pretty grim.'

'I heard you visited Norfolk when John McAdam went missing,' commented Fox.

'Yes. No more news, I suppose?'

'Absolutely nothing – it's a mystery,' replied Fox.

'I suppose Lomax and his merry men have given up,' said Tom.

'You may be right. I expect they have other problems on their plate.'

'Well, I haven't given up. In fact I was back on the North Norfolk coast a few days ago,' added Tom, not volunteering anything more.

Fox wanted to respond but Clarissa, who was hovering on the periphery, interrupted with plates of canapés. After being persuaded into a brief social circulation, he soon managed to round up Mike, Nigel and Scottie – leaving Tom with the ladies. The officers were hungry for information, each probing the other for news of developments. No one added much, until, that is, Scottie plucked up the courage to drop his bombshell.

'I'm convinced Llewellyn was innocent.'

'On what basis?' responded Fox pompously.

'I've been thinking about his behaviour on HMS *Athena*. I believe he was drugged, and then set up. In fact, I did take blood and urine samples from him on *Athena* and gave them to the MDP at Devonport. I suggested they check the alcohol levels, and perhaps test for drugs too. His breath did have an odd smell; not just alcohol. It's only just dawned on me – it could have been due to chloral. In other words, he may have been given a Mickey Finn – an alcoholic drink containing chloral. It would have knocked him flat.' Scott had not yet disclosed the results from the private Harley Street laboratory – there was less urgency following Llewellyn's sudden unexpected death. And he wasn't going to cause himself unnecessary trouble.

'You shouldn't be broadcasting your ideas, Paul – you had all better keep quiet about this. I'll pass on your suggestions,' said Fox sternly.

'Sounds like another inquisition for you, Scottie,' said Mike Morris.

Nigel Hannay interrupted. 'So, what are the implications?'

'Two murders, of course – Tolley's and Llewellyn's,' replied Scottie dogmatically.

'You can't possibly jump to that conclusion,' insisted Fox.

Mike made the visionary comment. 'And then there were four, or is it three?'

They knew what he meant.

Before the discussion could continue, Jane joined them and quickly prised Mike away. The social prowess of the other women, Jane's lack of it and the all-too-obvious attempts to make her feel at home had just turned the whole evening into a little corner of hell. She had had enough – and, in any case, it was time to rescue her childminder. Fox's presence and the turn of conversation had torpedoed the party. Nigel returned to base with Mike and Jane.

To Tom's surprise, Fox stayed on and bought him a drink. The women left them alone and went into a huddle with Paul Scott.

'Are you working with Claydon?' asked Tom.

'How did you know?' replied Fox.

'Just a guess – past associations. I encountered him quite often when we were involved in weapons trials, not that long ago. In fact he tried to persuade me against retiring.'

'I see.'

'Well, Andrew, I guess you are not going to tell me anything more about the troubles – there's obviously something very nasty going on at Devonport.'

'Do you really not know anything?' replied Fox assertively.

'Hardly anything – everyone's being very careful.'

'Getting back to Norfolk – did you find anything?' asked Fox.

'Not sure – it's all a bit suspicious. Maybe it has something to do with what's going on here.'

'Why would you think that?'

'Just wondered – odd coincidences.'

Clarissa appeared and invited them both to join the others for a late meal. Fox declined but made a final probe at Tom before leaving.

'So you think McAdam might be alive and operating in Norfolk.'

'I didn't say that.'

'I think you know more than you are saying. Well, be careful,' said Fox as he shook Tom's hand.

Fox departed briskly, nodding to Scottie and the women on his way out.

'What was all that about?' asked Clarissa.

'You guess is as good as mine – let's go and talk about more pleasant things,' said Tom as he escorted her to the dining room.

Monday 23rd November, Moscow

Admiral Alexai Mendeleyev was irritated by the instruction to meet General Chkalov urgently in his office at the Aquarium, the name of the old GRU (Military Intelligence) building at the Khodynka Airfield near Moscow.

Chkalov got straight to the point. 'I've received disturbing reports of incidents associated with your attempt to acquire British military material.'

'What incidents?' retorted Mendeleyev.

'Events such as people disappearing and dying – surely you are aware of this. Perhaps your agents are out of control.'

'Ah, just rumours and coincidences – probably exaggerated to discredit me.'

'Alexai, my agents are not stupid. There are concerns and I can't just ignore them in my briefing with the President tomorrow.'

'Of course the British are concerned,' replied Mendeleyev. 'They've lost important goods and top-secret information. But we've been careful – they have no evidence to implicate Russia. Our mission is going to plan. This will be a major coup – it will boost our weapons development programme and save considerable time and money.'

'I hope it's successful. But there are bigger things at stake if it goes wrong. I would like to tell the President that you have the operation under control, and that you will abort it immediately if you suspect trouble. I don't want to be landed with the damage limitation exercise.'

'Comrade, as I said, it's going to plan. If problems occur, I will sort them. There is no need to worry the President.'

14

Tuesday 24th November, Norfolk

A muddy green van drew quietly to a halt in the driveway of a small flint cottage in Saxlangham, a little village in farming country a few miles inland from the coast. Charles Fisher hopped out of the driving seat, stretched his limbs and took in a full chest of Norfolk air.

'Here we are again, then. Ironic, isn't it – I suppose this is what the wife would call her dream cottage in the country.'

'Bugger that for a lark – can't stand the bloody country,' retorted Jimmy Tarrant.

'Philistine!'

'Do what?'

'Never mind – give us a hand.'

The cottage backed onto fields at the end of a short cul-de-sac which ran straight into the road to Morston. It was well detached from the few neighbouring dwellings. Trees, overgrown hedges and typically high Norfolk stone walls provided more than adequate seclusion. Tremain had organised the 'safe house' months before.

Despite the delay in receiving the go-ahead, the operation was still on schedule. The plan had always been to retrieve the AMNACS device from the North Sea about four weeks after the drop. Spring tides were due again. But the imminence of the new moon and the shroud of blackness it plunged over coast and sea was the additional factor in the plan. Tom Falconer was half right.

After unloading the diving equipment and provisions, Tarrant slumped into an armchair with a can of lager and uttered his concerns. 'Glad we won't be here long – no television, no pubs, no women. Bloody hell.'

'No time for all that, mate. It's one o'clock – we'd better check out *Nine Bells* while the tide's still out and before it gets dark.'

'Yeah, that'll be fun – bound to be fucking vandalised.'

'Come on, you miserable bastard, shake a leg,' ordered Fisher.

Tarrant opened up his throat and emptied the can. 'Aahh! That's better.'

Grudgingly he followed Fisher to the van, making his point with a loud, dissident burp.

*

Within minutes they were in Morston and turning into Quay Lane. The car park was empty. There was no activity on the quayside, apart from a couple of twitchers glued to their binoculars, scanning the horizon for the elusive bird. The tide was still well out and the small boats were high and dry on the mud. Fisher and Tarrant pulled on their waders and plodded into the marshes carrying large diesel cans camouflaged with plastic bags.

Nine Bells was a small, utilitarian motor cruiser, a twenty-three-footer ideally suited for offshore fishing. Notable features were her strong, seaworthy semi-displacement hull and the bilge keels, which enabled her to remain upright when the tide went out. She was sitting at the edge of a tiny creek off the main channel which ran northwards from Morston Quay to the eastern reaches of Blakeney Pit. From the quay the short mast and the top of the wheelhouse were just visible – the rest of *Nine Bells* was hidden by the marshes.

The mercenaries unlatched and peeled back the blue canvas tonneau which covered and protected the open part of the boat behind the wheelhouse. They climbed aboard using the diving ladder at the stern. The wheelhouse was secured with detachable reinforced panels fixed firmly into place with heavy-duty padlocks.

Fisher opened up the cabins and looked around. 'All looks OK to me.'

'Blimey!' replied Tarrant.

'Perhaps people around here are honest.'

'Oh yeah – bloody spooky if you ask me,' said Tarrant, as he retrieved an excellent but well-worn pair of naval-issue binoculars from the cabin.

'Where did they come from?' asked Fisher.

'Don't know – probably Tremain's,' replied Tarrant, who knew they were not, and that they should have been thrown overboard on the previous excursion into the North Sea.

They topped up the fuel tank and made several trips to the van for reserve fuel cans and an array of electronic equipment. Before long the tide was coming in fast. They locked up the boat, waded ashore and sat in the van for some time – waiting and watching out for anything that might be suspicious.

London

Tom Falconer had left several messages on David Price's answerphone – the calls were not returned. He visited Price's office in High Holborn – it was closed. By now feeling very irritated, he decided to try the boat at St Katharine's marina. It was 6pm when he arrived. As he walked down the pontoon he noticed activity in Dan Bush's large white powerboat. But his attention was soon diverted to *Binnacles II* – the cabin lights were on. Tom jumped aboard, knocked on the door and immediately entered the cabin.

Price was alone. He stood up with a start, and set rigid.

'Where's my money, Price?'

'Who the hell do you think you are, Falconer? You're trespassing.'

'Hardly; you gave me the keys to come and go as I please. Remember?'

Price twitched and moved towards the door. Falconer blocked his way.

'I'm not going until I'm paid – and you're not going anywhere either.'

'I'm expecting clients any minute. Get off!' shouted Price.

Falconer didn't budge. Price reached for his mobile phone.

'I'm calling the police.'

Falconer snatched the phone from Price's hand and shoved him onto the settee. David Price was now looking nervous – his confidence was beginning to crack.

'Now, Price, I'll tell you what's going to happen. Either you give me the money you owe me or I am going to take you outside and dunk you in the water.'

'You're mad!' shouted Price.

With both hands Falconer grabbed Price's jacket and hauled him bodily off the settee. Price started to quake visibly.

'OK, OK – I'll write a cheque. I was going to anyway – there's no need for all this,' he squeaked.

'If it bounces I'll be back,' asserted Tom, sensing Price's fear of violence.

Price fumbled nervously as he wrote out the cheque.

Tom picked up one of the business cards on the table, looked at it and laughed. 'Entrepreneur – so that's what you call yourself, is it?'

Price looked crestfallen – the facade had disappeared.

'Thank you,' said Tom as Price handed him the cheque. 'I hope we won't be doing business again.'

The encounter was unpleasant – but Tom felt better for it nevertheless.

Wednesday 25th November, Norfolk

Harry White set out once again from Blakeney Quay. The tender was less full this time – just fuel for the heaters, a couple of good books, some tasty grub and a stock of favourite alcoholic beverages. He was looking forward to the next few days in Blakeney Pit. It was already too cold to spend long periods aboard the ketch – reluctantly he had decided to make this the last trip of the year. Unlike the last time, when he took Tom Falconer out, when he overdid the DIY and exhausted himself, he resolved to spend only this morning working on the boat. His handiwork needed just one final lick of varnish. He planned to be totally self-indulgent for the rest of the week, relaxing aboard his beloved boat, pampering himself and enjoying the solitude of the natural harbour.

*

Later that morning the mercenaries returned to Morston. Conspicuously, they carried fishing rods and nets from the van and left them prominently on display in the back of *Nine Bells* – not that anyone else was around to benefit from the ruse. Impatient to get into action, Tarrant poured scorn on the pussyfooting and playacting. But Fisher insisted they kept to the plan agreed with Tremain. They fitted and tested the radar, navigation and sonar equipment, locked up, and then returned to the cottage for another night. Everything was ready for their voyage into the North Sea tomorrow night – an exploratory trip to determine more accurately the location of the AMNACS package.

Thursday 26th November

At 6.30am Fisher and Tarrant returned to Morston. They parked the van just outside the village in a recess off the coast road. Loaded like packhorses with diving gear and emergency dinghy, they sneaked, unobserved in the darkness, along the road and down Quay Lane to the boat. Soon the tide had risen sufficiently to release the mooring lines. *Nine Bells* chugged gently through the cold, fine mist towards Blakeney Pit. Its running lights were off. Familiar with the anatomy of the harbour, Fisher used sonar to keep to the navigable channel and avoid the mudbanks. Tarrant sat on the bow, using a torch intermittently to check for obstacles. *Nine Bells* picked its way into the midst of a group of small boats moored in the deeper waters of the pit. They dropped anchors fore and aft and cut the engine.

It was calm. The engine noise had carried across the water to Harry White's ketch, which was moored a short distance away. Harry had worked late into the evening, despite his good intentions, and had celebrated the completion of the renovations with a couple of glasses of champagne before retiring. He was still asleep when the sudden cessation of the gentle drone of the diesel engine signalled something in his head. His sleep lightened; he turned over a couple of times in his comfortable, warm bunk and then plunged back into a deep sleep.

Tarrant rustled up some breakfast on the small galley stove tucked away in a corner of the wheelhouse. Fisher unravelled the canvas tonneau and fastened it back into place abaft. It was now cosy inside, like a caravan-cum-tent, and the gas stove provided some warmth. They checked the navigation charts ready for their expedition to the North Sea that coming evening and then settled down to a restful and inconspicuous day aboard.

In the daylight *Nine Bells* looked unoccupied. It was by now a very well-equipped little boat – but there was nothing particularly suspicious about it. It was no more conspicuous than other boats in the vicinity. No one could have seen the diving equipment. No one would have noticed the passive sonar detector designed specifically to pick up weak signals from the seabed – signals now being emitted from a device attached to the waterproof bag containing AMNACS.

Harry spent the morning in an armchair reading a book in the comfort of his newly appointed luxury salon. Around midday he went outside to stretch his limbs on the deck. He noticed the new boat, not far away. The view was partly obscured by the other boats. He retrieved his telescope and climbed onto the cabin roof. The first part of the boat's name was now visible. For the rest of the day Harry continued to watch and listen as inconspicuously as possible for signs of activity. He had just returned from the galley with a second helping of supper when he heard the noise outside. It was the sound of a diesel engine. Harry slid back the hatch to the cabin roof and peered out – it was as black as hell, and he could see nothing. The sound faded into the distance. He thought it was a boat going towards Blakeney Point, but there were no ship's lights. He summoned up courage to get his flashlight and direct it towards the position of the new boat. It had gone.

Harry thumbed through the local tide tables. The tide was well on the turn – just right for taking a boat out to sea. But this was odd. Few attempt to navigate in or out of Blakeney Harbour in the dark, especially this time of year. And why were the ship's lights off? It was getting late but Harry was sure Tom Falconer would be interested. He made a link call through the coast station on his VHF ship's radio.

London

Tom and Alice were just about to turn in for an early night when the phone rang.

'Tom, it's for you – Harry White.'

'Really? It must be something interesting.'

'Hi, Harry.'

'Tom – thought you would want to know ASAP about a suspicious boat that was moored briefly in the pit. It's just left with its lights off – possibly going out to sea.'

'Go on,' said Tom keenly.

'Don't have much detail. It's a small motor cruiser with a blue hull. The back was covered with a blue canvas when it was moored. I could only see part of the name from my boat – *Nine* something. I thought I'd set my alarm for 5am to see if it comes back on the tide tomorrow morning.'

'Harry – you're a wonder. This could be important. Please don't hesitate to phone if you see something. I'll contact you tomorrow anyway. Take care and keep a low profile. Thanks a million.'

Tom and Alice went through their photos of the boats in the local harbours.

'Look!' exclaimed Tom. 'A blue motor cruiser called *Nine Bells* moored at Morston. This can't be a coincidence. Let's see if Harry has more information first thing tomorrow – then we can decide what to do.'

'OK with me,' replied Alice. 'And if you are going to Norfolk, I'm coming too.'

15

Friday 27th November, North Sea and Norfolk coast

Soon after midnight, *Nine Bells* was in the North Sea close to the estimated position of AMNACS, some thirty miles north of Blakeney. The search was hampered by a rough sea tossing the boat about. This was no problem for the ex-marines. Tarrant was at the helm. Fisher monitored the navigation equipment and checked the map under the light of the chart table. The boat's external lights were still off. It was virtually a new moon and light from the stars was blocked out by an overcast sky.

They had a large area to cover in a short time. The estimated position of AMNACS could be out by up to two sea miles. The sonic emissions from the device on the seabed were purposefully weak and could only be detected up to distances of a few hundred metres. Trailing the sonar array in the sea behind her, *Nine Bells* trawled parallel four-mile courses back and forth, starting each leg of the search half a mile apart. Tarrant cut the engine for a few seconds every half-mile to allow Fisher to check the sonar and accurately record their bearings using the electronic navigation systems. They had already covered the high-probability grid and were well into the fifth trawl when Fisher picked up a weak signal on the sonar.

'Got it!'

'Thank God for that – now let's home in on it,' replied Tarrant.

After an hour of fine-tuning they narrowed the position of AMNACS to within fifty metres.

Tarrant was keen to attempt a dive or two. 'It's about twenty metres deep here – piece of cake,' he observed.

But time was short and they needed to get back before dawn.

'We need to keep to the plan,' urged Fisher. 'If we are being tracked, this trip will act as bait. We don't want to be caught with the bloody goods on board. We'll do the diving tomorrow night.'

By now the decks were awash with seawater. They returned at speed towards the Norfolk coast with the bilge pumps working overtime. It was still dark when they slowed down the engine and eased the boat carefully into the harbour entrance, taking care to avoid the hazardous Blakeney Wreck. They groped their way slowly along the tortuous three-mile channel, checking in turn each of the ten black buoys leading the way to the sheltered waters of the pit.

*

Clutching his third cup of coffee, Harry White returned to the deck. On watch for nearly three hours, he was frozen, but still keen. A halo of skylight had appeared on the horizon but the harbour was still cloaked in darkness. Harry's patience was about to be rewarded. The sound of a diesel engine returned. At first he could see nothing. Then the odd flashes of light gave the game away. The engine stopped and anchors were dropped nearby. Harry waited for sufficient light to scan the scene with his telescope. It was the same boat. He made the link call to London.

London

Tom was visibly excited by the news. He arranged to get back to Harry with more details – but they were definitely coming to Norfolk today. Alice persuaded Helen to cover for her at the shop. Tom paced the floor – he had an idea. Should he, shouldn't he? He phoned the lock-keeper at St Katharine's. High water at Tower Bridge was due mid-afternoon. Perfect, he thought, as he extracted Dan Bush's business card from his wallet. He picked up the phone, and hesitated. 'Why not? Nothing ventured, as they say.'

'What was that?' asked Alice.

'I just wondered if Dan Bush and his boat might be available.'

The secretary put the personal call straight through to Bush's office.

'Hi, Tom – an unexpected surprise. What can I do for you?'

'Tex – I apologise for imposing on you at work but something's come up that demands my urgent attention today. I need a good boat. So, I wondered if you might be free and interested in a little adventure in the North Sea.'

'Tom, it's a bit sudden. Of course I am interested. But today?'

'Yes – and soon. High water is due in a few hours.'

'Where would we be going?'

'Oh, yes – around East Anglia to the North Norfolk coast. We might be there for the weekend. Any chance?'

'It's possible, Tom. But what's it all about?'

'It's complicated – I'll tell you all about it at St Katharine's, if you're interested.'

'OK… is it all above board?'

'No problem, Dan – really.'

Tex examined his diary. 'I'll have to rearrange things. But yes, OK, I'll be there as soon as I can after one o'clock.'

'Terrific; I can promise you some interesting navigation.'

'I'm counting on it,' replied Tex.

Dan Bush sat stunned for a moment. He had just been given a hard sell, and he still knew nothing about the goods. A meeting was due to start in his office in half an hour. It was scheduled to finish at 1pm, but with Young Turks competing for airtime it would almost certainly drift on. He finished dictating an urgent letter and then asked his secretary to reschedule his afternoon appointments.

Two young executives, full of themselves, turned up to the meeting ten minutes late. Dan scowled and lashed out.

'Must I re-emphasise the fact that when I say I want to see improvements in the efficiency and effectiveness of our meetings, I mean it? Turning up on time would be a good start.'

Amid apologetic murmurs, Dan proceeded to dismember the agenda.

'Look, guys, there are some complex issues here for consideration. The working papers should have been circulated before the meeting – not during it. And I received the agenda only this morning – not good enough. We could be here for hours, wasting everybody's time.

In just ten minutes he had prioritised and halved the items on the agenda, and clarified the objectives of those remaining. The meeting finished at midday.

*

Alice was not overawed by the new arrangements. She wanted to join the men on the boat. But the plan required her to be shore-based overnight at Blakeney with the car and her mobile phone at the ready.

'Did you get back to that Inspector Lomax?' she asked.

'Oh hell, I forgot about him.'

Lomax had left a message on the answering machine. Tom played it back again. It was short but not sweet.

'Falconer, phone me PDQ.'

Tom had not really forgotten – he was procrastinating. What could he say about his activities in Norfolk? It was tricky.

'I'll leave it till we come back – might have more to tell him then.'

'Is that wise?' said Alice.

'Probably not.'

'Perhaps you should let the police investigate whatever it is in Blakeney Harbour.'

'It's not that simple,' added Tom. 'I'm not supposed to know about the happenings on HMS *Athena* etc. Don't want to drop Scottie in it either.'

'But if you do find something you will have to tell them.'

'That's true. But this could be a false alarm, and if it is I could be making trouble unnecessarily.'

Tom studied the navigation charts and packed. Alice dropped him at St Katharine's and then returned to the flat to sort out herself and book a room at the hotel in Blakeney.

Saturday 28th November, North Sea and North Norfolk

Skimming the waves at speed, the powerboat cut through the night towards the Blakeney Overfalls buoy. It was just after midnight. Tom used Tex's phone to let Harry White know that they would soon be mooring close to him in the pit. Adrenaline was working overtime. Dan Bush was manning the helm under a barrage of instructions. Once again, Tom gave the command to slow engines. He estimated their position from the red-flashing buoy and cross-checked it against the satellite navigation system.

'Can't be sure of the accuracy of this buoy, but the satnav seems to correlate well. Now for the tricky bit.'

'You mean it gets worse?' replied Tex.

'It's dead reckoning, satnav, echo sounder and crossed fingers from here on. The tide's against us, it's pitch black and there's a bloody great wreck without a light buoy on the sandbank at the entrance. Really need the help of an experienced local pilot. You'd either have to be a brilliant navigator or a maniac to try to get into Blakeney Harbour under these conditions. Never mind, we'll manage.'

'But you've done it before – haven't you?'

'No, that's what I mean – I must be mad.'

Tex didn't ask more questions, but followed Tom's instructions implicitly.

Using the latest marine technology they edged slowly into the deceptively difficult harbour entrance. Like a lowly protozoan using its tactile senses to work its way around an obstacle, the streamlined powerboat oscillated slowly back and forth, trying to avoid the sandbanks. Adding searchlight and eyes to the armament of instruments, they picked their way along the tortuous channel, counting off the black buoys one by one. Once in the pit they soon found the ketch. Harry was on the deck, waving. He had put out fenders and beckoned them to moor alongside.

Harry welcomed them aboard. He had prepared food. After introductions and a round of stiff Scotch whiskies, Harry updated Tom.

'They left in the dark earlier this evening – almost certainly making for the North Sea again.'

'Good,' replied Tom. 'If I'm right, they'll be back again before dawn. I'll keep watch.'

'I'll help,' said Harry and Tex simultaneously.

'Great. We'll have to play it by ear – depending on their next move. But first, I must contact Alice.'

She was lounging on the hotel bed, bored and aimlessly watching the television, when the phone rang.

'Darling, we're here – on Harry's boat at the moment. *Nine Bells* left the harbour again tonight. We're keeping a lookout for her return. I'll ring as soon as we know what we're doing – it may be before dawn.'

'That's fine – just glad to know you're all OK. Speak to you soon.'

The men stayed on Harry's boat, taking turns at the watch.

*

For an hour *Nine Bells* and her crew had bobbed about on the edge of the Outer Dowsing Channel. It was as if every ship in the North Sea had decided to use the channel that night. The mercenaries made every effort to maintain invisibility – the running lights were off and the mast with its electronic devices was lowered to reduce the radar signature. As soon as the last ship disappeared into the distance they raced to the bearings determined the night before and used the sonar detector to locate AMNACS as accurately as possible.

Tarrant made the first dive. His powerful lamp picked out details on the seabed, but visibility was limited. More useful was the portable underwater sonar equipment, which was gradually homing in on the weak signals. Methodically, Tarrant used fluorescent stakes to mark out parallel strips as he searched the seabed. After half an hour he returned to the boat, cold and empty-handed. Fisher immediately took his turn down below. He had been underwater only ten minutes when he struck lucky. Ahead of him was a hollow in the seabed. He followed it down – the signals became much stronger. Suddenly, there it was, partly concealed by vegetation on the substratum – a large bag merging imperceptibly with its surroundings. Fisher fixed a line to the bag and they hauled the goods aboard.

Without further ado they weighed anchor and with all haste abandoned Outer Dowsing. It was still very dark when *Nine Bells* crept back into the pit in Blakeney Harbour.

'So far, so good,' said Tarrant.

'Don't speak too soon – still got to find that pesky little channel to Morston,' replied Fisher.

*

Alice woke up with a start – her phone was ringing.

'Alice – this could be it!' said Tom. 'A boat's just passed us. It could be *Nine Bells* and we're pretty sure it's going to Morston. Take the car along the A149 to Morston and lie low. See if you can spot anything, like people coming out of Quay Lane with goods, car numberplates – anything we could use. We're taking the channel to Morston to check out the boats there. I'll contact you later – take your phone. Keep out of sight – it could be dangerous.'

'OK – on my way, sir.'

Alice put on her well-worn, tightly fitting light blue jeans, warm woolly socks and jumper, and a dark green anorak. Quickly, she threw her few things into a shoulder bag, including phone and camera, and made straight for the car.

*

Tom was intending to borrow Tex's inflatable dinghy to go it alone along the narrow and shallow channel to Morston. But Harry and Tex would have none of it.

'I'm coming too,' insisted Dan Bush. 'You haven't exactly been honest with me, Tom, but I'm not being left out of the action now.'

Harry volunteered to take them to Morston Harbour in his small tender. Tom was relieved and grateful – he could use the help. Initially, they used the outboard motor to save time getting into the channel.

Tom asked Harry to cut the motor. They listened – no sound of a diesel engine.

'The tide's coming in. That'll help us. Let's get rowing – we'll make less noise,' said Tom.

*

The drive to Morston took less than five minutes. Alice found Quay Lane easily and parked just opposite in a cul-de-sac on the other side of the narrow coast road. She turned off the lights, wound down the window, sat still and listened. It was still dark. Patches of mist clung close to the ground like wisps of cotton wool. Nothing seemed to be happening. She decided to investigate the quay on foot.

*

Revitalised by its pumping arteries, the harbour drew breath. No longer were the little boats lying idly at jaunty angles on the dried-out mudflats. The creeks were filling. The yachts lining Morston channel were now starting to float proudly with their masts pointing vertically to the sky. The trickling streams had grown into large, coalescing pools extending onto the banks. *Nine Bells* was now clinging to the side of a broken-down wooden landing stage. Pulling together, the mercenaries gave the stern rope one final hefty tug and hauled the boat as far as they could onto the boggy bank. A rough, stony track ran alongside the channel to the deserted harbour car park. Jimmy Tarrant unloaded the large sack containing AMNACS and stood on the soft verge, watching Fisher's silhouette dancing around in a puff of mist.

'What are you doing?'

'Closing up and securing the lines, of course,' snapped Fisher as he threw the diving gear onto the verge.

'Stop farting about and let's get the hell out of here.'

'We can't just leave her swinging about in the breeze with everything on display – it'll attract attention,' insisted Fisher.

'Jesus! We'll attract more attention if we stay here any longer. A light's just gone on in that house over there. I'm going – I'll wait for you in the van. You bring the diving gear.'

A small section of the missile was still attached to the AMNACS unit. The load was heavy. Tarrant was almost grateful for the counterweight of his bag of belongings on his other arm. Staggering momentarily like an overloaded donkey, his boots crunched loudly on the stony path. He struggled onto the soft verge and disappeared towards Quay Lane.

*

Alice flattened herself against the back wall of the public lavatory. The heavy footsteps were just a few yards away. She had seen nothing, but as soon as she heard footsteps crossing the deserted car park she decided to hide. She didn't want to be the next on the casualty list. Lights from a house in the lane provided some comfort – if necessary she could at least try screaming for help. The plodder entered Quay Lane and then stopped. Alice stayed transfixed to the wall, not even daring to turn her head. The ridiculousness of the situation struck her – it could just be someone walking their dog. But she waited there, flattened against the brick wall. A long time seemed to pass before the heavy steps continued up the lane once again. She tiptoed to the end of the wall, and stared in disbelief. A monstrous shadowy figure was disappearing into the haze. It was no man and his dog. She inched her way out, merging with the shrubs and shadows at the side of the lane. Alice kept the apparition just in sight and followed it towards the coast road.

Tarrant was walking out of the village towards Blakeney. Alice was still following him with great caution. She was sure he was up to no good. Why else would anyone keep stopping to look around? Just as she was wondering what to do next, Tarrant suddenly unburdened himself. Even without his luggage the man looked like a huge inverted triangle – built like a Viking, Alice thought. The rear door of a van swung into view from a recess in the road. Tarrant quickly loaded the goods, looked around as if waiting for something, and then climbed into the driver's seat. The van was facing away from Alice and partly hidden in the recess. She edged back towards the village. The road curved sharply and the van was soon completely out of sight. Alice tried to contact Tom with her mobile phone but could not connect to Tex's mobile.

*

Harry secured the tender to one of the outer landing stages in Morston Harbour. Tom and Dan Bush climbed ashore onto the adjacent bank.

'We'll have a quiet poke around the harbour and then check with Alice up on the main road,' said Tom.

'I'll hang around for a bit,' insisted Harry. 'If you're not back within the hour I'll assume you've gone elsewhere and won't need to get back to your boat immediately.'

'Really appreciate it, Harry.'

Fisher left the blue canvas tonneau where it was, crudely folded on the pile of ropes by the stern. He thought he heard activity in the distance. He secured the cabin, swung his legs over the side of *Nine Bells* and stepped silently up the bank to the path where his luggage was waiting. Instinct and training curbed the strong urge to rush off. He crouched and observed. A light flashed – not far away. Fisher picked up his goods and sidled silently towards a nearby sailing dinghy dry-berthed by the path. He squatted behind it.

Tom walked slowly along the bank using a torch aimed at the ground. Tex trailed some distance behind, as a backup – just in case. It seemed quiet. There was no obvious activity. Tom stopped frequently to inspect the moored boats, eventually stopping at one with a dark blue transom. The beam from the torch highlighted the name on the stern – it was *Nine Bells*. He waded a short distance into the water, leant over the starboard gunwale and stretched his hand towards the engine casing. It was hot. Fear quickly changed to panic as he sensed someone rushing up from behind. He managed to turn in time to avoid a crashing blow to his neck. Tom tried to fight back, but Fisher overpowered him and decked him with a punch to the face. He was about to finish the job when out of nowhere a screaming banshee launched at him. The Texan flung a wild right hook. The marine dodged it and then smashed a blow into his solar plexus. Dan Bush doubled up in agony, joining Tom on the ground. Fisher grabbed his luggage and ran.

*

Suddenly, the pounding of heavy footsteps erupted from the direction of Quay Lane. Alice threw herself into the gateway of a nearby cottage and crouched, once again finding herself trying to merge with a brick wall. She hoped it was Tom. But instead another Viking-like figure emerged. Without stopping, Fisher raced off in the direction of the van. Alice crept carefully to her car and very gently closed the door. She tried to contact Tom again, but without success. She was in a quandary – uncertain of what to do next. Down the road, an engine spluttered to life. It had to be the van. She had to follow it.

*

Harry heard the kerfuffle and crept carefully along the line of moored boats. He soon found Tom and Dan groaning and hobbling about. Harry shone his torch at Tom.

'My God – your face is a mess. You need an ambulance.'

'No,' replied Tom. 'I need to check if Alice is OK. What about you, Dan – do you need medical attention?'

'I think I'm OK – pride's hurting a bit. Try my mobile.'

'I'd rather not phone,' said Tom. 'If Alice is hiding, she won't want her phone ringing.'

'You'll be lucky to get a signal around here anyway,' added Harry.

'I'll pop up to the main road to see if she's there,' said Tom.

'We'll go with you – safety in numbers,' insisted Tex.

There was no sign of Alice or the Mini on the coast road. Tom, Tex and Harry returned to the tender and made their way back to the pit.

*

Alice was sure, at first. She hoped it was the same van that had turned into the road to Saxlangham. It had pulled well ahead – its presence now signalled only by the distant, fleeting, incandescent red glows from the brake lights as it took the bends in the road. There was nothing else to see but the dark, narrow and deserted road winding away through the fields in front of her. Alice needed all her concentration to keep away from the ditches lurking beneath the roadside vegetation. She dared not use full headlights.

The rear-view mirror had become a redundant accessory – until, that is, two round full-beam headlights began to glare at her from it. She cursed and put her foot down – the last thing she needed now was company. There was no sign of the van ahead, but the headlamps were closing fast. Soon they were right behind, intimidating her. She slowed down and the trailing vehicle pulled back a little. Ahead of her was a pull-in – access to a large wooden farm gate. She signalled, slowed right down and pulled into the recess. A large four-by-four shot past with its horn blaring. Alice followed the car at a respectful distance. It was now useful – piloting and illuminating the way, and diverting attention.

Fisher and Tarrant were entering Saxlangham when Alice's pilot car came tearing up behind them. Tarrant wasn't taking any chances. They did not want anyone seeing them turn off into the cul-de-sac. He slowed, pulled well over and allowed the four-by-four to squeeze by. Alice was still following at a distance. The van suddenly disappeared from view – it had turned off the road. Alice parked the Mini and got out. She crept nervously along the road. As she reached the cul-de-sac she heard car doors. Alice took the opportunity to get closer – picking her way very carefully in the dark. Peering through a gap in the hedgerow she saw Fisher throw the diving equipment into the garage. Tarrant put the AMNACS package into a large trunk, which they then loaded into the van.

As they locked up the garage and made their way to the cottage entrance, Alice could just hear them talking.

'We've got to get out of here now – never mind the plan,' insisted Tarrant.

'You're right,' replied Fisher. 'We could just make the 11am train at King's Cross – and it will give us more time to change onto the Highland train. Let's change into normal-looking clothes and get the hell out of here.'

As soon as they had gone in and closed the door, Alice groped her way back to the Mini. She tried to contact Tom again, but there was no answer. She examined the roadmap and pondered for a moment.

'What the hell! If they can do it – so can I,' she said to herself as she blasted off towards London. A weak urge to shout 'Geronimo' was quickly suppressed. She had serious doubts about her decision-making processes.

16

Saturday 28th November, London

Alice made good time to London and left the Mini in an underground car park near Bloomsbury. She ran to King's Cross Station and dashed across the concourse to the departures board. The only conspicuous 11am train was destined for Glasgow. She rushed to the platform – there were only a few minutes left before departure. A few stragglers hurried past her. She joined them – no one was checking tickets at the gate. Alice ran close to the carriages, trying to get a glimpse of the suspect men. She was well down the platform when she stopped for breath, and automatically looked back for a moment – then did a double take. A large Viking-like man was bundling a trunk into one of the rear carriages. He boarded the train before she could get a good look at him. She wasn't sure. The train was about to go. Dazed and exhausted, she dashed towards the nearest door. No, she couldn't possibly – but... she dithered. A guard shouted.

Alice scrambled aboard. She propped herself against the door and watched King's Cross Station disappear slowly out of sight.

Not even in her most absurd dreams did Alice ever think she would be pleased to find herself locked in a train lavatory. She stripped off her clothes and washed off the sweat as best she could with her hands and a generous supply of paper towels. Her face was still flushed but she was feeling better now and her brain was beginning to function again. The door handle rattled. Another passenger – the fourth – was trying to gain entry to the facility. Once again Alice shouted, 'Morning sickness' – how Freudian, she thought, but it did the trick. She quickly pulled her clothes back on, combed her hair and sat on the loo seat for a couple of minutes to compose herself. She was worried about Tom. She had eventually managed to leave a brief message on Dan Bush's answerphone but had not yet had a reply. And now she was on a train to Scotland – and had no ticket. She delved into her bag and with a sigh of relief found chequebook and plastic. But first, she needed to confirm whether the men were actually aboard.

Her pace became purposeful and brisk as she moved further along the train. It was fairly crowded but there were odd empty seats dotted around. Then, in one of the open carriages, she saw him sitting on a seat by the aisle. He must have moved forward from the first-class coaches at the rear. Trying to look as natural as possible, she stopped and inspected the seats. Her heart began to race. Alice was sure he was one of the men she saw in North Norfolk. She had difficulty persuading herself that he could not possibly suspect her.

Tarrant was gazing out of the window as Alice hovered by the empty seat opposite. She pressed her thighs against the table edge. His head turned slowly until his gaze suddenly fixed upon the shapely hips in front of him. He looked her up and down – he liked what he saw. But his face was mean, with no glimmer of warmth.

'God, I only just made it – didn't have time to get a ticket,' gasped Alice. 'Is this seat free?'

'Yes, love, no one's claimed it yet,' replied Tarrant.

'It is the Glasgow train, isn't it?'

'I hope so,' replied Tarrant, permitting a slight grin.

He stared at her but she avoided his gaze. Alice rummaged in her bag and then looked around. Then she noticed another big, well-built man sitting next to the window on the other side of the carriage. He was also staring at her. It was Fisher. Alice panicked internally but managed to continue looking around nonchalantly. There was no sign of the trunk, but the main storage area was at the end of the carriage.

Fisher and Tarrant were giving the impression of not being together. Fisher was dressed in a smart grey suit, a white shirt and a dark blue tie. He now looked more like a rugger-playing businessman likely to push a hard bargain. Tarrant still looked like a Viking on leave, despite his large, chunky white jumper and baggy black trousers.

Alice was jotting down a few notes in her diary when the guard arrived to inspect the tickets. He was a friendly-looking middle-aged man, well turned out in a smart uniform. He approached Alice first. Once again she took refuge in her bag, and took her time. The guard checked Tarrant's ticket without engaging him in conversation and then turned back to hover over Alice again. The delay had achieved nothing – she still didn't know their destination.

Alice brandished her chequebook and cards and smiled sweetly at the guard.

'I would have missed the train. It's most important that I get to Glasgow on time or I'll be in real trouble. Can I pay now – please?'

The guard was not unsympathetic. Alice winced at the price as she wrote out the cheque.

She closed her eyes and tried to relax for a few minutes, until the next ploy suggested itself. She stood up, put her bag on the seat and rummaged through it again, flaunting her backside at Tarrant. She then went in search of the buffet car. He didn't follow. She returned with sandwiches and tea, which she proceeded to devour rapidly.

She could not delay contacting Tom any longer and sought the sanctuary of an empty lavatory in another carriage. To her great relief, she got through to Dan Bush's phone.

'Tom – where are you? Are you OK?'

'I'm on the boat and I'm fine. But where on earth are you?'

'You won't believe this – I'm on a train to Glasgow.'

Alice enlarged on events.

'My God – you've done well. We only came across one of them at Morston. The timing fits. You said the second man came running out of Quay Lane to the van?'

'Yes.'

'That must be the one we had a tussle with,' said Tom.

'You what?! Did you get hurt?'

'Just a few bruises. Nothing to worry about – thanks to Tex, who helped to fend him off. Alice, be very careful. They'll be watching out for each other like hawks.'

'But who are they, and where does John McAdam fit into this?'

'I don't know – but it's just too much of a coincidence. You said you thought you saw them unloading diving equipment at Saxlangham?'

'I think so, but it was dark. The man sitting opposite me loaded a large trunk onto the train. I'll try to find out where they are going. Oh yes – one of them mentioned getting a connection to the Highlands. I'll stay on the train to Glasgow and phone you when I get there.'

'When will that be?' asked Tom.

'Sometime around 5pm, I think.'

'Alice, be careful.'

'Huh – you can talk. *Bye-eee.*'

Alice returned to her seat and gave Tarrant a quick smile. She snuggled into the upholstery and tried to snatch some sleep.

North Norfolk

Tom and Tex were now back in the powerboat in Blakeney Harbour. Tex was intrigued by events but unhappy with Tom's explanations.

'Tom – I want the truth this time. What the hell is going on?'

'I haven't lied to you. I just haven't told you everything. It's Royal Navy business and subject to the Official Secrets Act – you see my problem.'

Tom still needed Dan's help. He outlined the gist of events so far, suitably filtered and distilled – leaving out the murders. Tex's enthusiasm was boosted by the embellished, but true, tale of Alice's spunky sleuthing. He liked her – and he wanted to keep his end up too. His residual doubts were quelled when Tom announced that he would soon be contacting the police.

'Tex, we need to get out of Blakeney Harbour before the water levels get too low. I suggest we make immediately for the

Humber to pick up fuel and provisions and work things out from there. Are you game for this?'

'OK with me, Tom. Let's go.

Glasgow

It was bitterly cold and getting dark when the train drew into Glasgow Central Station. Fisher was at the head of the queue waiting by the door. Alice and Tarrant remained seated while the carriage cleared. She saw Fisher heading off down the platform at a pace despite his luggage. Alice disembarked with a show of enthusiasm. She kept Fisher in her sight but did not look back to see if Tarrant was following. Fisher stopped at a kiosk in the main hall and bought something. He unwrapped it slowly and scrutinised the passengers coming off the platform. Alice carried on purposefully towards the main station exit ahead of her. She noticed the other entrance at the side of the Central Hotel and doubled back through it, concealing herself behind a group of young people in walking gear who appeared to be waiting for their leader. She could just see Fisher between the moving gaps. He stayed put, looking around carefully for five minutes. Then Tarrant passed him with the trunk, which had sprouted a set of wheels. He had almost crossed the concourse to the main entrance before Fisher began to follow in the same direction. They left the station and walked slowly and separately down Buchanan Street, apparently stopping at random to look in the windows of the posh department stores. Alice followed them at a prudent distance. Eventually the mercenaries turned into George Street and then disappeared into the other main Glasgow station – Queen Street.

Alice felt vulnerable. She wished she had dashed into one of the stores to buy some clothes – anything to change her appearance. But she was frightened of losing them. She walked slowly up the stairs towards the entrance, keeping in the shadows, until she could just survey the main hall of the station. Tarrant was sitting on a seat in the middle of the main concourse with the trunk beside him. Then Fisher appeared with a newspaper – they seemed to be exchanging conversation. Tarrant looked annoyed. He got up and towed the trunk to the ticket hall on the other side of the station. He emerged ten minutes later and appeared to be coming towards the exit where Alice was trying to conceal herself. But just as she prepared to rush back down the stairs he changed course and disappeared into the Clyde Bar on the edge of the concourse. Fisher got up from his seat and made for the same venue.

Alice decided to chance it. She had to disguise herself somehow, and besides, she was freezing. She ran into the nearest suitable store and bought a warm, long black overcoat and matching hat with a large brim. She donned the new clothes and placed her conspicuous leather shoulder bag inside the generously proportioned carrier provided by the store, then hurried back to Queen Street Station. She needn't have rushed – Fisher and Tarrant were still sitting in the bar. She waited in a fast-food restaurant with a view of the main hall and platform entrances.

*

Tarrant emerged from the bar, moved close to the entrance to Platform 5 and sat on the trunk. Fisher headed for a phone box on the concourse. He braced himself for Tremain's response. He did not mention the fracas at Morston Quay – that would put paid to everything. Tremain was angry nevertheless.

Fisher reiterated. 'I told you – there were things that bothered us at Morston. May have been coincidence, but we couldn't take the chance. We had to move fast. Christ, man – we've got the goods and we'll miss the train if we mess about here any longer. Wouldn't be clever to spend the night sitting on the trunk in Glasgow, would it?'

'Damn it – you could have phoned before now,' replied Tremain. 'You were supposed to leave London from Euston Station. Did you get back to Saxlangham unobserved?'

'Yes – I said so,' said Fisher curtly.

Tremain continued. 'Get off the train at Arisaig and go straight to the boat. I'll contact you tomorrow around midday.'

'How?'

'Never mind – just lie low on the boat until I do.'

*

Fisher marched straight onto Platform 5. Tarrant followed soon after. Alice watched them board the train and then crossed the station to examine the information board and interrogate a ScotRail official. There was a queue in the ticket hall but it moved along quickly. Alice bought a ticket to Mallaig – the last stop on the line. The train was due to leave in ten minutes. She just had time to contact Tom.

He was upset. 'What happened to you? I've been worried.'

'No time to explain now. I've been tailing them. They've boarded a train to the West Highlands. It splits at Crianlarich. One bit goes on to Oban and the other to Mallaig. I think they're on the Mallaig bit. Does that make sense?'

'Oh yes – indeed it does. Mallaig's on the Morar coast. It's a busy fishing harbour this time of year, the perfect place to hitch a lift into the deep Atlantic.'

'I've got a ticket. I'll have to get aboard now.'

'It's dangerous!' exclaimed Tom. 'They've seen you.'

'I'm incognito – got a new hat and coat in Glasgow. I'm going, and yes, I will be careful. The train stops at several places on the way to Mallaig. They might get off before then. We need to know.'

'I'm not sure,' said Tom, hesitating.

'I am. Speak to you later.'

Alice bought a map from the bookstall and quickly boarded the rear end of the rear carriage. She moved cautiously along the rows of empty seats. There was a woman with two young children in the middle of the carriage. Alice sat near them in a window seat facing the engine. She placed the large carrier bag on the floor to hide her shoes and the jeans showing below her coat. She kept the hat on and buried her head in the map.

Soon the train was plunging through the Highland night on its five-hour journey through the lochs and mountains.

North Sea

The power cruiser was already well on the way to the Scottish coast when Alice called. Tom was surprised that Dan Bush had agreed so readily to his new suggestion that they cruise round the top of Scotland and then down to the port of Mallaig in the West Highlands. He felt the need to enlarge on his idea.

'Given the power of these engines we should get there by mid-afternoon tomorrow – and we'll have our own board, lodging and transport when we get there. We may need a boat to check out one or two things in the local harbours.'

Tex looked out from the bridge to the illuminated, swirling sea ahead of them. 'You did say you've navigated this route before?' he said, slightly nervously.

'Good God, yes! This is bread-and-butter stuff for me. I know the Scottish coast like the back of my hand.'

'But you skippered a warship, not a small fibreglass boat. I'm a bit worried about being holed by flotsam if we go too fast,' replied Tex.

'Don't worry, we'll keep a lookout – and these waters are relatively clear. We can go at full power when it gets light. But we will get tired – we need to take turns at the helm. We should stop for the odd break, perhaps at Aberdeen. You'll love this trip once we get the other side of Scotland – the voyage down the north-west coast through the Isles is magnificent.'

'Tom, let's just get there – alive.'

Scotland

The hermetically sealed diesel train with its electric doors was clean, comfortable, and warm – very warm. Alice began to swelter and undid the buttons on her overcoat. She slid across to the seat adjacent to the aisle in order to see the gangway in the next carriage through the communicating door. But it was difficult to see the passengers sitting either side of it.

A drinks trolley rattled behind her. 'Can I offer you something?' said a young man with a friendly smile.

'Yes please!' exclaimed Alice. 'I could murder a gin and tonic. And perhaps you could help me – do this coach and the next one go on to Mallaig?'

'That's right, madam – the train divides in about an hour.'

'And when do we reach Mallaig?'

'Not till 23.37. You might be pleased to know that I'm coming round again.'

'Thank goodness for that,' said Alice, returning his warm smile.

The train stopped at Helensburgh, where a few more people boarded. Alice felt less conspicuous. While they were still milling about she walked up the aisle and glanced into the next carriage. There was no mistaking Tarrant's bulk in the white jumper a few seats along, even though his back was towards her. She hurried back to her seat, satisfied that she would be able to see Tarrant if he moved into the gangway to get off the train.

Dog-tired, and helped by the alcohol, Alice soon fell fast asleep.

She woke with a start at 8.25pm. The train was leaving a station.

'Where are we?' she called to the woman with two children.

'We're just leaving Crianlarich.'

'Thanks.'

Alice made her way along the carriage to check if the men were still on the train. Tarrant was there, but now in a seat facing her way. She turned towards a table, made some purposeful movements over it and then returned to her seat. She had her new hat and coat on and he was some way off – but Alice was frightened. She couldn't see him now and he didn't seem to be looking for her. She slid across to the window seat, waited a while and then retrieved the mobile phone from her bag.

'Damn!'

The woman with the children gave a disapproving look.

'Sorry,' said Alice. 'Gadgets – guaranteed to let you down when you most need them.'

'Mobile phones don't work well up here,' said the woman.

'Great! Out of range?'

'Suppose so. They usually work in Fort William – try when we get there.'

'Thanks, that's really helpful,' replied Alice.

After two hours of nothing to see but blackness, hundreds of little lights scattered over the hills suddenly appeared through the window. It was Fort William – home of the Seaforth Highlanders. The train emptied. There were only four other people left in Alice's carriage, and two of them were railway employees. As far as Alice could tell, the 'Vikings' were still aboard. She tried the phone again. Fortunately the powerboat was not far offshore from a town.

'Tom, can't talk for long – phone problems. I'm at Fort William and I think they're on the train. So they may be going to Mallaig.'

'Great. Well done. We'll see you there tomorrow – probably mid-afternoon.'

'How?'

'We're on our way on Dan's boat. Look out for us in Mallaig Harbour.'

'Do you know your way?'

'Not you too! Really, Alice – it's been my job for twenty years.'

The train pulled out of Fort William, in reverse. Alice was now facing backwards. She caught a glimpse of Tarrant's jumper in the next carriage. He was hovering by the interconnecting door.

'Tom – I must go. See you tomorrow.'

'But where will you—'

She dropped the phone into the carrier bag, buttoned her coat and snuggled close to the window with her chin on her chest, as if asleep. Tarrant walked slowly down the carriage, stopped by her table, walked to the end and then returned. Squinting below the brim of her hat, Alice saw his legs pass by. She was terrified and did not dare look up for some time. Three stations later she raised her head and looked out. It was Loch Eil Outward Bound – there were seven more stations to Mallaig. She plucked up courage to move to the aisle seat. She could not see Tarrant.

Another hour passed – and then it happened. The train had stopped at Arisaig, a village on the Morar coast. Alice saw Tarrant's white jumper bobbing about in the next carriage. He was grappling with something, and then disappeared from sight. The doors closed and the train started to move off again. It was dark outside and she was in the spotlight in the well-lit train. She lowered her head so that the hat covered her face.

There were only two more stops: Morar and Mallaig, just minutes away. Alice crept down the carriage and through the connecting doors. There was no sign of Tarrant or Fisher – just a couple with climbing gear.

'Did you see two large men get off at the last station?' asked Alice.

'Yes,' said the man.

'Oh, pity I missed them – wanted to say goodbye. Are there hotels in Morar or Mallaig?'

'You won't find much open this time of year – your best bet is Mallaig. Haven't you booked?' enquired the woman.

'No – it's all been a bit last minute and I didn't expect to be so late.'

'Oh dear. We're going to Mallaig. There should be something near the station – we'll show you where to go.'

*

Tarrant and Fisher waited in the dark. No one else got off the train at Arisaig and there was no one to be seen inside or outside the station.

'Where's that bloody Hamish – I thought he was supposed to pick us up?' queried Tarrant.

'Perhaps Tremain has had problems changing the arrangements,' replied Fisher.

'He's had five hours, for Christ's sake – how long does it take? Hamish lives locally, doesn't he?'

'I don't know – and we're not supposed to know. Come on, we'd better find our way to the harbour – it's not far,' instructed Fisher.

'It is with this lot.'

Hamish was lurking behind an empty signal box a few yards from the station, keeping a lookout for strangers. He watched Fisher and Tarrant disappear into the darkness of the lane, which took a winding, downwards course to the harbour. He followed, stopping to pick up his van on the way.

The vehicle crept up slowly behind them. Its lights flashed. Fisher and Tarrant moved casually to the side of the lane. The van stopped alongside. Hamish lowered the window and called softly in his unmistakable craggy baritone voice.

'Really inconspicuous, aren't we, lads?' He laughed.

'About bloody time,' said Tarrant.

They drove onto the small stone jetty, which protruded a short distance into the expansive natural harbour. It was dark and deserted.

'Where's the boat gone?' asked Fisher.

'It's anchored in the deep water of the loch this time. I'm taking you out in this.' Hamish pointed to a tender moored by the jetty. 'Here's a few things to keep you going for a wee while – didn't have time to get much.' He produced two carrier bags and put them in the tender. 'There's fresh water on board.'

'Great,' said Tarrant sarcastically.

Even in the shelter of the harbour the sea was getting rough, and the temperature was close to freezing. The electric outboard motor struggled against the flow and the wind. Hamish delivered the two ex-marines to the small steel fishing vessel and returned immediately.

Tarrant rummaged through the carrier bags. 'Hamish – I forgive you,' he announced as he extracted a large bottle.

They sat huddled by the gas stove with cups of coffee and large glasses of malt whisky.

'Did you see anything suspicious on the train?' asked Fisher.

'N… no, it was almost empty after Fort William,' Tarrant replied.

'Did you get a good look at everyone?' added Fisher.

'Yeah, except for a woman huddled in a black hat and coat.'

'A long black coat and a hat with a large brim?'

'Yes, why?'

'I saw her at Queen Street Station,' replied Fisher.

'Well, you would, if she got the same train as us.'

'Yes, but she was waiting around in the station as long as us. Doesn't that suggest something?'

'What?'

'Maybe she was on the train from London too,' explained Fisher.

'Possibly. I couldn't see her face. She was tall,' observed Tarrant.

'That bird you spoke to on the London train was tall.'

'Yeah – nice bit of crumpet. Give me half an hour alone with her…'

'Seriously,' persisted Fisher, 'the woman with the black titfer – was she on the train when we got off here?'

'Yes, and she stayed on it – I saw her.'

'But you didn't see her face?'

'No.'

17

Sunday 29th November, Morar coast

The hotel was close to Mallaig Station and open until after midnight. Alice booked in and went straight to her room.

She woke abruptly at 7.30am to a chorus of seabirds and a soft, droning, swishing noise outside the bedroom window. The light was already beginning to peep in. Alice drew the curtains and watched spellbound as hundreds of herring gulls arrived in sheets and hovered just above the hotel roof, then gently glided away towards the harbour, only to be replaced by hundreds more. The ritual seemed never-ending. The fishing boats were landing in Mallaig – with their catches aboard. Alice was looking forward to her breakfast too.

The one train that ran on a Sunday on the single-track railway to Arisaig was in the afternoon. It was too far to walk and, in any case, Alice felt too conspicuous. The waitress gave her the number of a local man who hired out cars to tourists.

Mr Ross would not be hurried but agreed to get a hire car to the hotel around mid-morning.

Feeling human again, after a shower and an excellent cooked breakfast, Alice walked across the road to the harbour. The dozens of large fishing boats clustered along the piers were being tended proficiently by their small crews. Some of the men were coming ashore and making for their cars, which were parked close to the water. One of the fishermen, standing with an older man at the edge of the pier, called out to her. Unable to catch the words in the wind, she walked over to them.

'Are you OK? Can a' help you?' he repeated in a broad Highland accent.

'Oh, I see,' replied Alice. 'I'm fine, but thanks for asking – just looking. I'm surprised how busy it is.'

The older man, the skipper, chipped in. 'Ten million pounds' worth of fish caught here last year.'

'Really?! What sort?'

'Cod, plaice, skate, lobsters and prawns – lots of prawns. This is Europe's leading prawn-fishing harbour.'

'Are you a tourist?' asked the younger man.

'Sort of – I'm meeting a friend here. His boat's due in later today.'

'What kind of boat?' the skipper asked.

'A powerboat, quite a big one, but not as big as these boats. Where can he park it?'

The men eyed each other and the skipper gave her a wry smile. 'It gets a wee bit tricky when visitors compete for the moorings. Tell him he can moor alongside us.' He pointed proudly to his boat. 'I hope 'e knows what 'e's doing – need plenty of fenders or his boat will get damaged.'

'I think he does – he was in the navy.'

'Doin' what?'

'Commanding a frigate.'

'Oh, well then, we'll see how 'e does – 'e might like a jar with me later.'

'I'm sure he would. Thank you so much.'

Alice returned to the hotel. The lounge had an excellent view of the Inner Hebrides. The manageress pointed out the islands of Skye, Rùm and Eigg across the sea. They were becoming shrouded in mist, and the humpy, mountainous outline of Rùm, which was farther away, had almost disappeared.

Mr Ross eventually delivered the car – an old red VW. Alice drove straight to Arisaig and parked in a spot overlooking the harbour. She stayed in the car, took photographs and made some notes and sketches. The view was magnificent. The quiet natural harbour and loch was surrounded by gentle hills with snow-capped mountains in the distance. Across the slate-blue sea the island of Eigg was still visible, its unmistakable outline framed between the headlands of the harbour. Nothing appeared to be happening in the harbour. There was little activity in the village. There was nothing conspicuous – apart from Alice and the red VW.

*

Hamish had spotted the red car and trained his binoculars on the driver. He saw her taking photographs of the harbour – this wasn't the holiday season. When Alice returned to the coast road he followed her, keeping well back. She carried on past Morar. Hamish turned off there and waited a few minutes before continuing. He knew she must be going to Mallaig – there was nowhere else to go.

*

From his vantage point across the loch, Tremain adjusted his telescope and scanned Arisaig Harbour and the surrounding village. He picked up the phone again.

'You're sure she's alone?'

'I think so,' replied Hamish, who was now in Mallaig. 'She walked up and down the fishing pier a couple of times and then came to the pub for a snack.'

'It looks clear here,' remarked Tremain. 'I'm going to the harbour to check the goods. Keep an eye on her and contact me again here in an hour or so.'

*

At first the sailing dinghy seemed to be heading out to sea – then it changed course.

'It's coming towards us,' said Tarrant.

'Where did it come from?' asked Fisher.

'Across the loch – there must be an inlet or something by those wooded areas over there. It's coming fast.'

'It must be Tremain.'

'Doesn't look like him,' replied Tarrant.

'What?' Fisher took the binoculars. 'Might be some busybody – keep low; don't want him meddling.'

Although he had used it before on odd occasions, Tremain did not feel comfortable in his disguise, but it gave him the kick of excitement he loved.

The man with the thick black beard and soft blue peaked cap drew alongside the fishing boat. 'Look alive in there – help me aboard.'

The voice was familiar. Fisher cautiously looked over the side.

'Yes, it's me, idiot.' Tremain threw a line to Fisher, who caught it by reflex.

'What happened to the bloody password, then?' muttered Tarrant.

'Never mind all that,' said Tremain as he slithered onto the deck, crouched low and hobbled into the cabin. 'I hope you've been keeping out of sight.'

'We have,' replied Tarrant curtly.

'I haven't got much time – let's get down to business. First, show me the goods.'

Fisher opened the trunk and hauled out the sack. Tremain unfastened the seals and laid out the bounty on the deck. He examined the missile section containing the AMNACS unit – a grin spread across his face. He then turned his attention to the accompanying information which he scrutinised carefully. The grin changed into a broad smile of self-satisfaction.

'This is excellent – excellent. We're nearly there, but we must be careful, very careful indeed. Are you absolutely sure you weren't followed?'

'Reasonably sure,' said Fisher. 'Hamish was watching over us last night and no one else got off the train.'

Tremain continued. 'Hamish saw a woman in a red car looking over the harbour this morning. She was taking photographs. He hadn't seen her before but he knows the car – it's hired. She drove back to Mallaig. Hamish is keeping an eye on her. It's probably nothing.'

Tremain eyed Fisher and Tarrant suspiciously – they were looking uncomfortable. Fisher looked at Tarrant, as if for permission to speak, and then at the booty on the deck. He avoided Tremain's eyes.

'There was a woman who stayed on the train but we didn't get a good look at her. She was wearing a large black hat – it covered her face.'

'Hamish didn't mention a hat,' said Tremain. 'She has short black hair and is wearing a long black coat and blue jeans.'

'It's that tart!' exclaimed Tarrant. 'Is she tall?'

'Yes, she is. I thought you said you weren't followed? What the hell's going on?' The smile had gone.

'Probably just a coincidence – she may be on holiday. But it could be the woman who sat opposite me on the train from London.'

'I don't like it.' Tremain peered through the porthole. 'This puts us all in danger. Why the hell didn't you say something earlier?'

'Had no reason to suspect anything earlier,' replied Tarrant.

'If you had stuck to the original instructions, then we wouldn't be in this mess now.'

'How's that?' asserted Fisher.

'I had arranged for someone to cover you from Euston as an extra precaution. It was best you didn't know. Then you changed the schedule at the last moment and messed everything up.'

Neither Fisher nor Tarrant enlarged on the events in Morston, but they insisted they had not been followed to the cottage.

Tremain looked at his watch and repacked the goods into the waterproof bag. 'You two lie low. We'll try to get this boat out of here tomorrow. I need to send the final rendezvous message. But I daren't do that with all this uncertainty. I'll come back around midnight to go over the final arrangements with you. If I don't contact you by 2am, assume the worst and proceed with the emergency disposal procedure. My first job is to check out that woman.'

*

Alice had eventually managed to contact Tom on the boat. She checked out of the hotel and strolled around the town sightseeing to kill time. The boat was due to arrive sometime around mid-afternoon.

*

Tremain scooped up the phone impatiently. 'What happened to you?'

'I've been busy,' said Hamish. 'A fancy white motor cruiser has just moored alongside one of the fishing boats. Two fishermen helped with the mooring lines. The woman was there and they all seemed pleased to see each other.'

'Who was aboard the cruiser?'

'Two men – one helped her aboard with her luggage. He was a big man with a ginger beard.'

'We'd better see what they do next,' urged Tremain. 'I'll meet you outside the Fisherman's Mission in half an hour.'

He calmly put down the phone and stood rigid for a few seconds. Then he exploded, cursing loudly, and stamped his feet on the floor. The rage was short-lived. He readjusted his beard and cap and prepared to leave.

*

Tremain parked out of sight by the station and walked slowly towards the mission. He stopped and casually lit a pipe. Hamish saw him and stopped reading the noticeboard. He beckoned Tremain to follow him and walked across the road to the public house. They merged at the bar counter and ordered beers. Hamish directed Tremain's attention towards a couple leaning on the counter just beyond a group of fishermen. They were deep in conversation. The woman was tall and had short black hair. The man turned and put his arm around her. The profile was unmistakable. Tremain immediately recognised Tom Falconer.

Hamish moved closer to the couple and attempted to pick up bits of conversation in the hubbub. They seemed to be looking for someone or something. Whatever it was, they didn't seem very sure about it. They moved away from the counter. Falconer looked around a couple of times. His gaze passed straight through Tremain – there was no hint of recognition. They left the pub, and Hamish followed them.

Tremain waited a while and then walked to the other side of the harbour to get a look at the boat from across the water. The flashy, space-age powerboat was still there, sticking out like a sore thumb. He was surprised, even felt disapproval, at Falconer's choice of boat. He was relieved to get back to his little two-room bungalow overlooking the loch. His face was itching. He prised off the false beard and washed his inflamed red skin vigorously with cold water. He surveyed Arisaig Harbour and village with his telescope, and was not surprised when a red VW suddenly appeared. Hamish wasn't visible – but he was there too, somewhere, watching them.

Tremain poured himself a generous measure of Cragganmore and relaxed in an armchair. He had an idea, but it needed thinking through very carefully.

*

Tom and Alice surveyed Arisaig Harbour. She checked her notepad.

'Nothing seems to have moved since this morning.'

A dishevelled youth in grimy dungarees was propping up a shed on the waterside. Tom beckoned him from the car.

'It's a beautiful place.'

'Is it?' said the young man, waving his hand towards a row of fine villas with expensive cars parked outside. 'Just a second home for some.'

'No work?' enquired Tom.

'What do you think?'

Tom extracted a ten-pound note from Alice. 'I need some information – perhaps you could help us,' he said as he handed the note to the youth. 'Have you seen a couple of strangers here recently – two large, well-built men?'

'No. Ain't seen no one.'

'Have any boats left the harbour today?'

The young man put the note in his pocket. 'Let's see now.' He took his time. 'No, I don't think so. It's dead round here this time of year – nothing much moves.'

'Thanks anyway,' said Tom.

'What now?' asked Alice as she drove back to Mallaig.

'They must appear sooner or later.'

'Tom, face it, they might have taken a boat out last night.'

'It's difficult to be objective but…' Tom rubbed his face in an attempt to wipe away an overpowering desire to sleep, '… they must have been bloody tired last night too. It would make sense for them to lie low for a day. Perhaps tonight is the night.'

'Sounds like wishful thinking,' said Alice.

'Maybe.'

'Why are you so sure about another boat?'

'There must be. That's why they're here. This is an ideal place from which to take a boat into the deep Atlantic to make a drop to a boat or submarine without being spotted. They wouldn't have done it in the North Sea – too risky and too shallow for that sort of operation. And Mallaig is too busy – they would be conspicuous. Tell you what – we'll ask Tex to help us keep a lookout for boats leaving Arisaig tonight. At least he is getting some sleep – he'll be fresher than me. If we anchor strategically offshore our radar should detect boats coming out of Arisaig Harbour.'

'Tom, you are tired, you're not thinking straight. We're supposed to be having a drink in the pub with the fishermen tonight. I don't think we should snub them.'

'Oh God – I forgot. You're quite right. We also need to refuel the boat – can't do that until tomorrow morning, though.'

'Does Tex need to get back to London?' enquired Alice.

'Yes – he was having second thoughts about this adventure, until I embellished the story a little. He thinks you're some sort of secret agent. He likes you.'

'What?! You idiot.'

'Don't worry, it's all very vague. He's sworn not to say a word.'

'Idiot!'

'Anyway, he thinks the Hebrides are fantastic and wants to see more.'

'That's not the point, Tom. And talking of agents – you haven't contacted Inspector Lomax. The police can do this stuff better than us. And you could be putting us in danger.'

'We could spend hours trying to convince them to get things moving here. We just need a firmer lead. We're close to something important – I know it. We need to keep up surveillance a little longer – at a safe distance, of course. We must try – for Mary McAdam's sake if nothing else.'

'Oh, Tom! Really!'

'No, I mean it. Once the spooks get involved we'll never know the truth.'

'Well, as I'm now apparently a secret agent, here's my suggestion,' said Alice sarcastically. 'We have a good night's sleep and then in the morning we return by car to Arisaig Harbour to see if anything has changed. Then you can decide what to do next.'

'Good idea – works for me.'

*

The sleeper was worried. The coded message meant 'Pack and prepare to leave urgently'. It also demanded he contact Tremain directly – this was unusual. He left the base in his car. The guards were not a problem – it was not unusual for officers to get away from it all and visit a favourite hostelry in town.

Tremain, in disguise again, waited impatiently for the call in a public telephone booth at Mallaig Station. It was cold and wet, and the call was late. There was no one around, so he didn't have to pretend he was on the phone. It was too risky to make calls using his equipment, or any other near Arisaig. He cursed GCHQ. The seamier side of espionage had little appeal for him.

The sleeper rang from a public phone.

Tremain disguised his voice. 'Do you think Falconer is still trying to find out what happened to McAdam?'

'Yes. But he's also in some sort of trouble. The police have been trying to contact him without success.'

'Why?'

'Don't know. He's continued nosing around in North Norfolk.'

'Are you sure he's not working with the police?'

'I'm not sure of anything – just that they are trying to get hold of him.'

'I have some bad news for you, old chap. Things are moving fast in London. Apparently there's new information concerning events on HMS *Athena*. Something is about to break wide open at Devonport. I have limited information, as do you. But you may be the key target, and could be arrested in a matter of hours.'

The sleeper felt sick. He was momentarily confused – it didn't make sense. 'But security's been relaxed at the base.'

'*Exactly*,' replied Tremain emphatically. 'Here's the good news. I can get you to safety. But you've got to leave now without a word to anyone. It's hard, I know, but it's your only chance. We're all in trouble now.'

Tremain issued detailed instructions. The sleeper did not argue. He knew it might happen one day – and this was it.

*

Hamish phoned again.

'The boat is still in Mallaig Harbour. They've all gone to the pub, so I doubt they'll be doing much tonight.'

'Good. You get off now and have a rest,' replied Tremain. 'I'll probably need your help again early tomorrow morning. I'll contact you then with the details, when I've finally worked them out.'

'No problem.'

*

Tremain returned to the fishing boat in Arisaig Harbour. He went over the plans with Fisher and Tarrant. They were to leave

Arisaig tomorrow, make for the Outer Hebrides and then the deeper waters of the Atlantic to rendezvous with the submarine. It was straightforward and, as usual, the instructions were precise.

'There is something else I'd like you to help me with before you leave,' said Tremain hesitantly.

'It'll cost you,' said Tarrant, joking.

'Don't worry – there will be extra money for this. We need to incapacitate a couple of people first, to make sure they can't interfere with our plans. I'll be there to help you.'

'I don't like it,' said Fisher. 'I thought you said it was straightforward?'

'It's two men I'm talking about – not the woman. They are investigating the disappearance of that chap you eliminated in Norfolk. Somehow they've tracked you here. That woman must have followed you. Anyway, they don't know where you are now.'

Fisher exploded. 'Jesus! I'm getting out now.'

'Hold on, hold on. They are both wanted by the police. Whatever they're doing here, it's unofficial. If we can delay them and let the police find them tomorrow we'll have a clear run to finish the job. By the time they've explained themselves we will be long gone.'

'It's ridiculous,' said Fisher.

'It's the only way to complete the operation. Otherwise we must call it off now and disappear fast.'

Tremain enlarged on his plan. The mercenaries questioned him closely.

'So that it's all unofficial, I'll compensate you for this out of my own funds.'

Fisher pointed a finger into Tremain's face. 'This whole thing smells. You should know that I've left a letter to be opened in the event of my disappearing – and it's *not* with my wife, who has no knowledge of any of this. So I hope you don't have any plans for our disposal too.'

Tarrant looked at Fisher quizzically.

Tremain looked hurt. 'You shouldn't have done that. What if you get delayed accidentally?'

'We'll just have to make sure we're not, won't we? You could easily arrange for us and the boat to disappear in the Atlantic, without a trace – nice and tidy.'

'You're paranoid. There's nothing to fear on that count, I can assure you.' Tremain continued with the hurt expression. 'Well – it's up to you. Do we go ahead or not? It's all or nothing.'

Tarrant agreed. Fisher was eventually persuaded.

Tremain confirmed the mid-Atlantic rendezvous. Before retiring he poured himself a tot of his favourite malt, raised the glass and congratulated himself. The sleeper had been duped. That was one liability dealt with.

Now it was Falconer's turn.

PART THREE

THE RECKONING

18

Sunday 29th November, Devon

By early evening the sleeper was already on his six-hundred-mile journey from Plymouth to the Scottish Highlands. On reaching the M5 motorway at Exeter he stopped to refuel. He also had to contact his wife – it might be his last opportunity. Mixed emotions of anxiety and sadness welled up inside him. He was relieved when the answerphone replied.

'Darling, I have to disappear urgently. I may not be able to contact you again for some time. I'm so sorry. I had a secret life that I kept from you. You may hear terrible things about me. But always remember that I love you. Take care.'

As he put down the phone he wondered if she already knew about his other life. He did not know everything about hers.

Monday 30th November, Morar coast

At 7am the sleeper met Hamish at a prearranged place near Arisaig. Hamish drove him to a safe house close to Loch Morar, the deepest loch in Scotland. The nearby village of Morar lies between Arisaig and Mallaig. The sleeper freshened up and had a quick meal. Hamish reassured him and outlined the plan. Tremain would meet him in Morar Woods and take him to a safer hiding place. They would both stay there until appropriate documents and transport had been organised ready for their departure from the UK.

Hamish contacted Tremain. The next stage of the plan could commence.

*

Tom, Alice and Tex had had a good night's sleep on the powerboat in Mallaig Harbour. Tom felt duty-bound to rustle up the breakfast.

'This has all been a waste of time,' he muttered, fishing for sympathy but not expecting any.

Tex looked at Alice. She was staring into her coffee and looked downcast.

'Hey, guys, come on now – it's not that bad.'

'What do you suggest we do now, Tom?' asked Alice, raising her head and relieved to hear the upbeat response from the American.

'We could investigate Arisaig again – perhaps more thoroughly.'

'Or go home,' said Alice.

At that moment they were distracted by a movement outside. The boat rocked and then someone knocked on the cabin door. It was one of the fishermen. He handed Tom an envelope.

'I was asked to give you this by hand.'

'By whom?'

'Didn't give his name – never saw him before.'

Tom returned to the table and opened the letter. He read the hand-printed message, and read it again, before exploding. 'Bingo!'

'What?! What is it?' asked Alice, startled by the sudden expression of enthusiasm.

'It says, *Need your help urgently. Wait for call at 8.30am at station phone. Highly confidential. J.McA.*'

'John McAdam! Good God. It could be a trap,' blurted Alice.

'Well, you've got ten minutes to get to that phone, so you'll have to decide now,' said Tex.

Tom rushed onto the deck. The fisherman had gone. 'Damn!' He returned to the cabin for his coat. 'No time to discuss it – I'm going.'

'Tom, they know we are here,' said Alice, anxiously tugging at his arm.

'Yes. And we've drawn something out into the open. I want to find out what.'

'I could follow you and keep watch,' suggested Tex.

'A good idea – but no, I'll go alone. They may not have seen you yet – best to keep a few cards up our sleeves. I'll be OK at the station. Send out the search parties if I'm not back within half an hour.'

*

The first train of the day had left. The station was almost deserted. As soon as Tom found the telephone, it rang.

'Falconer speaking.'

A muffled voice answered. 'I have a message for you from John McAdam. Your presence is jeopardising important investigations. He would rather have you working with him than against him. Come immediately. Here are the instructions: drive to Morar on the A830; turn left into the road signposted to Bracora, stop at the kirk and find your next set of instructions under a brick behind the gatepost. Have you got all that?'

'Yes, but you must tell me more if you want my help.'

'If you carry on blundering about you will put a lot of people in danger. Hopefully, the other side hasn't seen you yet. Can't say more now – it's too risky. You must come alone. Don't talk about the instructions to anyone. McAdam needs your help. Go to your car and come straight away.'

'The car keys are on the boat – I need to get them.'

'OK – but hurry. If you are not in Morar within twenty minutes the instructions will be removed.'

Before Tom could speak again the sound of a disconnected telephone purred in his ear. He ran back to the boat and relayed the gist of the message to the others. 'I'm assuming someone is watching us – I can't hang about or they'll smell a rat. Alice, I'll have to borrow that hired VW – promise I'll take care of it.'

'Never mind the car. It's you I'm worried about, Tom – it's dangerous,' pleaded Alice.

'But what if it is John McAdam and he really does need help? It's now or never.'

Tex interjected. 'Alice is right. It is dangerous. You need someone to cover you. I'll climb along the boats and get onto the pier further down. If you slow down when you pass those parked trucks I can slip into the car unobserved. We can play it by ear from then on.'

'Are you sure?'

'Yes.'

'Thanks, Tex. I appreciate it – don't relish doing this alone.'

'It's madness – I'd better come too,' added Alice.

'I'd rather you stayed – in case,' replied Tom.

'In case what?'

'To call the police if you don't hear from us in, say, two hours.'

Tom turned to Tex. 'Don't s'pose you have a gun?'

'In the US, yes – right to bear arms and all that – but not here. But I do have a couple of flares – better than nothing. I'll bring them.'

Tom gave Tex a one-minute start. The American climbed onto the jetty behind the parked cars and crawled behind two lorries which were lined up side by side. He ran between them as the car slowed by the gap. Tom stopped the car and fastened his safety belt. Tex crawled out on all fours, reached up, opened the rear passenger door and hauled himself horizontally behind the front seats.

Within five minutes they were in Morar and turning off the A830. The church soon appeared on the left. Tom found the envelope under the brick behind the gate. Back in the car, he read out the instructions in a hushed voice, trying not to move his lips.

'Continue along this road for 1.5 miles, then slow down. Stop at the portable danger sign. Leave the car and do not return to it. Walk forty paces north. Stick and stone marks next instruction.'

'Is this for real?' whispered Tex from the back.

'It's like *Boys' Own* comic stuff. They're covering their tracks,' said Tom.

'And yours,' replied Tex.

'Yes.'

Beyond the church the narrow road to Bracora ran alongside Loch Morar, which extended inland for several miles. To their left was open country, which soon turned into woods. After four minutes, Tom slowed down.

'We're not quite there yet but the woods are coming to an end. It's open country ahead. You'd better slip out here while you have some cover.'

'OK. I'll try to keep you in sight. Use the flare, or shout "Tex" if you need me in a hurry. Good luck, Tom.'

'And you.'

Hills and mountains stretched into the distance. Patches of fog drifted over the lower regions and merged with the woods. Tom drove slowly on for another half-mile before the red triangle at the side of the road suddenly appeared. It was cold and deathly quiet. He looked back anxiously towards the woods. The mist obscured them. Neither could he see Tex. The low ground in front of him was also shrouded in gloomy wisps of fog. He summoned up his courage and walked forty paces into it. The stick was not immediately obvious. He placed his coat on the ground as a marker and methodically worked his way around it. After a two-minute search he found a short stick. The message was under a nearby stone. Following the new instructions he started on a half-mile trek towards the large hill in front of him. The three rocks halfway up the hill were easily visible. Tom made for the middle rock as instructed. The next message was behind it. The instructions were much more detailed.

Tom screwed up the message and threw it to the ground in disgust. He flopped onto the heather. 'Bloody ridiculous!'

Was this all a ploy to get him out of the way? He tried to think objectively. The urge to know the truth about McAdam kept coming back. Tom retrieved the note and continued on.

The trail took him on a winding and concealed course around screes, up and down hills and eventually into open ground leading to woods.

To avoid being obvious, Dan Bush had taken a long, circuitous route to the hills. Tex was fairly sure Tom had gone in that general direction. He climbed onto a rocky prominence and surveyed the landscape. He saw a figure in the distance walking across open country and then disappearing into the woods. It could have been Tom, but it was a long way off. His heart sank. It would take a long time to reach the woods unobserved – and tracking Tom in them would be difficult.

The sleeper had already been dropped in the woods close to the rendezvous point. He was waiting impatiently for a signal. Unknown to him, Tremain, Fisher and Tarrant were also hiding nearby, waiting for Falconer's arrival.

Tom was becoming disorientated. The trail twisted and turned through the trees. It was dark under the canopy. Ghostlike wisps of mist hung about in pockets over the uneven, sloping ground. There were occasional noises: a bird going about its business; the cracking of twigs, or something. Then there was the silence in between, the oppressive silence which magnified every little sound. Eventually the last sign came into view at the edge of a small clearing. He now had to walk across the clearing back into dense woods to the rendezvous point. Tom was frightened – his heart thumped rapidly in his chest. He slowed down and stepped lightly over the ground, and then purposely deviated from the intended course at the last moment, hoping for some slight advantage. He stopped. In the midst of the tall firs it was dark and shadowy – and quiet, very quiet. Tom stood with his back pressed against a large tree trunk. He looked at the instructions again. This was it – he now had to give the signal.

Tom whistled the national anthem until his mouth dried up with fear after a couple of minutes. Nothing happened. He slid slowly down the tree trunk and sat on the ground. He hoped it was just a hoax to get him out of the way for a while. Then something cracked a few yards away, behind the tree. It sounded like a foot on a twig. Tom went rigid for a moment and then forced himself up. Something was there. He saw it out of the corner of his eye. It moved slowly towards his left side and then stopped. Tom was paralysed for a moment – he could not turn his head.

'Tremain?'

The hesitant voice came again. 'Tremain – is that you?'

Tom's thoughts raced as he turned slowly towards the figure in the shadows. *Who the hell is Tremain?* Instinct told him not to answer. The voice puzzled him. It had a strained, anxious quality, but there was something else – it was familiar. He could not yet see the face clearly. But the bear-like outline of the man hovering in the shadows confirmed his worst suspicion. It was not John McAdam. It was Nigel Hannay.

The men eyed each other warily. Neither spoke for several seconds – the wrong word might be their last.

Hannay forced a grin and broke the silence. 'Well, well – I never dreamed it was you, Tom.'

'Who did you expect, then?'

Hannay ignored the question. He was confused. He wanted it to be Tremain – it was his only way out. He couldn't go back. They would be looking for him soon. But how could Falconer possibly be Tremain? Something was wrong.

'First things first,' said Hannay. 'Which project?'

Tom hesitated – the reply had to be correct. He took a chance and guessed. 'Athena.'

It was the wrong answer. Hannay said nothing but his face gave him away.

'I'm waiting for John McAdam. How about you?' said Tom, as he put his hand in his coat pocket and clutched the flare.

'McAdam? I don't understand.'

'What happened in Norfolk?' asked Tom.

'I don't know. Do you?'

'No. So who arranged this meeting?'

Suddenly, Hannay pulled out a pistol and pointed it at Tom. 'Do exactly as I say. No rapid movements. Take your hands slowly out of your pockets and raise them above your head.'

Tom obeyed, slowly. 'So we've both been double-crossed.'

Hannay did not reply. He was nervous and looked around cautiously. A movement in the woods distracted him. Tom stepped sideways and launched a rugger tackle into Hannay's body. Hannay dropped the gun. The men fought briefly but Hannay soon overpowered Tom. After two heavy punches to the head, Tom sank, unconscious, to the ground.

Before Hannay could retrieve the gun he was suddenly attacked from behind. Fisher and Tarrant rendered him unconscious.

Tremain appeared. He picked up the gun and wiped it clean. 'This is very convenient – couldn't have arranged things better myself. Prop this one against the tree.'

Fisher obliged. Hannay's head flopped limply onto his chest.

'Step aside,' ordered Tremain as he held the gun close to Tom and pointed it at Hannay.

'What the hell are you doing?' said Fisher.

'Tidying things up, once and for all.'

Tremain pulled the trigger. The sharp crack echoed through the woods. Hannay's body slumped to the ground, with a hole in its chest.

Fisher jumped at Tremain and disarmed him. 'Christ! You bloody fool.' He pointed at Tom, who was still out for the count. 'And what do we do with him?'

Tremain was not intimidated by the ex-marine. 'Just wait, will you?! Everything's planned and under control. He knows nothing. The police are looking for him. We'll give them something to occupy their time and divert attention away from us. Give me the gun – we need to make him the suspect. An anonymous phone call will tip off the police.'

Tremain wiped the gun clean again and wrapped Tom's fingers around it. He then placed it beneath some leaves a few yards from the body. On the double, the mercenaries rushed Tom's groaning, now semi-conscious, bulk through the woods and dumped him two hundred yards from the corpse.

Tremain was pleased with himself. Hannay had been silenced and Falconer had been framed for his murder.

19

There was no doubt – it was a gunshot. Immediately he heard it, Tex started to work his way around the woods, making short, stealthy excursions in among the trees. He looked upwards, hoping to see a flare, but the trees and the elevated ground obscured his view of the sky. Another inland loch appeared, limiting the northern reach of the woods. He stopped at the water, wondering what to do next. He had to get onto higher ground. Suppressing his fear, Dan Bush ran half a mile to the foot of a hill and marched up it until he could see over the tops of the trees. He surveyed the woods and cupped his ears in an attempt to capture distant sounds. He stayed five minutes – but there was nothing significant. His initial reaction was to get help. But that would take time. And what if Tom was injured and in need of urgent assistance? He looked over the tops of the trees again. The woods were not that extensive – about a mile across.

Caution had had a chance – it was time to be bold. Tex hurled himself towards the trees, taking long strides across the open ground. At first he made for the northern edge, intending to search the woods in a zigzag fashion. But halfway he changed his mind and charged straight through the middle, stopping every minute to shout, 'Tom!' His regular sessions at the health club were paying off. Now adrenaline was pushing him forward and hype was suppressing fear.

Much sooner than expected he ground to a halt at a river which crossed the woods from north to south, linking the lochs.

'Tom!'

He turned to each point of the compass and shouted again, even louder. After a minute he repeated the process and waited in silence.

Suddenly, a faint voice in the distance called his name. Dan hurried through the dense shadowy array of tree trunks. He could not see far ahead. He stopped and called again. A groaning reply came back immediately, louder this time, not far to his left. He ran on, rushing in and out of the trees.

And suddenly, there it was – the sight. Tom Falconer was staggering around holding his head, with blood all over his face. It seemed familiar.

'Tex – am I pleased to see you. We've no time to lose – help me to the car.'

'But what happened?'

'I'll explain when we get back – but we must hurry.'

'But are you fit enough? Were you shot?'

'Shot?!' exclaimed Tom.

'I heard a shot,' replied Tex.

Tom examined his head. 'Not sure, but I seem to be alive and kicking. There was a gun, but I can't remember what happened.'

'Better go straight to the police,' urged Tex.

'No, not yet – we must get back to the boat first.'

Tom struggled. Tex held his arm. They made their way slowly towards the car.

*

Tremain, Fisher and Tarrant were back in Arisaig. Hamish would soon be joining the mercenaries to take them out to the boat in Arisaig Harbour.

'This is where we say goodbye,' announced Tremain. 'You should have a smooth run from here on. Send me a message as soon as you return from the Atlantic. Good luck.'

'Yeah, we need it,' replied Tarrant. 'Don't try the dirty on us – or we'll come looking for you.'

'Just do your job.'

Without another word Tremain started his journey back to the south. He needed to keep his alibi intact. He stopped briefly on the outskirts of Arisaig to make the anonymous call to the local police at Mallaig.

*

Back in the white powerboat in Mallaig Harbour, Tom's wounds were being cleaned and dressed by Alice and Tex. His refusal to be taken to a doctor increased Alice's concern, and her anger. Tom attempted to defuse the situation by announcing that he would contact the MDP immediately.

'You will both learn more about what happened when I explain events to the police,' he said, as he borrowed Alice's mobile phone. 'It's almost unbelievable – but it makes sense now.'

Tom eventually got through to Lomax. He waited for a lull in the reading of the Riot Act.

'Inspector – I have vital information. It's urgent – please just listen for a minute. As you know, I also have been trying to make sense of John McAdam's disappearance. I found nothing else relevant to that in North Norfolk – but I did notice other events. These might be related to whatever happened on HMS *Athena* in the North Sea. No one would say much about that but I gathered that something important went missing. The point is – I noticed a suspicious boat bringing goods into Morston Harbour at night. I tried to investigate but got attacked. Fortunately a friend helped fend off the man. I won't go into details of how I know, but two large, fit men, probably military or ex-military, travelled with goods from North Norfolk to King's Cross Station and then by train to the West Highlands of Scotland. They got off at Arisaig – a very convenient place to take a boat out to the Atlantic.'

'So what?' interrupted Lomax.

'The Atlantic beyond the Outer Hebrides is an ideal place to make a drop, to a submarine or another boat.'

'Falconer, this is fanciful. Look here—'

Before Lomax could continue, Tom interrupted. 'No – please listen. It gets worse – much worse. I came round to this part of Scotland in a friend's boat to try to investigate. I was just beginning to get despondent, thinking I was deluded and it was all a waste of time, when it happened. I got anonymous messages to meet John McAdam in woods near Loch Morar, a stone's throw from Arisaig. But it wasn't McAdam – it was Lieutenant Commander Nigel Hannay. He was expecting to meet someone called Tremain and initially thought it was me using an alias. He knew nothing about McAdam, allegedly.

So, we had both been set up. When he realised I wasn't this Tremain person he pulled a gun on me. We fought and he left me unconscious. Fortunately, my friend found me and brought me back to his boat in Mallaig Harbour, where I'm phoning from now.'

There was silence. Tom looked at Alice. Her eyes were wide and staring and her jaw had dropped in astonishment.

'There's something else,' continued Tom. 'My friend heard a gunshot but I haven't been hit. When I came round, Hannay was nowhere to be seen.'

'When did this happen?' asked Lomax.

'Just over an hour ago. Look, Inspector, I must go now – got a stinking headache which might need medical attention. I'll give you this phone number and details of our boat etc. Oh yes, I forgot to mention it – the suspect motor cruiser in Morston Harbour was called *Nine Bells*. It may still be there.'

'Falconer, you must report the incident to the local police as soon as possible. With different forces and organisations involved I have to be careful not to tread on more toes. I'll contact you later.'

Tom gave Lomax the details and smartly cut off the phone.

'So, Nigel Hannay is the traitor,' exclaimed Alice.

'It all fits,' replied Tom, hoping Alice would not mention the murders in front of Tex.

She didn't.

'By the way, I haven't got a stinking headache – just wanted to get off the phone,' added Tom. 'I feel OK now. I'll understand if you both object, but I really would like to go to Arisaig Harbour to see if any boats have left since we last checked.'

'But, Tom,' Alice replied, 'they, whoever *they* are, know we are here in a bloody great white boat. We'll be a bit obvious.'

'*They* should have gone by now – just need to know if a boat has left. In any case, this boat can outrun any other boat I've seen here.'

'Oh, really?!' exclaimed Alice.

Dan Bush intervened. 'It's fascinating. There are obviously things I shouldn't know about – so I won't ask. But who is Nigel Hannay?'

'He was a senior officer on my frigate,' replied Tom. He was a friend as well as a colleague – or so I thought.'

'I'm game for the trip to Arisaig, after we've refuelled,' announced Tex.

'OK,' said Alice. 'Two to one – I give in. Let's go.'

The Inner Hebrides

Arisaig and the Morar coast were now ten miles behind them and fast disappearing out of sight. Fisher took the boat round the southern tip of Eigg, as close as he dared. The sea could be treacherous around the islands – rocks under the surface lay in wait for the inexperienced. They had reached the Sound of Eigg, the stretch of sea lying between Eigg and the smaller island of Muck to the south-west. These, and the nearby islands of Rùm and Canna, constitute the Small Isles of the Inner Hebrides, lying just south of the much larger, and better known, island of Skye. The Small Isles are not insignificant – their prominent and characterful mountains reach up far above the sea. The Inner Hebrides formed a convenient barrier. Once beyond them, to the west, their boat would be undetectable from the Morar coast.

Tarrant put down the binoculars and drew a sigh of relief. 'So far, so good.'

'Nothing following us?' enquired Fisher.

'Nothing yet.'

'I'll be happier when we get to the Outer Hebrides and nothing's following us,' added Fisher.

'I won't be happy until it's all over,' said Tarrant. 'I've got a bad feeling about this trip. By the way, did you really leave a letter to be opened if you don't return?'

'No.'

'It was a good idea to say that,' added Tarrant.

'Suddenly sprung to mind – I don't trust the bugger. We may be pawns in Tremain's game, but we can spoil it for him, and he knows it. Trouble is,' continued Fisher, 'Tremain may not be our only problem.'

'Yeah – especially with a corpse waiting for the police at Morar. And there's that bloke and the woman.'

'I wasn't thinking of them. I have a nasty feeling about Tremain and his network – too many cooks.'

'What do you mean?' queried Tarrant.

'I mean, who's really in charge now? We know it's a Russian operation. But what's happening with their intelligence network now that Gorbachev's gone and the KGB's cracked up?'

'See what you mean, old mate.' Tarrant removed a long package from his bag and unwrapped it. 'I don't trust any bugger.'

Fisher looked at him and laughed.

Tarrant brandished a sub-machine gun and loaded the magazine ready for action.

*

The powerboat had departed from Mallaig Harbour on the start of its eight-mile journey along the coast. Tom was at the helm – navigation into Arisaig could be tricky. Tex was happy to watch.

'Keep a lookout for anything crossing,' called Tom.

'I am,' replied Alice, as she picked up the binoculars once again.

There were no boats going from the mainland to the islands. Soon the north point of Muck lined up with the south point of Eigg, providing Tom with the leading line, the recommended navigation route, for Loch nan Ceall and Arisaig Harbour. He found the south channel and followed the perches along its winding course into the loch.

Alice carefully scanned the boats in Arisaig Harbour as they came into view. She referred to her sketches and looked through the glasses again, and then repeated the operation quickly.

'What is it?' asked Tex.

'Don't get too excited yet, but I think there's a boat missing,' she replied cautiously.

'Where? What sort of boat?' demanded Tom instantly.

Alice pointed to an assortment of boats, mostly small ones, anchored close together. 'I'm sure there was another boat to the side of that group. Take us nearer. I need to see them from another angle to be sure.'

Tom obeyed without saying another word. But his excitement was obvious. She wanted to be absolutely sure before committing herself again.

Three minutes passed.

'Yes – definitely.'

'Show me,' said Tom as he stopped the engines.

They looked at Alice's sketches.

'This one,' she said, pointing to a squiggle among a lot of other squiggles.

'A fishing boat?' queried Tom.

'Yes, that sort of boat. A bit like those at Mallaig but smaller. It was definitely here yesterday. I've taken photographs but they need developing.'

Tex interjected. 'Tom, you were right. They must have left on the tide earlier this morning, while you were conveniently out of the way.'

'But where are they now?' asked Alice.

'In the Sea of the Hebrides on the other side of those islands, I expect,' replied Tom. 'I would like to try to confirm that before we call in the heavy mob. If we keep our distance we may see them before they can see us. We haven't a minute to lose – let's go.'

20

Early afternoon, Monday 30th November

The body had been found. Initially, the police inspector covering the Morar district was in charge of the crime scene. After securing the area around the body he followed protocol and informed the office of the procurator fiscal. Apart from confirming death, the local police took care not to disturb the body or its surrounds. But they were assuming murder – there was blood on the clothes covering the chest and there were reports of a gunshot. Accordingly, the Specialist Crime Division activated a Major Investigation Team. Forensic and crime scene specialists were flown in from Glasgow.

Initial examination of the body confirmed a bullet wound in the chest. Evidence of identification was found in a wallet. Further enquiries confirmed that Nigel Hannay was a serving naval officer, and he was AWOL. The Ministry of Defence Police were now also involved.

A wider search of the area uncovered the gun, which was sent away for urgent forensic examination. The body was moved to Glasgow and arrangements were made to contact Clarissa Hannay.

News of the death soon reached Inspector Adrian Lomax of the MDP. He was already aware of Hannay's absence. This all appeared to make Tom Falconer's account of events more credible. Lomax had fallen out of favour. His own investigations in Devonport had disappointed the intelligence agents, who had, up to now, supported him. He took a chance and relayed recent events and his and Falconer's views to the relevant agencies.

Soon, Lomax and his sergeant, and agents from Special Branch and Intelligence, were on flights to the West Highlands of Scotland.

*

Dan Bush's motor cruiser was well on the way to the Outer Hebrides when Alice called out from the flybridge.

'Tom, I can see the top of a boat in the distance – just masts and things.'

Tom took the binoculars and scoured the horizon. 'Yes. It looks like a fishing trawler.'

He asked Tex to slow down to a slow cruising speed. 'If we keep back at this distance they may not see us – their wheelhouse is lower than those structures. I want to know if they're going on beyond the Hebrides.'

'Of course, it might just be an innocent fishing boat going about its normal business,' observed Tex.

'I know,' replied Tom. 'I'll contact Inspector Lomax when we reach the Outer Hebrides and then we can return to Mallaig. If there's something suspicious the navy can sort it out.'

Dusk had already descended when the mercenaries sailed past the southern tip of the Outer Hebrides. Their lights remained off. This was suspicious. Tom insisted on continuing for a short while, tracking the boat's direction with radar. He transmitted details to Lomax's office. Tex turned the boat around and made for Mallaig at full speed.

It was just after 8pm when the white motor cruiser berthed in Mallaig Harbour. The police were waiting. Tom Falconer was arrested and cautioned. Dan Bush and Alice Silk were also accompanied to the local police station for questioning.

*

Lomax and the officer from Special Branch listened in as the local inspector initiated the interview with Falconer.

'You admitted to being with Lieutenant Commander Hannay in the woods. He was killed around that time. We've now confirmed that your fingerprints are on the gun that killed him. And your clothes have evidence of gunshot residue on them. Just admit it, Falconer – you killed him.'

'No – I didn't! Hannay pulled a gun on me and we fought. I was knocked unconscious and can remember little else. But I'm sure he was alive up to that point.'

'OK – perhaps it was self-defence or an accident,' suggested the inspector. 'Perhaps you struggled and the gun went off, killing Hannay instead of you.'

'No, I don't think so. I'm sure he dropped the gun but I can't remember anything else. When I came round I was alone and in a different part of the woods. Dan Bush can confirm that he found me covered in blood, wandering around in a daze.'

'I'm sorry, Falconer, but the evidence is stacked against you. You have a right to a solicitor – I'd advise you to get one.'

At that moment the door to the interview room opened and the inspector was beckoned by a chief inspector from Glasgow. The interview was terminated and Falconer was left in the room under the care of a constable.

The local inspector, Lomax and the Special Branch officer grouped around the whiteboard in the small office as the chief inspector presented new information.

'There's evidence that something was dragged from the crime scene to the place where Bush claimed to have found Falconer. There was a blood trail – it was Falconer's blood. And there was evidence of other people in the region of Hannay's body. Investigations are ongoing.'

Lomax interrupted. 'This all fits with Falconer's account of events. Hannay is already implicated in matters affecting national security. There are good reasons for believing Commander Falconer's view that something big is about to happen in the Atlantic off the Scottish coast. He thought both he and Hannay had been set up – they were both expecting to meet different people in the woods. They were obstacles getting in the way of something – something that may be happening while we are pratting about here. Can't say more, for obvious reasons.'

Lomax looked to the Special Branch officer for support. He was nodding in agreement.

*

By midnight, Intelligence and Special Branch had trumped local police involvement, which now assumed a supportive role.

Additional resources had been brought in – including armed officers from Fort William.

Tom and Alice had been reinterviewed, but together this time, to get a quicker and more joined-up picture of events. Further investigations in North Norfolk were initiated – particularly concerning the cottage used by the suspects. *Nine Bells* in Morston Harbour was already under investigation. It had yielded useful information which had only just been relayed to Inspector Lomax. McAdam's binoculars and one of his boots had been found on the boat. CCTV data was currently being sought from the London and Glasgow train stations used by Alice and the mercenaries.

Tom insisted that Dan Bush had had nothing to do with their sleuthing and that he just provided the boat and came to his rescue on a couple of occasions. Tex had threatened to contact the American Consulate about his detainment. He was persuaded not to do that in return for release back to his boat. The last thing Intelligence wanted at this stage was American involvement too. Tex agreed to have an armed officer on board for protection – and to ensure he didn't make contact with anyone. Tom and Alice were eventually allowed to join him on the boat, accompanied by Lomax and his sergeant.

A British frigate in the North Atlantic had just detected unknown fast submarine activity. This, together with the information coming out of Scotland, was sufficient to activate an emergency COBRA (Cabinet Office Briefing Room A) security meeting at 70 Whitehall. The Ministry of Defence activated the clandestine 'Bikini State Red'. This was a non-public alert state enabling relevant military and other groups to coordinate and react appropriately to actual or perceived national security threats.

4am, Tuesday 1st December

The Russian Kashalot submarine had been lying quietly in the deeper waters of the Atlantic for two hours, five miles from the agreed pickup coordinates. This class of vessel is nuclear-powered, has a titanium hull and is capable of underwater speeds of up to 35mph. It ascended briefly from its current depth of one hundred metres to just ten metres below the surface to receive final confirmation of instructions via VLF (very low frequency) radio. The commanding officer was concerned – the original instructions had been changed.

*

The fishing boat was now only half an hour from the rendezvous point, some 120 miles from the Outer Hebrides.

'Let's prepare for the worst,' said Fisher.

'Yeah – the guns are ready,' replied Tarrant.

'Not just that. We need to get our life jackets on, sort out the lifeboat and find the emergency beacons.'

'OK – but the life raft is just a small inflatable with no outboard.'

'It'll do – better than nothing,' said Fisher.

'So you really are expecting trouble, then?' added Tarrant.

'Yes – gut feeling.'

Fisher cut the engines at the rendezvous point. The sea was relatively calm. It was pitch black outside. As instructed, they waited in silence for a few minutes. The submarine had moved closer and was also waiting silently. It had detected the fishing boat some way off. Fisher sent the agreed signals. He started and stopped the boat engines four times using specific time intervals.

The submarine came closer to the surface and surveyed the boat with its periscope. Fisher confirmed readiness with a brief Morse signal on the mast lights.

Fisher scoured the water with a torch. A frogman appeared. Fisher lowered a rope ladder. The frogman climbed aboard and shook Fisher's hand. It all seemed friendly enough. A line was attached to the package containing AMNACS and the frogman started back down the ladder, with the goods, towards the sea. It seemed to be going to plan. But then three Russian Special Forces agents climbed aboard the other side of the boat. Tarrant, who had been staying out of sight, suddenly appeared and sprayed the boarders with bullets. Fisher picked up his sub-machine gun and shot at the AMNACS package before it disappeared below the water.

The ensuing gun battle was short-lived. Tarrant was lying on the deck, motionless. Fisher was wounded and losing blood. One of the Russians was dead. The others disappeared rapidly back to the submarine, but not before clamping a limpet mine to the hull of the fishing boat. The submarine left at speed. Fisher crawled over to check Tarrant. He was dead. Blood was gushing from Fisher's leg. He attempted to stem the flow. But he also had more serious wounds.

After fifteen minutes the limpet mine exploded, blowing a hole in the submerged hull. The boat listed and began to sink. Fisher crawled over the sloping deck to the dinghy and threw it, and himself, overboard.

*

A mutual respect had developed between Inspector Adrian Lomax and Tom Falconer. They were now bouncing ideas off each other. They had both come to the conclusion that someone in a high position with access to classified naval information had directed operations in the North Sea and in Scotland. Hannay was obviously the traitor on HMS *Athena*. But he was just a pawn in the plan, as were the heavies tracked from Norfolk to Scotland.

The security agencies had taken Falconer's suggestions seriously. His data on the course of the fishing boat, and Alice's photographs, were being investigated intensively. Two frigates with submarine detection equipment were already sailing towards the deep Atlantic to the west of the Outer Hebrides. Military helicopters were flying towards possible locations of the fishing boat.

A flare suddenly lit up the sky. One of the helicopters flew towards it using a powerful light to search the sea. Fisher saw it in the distance and released another flare from the dinghy. The pilot soon spotted him and the half-sunk boat. Special Forces helped the injured Fisher aboard the helicopter. He was given emergency treatment for haemorrhagic shock.

*

Lomax did not want to spend another night aboard Tex's motor cruiser – he felt awkward. There was tension in the air. Dan Bush and Alice Silk had pressing business in London and wanted to leave as soon as possible. Lomax promised to try to sort things out.

It was 8.30am when he entered Mallaig Police Station. The navy and various agencies had been busy overnight. A Special Branch officer took Lomax to a quiet corner.

'The information from you and Falconer has yielded results. Frigates detected an explosion in the area of interest and an unidentified submarine moving fast to the north. Also, a partially sunk fishing boat has been found and an injured man was rescued from a dinghy nearby. He's been transferred to a trauma unit at Fort William. He is in a serious condition but we're hoping to interview him soon. The boat is being examined as we speak. Two dead men and weapons have been found on it.'

A slight smile of satisfaction spread across Lomax's face. 'Well, that's a relief. At least everyone's time hasn't been wasted. Tom Falconer's friends on the powerboat are getting tetchy – they need to get back to London ASAP. I can get hold of them again if necessary. We may run into *American problems* if we detain Dan Bush any longer.'

'I agree. But Falconer needs to stay – we may need his help. And there's the little problem of Hannay's murder. Sort out the formalities and let the Texan and the woman go.'

*

Lomax looked uncharacteristically jolly when he returned to the boat.

'Tom, I've got important news – we need to speak in private.'

Lomax recounted the events of the night.

Tom took a deep breath of relief. 'Wow! This may sound thoughtless, but thank God for that. I was beginning to seriously doubt my sanity.'

'There's one problem, though,' added Lomax. 'Special Branch insists you stay for a while. But your partner and the American can go.'

They joined the others in the salon. Looking at Alice and Tex, Lomax announced the good news.

'I've persuaded Special Branch to let you leave – today, if you wish. Unfortunately, we need to hang on to Tom for a bit longer. My sergeant and I will be moving into the local hotel for a day or two. I know you'll want to discuss things privately, so I'll make myself scarce.'

Just before his hurried departure, Lomax turned to Tom and whispered. 'It's Bikini State Red – there may be more twists and turns to come.'

21

Tuesday 1st December

Dan Bush checked his bag and hurried onto the deck. He had only minutes left to catch the 10.25 train – the next one was not due at Mallaig until late afternoon.

'I should get to London by early evening,' he called out as he stepped ashore. 'I'll be in touch tomorrow.'

'Thanks for all your help,' replied Tom. 'And don't worry about the boat – I'll keep an eye on her.'

Tom clambered back into the warmth of the salon.

'How about another coffee?' said Alice, hoping to corner him for a moment.

'Yes please. Let's relax while we can. God knows what's in store for me next.'

'Tom, I need to get back to London too. I'll stay here for at least one more night – so I know what's happening. I suggest I book a double room in the hotel. It'll be much more comfortable.

Lovely though this boat is, I don't think I could stand another day using the heads. And I need to sort my clothes before I start looking like a tramp. Hopefully, the police will have no objection to you moving from the boat to the hotel.'

'Excellent idea; go ahead and book us in. You could move in straightaway. I'll join you if and when I get the all-clear from Lomax or whoever else now has the last word.'

Tom phoned Adrian Lomax and attempted to justify the move. 'I'd be putting myself under "hotel arrest" at my own expense. And I'd be nearer to you lot, should you need me in a hurry.'

He needn't have worried – Lomax jumped at the idea. This would be convenient – things were moving fast. He needed Falconer close by in case they were suddenly required urgently in Glasgow.

'Go ahead – I'll take responsibility and let the other parties know about the arrangement. My sergeant will liaise with you.'

Tom and Alice put their luggage in the VW, which was still parked nearby on the quay. They returned to the boat to make final checks and lock up. As they stepped ashore again, Tom spoke to one of the friendly fishermen.

'What was that about?' enquired Alice.

'I offered him a few quid to keep an eye on the boat. He agreed – but would settle for a drink sometime. And a gossip, I suspect – they've probably already heard things on the ships' radios.'

'They are so helpful,' said Alice, 'especially given the tough lives they must have here every day.'

'That's mariners for you,' observed Tom. 'But don't get on their wrong side.'

*

Emergency surgery had stemmed an internal haemorrhage but Fisher's injuries were still life-threatening. Doctors at Fort William were trying to stabilise him before transfer to a specialist unit in Glasgow. His general condition was poor. But he had regained consciousness some time before anyone had realised. He lay still, with eyes closed, listening to the discussions between the medical staff, and between the medical staff and the police, who were desperate to interview him. Fisher assumed he was dying. Tremain was going to pay.

Suddenly, Fisher opened his eyes and shouted. 'I demand to talk to the police now – before I fucking die.'

Despite the concerns of the medical staff, he got his way. A chief inspector and a Special Branch officer were soon at the bedside, with a recorder running. Fisher gave them a brief account of events in the Atlantic. The Special Branch officer showed him photographs of the two dead men extracted from the fishing boat.

'That's my mate – he died fighting, trying to save me,' said Fisher, pointing to the picture of Jimmy Tarrant. 'The other one came from the sub, firing at us.'

Fisher was becoming restless. He cut short the continuing cross-questioning. 'It's Tremain you need to find. He's responsible for all this. Jimmy Tarrant and I were just foot soldiers. He organised things in Norfolk and the drop in the Atlantic.'

'OK, OK,' interrupted the Special Branch officer, 'but who is Tremain?'

'I don't know – and that's probably not his real name. But he's naval – senior navy, I'd say. He's a pushy bugger with a plummy accent.'

'What does he look like?'

'He's tall with piercing brown eyes, a high forehead and dark hair greying at the edges.'

'How old?'

'Fifties, probably.'

'Do you know anything about a shooting in woods near Arisaig yesterday?'

'Oh yeah – that was Tremain too.'

The chief inspector showed Fisher a photograph of Tom Falconer. 'Is this Tremain?'

'No, no – does it look like the bloke I just described? You've got it all wrong. No – this man had a fight in the woods with someone called Hannay. Hannay knocked him out. Tremain shot Hannay and then wrapped this bloke's hand round the gun. That's where we came in – to clear up the mess.'

Fisher pointed at Falconer's photograph. 'He was poking about in Norfolk too. But he isn't Tremain. Oh, I forgot to say – Tremain sometimes disguises himself with a black beard.'

Fisher was becoming vague and his speech was slurred. The doctors intervened with emergency procedures.

*

By early afternoon Tom and Alice had settled into their comfortable hotel room. Tom was just pouring them drinks when Lomax knocked at the door.

'I need you both to look at some photos – but separately.'

Lomax spread six pictures over the bed. One was of Fisher, sent from Fort William. Two were of the dead men found on the boat. Their photos were sent from the morgue in Glasgow. The other photos were of randomly selected individuals who had nothing to do with the investigation.

Tom went first. 'The only one I recognise is him – we had a brawl at Morston. He ran off when Dan Bush came to my rescue.'

Alice picked out the two 'Vikings' that she saw in Norfolk and later on the trains from London to Arisaig. They had identified Fisher and Tarrant.

Lomax looked relieved but gave little away. He left in a hurry.

'Meet me in the bar this evening, say around seven o'clock. I may have more news for you by then.'

*

Charles Fisher died during the afternoon. The chief inspector and the Special Branch officer left Fort William and returned fast to Mallaig Police Station. They updated Intelligence and MDP officers, including Lomax. The consensus was that Falconer probably did not kill Hannay. The investigation would now focus on identifying and finding the arch-traitor Tremain.

*

Lomax was late. Tom and Alice were not bothered – they were enjoying their freedom in the luxury of the hotel lounge.

'Sorry,' said Lomax apologetically, 'a lot has happened in the last few hours and I've just returned from a key briefing.'

'Is there any good news?' enquired Tom.

'Basically – yes. There was a submarine in contact with that fishing boat, just as you suspected – almost certainly Russian. I'll fill you in later. And, you'll be pleased to hear that you're not being charged with Hannay's murder.'

'Thank God!' exclaimed Tom.

Alice hugged him.

Lomax continued. 'But you may still be able to help us. Can you stay for another day or two?'

'I'll be around until Dan Bush returns. I'm helping him take the boat back to London. It's the least I can do given all the hassle we've put him through. Hopefully, that will be at the weekend.'

'Great – really appreciate your help, Tom. The operations in the North Sea and in the Atlantic appear to have been organised by a traitor known as Tremain – probably an alias. It appears he also killed Hannay. We need to identify the bugger ASAP. Given your previous experience with weapons trials and the various people and groups involved, perhaps you could give the matter some thought?'

*

Tremain was unaware of the course of events in the Atlantic. But he was worried. It was now midnight and Charles Fisher had not yet made contact. And worse, the Russians appeared to have excommunicated him – none of the confidential phone links were working. Tremain no longer felt in control. His false alibi was now critical.

Wednesday 2nd December, Moscow, 10am (four hours ahead of UK time)

News of the debacle in the Atlantic had been transmitted from the Russian submarine to Moscow overnight. The President was furious. He called an emergency meeting in the Kremlin with General Chkalov and other senior Russian Intelligence agents. Admiral Alexai Mendeleyev was excluded. He was now in disgrace and no longer in charge of the operation. Chkalov's agent in Britain had previously flagged up rumours of problems in the North Sea and at a British naval base – such as disappearances and unexplained deaths. And now there was a politically damaging fiasco involving a Russian submarine.

'Did anything useful come out of this mission?' asked one of the Intelligence officers.

'AMNACS was damaged in the fracas but we managed to retrieve it,' replied Chkalov. 'We might get something useful from it.'

'It's a disaster!' blasted the President. 'We need to sever all connections to this operation – I don't want an international crisis. Activate damage-limitation protocols immediately.'

Turning to Chkalov, he added, 'From now on I want tighter control over all our agents, and especially dissident agents from the old regime.'

'Tremain is now a liability,' asserted Chkalov. 'If cornered by the British he might turn to save his skin. He knows too much. We have already closed down communications with him. I have an agent in deep cover who is well placed to sort out the problem.'

'Go ahead – and keep me updated, daily,' replied the President.

They were not yet aware of the murder of the sleeper, Lieutenant Commander Nigel Hannay.

Mallaig, 9am

After a good night's sleep, their best for days, Tom and Alice were late rising.

'I must try to get the morning train to Glasgow,' announced Alice, 'so I can get back to London today. Helen will be wondering what the hell her so-called business partner is up to.'

'Good – back to some sort of normality, hopefully,' replied Tom.

Alice had just finished packing when her mobile phone rang. 'Hello?'

'Alice – Helen here. Sorry to trouble you but I've had a call from someone who is desperate to contact you.'

'My God, how weird – I was just saying to Tom how guilty I feel for mucking you about.'

'Don't worry about that. I think you may have another problem. A woman called Clarissa Hannay phoned me at the shop. She tried your home but got no answer. She wondered if I had another telephone number for you. I said I would try to contact you and took her number. I didn't like to give her your mobile number without asking you first. She sounded distraught.'

'Oh dear, poor Clarissa,' replied Alice. 'Yes, I'll get back to her. Helen, thanks for holding the fort. I'll explain everything tomorrow.'

'That's OK. You just sort yourself out first.'

Helen gave her Clarissa's mobile number.

'What's happening?' asked Tom.

'Clarissa's in a state and wants to talk to me.'

'It's a bit tricky, given the way things have turned out,' replied Tom.

'I know, but I can hardly ignore her – that would be horrible.'

Alice phoned. 'Hi, Clarissa, I eventually got your message. We've been on a boat sailing round the coast – phone out of range most of the time.'

'Oh, Alice – thank goodness. I really don't want to talk to anyone else at the moment. I don't know which way to turn. Nigel got involved in something ghastly in Scotland. He's been killed. I'm in Glasgow at the moment. I've just seen his body. The whole thing is a nightmare. Can we meet sometime soon please?'

'God, how awful! Clarissa, I'm so sorry. Yes, of course I'll meet you. I'll be in London tomorrow – is that any use?'

'Yes. I'm booked on a train from Glasgow tomorrow morning – it gets to Euston at 2.10pm.'

'I'll meet you at the station and we'll sort things out then,' replied Alice.

'Thank you so much. You're a real friend – and I need one at the moment.'

'Take care, Clarissa. I'll see you tomorrow.'

After turning off her phone, Alice cut in before Tom could speak. 'Don't worry. I won't admit to knowing already about Nigel's murder or say anything about our ventures in Scotland. As far as Helen and Clarissa are concerned, we were just on a boat trip around the coast. I like Clarissa and I regard her as a friend. It would appear most suspicious if I refused to see her. When you see Inspector Lomax later today, to discuss things I'm not supposed to know about, perhaps you could tell him that I'm seeing Clarissa tomorrow, and that I will be careful?'

Tom smiled. 'I'm beginning to wonder if you really *are* a secret agent.'

'I might be,' replied Alice, straight-faced. 'But I couldn't possibly tell you – or you know what I might have to do. Anyway, I need to get a move on or I'll miss my train. Hope I don't bump into Clarissa in Glasgow – that would be awkward.'

*

Tom met Adrian Lomax in the lounge at midday. He gave him the message from Alice.

'I'm glad she's on our side,' said Lomax, grinning.

'So you're happy with her meeting Hannay's wife then?'

'Not entirely, Tom. But I can hardly stop her seeing her friend – a friend who has just lost her husband. I'm sure she'll be careful. I'll let Special Branch know that Miss Silk has informed me. That should pre-empt unnecessary suspicion.'

Lomax continued. 'We need to get down to other business. Although strictly speaking you are still subject to the Official Secrets Act, this affair has moved to a higher level. I ought to get clearance for some of the things we are about to discuss, but I trust you and I'm taking a chance. I'm in and out of favour with the spooks – in favour at the moment, thanks largely to you and Miss Silk. Let me fill you in on the situation up to now, as far as I know it. The men using the boat *Nine Bells* in Norfolk are the same two men who were on the fishing vessel you tracked to the Atlantic. They were ex-marines. For some reason there was a gun battle between them and the Russian submariners. One of the ex-marines was killed and the other was picked up injured and flown to Fort William. He also died – but not before giving up some useful information to the police. As I mentioned before, he said that someone known as Tremain had organised everything and was responsible for Hannay's death. Tom, have you had any thoughts about who Tremain might really be?'

'I've had one nagging thought for some time. Why was Rear Admiral Richard Claydon so put out when I unexpectedly announced I was taking early retirement from the navy? And is it a coincidence that Nigel Hannay was the principal warfare officer on my ship? Also, Claydon would have had the knowledge needed and been in a position to organise such a complex operation.'

'Fascinating,' replied Lomax. 'The rough description of Tremain given by the mercenary before he died fits Claydon to a T. Claydon is currently supposed to be on holiday. It's above my pay grade now, but spooks and others are investigating him as we speak. They may or may not keep me in the loop.'

'Any news about John McAdam?' asked Tom. 'He was the reason I first got involved in all this.'

'Not much. There was evidence that he might have been on *Nine Bells* in Norfolk at some stage.'

'Oh – what evidence?'

'They found his binoculars and a boot. The boat had been so awash with water that there was little useful forensic evidence left. But a fingerprint from one of the ex-marines was found on McAdam's binoculars. The dying mercenary provided no additional useful information about McAdam – his condition had worsened by the time they got round to those questions.'

'And then there's the weird messages I got about McAdam wanting to meet me up here,' added Tom. 'But, clearly, he wasn't around.'

'It's still a mystery,' replied Lomax. Given the other events and findings, I doubt much resource is going into John McAdam right now. But I'll do what I can.'

'I'd appreciated that, Adrian.'

'Well, I must be off now, Tom. I'll keep you posted. And let me know if you hear anything interesting from your good lady.'

22

Thursday 3rd December, London

Alice felt refreshed after a quiet night in her own bed in her own place. It was past 11pm when she eventually got back from Euston Station. She was tired and took a cab – she couldn't face the hassle of retrieving her car late at night from the underground car park in Bloomsbury.

She looked again at the letter that had arrived while she was away. It was from the company that had offered her that fantastic job. Alice was surprised that they were still so eager to see her. She had replied briefly two weeks ago, just acknowledging their original offer and asking for time to think about it. Now she phoned the director and made an appointment to meet him next week.

By 10am Alice was in Bloomsbury picking up the Mini. There were no problems. The car park attendant had been there for years and knew Alice by sight. And there were two more days left on her permit. She drove straight to the shop at Hampstead.

Helen Lane was pleased with herself. 'We've sold quite a lot in the last week. I suppose it's the run-up to Christmas – let's hope it continues.'

Alice gave her a truncated version of her activities and problems while she'd been away.

'And Clarissa's husband has died. She's terribly upset. I said I'd meet her at Euston this afternoon. But I'm hoping other things will get back to normal soon. I'm really sorry I haven't been around to do my bit here.'

'Don't worry,' said Helen. 'It was good for me – coping on my own for a while. But I'm glad you're back. By the way, what happened about that job?'

'Well,' said Alice, 'I'm seeing someone about it next week. This is what I've decided. I want to remain a free agent and make a go of our business venture. Becoming an employee of that company would cause conflicts. So, I might offer myself on a consultancy basis – subject to contract, as they say.'

'Are you sure, Alice? What if they say no to that?'

'Tough – it's their loss.'

'Well, I must admit I'm relieved,' said Helen.

'And furthermore,' added Alice, 'I'll be here tomorrow and Saturday – so if you want a break, please feel free. It's the least I can do.'

'I'm just pleased you're back – but I might take you up on the Saturday offer,' replied Helen, smiling.

'Great – well, I must be off, once again. See you tomorrow.'

*

Alice drove back to the car park in Bloomsbury and walked to Euston Station. She met Clarissa at the platform entrance and gave her a long, comforting hug. Clarissa looked drawn – her usual bubbly personality was absent.

'Clarissa, you look so tired – would you like to stay overnight at my place?'

'I'd love to but I have to get down to the New Forest tonight – there are now problems at home. It goes from bad to worse,' continued Clarissa. 'I'll tell you about it later.'

'Let's walk to Bloomsbury,' said Alice, picking up some of Clarissa's luggage. 'It's not far and I know a quiet Italian restaurant there – you must be hungry.'

'That would be nice. I'll get a train from Waterloo to Southampton later this afternoon.'

*

The waiter filled their glasses with a dry white wine and left the bottle on the table.

'So what's happening at your house?' asked Alice.

'Margaret, my housekeeper, phoned to say that the police turned up unannounced with a warrant to search the property. They've taken away Nigel's stuff – and my work and IT equipment as well. And they were so rude – the poor woman was beside herself. That's why I need to get back today.'

'I don't know how you're managing to cope with all this.'

Clarissa burst into tears. 'I'm not, Alice – I'm not,' she said as she replenished her glass. 'I'll give you my account of events. I've nothing to hide, and you are welcome to tell Tom if you wish.

'Nigel left me a strange recorded message on our answerphone. He said he'd been involved in something bad and had to disappear immediately. Fortunately, he also said he was sorry that he had never told me about his other life, whatever that was. I hope the police or Security Service will take that into account. Then I was contacted by the police, who told me that Nigel was dead and that I must come to Glasgow immediately. Apparently he was shot. The Security Service agents gave me the third degree, implying that I must have known that my husband was a traitor. They wouldn't tell me when his body might be released for the funeral. There's all this procurator fiscal nonsense in Scotland – I sometimes wonder if we're in the same country. Anyway, you'll understand why I'm too embarrassed to contact Nigel's friends and colleagues at Devonport. Sorry to burden you with all this, Alice, but I do think of you as a friend I can trust. Well, that's it – enough of me. What have you and Tom been up to?'

Alice had to tread carefully. She did not want Clarissa to know that she and Tom already knew Nigel was a traitor, and that he was dead.

'Not much to tell,' she said. 'As you know, Tom was trying to find out what happened to John McAdam. I think he ruffled feathers. The MoD Police accused him of interfering. It didn't get anywhere. Tom started to set up a motor cruising course but it foundered because his business partner ran into difficulties. And we've just had a bit of a cruise around the coast on friend's boat. He's an American we met at St Katharine's marina. Anyway, all in all there's nothing much to report. I'm not sure where everything's going at the moment.'

Alice hoped Clarissa would take the bait to divert the conversation.

'But surely you and Tom are OK?' asked Clarissa.

'I hope so. Anyway, I'm more concerned about you. Can I help?'

'There is one thing – I hardly like to ask,' said Clarissa hesitantly. 'If and when I get Nigel's body back, I would be so grateful if you and Tom would consider coming to his funeral. I doubt he'll be buried with military honours and I don't think I dare invite anyone from Devonport.'

'Of course I will, Clarissa – and I'm sure Tom will too.'

Clarissa insisted on taking a taxi to Waterloo Station. Alice collected her car and drove straight back to Belgravia.

On her third attempt she got through to Tom in his hotel room.

'Tom, you really must get a mobile phone and join the modern world.'

'Sorry. I've been sorting things out ready to leave Mallaig – taking the car back, refuelling the boat and having a jar with those fishermen.'

'So when are you leaving, then?'

'I'm hoping to start back with Tex tomorrow afternoon. He's getting the overnight sleeper to Glasgow this evening. We should get back into St Katharine's on Monday morning – tides willing. I'll give you more details when we finally get underway.'

'Can't wait to get you back,' replied Alice. 'I met Clarissa in London. She's distraught. Not only has she lost her husband but the police have turned over her house. She feels terribly isolated and is too embarrassed to contact people at Devonport. Tom, I said I would attend Nigel's funeral when she eventually gets his body back. Would you come too? She'd really appreciate it.'

'Poor Clarissa – of course I'll go.'

'Thanks, Tom – I'll let her know. Well, see you soon. Love you.'

Friday 4th December, Plymouth

Inspector Adrian Lomax had returned to Devonport the previous evening. This morning he was in Plymouth Harbour scouring the entrance with binoculars. Eventually, Richard Claydon's small yacht *Topsy 2* appeared. The boat sailed slowly round the harbour to its mooring. It was definitely the rear admiral on board – and he was making himself very visible. After half an hour he climbed ashore and made for a nearby bar. Lomax followed him in and sat inconspicuously on the other side of the room. It was busy. Claydon had soon struck up conversations with cronies and was displaying a rather overdone bonhomie with the barman. Lomax had to tread carefully. Claydon was a powerful man with important connections. Boarding and searching his yacht would be asking for trouble. And what exactly would they be looking for?

Back in his office, Lomax contacted the other MDP officers investigating Ramsgate Harbour. Claydon had said to several people that he was sailing from Plymouth to Ramsgate, resting a day, and then sailing back to Plymouth. The contacts in Ramsgate confirmed that Claydon had arrived there about three days ago. This meant that his apparent sailing time from Plymouth to Ramsgate was around two days. As this was a three-hundred mile course, Claydon would have had insufficient time to stop off somewhere to get to the Scottish Highlands and back. There were plenty of witnesses to confirm the times that *Topsy 2*, with Claydon aboard, had left and arrived at Plymouth and Ramsgate Harbours.

Richard Claydon's alibi appeared to be watertight.

23

Monday 7th December, Devonport

Inspector Lomax had arranged to meet Rear Admiral Claydon and Captain Fox, the most senior officers directly concerned with Project Athena. The official objective was to update them on events so far. Fox arrived on time at 11am. By 11.15 there was no sign of Claydon. Fox was becoming agitated. Lomax tried phoning, but there was no answer. Fox decided to search likely places in the base, but Claydon could not be found. The meeting was postponed.

This gave Lomax the excuse he needed. He collected his sergeant and they made for Plymouth Harbour. *Topsy 2* looked unoccupied from the outside.

Lomax called out from the pontoon. 'Rear Admiral – are you aboard, sir?'

There was no answer.

They stepped onto the boat. The cabin door was unlocked. The sergeant opened the door and they entered cautiously.

Someone appeared to be asleep on a chair. Lomax called out again. There was no response. They moved round to the front of the chair. Rear Admiral Claydon was sitting back with his head slumped forward on his chest. There was a bloody wound on his temple. A revolver was lying on the deck a couple of feet from the chair. There was no pulse. Lomax called in the crime scene team.

Superficially at least, it looked like suicide. Forensic tests indicated that a single bullet had been fired at very close range into the right temple with an exit wound on the other side of the head. The low ambient temperature may have slowed the post-mortem changes, but the degree of rigor mortis and lack of significant putrefaction suggested that death may have occurred on Saturday evening or Sunday morning. There was little else of note at the scene – apart from faint imprints from small shoes. Witnesses were quick to tell Lomax that Claydon frequently had 'lady visitors' on his yacht.

Later in the day a Special Branch officer and an MDP chief inspector met with Lomax in his office.

'The consensus so far is that the rear admiral committed suicide,' said Lomax, adding, 'The gun was unregistered, but only Claydon's fingerprints were found on it.'

'Well, it fits,' added the Special Branch officer. 'We were obviously closing in on "Tremain", and we can now assume Tremain was indeed Claydon.'

'That would be convenient and a relief, but there are some awkward loose ends, such as Claydon's yacht holiday alibi,' said Lomax.

'We need to tidy this up as soon as possible,' urged the chief inspector.

'We are actively investigating the alibi – there may be flaws in it,' added Lomax.

London

Dan Bush's motor cruiser had at last returned to its mooring at St Katharine's. It was early afternoon by the time Tex and Tom locked up and stepped ashore with their luggage.

'Hey, Tom – *Binnacles II* has a "for-sale" notice on it.'

'So it has. I'm not surprised. But I shan't be making an offer.'

'I need to get straight back home for a clean-up,' said Tex. 'I've a lot of work to catch up on – and I need to call into the office later today. Perhaps we could all meet up before Christmas? Give me a call soon.'

'Will do. Thanks again for all your help. I know it's caused problems.'

'But it certainly was exciting. Take care, Tom.'

*

Back in Belgravia, Tom checked the answerphone. Lomax had rung twice. Tom got straight back to him.

'Tom, there have been major developments at Plymouth. I can't go into details on the phone for obvious reasons. I realise you've only just got back to London, but could you and Miss Silk possibly come down to Plymouth? You may both be able to help me clear up some loose ends.'

Tom contacted Alice at the shop and then got back to Lomax. 'Yes, I'll book a room at the Drum Hotel. I should be there around 2pm on Wednesday. Alice can't make it until late Thursday – she's got a job interview and other commitments in London.'

'That's terrific. I'll meet you at the Drum.'

Wednesday 9th December, 11am, Moscow time

General Chkalov arrived at the Kremlin for an audience with the President.

'I have good news today,' he announced. 'The Tremain problem has been solved.'

'That's good, but how?' responded the President.

'He has conveniently committed suicide.'

'Without our help, of course,' added the President.

'Of course – and everything has been tidied up neatly.'

'And the British are keeping quiet about everything,' continued the President. 'I suspect the whole affair is an embarrassment. Their lack of security makes them look like fools. Your agent has done well. If there are no further difficulties, we should consider honouring him with a commendation.'

'Yes, *she* has done well,' added Chkalov.

'She?!' exclaimed the President.

'Oh yes – she's one of my best.'

2pm, Plymouth

Lomax was already waiting in reception when Tom arrived at the Drum Hotel. He didn't want to be seen having a discussion in the lounge, so they went straight to Tom's room.

'This is in confidence, Tom. Claydon was found dead on his yacht on Monday – looked like suicide.'

'Ooh – I was about to say it couldn't happen to a nicer chap, but I'll withdraw the remark. Well, it all points to his involvement, I guess.'

'Conveniently, yes. But his alibi still appears intact,' added Lomax. 'He was apparently on a sailing holiday alone on his yacht, sailing from Plymouth to Ramsgate and back again. People at those harbours confirmed his arrival and departure times. There's no way he would have had time to get to the Highlands, do whatever he was supposed to have done there and then get back to Ramsgate. We wondered about the use of two similar boats but we found no evidence of a duplicate boat in havens or harbours near Plymouth.'

'Were there sightings in the Channel after leaving Plymouth?' asked Tom.

'No, nothing definite – but his yacht is small. Also, it was getting dark when he left. Perhaps we could go over this again when you've had time to think about it.'

'I suggest we get Alice involved in solving the conundrum – she is good at that sort of thing,' added Tom. 'We could present it as a puzzle without giving away state secrets.'

'Good idea,' replied Lomax. 'Perhaps we could all get together on Friday morning?'

*

In the evening, Tom phoned Alice.

'How did the job interview go?'

'Quite well,' replied Alice. 'They weren't entirely happy about not owning me as an employee, but we came to an amicable agreement. They are going to try to work out a suitable consultancy contract that won't compromise their confidentiality requirements and is also compatible with me continuing my other activities.'

'That sounds great.'

'I told Helen when I got back to the shop this afternoon. She was so relieved. Mind, I haven't seen the contract yet.'

'Some things are coming together,' said Tom. 'But there are some problems down here in Plymouth – can't talk about them on the phone. Adrian Lomax would like to pick both our brains on Friday morning – is that OK?'

'Yes, I should be in Plymouth late tomorrow afternoon.'

'In that case I'll try to contact Scottie to see if he can join us for a drink at the hotel tomorrow evening.'

'Yes, do,' said Alice. 'Actually, I feel guilty that I haven't contacted Jenny since she's been back in London – I'll do that tonight.'

Thursday 10th December, Plymouth

Paul Scott met Tom in the hotel lounge in the evening.

'Alice will be joining us a little later. It gives us a chance to discuss confidential naval matters,' said Tom.

'Things are becoming clearer, even though we haven't been told everything,' said Scottie. 'Nigel Hannay was obviously the traitor on *Athena*. The MDP, and others, may now be wondering if Hannay also murdered David Llewellyn. That's between you and me.'

'I assume you've heard that Hannay was murdered in Scotland?' added Tom.

'Really?! We knew he had disappeared but not that he was dead. What happened?'

'The police and the spooks would like to hush things up. But Clarissa knows what happened to him and I doubt she'll keep quiet. I'm not sure of all the details, but he was shot. I know this because, believe it or not, I've been working closely with Inspector Adrian Lomax. Please keep all this to yourself.'

Alice arrived. 'I spoke to Jenny last night,' she said, grinning at Scottie. 'So, she's moved into your London flat, then.'

'Yes, we thought we would try living together. And it saves money.'

'Wow, you two are getting serious,' said Tom.

'I hope so. With all the problems here we've only had a few days together in London so far. And I may be at sea again after Christmas – don't know the details yet.'

'Well, Tom and I survived all those upheavals and we're still together, so far,' said Alice. 'I do hope it all works out for you both. Jenny sounded chirpy.'

'That's a relief,' replied Scottie. 'I left her to rearrange and sort things in the flat.'

'Oh yes – Jenny would be good at that,' added Tom, laughing.

They agreed to all meet up somehow, somewhere, before Christmas.

After Scottie's departure Alice was keen to talk about Christmas arrangements. 'I need to confirm dates with Mum. She's expecting me to stay with her in Essex on Christmas Day and Boxing Day. Is that all right with you, Tom?'

'Yes, of course. And I need to check with my brother up north – my father's staying with him and his family.'

'I'd rather it was just you and I together for Christmas,' added Alice, 'but Mum will probably be on her own. Her friends will have their own commitments. She'll be vulnerable if my father decides to turn up – although that's not very likely.'

'Can he be violent?' asked Tom.

'Not so far, but he is controlling and very persuasive. I can handle him.'

'I'm sure you can,' said Tom.

Friday 11th December

Lomax met Tom and Alice at Plymouth Harbour. He took them to a pontoon which was partly cordoned off with crime scene tape.

'That's the boat in question,' said Lomax, pointing at *Topsy 2*. He didn't want to mention Claydon's name in Alice's presence. He wasn't sure how much she knew, or even if she was involved in some way. He gauged her reactions.

'Miss Silk, I've asked you and Tom here to help me solve a puzzle.'

Alice interrupted. 'Please – you can call me Alice, if I can call you Adrian. After all, I'm assuming this is informal or you wouldn't be involving me at all.'

'Quite right – OK.'

Lomax outlined the problem of the yacht journey to Ramsgate.

'Are we talking about that Tremain character? I know about the murder in Scotland,' said Alice. 'Don't worry, I shan't tell anyone.'

'Yes, we think this could be Tremain's boat.'

'So,' said Alice, 'if he had to get to Scotland and then to Ramsgate during the supposed time of the outward voyage, then he must have moored the first boat nearby and used a second, identical boat, this one, for the return journey from Ramsgate. And he must have used a car to get to Scotland.'

'Yes, that seems to be the only way he could have done it,' replied Lomax. 'The problem is, we have searched harbours and moorings near here for another boat called *Topsy 2* without success.'

'Wait – let me think,' said Alice.

The men watched silently.

'That's it,' she said after a few seconds. 'I would have used a second boat name, changing the names around as appropriate after leaving the harbours. So, the first boat should now be moored in a harbour near Plymouth, but with a different name.'

'And hold on,' said Tom, looking at the yacht. 'The nameplates are bolted on. Let's unbolt one and see what's on the other side.'

Lomax retrieved some tools from his car and proceeded to unbolt the nameplate nearest to the pontoon. 'Yes!' he cried as he turned the plate over. Her other name was *Joyrider*.

'So,' said Alice, not batting an eyelid, 'the second boat, this one, was kept somewhere near Ramsgate under the name *Joyrider*. Tremain must have changed it to *Topsy 2* before entering Ramsgate Harbour and then sailed back here. The original boat that sailed out from here as *Topsy 2* is now sitting somewhere near Plymouth under another name – which might also be *Joyrider*. And the name on the hidden side of its nameplate should be *Topsy 2*.'

'You're brilliant,' replied Lomax. 'And well spotted, Tom. We'll check the Small Ships Register for those names. It would be wiser to have used just two names on the two boats, in case some harbour master decides to be nosy and checks up. I'll get the search parties out to do more thorough checks in the local harbours and havens.'

Lomax had more questions for Alice. He persuaded them to join him for a drink in the local bar.

'How was Mrs Hannay when you saw her last week?'

'She was beside herself and tearful. It was bad enough finding out that her husband was a traitor and had been shot dead. On top of that, she also had to suffer the indignity of having her house turned over by the heavy mob while she was in Scotland. I feel so sorry for Clarissa – she's a lovely lady. Whatever Nigel did or didn't do, I've little doubt that they loved each other. We just had a brief meal together after I met her at Euston. She had to dash off to sort out the mess at her home in Lyndhurst.'

'This will sound insensitive, but sometimes I have to ask awkward questions,' said Lomax. 'Do you think she had any prior knowledge, or even a suspicion, of her husband's clandestine activities?'

'I don't know. I've no reason to think that she did. It seemed to come as a complete surprise to her. She did mention a recorded message, the last call from Nigel. He mentioned something about his other life of which she knew nothing. But I guess the spooks must have retrieved that message already.'

'OK – sorry I had to ask,' replied Lomax. By the way, have you been in contact since your meeting?'

'No. Clarissa was having trouble getting Nigel's body released. She'll contact us when she has a date for the funeral.'

'You've both been most helpful. I'll try to acknowledge your help officially but I have to tread very carefully. I'm sure you understand.'

'Don't worry about that,' said Tom. 'But we would like to know the outcome of the search for a second boat.'

'No problem.'

Saturday 12th December

It was late morning when a small yacht named *Joyrider* was found at Brixham Harbour, about fifty miles by sea around the coast from Plymouth. Lomax and his team descended on the area, which had already been cordoned off. The boat's nameplate was unbolted. There was another name on the other side – *Topsy 2*.

*

By now, Tom and Alice were already on their way back to London. Alice pondered over Clarissa's movements. She hadn't mentioned it in the presence of Lomax, but she had tried several times to contact Clarissa at home over the weekend. There had been no reply. She mentioned it to Tom. He didn't seem bothered.

'Actually, I couldn't get hold of *you* over the weekend,' he said. 'Is that suspicious too?'

24

Wednesday 16th December, London

Adrian Lomax had never before been summoned to a meeting at the Ministry of Defence at Whitehall. He felt slightly intimidated by the large gathering of high-ranking people from the navy, civil service, MDP, Special Branch and Military Intelligence.

'Inspector, tell us about your recent investigations,' commanded the chairman.

Lomax explained how Claydon's two-boat alibi worked. He then presented additional new evidence.

'Forensic investigations on the first boat, now at Brixham Harbour, showed that Claydon had been aboard. Local enquiries revealed that a tall man with a thick black beard was seen bringing that boat, then named *Joyrider*, into the harbour. A false black beard has since been recovered from Claydon's belongings on the second boat, now moored at Plymouth Harbour. We produced a photofit of Rear Admiral Claydon with the beard. In the last couple of days we have been touting this around Brixham Harbour and in Mallaig and Arisaig in the Highlands. He was recognised by a few people in all these locations. This, together with the testimony of the dying ex-marine, who worked with Tremain in North Norfolk and in Scotland, provides convincing evidence that Claydon was Tremain. So, he appears to be the traitor-in-chief. As you've probably heard already, Claydon was found shot on his yacht at Plymouth. The evidence suggested suicide.'

'And what is the current situation regarding Lieutenant David Llewellyn?' asked an MDP superintendent.

'We think he was set up by Lieutenant Commander Hannay to be the fall guy on HMS *Athena*. We now have evidence that Llewellyn was drugged with chloral on the night that Dr Tolley was murdered and the AMNACS device disappeared. Personally, I think he was innocent of all the charges initially brought against him. Llewellyn was found hanged at Devonport. It looked like suicide, but could have been murder. So far, the evidence against Hannay for Llewellyn's death is circumstantial.'

Lomax was asked about John McAdam and Clarissa Hannay.

'There is no firm evidence to support their active involvement in these events,' he asserted.

Before he could elaborate on the McAdam situation, he was cut short by the chairman. 'Thank you, Inspector – your findings have been most helpful. That's all for now. Please wait outside.'

The meeting continued for another half-hour. It had reached the summing-up and future strategy stage. Claydon and Hannay were confirmed as the key traitors. As far as possible, details of the affair would remain secret. There would be no official condemnation of the Russians – unless they caused further trouble. Bikini State Red would be appropriately downgraded. AMNACS had been a success and its development would continue. Another sea trial was planned for the following year.

After the meeting the MDP superintendent invited Lomax to lunch.

'Adrian, that was impressive. Some were surprised that you're still an inspector. I'd like to push for your promotion.'

'I'd appreciate that, thank you. I'll try not to tread on toes in the meantime.'

'I don't think you need to worry about that. We need more plain speaking.'

'In that case,' added Lomax, 'perhaps I could continue investigations into John McAdam's disappearance? The meeting didn't seem keen to pursue that.'

'They had more pressing things to consider. But, yes, I think you should try to bring that matter to a close. Talking of other matters, you should probably stop investigating Clarissa Hannay. She has already made a hell of a fuss. And you might be treading on the spooks' toes. Apparently, that lady is still of interest to them.'

*

Alice had had a busy day at the shop. Tom poured her a drink.

'There were two phone calls this afternoon,' he announced. 'One was from Adrian Lomax. They found the other boat with the two names at Brixham Harbour, just round the coast from Plymouth. He sends his thanks to you again – he thinks you're a genius. He's now concentrating on John McAdam's disappearance.'

'Great,' said Alice. 'What was the other call?'

'It was from Clarissa. She's got Nigel's body back from Scotland – apparently after making trouble and threatening to go to the press and her MP. The funeral is this Friday. Short notice, but I said we would both go. I've got all the details.'

'Good. We must go. But I'm feeling slightly nervous about it.'

'I know,' replied Tom. 'Apart from feeling sorry for Clarissa and offering our condolences, it's difficult to know what to talk about.'

They were just relaxing after supper when the phone rang. Alice answered.

'Hi, Jenny – how's things?'

'Good. Paul will be coming home on leave this weekend until after Christmas. I wondered if we could meet up sometime next week?'

'That would be great. We're off to see our families over the Christmas period. Next Tuesday would suit us.'

'That's fine,' replied Jenny.

'OK. So come to us for a little soirée on Tuesday evening?'

'Love to,' replied Jenny enthusiastically.

'Scottie's back in London at the weekend,' said Alice as she replaced the receiver. 'Jenny sounded keen to come here. If you're happy with the arrangement I'll invite Helen too.'

'Good idea,' replied Tom. 'And I'll see if Tex is available – that'll even up the pairs.'

Friday 18th December

Tom and Alice drove from London to the crematorium at Southampton.

'We're early – let's wait a while before we go in,' said Tom.

'Good idea. Glad we came by car, so we can leave as soon as politely possible.'

There was just one lady in the waiting room for the small chapel. They recognised her. Margaret was the Hannays' housekeeper. Just as they started to talk, the hearse arrived. Clarissa and Nigel Hannay's mother followed in Clarissa's car. The service was due to start in a few minutes. No one else arrived, apart from the friendly minister. The chapel felt starkly empty.

The service was short and sympathetic, but with little allusion to God or Christian belief. Nigel's mother was unhappy with the proceedings but respected the fact that both her son and Clarissa were atheists. Clarissa had tried to compromise. After the cremation she invited Tom and Alice to join them in a local inn for a small buffet lunch.

Nigel's mother was too upset about her son's death to say much. But eventually she asked Clarissa the awkward question once again.

'Why did my son not have a proper funeral with more naval colleagues present?'

Clarissa hesitated – she did not want to say that Nigel had been a traitor and was now hated.

Tom came to the rescue. 'Nigel served with me for many years. He was an excellent officer and a credit to the navy. As I understand things, he was involved in very secret undercover work. This was dangerous and he gave his life. Unfortunately for you and Clarissa, and for us, we will never know exactly what happened. I believe his work had implications for national security. So, officially, little can be revealed and a degree of cover-up is necessary – for now at least. Let's just celebrate the Nigel we all knew and loved.'

'Thank you, Tom. That means a lot,' said Clarissa, looking pensively towards Nigel's mother.

'Yes, thank you,' she added tearfully.

After a short while, Tom looked at his watch. 'Clarissa, we need to make a move soon or we'll get stuck in the rush hour in the dark in London.'

'Of course – thank you both so much for coming. I'll see you to your car,' she replied, with a look suggesting she'd like to talk in private.

*

'It seems he was a traitor,' said Clarissa. 'Was he working for the Russians?'

'I'm not privy to that information,' replied Tom. 'It's possible – after all, who else?'

Clarissa was about to ask another question when Alice interrupted her flow.

'So what are your plans now?'

'I'm selling up once probate's sorted – just need to move away and start a new life.'

'Well, good luck, Clarissa. And keep in touch,' said Alice, opening the car door.

Clarissa stood waving them goodbye until they were out of sight.

'She was fishing for information just now,' said Alice.

'Yes – and she was asking a lot of questions during our last visit. And perhaps she's always had suspicions about Nigel.'

'I wonder what she'll do now?' queried Alice. 'She worked in the diplomatic area. That might be difficult now, given what's happened. She is multilingual – I wonder if that included Russian.'

'Interesting thought,' said Tom. 'Anyway, thank goodness that's over – I could kill a drink.'

'Yes, same here. But you did well, Tom. Those were very kind and very diplomatic things you said about Nigel. You never fail to surprise me.'

'I hope that's a good thing,' replied Tom, smiling.

Sunday 20th December

Feeling the need for some exercise after breakfast, Tom took a stroll around Belgrave Square. He also wanted to have a quiet think about the future.

'Is everything all right?' asked Alice on his return. 'You look thoughtful.'

Tom took her hand. 'As it's peaceful and pleasant at the moment, and we don't have to shoot off somewhere, let's talk about us,' he said.

'Is there another woman?' replied Alice, laughing.

'No, dear – just us, I hope. Alice, I'm floundering around at the moment, not sure where I'm going exactly. You, on the other hand, have firm plans and prospects. I don't want to get in your way or become a burden. Of course, I'll help in any way I can. What I'm trying to say, with difficulty, is – are you happy to continue as we are?'

'Of course I am, as long as you are – you silly old thing.'

'Oh, I am. And perhaps, when everything's settled down a bit, we could think about taking things further?'

'Tom, I'm not a commitment freak and I'm not gagging for marriage and kids. If you're happy with our arrangement, so am I.'

They embraced and kissed. Tom's relief was palpable.

'While we're on the subject of getting back to a normal life, whatever that is,' added Tom, 'I was thinking about doing a bit of oil painting again. Problem is, I haven't really got the space here.'

'Tom, that's a great idea. Actually, you could use the workroom at the back of the shop.'

'Are you sure?'

'Yes. I use it occasionally for cleaning old paintings but I'm sure we can work around each other. Obviously, I should check with Helen first, but I doubt she'll object.'

'Alice, I'm just an amateur and not very good. I don't want to be an embarrassment.'

'Nonsense – come with me to the shop tomorrow. Bring some of your work.'

Tuesday 22nd December

Helen accompanied Alice back from the shop. Background music was playing when they arrived. Tom was making a manful effort at sorting out the spread for the party. Helen rushed to him and gave him a long hug.

'Tom, you've done a great job,' said Alice. 'Let us take over and you can pour the drinks. And Helen had an idea about your paintings.'

'Really – not the bin?' replied Tom.

'No!' said Helen. 'Don't be silly. Your paintings are nice and pleasant – they would brighten up any room. I was wondering if you would consider producing a few small works that we could put in our window, with a note saying that some of the proceeds will go to local good causes? That would be good publicity for our business.'

'I think it's a great idea, Tom,' added Alice.

'Well, I'm flattered, but I can't compete with trained professional artists.'

'You won't be,' said Helen. 'We will just say you're a local part-time artist. The price tags will be appropriate and the mention of charitable intentions will be a bonus in our favour.'

'OK – I'll give it a go. I need a new challenge.'

'It will be great having you around,' said Alice.

'Yes,' added Helen, 'and you can keep us girls in order.'

'Not much chance of that,' replied Tom.

Within the hour, Scottie and Jenny arrived. Tom and Scottie were soon having a chat together away from the ladies.

'It's back to square one,' said Scottie. 'Sea trials on the weapons system you're officially not supposed to know about are starting again at the end of March. It's on HMS *Athena* again, with Appleby in charge. Mike Morris is going – he'll be working with Appleby's original principal warfare officer. So, he's doing all right. Of course, they, unlike me, will be spending some time at AWRE after Christmas.'

'I must send Mike a card. But what about Captain Fox?' asked Tom.

'He's not involved now – not flavour of the month. Appleby's criticisms of his security arrangements were taken seriously. Someone still living had to be made a scapegoat, I suppose.'

'You're in danger of becoming a cynic like me,' joked Tom.

Alice was relieved when Dan Bush arrived without arm candy. She was quick to pair him up with Helen.

'Dan, are you in the UK for Christmas?' asked Alice.

'Yes. It's not worth all the hassle of travelling at this time of year for just a few days in the US. And I'm up to my eyes in work at the moment. Fortunately, my sister and her husband are coming to stay with me for a week over the holiday period – they love London. And by the way, in the New Year I'd like to invite all of you to my apartment in the Barbican.'

'You're on,' said Jenny.

'We won't be around over Christmas,' said Tom. 'We're off to do family duties – but separately.'

'Well, it's just me and Mum this year – a nice quiet Christmas,' said Helen. 'Larger gatherings of our family almost always end with someone having a row.'

'Oh dear,' said Scottie, looking at Jenny. 'What have we let ourselves in for?'

Jenny enlarged. 'Paul's coming to my family on Christmas Day and I'm going to his on Boxing Day.'

After a short lull in the conversation, Scottie winked at Jenny. She extracted something from her handbag. Scottie tapped on the table and coughed for attention.

'Please top up your glasses. I've an important announcement to make. I asked Jenny to marry me. And she said yes – foolish girl.'

Jenny slipped on the engagement ring and displayed it proudly. The spontaneous hugging, clapping, toasting and congratulations lasted several minutes.

'That's fantastic,' said Alice. 'So, when is the big day?'

'Probably in late February – we've yet to arrange the exact date and place,' said Jenny. 'We'd like you all to come if you can.'

'Yes indeed,' added Scottie. 'We're hoping to get married at least three weeks before I set sail again.'

25

The Following Year
Sunday 10th January, London

'That was an eventful evening,' said Tom, clutching his second strong coffee.

'And Dan's apartment really was something,' added Alice. 'I've often passed Shakespeare Tower on my way through the Barbican but I've never been inside before. The view from those upper floors is amazing – I thought Helen's eyes were going to pop out.'

'Yeah – and apparently his company pays the rent. That's what I call a perk.'

'So, Tom, tell me about the project that Dan was discussing with you.'

'Well, it involves sailing round those parts of the Scottish coast with offshore oil rigs. Two of his techno-buddies have developed a device for fast, accurate three-dimensional imaging of objects on the sea bed. It's of potential use in the oil industry. At present, this sort of work often involves AUVs, autonomous underwater vehicles. This new device would be simpler to use because it can be trailed behind a boat. Tex wants to do preliminary tests around the east coast of Scotland in April using his boat. He asked me to join them as the navigation expert. He thought it would look good on their report.'

'It sounds interesting.'

'Yes – I'm going over details with him at his office tomorrow. As the North Norfolk coast is not far off the proposed route, I suggested we might stop at Blakeney Harbour overnight. Tex was quite keen. He'd also like to meet up with Harry White again. I'll contact Harry to see if he'll be on his boat over that period. We owe him more than he will ever know, so I'd like to thank him again for all his help. Also, talking of maritime matters, I'm definitely going to book myself onto an RYA motor cruising instructors' course later this year. It will help keep other options open for me.'

'I'm so pleased, Tom – things are coming together for you. And you've produced two lovely little paintings for the shop,' added Alice.

'Yes – no more excuses for moping about aimlessly.'

Tom continued. 'So, Paul and Jenny have finalised their wedding plans then.'

'Yes,' said Alice enthusiastically, 'the wedding's in six weeks' time at Kensington Register Office. They have everything well worked out. After the ceremony cars are taking the guests to the wedding reception at a hotel in Cromwell Road.'

'Yes, very well organised. And I'm best man. I feel a bit anxious.'

'You'll be fine. Jenny's younger sister will be the bridesmaid,' added Alice. 'And they reconfirmed that they want simple low-key hen and stag parties – hers in London and his in Plymouth, so his naval colleagues can get to it.'

'I'm assuming "low-key" means that I won't have to find a stripper,' said Tom.

'I don't want to know,' replied Alice, laughing. 'Jenny's hoping to get Mike's wife along to the hen party – she has made a big effort to make friends with her.'

'That's good. Scottie and Mike have endured a lot together over the last few months – they are already close friends. They'll be the last of my old mates still sailing together.'

Tuesday 16th February

The postcard was waiting for them on their return from the shop.

'Look, Tom – it's from Clarissa. It just says she's off to start a new life, but doesn't say where. She thanks us for our help and kindness. It appears to have been posted at Heathrow – I guess she's going abroad. She hasn't put a contact address or telephone number.'

'That may be the last we'll hear of her,' said Tom.

Alice tried to contact Clarissa's mobile phone. It appeared to be out of action.

'It's a bit suspicious given all the circumstances,' added Tom. 'I think we should keep this to ourselves. I don't want to get embroiled again with the Intelligence Services.'

'I agree,' said Alice. 'If Clarissa wants to contact us again, she can.'

Saturday 20th February

The wedding breakfast was nearly over by the time Tom concluded his best man's speech.

'That was the last of the nautical jokes – you'll be glad to hear. Paul and Jenny, I'm sure you will both have a very successful voyage together – with a good skipper. What was that? Is that Jenny? I couldn't possibly say.

'Anyway, ladies and gentlemen, please join me in toasting the bride and groom, Jenny and Paul, and in wishing them a long and happy marriage.'

The sentiments were heartily endorsed by all the guests, as they finished their puddings. After a couple more speeches the dancing started and Jenny gave the bridal bouquet to the bridesmaid, her younger sister. Paul and Jenny Scott left early for their flat in nearby Holland Park. They would be starting their honeymoon proper tomorrow, in Cornwall.

Tom and Alice managed to corner Mike and Jane Morris for a chat. Jane seemed more at ease than on previous social occasions.

'They've arranged for us to stay overnight at this hotel,' she said; adding, 'Jenny's such a nice, down-to-earth woman.'

'And we'll probably be seeing quite a lot of Paul and Jenny over the next few months,' added Mike.

'I gather you're off to the North Atlantic on the *Athena* again?' queried Tom.

'Yes. And apparently, I'll be the key weapons engineer on the forthcoming trials.'

'I'm not surprised!' said Tom. 'You should be well on the way to lieutenant commander.'

'I hope so,' replied Mike, putting his arm around Jane.

'Perhaps we could meet up a bit more now that all that ghastly business has settled down,' said Alice.

'Yes, I'd like that,' replied Mike.

After a protracted round of goodbyes to all the guests, Tom and Alice left as soon as prudently possible.

'That went well,' said Alice.

'Yes, but I was hoping Jenny would throw her bouquet to you,' replied Tom jovially.

'Jenny was being diplomatic.'

Wednesday 10th March

Adrian Lomax was in London and wanted to meet up with Tom and Alice. They invited him for an evening meal at their flat.

Lomax struggled in with a case of malt whisky. 'Just a small token of my appreciation,' he said, as they welcomed him.

'Well, thank you, Adrian – but you shouldn't have,' protested Alice.

'Oh yes I should. Your help has been invaluable. I'm back in favour again and I've just been promoted to chief inspector.'

'That's fantastic – congratulations,' said Tom. 'It's long overdue.'

'Hear, hear,' added Alice, handing round the drinks.

'Thank you,' replied Lomax. 'I also wanted to touch base with you on a couple of outstanding matters. Firstly, have you heard from Clarissa Hannay recently?'

'Not recently,' replied Alice, deadpan, trying to conceal any hint of lying. 'I tried her phones but they seemed to be out of action. Do you have any news?'

'She's sold her house and transferred her funds abroad. She was traced to Eastern Europe and then she disappeared. Officially, even I'm not supposed to know about that.'

'Where was she at the time of Claydon's death?' asked Tom.

'Good question,' replied Lomax. 'We don't know – and I think the powers that be want to keep it that way. For God's sake, don't repeat any of this.'

'We won't – and we won't mention the obvious conclusions,' added Tom.

'I've already said too much on that matter,' reiterated Lomax. 'However, I have been able to continue investigating John McAdam. But don't get too excited – we're no further forward on the cause of his disappearance on the 27th September. The good news is that there is no evidence to suggest that he was actively involved in the retrieval of the goods from the North Sea, or any of the events in Scotland. From your observations, Alice, we know that he did not accompany the ex-marines, the mercenaries, from North Norfolk to Scotland. Forensic evidence at the cottage in Saxlangham confirmed the presence of the mercenaries, and also that Claydon had been there at some stage. But there was no evidence that McAdam had been there. Tom, Claydon must have known that McAdam was out of the way when he took the risk of using his name as a ploy to distract you in Scotland.'

Tom interrupted. 'And you did find some of John's belongings on *Nine Bells*.'

'That's right – his binoculars and one boot, which was under a pile of ropes. His wife confirmed that they were his. The binoculars were found in the cabin with fingerprints from one of the mercenaries on them. But there was no forensic evidence to confirm that McAdam had been in the boat's cabin.

Unfortunately, the open part of the boat was so awash with water that forensic investigations were next to useless. The presence or absence of blood could not be confirmed. One problem is the uncertain timeline relating to his actual presence on *Nine Bells*. We have little information on the movement of the boat over that period.'

'But surely he was most likely on the boat around the time of his disappearance?' said Alice.

'And it was spring tides – a time when they were more likely to have taken the boat out of Morston for a few hours,' added Tom.

'Yes, I agree. That's the most obvious scenario. He may have come across the boat while birdwatching and somehow got in the way or became too inquisitive. He may have been killed and possibly dumped at sea. The problem is,' continued Lomax, 'we can't be sure of anything until we find John McAdam or his body. He's just missing. That causes all sorts of problems for the navy, the coroner and Mary McAdam.'

'God – poor Mary,' remarked Tom. 'The navy won't cough up the widow's pension without the death certificate.'

'That's why I'm going to make a strong case for his death at sea,' continued Lomax. 'In my view the circumstantial evidence is now overwhelming. The problem is that some evidence cannot be made public. I've spoken to Mrs McAdam about my intention. Obviously, she's upset – but she accepts that this may be the best way forward. We may still run into bureaucratic obstacles in terms of the death certificate. One possible tactic occurred to me, unofficially. When Clarissa Hannay made trouble because of the delay in getting her husband's body released, either rules were bent or officials got a kicking. National security trumped bureaucracy. Perhaps, if necessary, Mary McAdam could try a similar tactic. But she should get advice.'

'Tom, let's talk to Mary,' urged Alice. 'We could give her support and take up the cudgels on her behalf. We can take the flak and keep Mary out of the firing line.'

'You're on – I feel guilty I haven't done more to help her.'

'Good luck,' said Lomax. 'But try not to drop me in it.'

'We won't,' replied Tom. 'We appreciate all the effort you've put into this.'

Thursday 1st April

Tom stayed at home to prepare for his venture with Dan Bush and colleagues. They were due to sail from St Katharine's to the North Sea at the weekend. Harry White was already on his boat in Blakeney Pit and was keen to meet up with them again.

Tom had more or less finished by early afternoon and poured himself a stiff cognac. As he relaxed in a comfortable armchair an idea came into his head. It was daft, but it kept coming back.

He was topping up his glass again when Alice returned from the shop.

'Are we celebrating?' she enquired.

'No, I'm just relaxing – and trying to drown a stupid idea.'

'Tell me.'

'I was thinking about the whole ghastly business in Norfolk, Scotland, Devonport and so on. We've been involved in so many aspects, sometimes actively. And we were privy to a lot of sensitive information. Some might say that the whole affair is just too unbelievable, but I think it's got potential for a novel.'

'You're not serious,' replied Alice, looking concerned. 'What about the Official Secrets Act and all that?'

'The names and characteristics of people and other things involved would have to be changed. There would need to be a decent time lapse before attempting to publish – probably several years. The Ministry of Defence and the Secret Intelligence Service will be trying to keep a low profile on this mess. They will be less likely to make a fuss if sensitive material or events are not specifically identifiable. Even the odd village might need to be fictional or ambiguous.'

'So you and I won't be recognisable, then?' queried Alice.

'No. I'll take the opportunity to big myself up. But you will have to remain beautiful.'

'Thanks for that,' said Alice, laughing. 'Well, it should keep you out of mischief – or will it? Have you ever written a story before?'

'No; there's the rub. But you could help.'

'That sounds like a recipe for divorce.'

'So, you might be considering marriage, then?' queried Tom.

'Oh dear – another Freudian slip. Well, you could wine and dine me when you return from your trip,' replied Alice, giving him a comforting hug.

'By the way,' she added quickly, changing the subject, 'have you thought of a title for this book?'

'Hmm – I was toying with *When Nine Bells Toll*.'

'You're having me on, of course. I have noticed the date today, Tom.'

'Oh no, darling – I'm not fooling.'

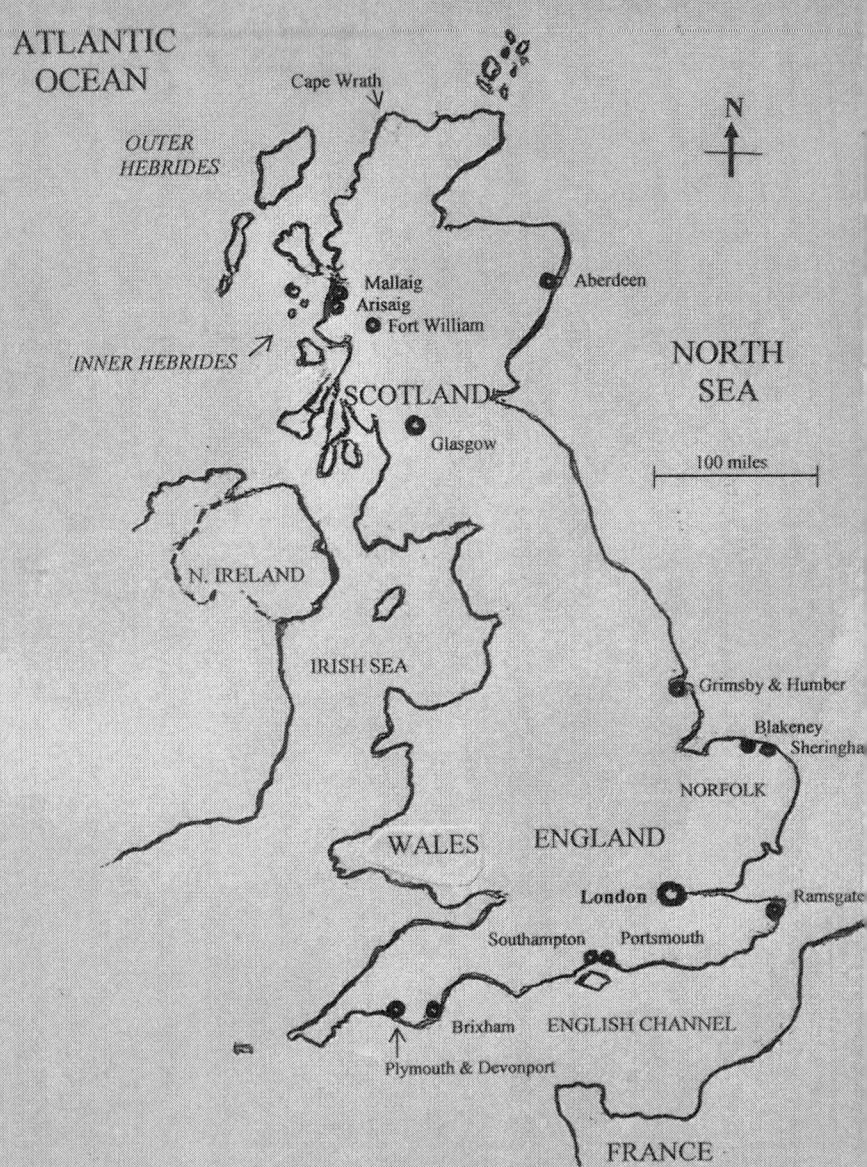

MAP of the UNITED KINGDOM & SURROUNDING WATERS

This shows towns, ports and coastal areas relevant to the story. It is an approximation